ICE ABOVE, DEATH BELOW!

With his glance locked on the frantic efforts of the chief and his men as they tried to stem the rush of flooding water, Captain Matt Colter barked into the intercom, "It's the port circ pump, Al. The chief's on it now, but the engine room is flooding badly. I'm ordering emergency ascent."

"Skipper, as of ten minutes ago we had a pretty thick sheet of ice above us," the XO replied from the control room. "Even if we do take her up, there's no telling how close the nearest lead will be."

"We've got no choice," the captain said. "Crank up the old ice machine and pray there's some open water nearby!"

And with that, Colter replaced the intercom and rushed down into the engine room's flooded confines as the fight to save the *Defiance* began in earnest.

BOOK YOUR PLACE ON OUR WEBSITE AND MAKE THE READING CONNECTION!

We've created a customized website just for our very special readers, where you can get the inside scoop on everything that's going on with Zebra, Pinnacle and Kensington books.

When you come online, you'll have the exciting opportunity to:

- View covers of upcoming books
- Read sample chapters
- Learn about our future publishing schedule (listed by publication month *and author*)
- Find out when your favorite authors will be visiting a city near you
- Search for and order backlist books from our online catalog
- Check out author bios and background information
- Send e-mail to your favorite authors
- Meet the Kensington staff online
- Join us in weekly chats with authors, readers and other guests
- Get writing guidelines
- AND MUCH MORE!

Visit our website at
http://www.zebrabooks.com

RICHARD P. HENRICK

UNDER THE ICE

Zebra Books
Kensington Publishing Corp.

http://www.zebrabooks.com

ZEBRA BOOKS

are published by

Kensington Publishing Corp.
850 Third Avenue
New York, NY 10022

First printing: November, 1989
10 9 8 7 6 5 4 3

Printed in the United States of America

"The lure of the North! It is a strange and powerful thing. More than once I have come back from the great frozen spaces, battered, worn and baffled, sometimes maimed, telling myself that I had made my last journey thither. . . . But somehow, it was never many months before the old restless feeling came over me. And I began to long for the great white desolation, the battles with the ice and the gales . . . the silence, and the vastness of the great, white lonely North."

— Admiral Robert E. Peary, USN

"Star Wars will not work without the early warning system, and that depends on Canada. There is no military scenario in the northern hemisphere in which Canada (or at least Canadian real estate) does not play a crucial role."

— William Arkin

"Our doubts are traitors,
And make us lose the good we oft might win
By fearing to attempt."

— Shakespeare

The author wishes to thank Calgary's Glenbow Museum, and the staff of Banff Centre, who helped make my stay at the Leighton Artist's Colony a comfortable, enjoyable one.

Chapter One

The wind blew in cold, northernly gusts. Oblivious to the icy chill, Ootah directed his gaze solely at the narrow pool of open water that lay at his feet. Warmed by his double-thick, caribou-skin parka, the twenty-nine-year-old Inuit hunter patiently waited for a ringed seal to surface and breathe. When one of these sleek mammals showed itself, he would spear it with the ivory-tipped harpoon that he carried at his side. And once again his mouth would be filled with the sweet taste of fresh, red meat.

It had been three days since he had last eaten, and his stomach growled noisily. Since he hadn't been forced to choose the life of a hunter, he had long since learned to live with his hunger. Yet could he say the same for his wife, young son, and sick father who waited for him back at the igloo? Surely they had consumed the last of the seal meat, leaving them with nothing but frozen snow to fill their empty bellies. It was thus for his family's sake that Ootah remained at his icy vigil, with nothing but his hunger and the howling wind for company.

Silently staring into the dark blue depths, Ootah projected his will downward, into the liquid realm of the elusive creature he so desperately sought. It had been his father who long ago taught him the utter importance of treating one's prey as an equal. To insure a successful hunt, the hunter had to make contact with the animal's spirit. For it was well known that if animals are not treated with respect, both when alive and dead, they will not allow themselves to be killed.

Ootah couldn't help but wonder what force was keeping the seals away. Open water was a rarity in this portion of the ice pack. Even with the constant probing of his harpoon, it was a constant battle to keep the pool from freezing over. Since the seals were dependent upon fresh air, there could be no more convenient spot for them to ascend and refresh themselves. With this hope in mind, he began mumbling a sacred prayer designed to call the seals upward.

The words of his chant came from deep in his throat, and were delivered with a hoarse resonance. As the monotonous, atonal chant broke from his chapped lips, he searched the water's surface with a renewed intensity. Bending over at the waist to get a better view, he momentarily lost his balance when a particularly violent gust of wind hit him full in the back. For a single terrifying moment he found himself teetering on the edge of the ice. To fall forward into the frigid waters of the pool meant almost certain death, and he desperately struck out with his harpoon to regain his balance.

Fate was with him as the ivory spear point firmly embedded itself in the pack ice. With his heart beating madly away in his chest, Ootah exhaled a long sigh of relief. Only then did he identify the black force that had almost sent him plunging to his watery grave, and was most likely keeping the seals away as well. There was no doubt in his mind that Tornarsuk, the great devil who travels on the wind, had paid him a visit. Ever thankful that he had survived this confrontation, Ootah once again raised his voice in prayer. Yet this time his petitions were directed solely toward the spirits of his deceased ancestors, who had intervened on his behalf in this most eternal of earthly struggles.

With the life-force flowing full in his veins, Ootah scanned the Arctic heavens, his prayers of thanks barely audible in the still-gusting wind. A sun that had not set for over six moon cycles now lay low in the gray sky, its light muted and diffused. All too soon it would be dropping beneath the horizon altogether, as the winter arrived in a shroud of perpetual darkness.

The new season signaled a time of change. The cold would intensify, and as the ice pack further solidified, new hunting grounds would form in the waters to the north. Hopefully they would be more prolific than the ones he presently stalked. Otherwise, he would have no choice but to return his family to the white man's city from which they had originally ventured nine months ago.

Merely considering such an alternative sickened Ootah. His brief time spent in the white man's world was far from pleasant. It all began a year ago, when the scarlet-coated policeman arrived from the south and ordered Ootah to convey his family to the city of Arctic Bay on Baffin Island's northern tip. He did so without question and was somewhat shocked when the Canadian officials there informed him that his son would be taken from them and forced to attend a state-run school. He reluctantly complied with the law, and took up residence in the settlement to be as near to the boy as possible.

For the first few months the time passed quickly. The house that was provided for them was filled with

11

many amazing devices, and Ootah and his wife Akatingwah found themselves with a whole new world to learn of and marvel at. Yet the surrounding land was almost barren of game, and Ootah was forced to take government handouts in order for his family to survive.

They were not the only Inuit to be called to the city, and Ootah watched how the white man's culture changed his brothers. Also driven to accepting government welfare, they seemed to readily abandon their ancestral ways to become as much like the whites as possible. Dressed in bluejeans and sweatshirts, the Inuit gave up their dog teams for snowmobiles and pickup trucks. Canned food replaced fresh, red meat, and the men learned to ease their anxieties by consuming vast amounts of alcohol.

Ootah had fallen into this dangerous trap himself, and was well on his way to completely losing his identity when the hand of fate intervened to save him. It had all come to pass nine months ago, when he received word that his mother was on her death bed. Borrowing a neighbor's snowmobile, he dressed himself in a nylon ski outfit, that he had purchased on credit from the Hudson's Bay Company, and took off across the frozen Admiralty Inlet for the Brodeur Peninsula, where his father had set up his spring camp.

As it turned out, he arrived just in time to view his mother breathe her last breath. Though she had been unconscious throughout most of her brief illness, she awoke from her coma just as Ootah came storming through the door of their ramshackle snow cabin. He would take to his own grave the moment when her pained glance locked onto his face and figure. For instead of acknowledging his presence, she greeted him with the cool indifference of a complete stranger.

12

Ootah couldn't help but be puzzled. Had her illness distorted her mind so that she couldn't even recognize her only son, or had she indeed not recognized him because of his alien garb? He would never learn the answer to this question, for less than five minutes later she left this earth for all time, to join her ancestors.

Ootah's father had been perched in the cabin's shadows, and as his mate of fifty years passed into the land beyond, he vented his sorrow with a gut-wrenching wail. In all his life, Ootah had never seen Nakusiak lose control like this. Yet his cries of grief were short-lived; all too soon he regained his composure and somberly initiated the burial procedures.

Hardly a word was spoken between them as they wrapped the still-warm corpse in a shroud of sealskin. According to Inuit custom, a stout line was wrapped around her shoulders and the body thusly dragged headfirst out of the cabin. Nakusiak had prepared a shallow grave in a nearby ravine. Here the body was deposited, along with a variety of objects that the deceased would need in the afterlife. These included a soapstone lamp, some flints, a variety of cooking utensils, and some dried caribou meat. Only after the corpse was subsequently covered by a thick mantle of loose stones, to protect it from marauding animals, did Ootah's father directly address him.

"What is the identity of this stranger that stands before me? Surely it's not the same son who crawled from the loins of the proud woman we just buried."

Suddenly aware of his alien costume, Ootah blushed with shame, and tears fell from his eyes. Sensing his discomfort, Nakusiak continued, this time a bit more compassionately.

"Though you may have tried to cover it with the clothing of the white man, I sense that the blood of the Inuit still flows inside you. Never again try to hide this fact, or eternal disgrace shall be your reward."

Ootah humbly nodded. "I have shamed the family enough for one life, Father. When I first entered the cabin and Mother set her eyes on me, I thought it was her illness that prevented her from identifying me. But now I know differently."

Ripping off the nylon ski jacket he was wearing, Ootah added. "I have been gone too long. The white man's ways have indeed blinded me. Is it too late for me to return to the path of the people?"

A wise grin turned the corners of Nakusiak's cracked lips as he answered. "If your heart is pure, of course it isn't, my son. So come, join me around the fire-circle, and we'll discuss your homecoming."

The two talked long into the night, and as a result of this meeting of souls, a plan was formulated. With Nakusiak's invaluable assistance, Ootah would return to Arctic Bay. Here he would gather together his wife and son, and as soon as the first opportunity presented itself, free them from the alien world of the white man.

The scheme worked perfectly, and nine months ago, Ootah and his family returned to the ways of their ancestors. Gratefully, Ootah accepted his father into his camp. Together with a team of powerful huskies, they lived off the land.

The summer just passed had been a bountiful one. The caribou herds ran full, and ducks and hare were abundant just as they had been in the old days. Taking this as a good omen, they moved back into Baffin Island's rugged Brodeur Peninsula to await the winter.

It was at the beginning of the last moon cycle that Nakusiak took ill with a deep cough that brought blood to his lips. Powhuktuk the shaman was called in. Yet even the miracle worker's most potent spells failed to slake the fiery fever that burned in Naku-siak's brow.

Without his father's help, Ootah was forced to go on the hunt by himself. Since the caribou had long since migrated to the south, seal was the meat that would now fill their bellies.

At first Ootah met with some success; a pair of fat ringed seals fell to his harpoon. Yet now that Tornar-suk had returned, their cache was empty, and would continue to be so until the demon was exorcised. Well aware that his father's rapidly weakening condition was only that much more aggravated by lack of nour-ishment, Ootah projected his voice in renewed prayer.

Utilizing the blunt end of his harpoon to crack the ice that had gathered at the pool's edges, he returned his ponderings to the hunt. Oblivious to the howling wind, he once again turned his back to the furious, demonic gusts and approached the open water. New purpose filled his being as he directed his chants to the spirit of the seal.

"To you, whose sweet flesh fills the stomachs of hungry babies, I call. Ascend from the icy depths and surrender your life-giving essence to those in need. I implore you, spirit of the seal, do not forsake us!"

With one hand still holding the ivory-tipped har-poon, Ootah reached into his parka's central pouch and pulled out a large eider feather. Bending down at the pool's edge, he then dropped this object into the deep blue water.

Ootah's eyes were glued to the floating feather as he cocked his harpoon above his right ear and cried out passionately.

"Begone with you, Tornarsuk, you who cause mothers to weep and babies to go to bed hungry! Return to the black abyss from which you crawled and bother us no more with your evil presence."

This forceful petition was met by an angry gust of frigid wind, and for one fleeing second Ootah doubted his prayer's effectiveness. Yet this moment of uncertainty was followed by a sudden, unexpected drop in the wind's velocity. Able to stand fully erect now without fear of being blown over, Ootah watched as a series of bubbles burst onto the pool's surface. Expecting the feather to next fly upward as a result of a seal's exhalation, he readied himself to plunge the tip of the harpoon downward. More bubbles reached the surface, and when a seal still failed to show itself, Ootah's voice muttered to the wind.

"Come on, brother seal don't be afraid to show yourself."

When another series of even larger bubbles broke on top of the pool, the Inuit spoke out excitedly. "Perhaps what we have down below is not a seal after all. Could it be that your cousin the whale will soon be making an appearance?"

Stirred by such a thought, Ootah prepared himself to greet this unexpected visitor. A whale would definitely be more difficult to fatally wound, yet its abundant flesh would feed his family for weeks on end. Turning to his right, he bent down and reached out for the coil of sinew rope that lay beside him. With one end of this line already firmly attached to an inflated walrus-bladder float, Ootah tied its free end to his harpoon's hilt. If the whale wasn't too large, this crude but effective system would hopefully keep the beast from sinking to the depths once it was speared.

Returning to the pool, Ootah once again cocked the harpoon above his right ear. The bubbles were breaking the surface with a furious regularity now, and peering intently downward to find their source, the Inuit imagined that he could just view a massive, black object ascending with a vengeance.

Though he was well prepared to strike out at the creature regardless of its size, Ootah never had the chance. For before he could make good his attack, the thick pack ice beneath him shattered with an ear-splitting concussion that sent him reeling to the icy ground. He struck the ice with such force that for an agonizing moment he had the breath knocked out of him. Struggling merely to breathe, he impotently looked on as the pack ice beneath him violently shook to yet another rumbling, bone-shattering blow.

Well aware that no earthly animal was responsible for such an intense disturbance, Ootah dared to think of the true nature of the one responsible. He had heard the tales of the elders, in which Tornarsuk, the devil, took the form of a frightening sea monster that swallowed both men and kayaks whole. Surely the evil one had taken on such an incarnation. And since it was only a matter of time before the great beast was able to crack the pack ice and get to him, Ootah valiantly struggled to regain his breath and stand.

His lungs were burning with pain as he scrambled to his knees. Unable to fully stand erect because of his trembling limbs, he turned from the ever-widening pool and crawled off on all fours like a terrified infant who had yet to learn to walk. Daring not to look back, he managed to reach his dogsled; he had left it behind a nearby hummock.

Though his dogs were also weak with hunger, they seemed just as anxious to leave this cursed place as the Inuit. Without even having to put a whip to them, the pack broke for the distant horizon, their excited howls all but swallowed by the maddening beat of Ootah's pulse and the gusting cry of the rising wind.

Thirty-five feet below that same Arctic ice pack, the hull of the *Sturgeon*-class attack submarine, USS *Defiance,* was still reverberating after its unsuccessful attempt to break through to the surface. In the vessel's control center, Captain Mathew Colter cried out firmly, his voice deep with concern.

"Take her down, emergency!"

Still shaken by their all-too-recent, unexpected collision with the ice, the sub's diving officer, Lieutenant Don Marshall, reached forward with trembling hands to address his console. Seconds later, the vent to the negative tank opened with a pop of compressed air, and as tons of seawater flooded into the *Defiance,* the sub shuddered and began to descend.

Practically screaming to be heard over the deafening roar of venting air, Marshall addressed the crewcut, veteran sailor seated to his right. "Blow that negative to the mark, Chief!"

With one eye on the depth gauge, that was mounted on the forward bulkhead, Matt Colter added. "Shut the flood, vent negative."

As these orders were carried out, another roaring blast of compressed air filled the control room. His gaze still riveted on the depth gauge, the captain allowed himself a brief sigh of relief only when the counter hit the three-hundred-and-sixty-foot level and remained constant.

Colter's hand went to his pant's pocket, to remove a white handkerchief. He mopped dry his sweat-stained forehead, repocketed the handkerchief, and quickly scanned the hushed compartment. It was as his intense glance locked on a tall, thin, mustached officer who was standing beside the chart table, that the captain exploded in rage.

"Damn it, Al! I thought you said we had open water up there? The way we smacked into that pack

18

ice, it's a miracle we didn't split open our sail or damage the rudder."

Not used to having to make excuses, Lieutenant Commander Al Layman, the sub's executive officer, nervously cleared his throat. "I'm sorry, Skipper, but the ice machine definitely gave us a green light."

"Damn that friggin' machine!" cursed Colter. "That's the third time this week it almost got us killed."

"I realize that, Skipper," offered the XO. "I guess it still has some bugs in it."

Colter shook his head. "That's an understatement if I ever heard one. As far as I'm concerned, they can rip that whole damn unit out and replace it with the gear we used to carry. The old ice machine never failed us, even if it was based on technology that was over three decades old."

Having vented his frustration, the captain crossed the control room to join his second-in-command.

"I'm sorry if I snapped at you, Al. I realize it's not your fault Command gives us gear that's not properly tested."

"No apologies necessary, Skipper," countered the XO, whose gangly frame was a good four inches taller than Matt Colter's. "After all, I was the one picked to operate the unit. I only wish my training was a bit more extensive. One week isn't a hell of a lot of time to learn the intracacies of a complicated system such as this one. Who knows, maybe the laser was calibrated improperly."

The captain grunted. "That shouldn't be our concern, Al. It's evident that the engineer who dreamed up this newfangled process failed to think it out completely. And unfortunately, we were picked to be the human guinea pigs who almost lost our lives because of a pencil pusher's incompetence. What I wouldn't give for five minutes alone with the fellow responsible for this boondoggle. He needs to be reminded that human lives are at stake out here."

"They should have sent him along," offered the XO. "I guarantee you, the first time we smacked into the pack ice, he would have gotten that gear working properly."

"Either that, or he'd have died from fright while trying," jested Matt Colter.

A grin turned the corners of the XO's mouth. "Since we have no reliable way of determining if there's clear water above, how are we going to complete the rest of our mission?"

"We're not going to even try," answered the captain. "As far as I'm concerned, the safety of this crew takes number-one priority. It would be foolhardy to try another ascent. And since our orders revolve around surfacing in a variety of ice conditions, I've no alternative but to send us packing, back to New London. So, how about charting us the quickest route back to the Davis Strait?"

"Aye, aye, Skipper," returned the XO, relief clearly painted on his handsome face.

Well aware that barring any mechanical difficulties they'd be home in another five and a half days, Matt Colter excused himself and went to his quarters. A combination of emotional stress and a simple lack of sleep had finally caught up with him. Confident that his XO was well qualified to take over, Colter gratefully closed the door of his cabin behind him. Without even bothering to take off his shoes, he collapsed on his narrow mattress and was instantly asleep.

He awoke with a start, precisely four hours later. Having emerged from a vivid dream, it took him several confusing seconds to reorient himself. The soft glowing lights of the digital depth, speed, and course indicators mounted on the bulkhead at the foot of his bunk finally brought him back to full waking consciousness. The rest of his cabin was pitch black, and he momentarily remained on his bunk unmoving.

Except for a distant muted whine, there was no indication that the three-hundred-foot-long vessel that surrounded him was even moving. But Colter knew differently. The *Defiance* was currently four hundred feet beneath the frozen waters of Lancaster Sound, moving along at a crisp twenty-five knots. Their course was taking them due eastward and would soon turn to the southeast, once they reached the Davis Straits. The ship would remain on this heading for almost two-thousand miles, until the coast of Newfoundland was attained. Here they would round Cape Race and turn to the southwest, for yet another thousand-mile jaunt to their home port.

Throughout this entire trip, not once was the *Defiance* scheduled to break the water's surface. They would do so only upon reaching Long Island Sound. Thus they would be traveling oblivious to the fickle state of the tempestuous seas above. This was quite all right with Matt Colter, who was as prone to seasickness as any other normal mortal.

He would never forget his first encounter with this sailor's arch nemesis. He had only been a lad at the time. It was spring break, and his Uncle Bill had invited him down to Sarasota, Florida. This was to be Matt's first trip all on his own, and he boarded the prop-driven airplane with a promise to his parents to be on his best behavior.

Bill was his father's older brother, and had always been Matt's favorite relative. They only got to spend time together during those all-too-brief, yearly family reunions, during which his uncle never failed to enchant him with tales of the sea.

His uncle had been a submarine captain during World War II. Yet it wasn't until Mathew arrived at his Florida home that he learned Bill's ship had been responsible for sinking over a dozen Japanese surface vessels.

Anxious to learn more about his uncle's wartime experiences, Matt eagerly accepted an invitation to join him for a day of sailing on Sarasota Bay. This was the youngster's first excursion on a body of water larger than the Arkansas lake he grew up on, and he was thrilled beyond belief.

The day started off splendidly. The sky was clear, the air warm, with a moderate breeze blowing in from the west. His uncle was an expert mariner, who handled his thirty-five-foot sloop with the ease of a veteran sailor. He was quick to teach his inquisitive nephew the basics of seamanship, and in no time at all, Matt was at the helm, guiding them through the channel markers.

Invigorated by the warm sun, cool ocean spray, and the ease with which the boat handled, Matt found himself entranced by his uncle's war stories. He was particularly fascinated by the type of vessel Bill had commanded. He found that the very word submarine had an exotic ring to it. Able to utilize the black ocean depths to sneak up on the enemy and then deliver a fatal blow, the submarine was an effective killer.

In the course of his stories, Bill made certain to explain the submarine's shortcomings as well. Dependent upon limited battery power when submerged, and air-guzzling diesels when topside, the submarine was a far from a perfect weapon. Yet Bill explained that new technology would change all this.

Matt had a basic understanding of nuclear power from school, yet he'd never dreamed it could be adapted to propel a submarine, thus freeing the craft from having to ascend to the surface at all. The first nuclear-powered submarine was called *Nautilus*, and was already on sea trials. His uncle was a great advocate of such a warship, and promised to keep Matt informed on its future deployment.

While Matt was visualizing a vessel that could travel around the world submerged, without refueling, a distant rumble of thunder sounded. Quick to point out the rapidly advancing storm, Bill replaced Matt at the helm and turned the sloop back toward port.

Matt could just make out the marina when the first violent gust of wind hit them. Moments later, a torrent of rain soaked them to the bone. Ordered down into the enclosed cabin, he prepared himself to ride out the storm. Confident in his uncle's ability to see them out of harm's way, he looked at this experience as a great adventure. Yet as the boat continued to rock to and fro, any such pleasant ponderings on his part were soon replaced by sheer misery for a wave of nausea overcame him.

Never had he been so miserable in his short lifetime! Even after he'd deposited the remains of his breakfast and lunch on the deck, the nausea would not leave him. Dizzy and flushed, he emptied his stomach completely before succumbing to a disorienting wave of dizziness. As it turned out, his uncle got them safely ashore and Matt returned home with a new respect for the sea. He also found himself with an exciting new goal in life. For he had decided to be a nuclear submariner.

Inwardly grinning at this long-forgotten recollection, Captain Mathew Colter peered out into the black void of his cabin. Over thirty years had passed since that fated day on Sarasota Bay. In that time he

23

had grown to manhood and subsequently followed his childhood dream to the very end. Proud of this fact and never sorry for the difficult career he had chosen, he nonetheless regretted that his Uncle Bill had not lived long enough to see him get his dolphins. Stricken with cancer, Bill had passed away on the same day that Matt was accepted into the Naval Academy. Though he wasn't able to be with his uncle at the end, Matt dedicated his stay at Annapolis to him, and he graduated in the top ten percent of his class. Submarine school followed, and after a decade of hard work, he finally got a command of his own.

The *Defiance* was the type of vessel that his uncle had dreamed about. Powered by a single water-cooled nuclear reactor that could go years between refueling, Matt's present command was a first line man-of-war. Should the *Defiance* ever be called upon to do so, she could hit the enemy with an awesome amount of firepower that included a mix of Mk48 dual-purpose torpedoes, nuclear-tipped SUBROC antisubmarine missiles, Harpoon antiship rockets, and even a newly fitted complement of long-range Tomahawk cruise missiles. To make certain that these weapons hit their mark, a sophisticated fire-control system had been incorporated into the *Defiance*'s hull, and she was outfitted with the latest in sonar and communication equipment.

Manned by a crew of one hundred and seven of the US Navy's best, the *Defiance* was a proud ship with a proud tradition. Ever grateful for the opportunity to lead these brave men into battle if that should become necessary, Matt Colter restlessly stirred. Only then did he realize that he was lying there completely clothed. This was not the first time he had fallen asleep in such formal attire, and he stiffly sat up, intending to wash and change into a fresh uniform.

Standing before his pullman-type metal washbasin, Matt soaked his face with cool water. Deciding not to shave, he momentarily caught his reflection in the wall-mounted mirror. Surprisingly enough, the tired face that stared back at him could easily have been a twin of his Uncle Bill in earlier days. He had the same short, spiky blond hair, deep blue eyes, highly etched cheekbones, and rounded, dimpled chin.

With this thought in mind, Matt wondered how his uncle would have handled their present mission. Would he have ordered them to return over a week early as Matt had done, or would he have attempted yet another series of ascents to the frozen Arctic ice pack?

If it had been wartime, and the success of their mission depended upon such an ascent, Matt did not doubt that he would have given it another try. Yet the way he saw it, they had absolutely nothing to gain by such an attempt at this time and place.

It was evident that the new surface-scanning Fathometer still had quite a few bugs in it. It was a far from a reliable system, and until these flaws were worked out, it placed the entire crew in jeopardy. Thus as captain of the *Defiance,* Matt had no choice but to cut their mission short before the ship was once again needlessly endangered.

The theory behind such a device was fairly basic. In reality it was but a converted Fathometer, mounted on the topside of the submarine. The older machines utilized sound waves to determine the location of any surface ice. The device that had been installed on the *Defiance* used a sophisticated laser that was supposed not only to locate the smallest of usable open leads above, but also to interface with the boat's navigation system to help the sub undergo a precise ascent.

Without such an instrument, the control-room

crew had no reliable way of knowing what lay above them. Though sturdily built, a submarine could be readily damaged by a collision. Thick pack ice could be extremely unyielding, its submerged razor-sharp ridges able to easily puncture even the sturdiest of steel hulls.

One unusual feature of the Arctic ice fields was that even in the coldest parts of winter, open leads, or polynyas formed. Such openings extended from a few yards to many miles, and provided a submarine a safe haven in which to surface.

Matt Colter had been on several past Arctic missions during which time ascents to the surface were made. In each instance, even with perfectly functioning equipment, the atmosphere inside the control room had been tense as the submarine rose to meet its fate. Collisions with the ice weren't unknown, and on one submerged ridge they had even damaged their vulnerable rudder. Yet their hull had remained intact, and after a series of makeshift repairs, they'd continued on with their patrol.

The *Defiance* had a specially strengthened sail, or conning tower, that could puncture up to a foot of solid ice. During the last week they had attempted to surface in three different, promising polynyas. Yet each time their best efforts were thwarted by an impenetrable sheet of ice that produced a deafening, bone-jarring jolt. Fortunately, most of the damage was limited to their nerves. But would they be so lucky the next time? Determined not to buck the odds, Matt had made the difficult decision to cut short their cruise and return to port. Certain that his uncle would have made the same choice, he mentally prepared himself for the icy reception that would be awaiting him in New London.

The scent of perking coffee met his nostrils, and he

was suddenly aware that he had passed by both breakfast and lunch. Determined to make up for these missed meals, he turned away from the washbasin to change into a fresh set of coveralls and go to the nearby wardroom.

Chapter Two

A full moon cycle had passed since Ootah's terrifying confrontation with Tornarsuk on the ice pack. In this time span, the Inuit hunter had succeeded in closing up his camp and moving his family out of that cursed spot. They traveled to the north, finally halting on the shore of the great ice sea known to the whites as Lancaster Sound. Here the fates were with him, and his harpoon took down a fat walrus. The meat of this animal was sweet and nourishing, and with their bellies finally filled, life was once again bearable.

Even Ootah's father seemed a bit stronger. Though the cough that brought blood to his lips was still with him, Nakusiak was as feisty as ever. Demanding that he share equally in the workload, the old-timer helped build their snowhouse. Quick to remind his son to locate the entrance to the igloo below ground level, so that the cold air that would otherwise enter their living space would be trapped, Nakusiak supervised the placement of the last of the smooth ice blocks into the structure's rounded roof. Afterward, he assisted Akatingwah in butchering the massive walrus Ootah had triumphantly dragged into their new camp.

With the first winter storm of the season howling madly outside, they settled in to wait for the icy tempest to vent itself. Nakusiak was more than content to take his young grandson aside and teach him the ancient Inuit throat songs. While these resonant tones filled the interior of the igloo, Ootah stripped off his clothes and slipped under the thick fur blankets with Akatingwah close at his side.

His mate's skin was warm and soft as they embraced in the way of a man and a woman. His fingers' touch aroused the sensitive buds of her ripe breasts, and as her breath quickened, Ootah slipped his manhood deep inside her. With Nakusiak's spirited song providing the perfect accompaniment, Ootah pulled his hips back until only the tip of his erect phallus touched the lips of his wife's pulsating love channel. Sensing her need, he slowly plunged his hips downward until his all was given. He repeated this process until an ever-quickening rhythm was established. Akatingwah moaned softly in delight, and as her embrace tightened, Ootah sensed a sudden flow of hot fluid from deep inside her. It was then that his own seed rose, and a rapturous pleasure beyond description filled his being as he deposited the milk of life into her wet depths. If the fates so willed it, an infant would next be crawling from Akatingwah's loins when the summer returned to the land of the Inuit.

With his mate still locked tightly in his embrace, Ootah listened as her previously pounding pulse slowly returned to normal. While beyond, his father's monotonous song continued, the distant howling wind a fitting accompaniment.

Ootah's dream was soon in coming. In this vision, he was conveyed high into the rugged mountains that lay to the east of Arctic Bay. It must have been summer, for no snow lay upon the ground. In its place, an unending carpet of bright red and gold wildflowers stretched to the horizon. As he climbed down to the floor of a particularly luxuriant valley, he spotted a herd of musk oxen grazing before him. Upon viewing the Inuit, the round-shouldered, shaggy beasts immediately took up a defensive circle, with the lead bull lowering its horned head and stepping forth to do battle. Strangely enough, even though he wasn't armed, Ootah advanced to meet the bull's challenge.

The razor-sharp horns of a fully grown musk ox were not something to take lightly. Many times Ootah had seen predators as crafty as the wolf and as strong as the bear fall victim to a fatal gore wound. Yet completely oblivious to the dangers involved, he found himself walking down to meet the beast, with not even a stick to protect himself.

Ootah was actually close enough to smell the musk ox's strong scent, to see it's bulging, red-veined eyes, when the first wave of fear possessed him. This fear turned to sheer terror when the beast bellowed loudly and took several bold steps forward. Suddenly halting in his tracks, Ootah sensed his precarious position. Yet as he turned to run away, he found that his lower limbs were inexplicably weighted down, so that even the most tentative step was impossible to achieve. Again the angry beast bellowed, and just as the bull lowered its head to initiate the final charge, a deafening boom of thunder filled the air. Looking up into the sky, Ootah viewed an intense, fireball of glowing red light that blotted out even the sun with its intensity. Another thunderous peal filled the air, and as this blast echoed in the distance, the fireball flared up and then dissipated, until not a trace of it was left above.

An icy gust of wind hit him full in the back, and as

Ootah returned his attention back to the musk oxen, his eyes opened wide with disbelief upon noting that they too had completely vanished. In their place was a wide, circular lake. This pond was completely frozen over, except for a tiny opening in the pool's exact center. Curious as to what lay exposed inside this hole, Ootah walked over to examine it more closely.

The Inuit was somewhat shocked to find a large eider feather floating on the circular pool's surface. Viewing this familiar object, that was designed to fly up into the air and warn the hunter of a surfacing seal, filled Ootah with dread. Ever mindful of his last terrifying seal hunt on the pack ice a week ago, he attempted to back away from the open water. Unfortunately, this simple feat proved impossible, for his boots were frozen solidly to the ice below.

An angry gust of frigid wind scoured the valley, and finding himself chilled to the bone, Ootah had no choice but to look down to the waters of the pool. Goosebumps formed on his shivering skin as he spotted a myriad of bubbles swirling to the surface. And below, he could just make out a dark menacing shape rising from the black depths. Unable to keep his eyes off this mysterious object, he gasped in horror upon identifying it as a human being. Its puckered hand beckoning him forward, and Ootah cried out in revulsion as he sighted the floating body's head — for it was that of his dead mother!

It was at this point in the nightmare that he awoke. The vision of his mother's white, unseeing eyes was still clear in his consciousness as he stared out into the black depths of the igloo. Surely this was no ordinary dream, but one that had been placed before his eyes by the great deceiver himself — Tornarsuk!

Chilled by this realization, he scanned the darkened interior of the snowhouse as if seeing it for the very first time. The bare light of a soapstone lamp flickered alive at the igloo's center, providing just enough illumination for Ootah to see the thick fur pelts covering the adjoining pallet where his father and son slept. Nakusiak's snores filled the circular room with a resonant roar, while somewhere beyond gusted the ever-present howling wind.

Unable to fall back to sleep, Ootah decided to see how his dogs had weathered the storm. Slipping out of the covers, he dressed himself in his double-thick, caribou-skin parka, pulled on his boots and mittens, and silently crawled through the igloo's sole exit.

Outside, he was met by a blast of numbingly cold Arctic air. Taking a moment to catch his breath, he peered over a newly formed snowdrift and caught sight of the dawn sun as it just broke the distant horizon. Even at noon, the muted orange ball would not climb much higher into the sky than it already was. Ootah was well aware that all too soon it would not even bother rising at all, as perpetual night ruled the Arctic winter.

The storm that had first arrived two nights ago had finally passed, leaving in its wake a crystal-clear, dark blue sky and mounds of freshly fallen, powdery snow. The morning star twinkled in the heavens, and Ootah turned to check on the condition of his dogs.

He had built a windbreak for his team on the opposite side of the igloo. Though the drifting snow made finding this protective barrier difficult, he was thankful to find it still standing. He brushed away the loose snow and found his team of seven huskies gathered in a tight embryonic ball. First to open his eyes and spot the gawking human was Arnuk, Ootah's lead dog. This would be Arnuk's twelfth winter, and though getting old in years, he was still the dominant member of the pack.

Quick to his feet, Arnuk howled in delight and moved over to playfully nuzzle his master. As the others awakened and shook the loose snow off their backs, Ootah walked over to the igloo, where a large, hollowed-out block of ice protected their cache of walrus meat. Cutting off several large chunks of frozen flesh from the hind quarter, he proceeded to feed his faithful pack. For they needed strength just like humans did, and when meat was available, all was shared equally.

While his dogs gratefully consumed their morning meal, Ootah turned his attention to the new sled that he had been working on when the storm arrived two days ago. He brushed away powdery snow, and found it behind the same barrier that had sheltered his dogs. Only a few days' work need be done on it before it was ready to hit the ice.

He had designed it to carry his ailing father. Though Nakusiak hated to admit it, his illness had greatly sapped his once-formidable strength, and it was a struggle for him merely to stand, let alone keep up with them when they were on the move to new hunting grounds. Built much like the sleds of their ancestors, its runners were formed from frozen char that had been split and tightly wrapped in soaked caribou hides. Walrus tusks and whalebones comprised the body, on which a caribou hide would soon be stretched to hold Nakusiak.

Ootah's current job was to make the runners as smooth as possible. He did so by chewing up large mouthfuls of snow and then spraying this liquid onto the existing runners. He was well into this tedious task, when a deep voice boomed out from behind.

"Well my son, you're certainly up early. What demon could possibly have pulled you away from the warm body of your comely wife?"

33

Noting the unusual manner in which Nakusiak phrased this question, Ootah looked his father full in the eye and explained every detail of his recent nightmare. When he finished describing his horrifying vision, he looked on as Nakusiak grunted.

"You are correct in ascribing this dream to Tornarsuk, my son. For you see, I had a similar vision."

Puzzlement etched Ootah's face as he questioned. "But what does such a shared nightmare mean, Father? Is it a presentiment of an even greater evil yet to come?"

Nakusiak somberly nodded. "I'm afraid that it is, my son. The songs of the grandfathers tell of a time in the not so distant future when a star shall fall to earth. Sent from the Great Spirit, this comet shall explode in the dawn sky for all to see as a signal that the time of prophecy is upon us. As the tail of this comet falls to earth, mankind shall face the final trial. And if the Great Spirit finds the people unworthy, he shall cleanse the earth with fire, and death will walk everywhere."

"But how do we insure that such a terrible fate won't befall us?" quizzed Ootah.

Reaching into the pocket of his parka, Nakusiak removed a hand-sized bone amulet that had a piece of sinew strung through it. "This holy amulet was carved by my grandfather, Anoteelik, who was a great shaman of the people. He, too, dreamed of the cursed pool and the exploding comet that signaled the end of time. My time on this earth is almost over, my son. It's now up to you to wear this holy amulet over your heart, and if the flow of your spirit is pure, perhaps the Great Spirit will intercede, and the people will be reprieved."

As he handed the necklace to Ootah, Nakusiak was consumed by a fit of violent coughing. Blood red spittle drooled off his lips and dropped down to stain the white snow below.

"Come, Father, you've been out here in the cold long enough. You must take better care of yourself."

Ootah's pleas were met with an angry smirk. "Stop coddling me, boy! Don't forget who it was who brought you into the world. Now just swear to me that you'll wear this amulet always, and that your meditations will be as pure as the snow that my life fluid has just violated."

Well aware of his father's stubbornness, Ootah meekly nodded, and slipped the sinew necklace over his neck. He could only look on helplessly as Nakusiak was once again consumed by a coughing fit. Grasping the flat bone amulet with one of his mittened hands, Ootah angled his gaze to the distant horizon. There the fiery, golden-hued Arctic dawn continued to fight off the black tide of winter, in an eternal battle that began at the very beginning of time.

From a windswept plateau eighty-five miles due east of Ootah's camp, another individual watched the Arctic dawn develop. Bundled in his down parka, Ensign Graham Chapman of the Royal Canadian Navy felt sadly out of place. The Calgary native had originally enlisted in the armed forces as a way of bringing badly needed adventure into his life. And for the first couple of months, he hadn't been the least bit disappointed.

Having never traveled farther than Edmonton in his home province of Alberta, Graham initially had been sent packing to Halifax, Nova Scotia. There he underwent basic training. His naturally high aptitude got him an invitation to attend the Naval Officer's training center in Esquimalt, British Columbia. Once again he crossed the wide breadth of his native country, seeing magnificent sights he'd never dreamed existed. He was most impressed with the ultrasophisticated city of Vancouver, and it was in this exciting metropolis that he spent many a cherished weekend leave.

In order to be as close to Vancouver as possible, he took a position on the staff of the vice admiral in charge of the Second Destroyer Squadron based in Esquimalt. Such duty demanded limited sea time, and gave him an opportunity to get his own apartment in nearby Vancouver.

For the son of an itinerant oil-well driller, this was like a dream come true. The petroleum business was in the midst of lean times, and if he'd stayed in Calgary, he'd most likely been on the dole like the majority of the boys he grew up with. Yet here he had a position that commanded respect, he was making a decent wage, and he was living in one of the most exciting cities in all of Canada.

Unfortunately, all too soon his luck was to run out. It started that morning he was ordered into his superiors office, and asked if he wanted to take a position of the utmost sensitivity. Fooled into thinking that this was some sort of promotion, he immediately accepted. Little did he realize what he was getting himself involved with.

Graham's new job certainly started on an upscale beat as he was soon on a plane bound for balmy California. Though he never made it to Hollywood, his duty did take him to Beale Air Force base, north of the city of Sacramento. At this supersecret installation he was to learn a whole new craft that would eventually take him from the land of surfers and bikinis to his current forsaken assignment in the frozen wastelands of the Canadian Arctic.

Totally sickened by the abrupt turn in his luck, Graham could only sigh heavily and shrug his broad shoulders. Like a wildcatter he had gambled his future on a single throw of the dice, and he had lost. It was as simple as that. And now he would have to pay the consequences.

Absently gazing out to the eastern horizon as the Arctic dawn continued to take shape, Graham mentally calculated that he had at least one hundred and eighty days left at this icebound outpost. After that time, command had promised he'd be transferred back to Esquimalt with a full rank's promotion. Though it didn't seem like that long a time, six months was an eternity here at the distant early warning station known as Polestar. Making matters even worse was the fact that he was the only Canadian in a complement of fifty-five grubby Yanks. Why the only thing he had to look forward to were the weekly trips into Arctic Bay to pick up supplies and the mail. And even those trips were depressing, for the so-called town was little more than a collection of dilapidated Jamesway huts, holding an odd collection of squalid Eskimos.

If only his work was interesting, at least that portion of his stay would go quickly. But most of his duty time was spent perched before a radar screen, waiting for a Russian sneak attack that in all probability would never come to pass.

Polestar was the newest addition to the legendary DEW line, that was first built in the 1950's to monitor the approach of Soviet prop-driven long-range bombers. Since that time, the character of the enemy's strategic forces had drastically changed, and it was the threat of a surprise attack by the so-called Stealth aircraft that most concerned them.

To track these sophisticated planes from their take-off phase onward, Polestar relied on a revolutionary new technology known as Over-the-Horizon-Back-scatter, or OTH-B for short. The system could cover airspace for a distance of over 2,000 miles. It did so by projecting a high-frequency signal off the ionosphere. The reflected echo returned to the sending installation by a similar route, and was all but resistant to enemy jamming because the Soviets were still confused as to the exact frequencies that were being utilized.

Though Graham didn't doubt the system's effectiveness, what he did have misgivings about was the necessity of such an installation's existence in the first place. Just as the strategic delivery systems had changed over the years, so had the statesmen that controlled them. Unlike in the 1950's, today every responsible citizen of the planet understood the folly of nuclear war. Such a conflict would have no winners, for the resulting radioactivity would poison the atmosphere and create a living hell for any unlucky survivors.

A new generation of enlightened leaders was currently changing the character of enemy number one. The Soviet Union was no longer the evil empire it had been rumored to be in the past. Socialism was gradually mutating, blending in capitalism and free enterprise to insure its future survival.

Currently leading the Soviets into the twenty-first century was an energetic, charismatic Premier by the name of Alexander Suratov. Graham liked the man from the very first time he saw him speaking on the evening news. He was young, dashing, and full of vigor.

Publicly admitting that the unparalleled arms race that had taken place during the last four decades was decimating the Soviet economy, Suratov was an exponent of total nuclear disarmament. To begin this long, difficult process, he advocated creating nuclear-free zones throughout the globe. One of the first regions he'd picked to ban such weapons was the Arctic. And to prove the seriousness of his intentions, he was about to embark on an unprecedented journey to Ottawa, where he was scheduled to meet with both the Canadian Prime Minister and the US President to sign an Arctic demilitarization treaty. This was a bold first step, and Graham prayed that the three leaders would reach an accord quickly.

Well aware that the plane carrying the Soviet Premier would soon be showing up on their radar screen, Ensign Graham Chapman turned to take in the installation that would be tracking this aircraft. Polestar was comprised of four massive OTH-B radar units. Each of these flattened, octagonal-shaped radars was as large as a seven-story building, and was pointed northward. An enclosed walkway had been mounted on top of the permafrost. It connected the four separate radar arrays to a central structure. This massive building housed the control room, living quarters, mess hall, recreation room, and power plant. Though all the comforts of home had been included inside its thick walls, Graham still felt suffocated. Thus the reason for this morning's early, subzero constitutional.

No stranger to cold weather, the young ensign surveyed the bleak landscape and disgustedly spit. Last night, thoughts of desertion had actually crossed his mind. Yet in this isolated, godforsaken wilderness there wasn't even anywhere close by to desert to!

Shivering when a cold gust of Arctic wind hit him full in the face, Graham turned back toward the compound just as a high-pitched whistle broke the frigid

39

air. A single individual wearing a bright orange parka could be seen standing beside one of the structure's entryways, waving his arms. As he put his ungloved hands to his mouth, this figure's deep, bass voice clearly boomed out.

"Hey, Canuck, are you going to join me or not?"

Only then did Graham remember his earlier promise to have a drink with one of his co-workers. Signaling that he had heard himself called, the Calgary native began his way back to the compound.

"I heard that you Canadians were a hearty lot, but this is stretching it a bit," greeted Air Force Master Sergeant Jim Stanfield. "Do you realize that with the wind chill it's twenty degrees below zero out here?"

As the likable New Yorker led them inside, Graham replied, "Your blood just needs a little thickening, Sergeant."

The interior passageway that both of them were soon walking down was so well heated that Graham had to remove his parka to keep from sweating.

"See anything interesting out there, Ensign?" quizzed the American, who continued leading the way.

"Actually, I was just taking in the sunrise," returned Graham. "Pretty soon, we'll be losing it altogether."

"Ah, the infamous black Arctic winters," reflected Stanfield. "I always was a night person, so this should suit me just fine."

They passed by a bisecting corridor that led to the central control room, and the American continued. "I know some would say it's a bit early, but are you still up for that drink? I don't know about you, but after that nine-hour shift we just completed, I certainly need to unwind before hitting the chow line and then the rack."

"I think that I could manage a nice hot toddy,"

40

answered Graham, who followed his escort into the recreation room. Part health club, part library, the rec room was currently deserted except for a single portly figure grinding away on an exercise bike.

"That's the way, Smitty," greeted Jim Stanfield playfully. "Maybe next time you'll think twice before taking a second helping of Cooky's pie."

"Up yours, Stanfield!" managed the sweat-stained bike rider, between gasps of air.

Grinning at this response, the American master sergeant ducked into yet another corridor. Graham Chapman remained close on his heels. The lighting was subdued in this portion of the complex, and in the distance echoed the spirited sounds of recorded reggae music.

The corridor led them to a narrow entranceway. Here the door had been removed and replaced with long ribbons of green crepe paper that extended from the top portion of the frame. A bamboo sign was hung above this portal. It read, The Golden Ussuk Club—Member's Only!

Inside, a warm, clublike atmosphere prevailed. Tropical plants lined the walls, and a half-dozen cozy bamboo booths were set to the side of a central bar behind which was an expertly rendered mural of Waikiki beach.

Two khaki-uniformed figures sat in one of these booths, sipping their beers and in the midst of a spirited conversation. Jim Stanfield gave them a brief wave before leading Graham over to the bar and commenting.

"Sounds like Jonsey and Pops are talking football again. You know, a damn war could break out, and those two would still be carrying on about whether or not the Bears' defense was overrated."

Graham chuckled at this and sat down on one of

the bamboo bar stools while his Yank drinking companion walked behind the self-service bar, donned an apron, and asked in his best imitation cockney accent.

"What will it be, mate?"

"A hot buttered rum would certainly warm the cockles of my heart," answered Graham.

"Sounds good to me. In fact, I'll join you. Two of Doc Stanfield's famous hot rum toddy's on the way."

While the American expertly mixed their drinks, Graham glanced up at the series of nine-inch-long, rectangularly shaped bones that were hung on the wall just above the mural. There were two dozen altogether. Though their scientific name was Ussuk, the natives knew them simply as walrus penis bones.

Looking down to lose himself in the mural, the Canadian admired the stretch of pure white sand, the crystal blue water, palm trees, and the distinctive volcanic formation known as Diamond Head. He had never been to Hawaii, but as soon as his orders arrived transferring him from Polestar, he promised himself that his first extended leave would take him straight to the exquisite tropical setting displayed on the wall before him.

From the other side of the bar, Jim Stanfield noted the forlorn expression that was etched on the young Canadian's innocent face as he studied the mural. He had seen this same look before, and made certain to pour a bit more of the dark, Virgin Island rum into his co-worker's mug. He topped this off with a half-cup of hot water, a dash of cinnamon, some cloves, and a dab of rich butter.

"Bottom's up, mate," interrupted the Yank as he picked up his own mug in toast.

Suddenly brought back to reality, Graham solemnly reached out for his drink.

"Now come on, lad. Things can't be as bad as all

that," reflected the American. "Just think, we could have been left out in this icebox without a drop of booze to console us. Now that would be serious!"

Graham couldn't help but laugh at this innocent statement, and seeing this, Jim Stanfield added. "That's more like it. Now are you just going to sit there, or are you going to try some of my magical elixir that's guaranteed to cure what ails you?"

The Canadian lifted up the white enamel mug, took an appreciative sniff of the fragrant steam rising from its golden surface, and toasted. "To your health, my friend."

"And to yours," returned the American, who raised his mug to his lips and took a cautious sip. Instantly liking what he tasted, his rugged face lit up in a full smile.

"This is just what the doctor ordered. Finish this baby off, and I promise you that those homesick blues will be gone."

"How did you know that I was homesick?" questioned Graham, in between sips of his toddy.

The American winked. "I don't know, lad. Just call it an educated guess. May I ask where you were stationed when you got the orders sending you on your way to Polestar?"

"I was in Esquimalt, British Columbia," Graham answered directly.

"I know the place," replied the Yank. "Me and the wife spent part of our honeymoon on Vancouver Island and really loved every moment of it. Why with those thick coastal woods and all, it's hard to believe that there's even a military base hidden away out there."

Graham nodded. "It's beautiful country, all right. Having spent most of my life as an Alberta flatlander, those coastal mountains were like a breath of fresh air. Have you ever been to Waikiki beach, Sergeant?"

Stanfield took a long drink before answering. "That's Jim to you, and yes, I have been to the island of Oahu. In fact, I was stationed at Hickam Air Force base when I got the papers sending me to the Arctic."

With his gaze locked on the mural, Graham sighed. "You must have been really disappointed with your new assignment. Hawaii sounds to me like it's the closest thing to paradise we have on this earth."

"Believe it or not, I actually requested this transfer," revealed the grinning American. "You see, I was brought up on a farm in upstate New York, and all that Hawaiian sunshine was finally starting to get to me. There's certainly nothing wrong with the cold, as long as you're dressed for it. If you ask me, it makes a man feel totally alive."

"I beg to differ with you, Jim. All my life I've had nothing but fickle Canadian weather. When it finally does warm up in the summer, the mosquitoes and flies are so bad that you really can't enjoy yourself. And the winters, why they're the worst. I'm sick and tired of having cabin fever for six months of the year. You can give me a warm beach and a shapely Polynesian lady any day of the week, and I guarantee you won't be hearing any complaints from me."

Jim Stanfield chuckled. "I still say that it would get to you eventually. In a couple of months you'd be begging for a cool spell, so that you could finally stop sweating. Although, I must admit, this Arctic weather is a bit extreme. How long are you up here for?"

"Six months," replied the Canadian. "And you?"

"The same," answered Stanfield as he warmed his large hands on the sides of his mug.

"Isn't that an awfully long time to be away from your wife?" asked Graham.

The American polished off the rest of his drink

before answering. "Not really. You see, we split up this past spring. The last I heard from her, she was living in Waikiki with a Hawaiian surfing instructor. I should have known that she would go native on me. That one was never satisfied from the very start."

Conscious now of why the American had most likely requested a transfer to such an isolated outpost, Graham turned his attention back to his drink. The rum was strong, and he could already feel its soothing effects. No longer feeling all alone in his misery, the Canadian began tapping his foot to the spirited reggae music that continued to blare forth from the room's excellent stereo speakers. Ironically enough, he identified the song that was currently playing as Bob Marley's, "No Woman, No Cry." While wondering if his suddenly morose drinking companion had ever really listened to the clever lyrics to this piece, Graham became aware of another's presence behind him. He turned and set his eyes on a tall, khaki-uniformed black man who hurriedly entered the room and spoke excitedly.

"Ah, I should have known I'd find you in here, Stanfield. You asked me to let you know the moment we had the *Flying Kremlin* on the scope. Well, we've got 'em all right, clear as day, just leaving Siberian air space."

This surprise revelation served to immediately divert the broad-shouldered New Yorker from his thoughtful reverie. Catching his drinking companion's eye, Stanfield winked.

"Well, Canuck, shall we go and see what a real live Ilyushin-76 looks like on an OTH-B?"

Already standing, Graham polished off the rest of his drink and turned for the exit. Master Sergeant Jim Stanfield followed him, all the while busily ripping off the apron that he had previously neglected to remove.

They arrived in the central control room along with several other curious observers, likewise drawn from other portions of the compound. To facilitate their viewing, the commander had activated the main display screen. Fully occupying one entire wall of the cavernous room, the screen was filled with a large polar projection map. A constant circular blue light, that was set on the northern extremity of Baffin Island corresponded to their current position, while the only other visual illumination was a flashing red star, located off the coast of central Siberia. It proved to be the senior duty officer, Captain Carl Schluter, who provided them with the latest update.

"They should have crossed Severnaya Zemlya by now. From here on in, there's nothing but the frozen Arctic ocean between them and Ellesmere Island.

"We picked up the first blip about a quarter of an hour ago. Conditions in the ionosphere are excellent today, and we tagged 'em way beyond the two-thousand-mile threshold. The prearranged flight plan will take them over the pole in another hour. Interestingly enough, they seemed to take off a little early, though there's a pretty brisk tail wind that could be helping them out a bit. That means in less than three hours they'll be almost directly overhead. Just to insure that they aren't carrying any ELINT gear aboard, we'll be going off-line long before then. Thule will take over for us at that point. We all know the Soviets would just love to get a definite trace of our frequencies, and we're not about to let them have the opportunity.

"Their ETA in Ottawa . . ."

While the bespectacled American captain continued his emotionless briefing, Graham couldn't help but ponder one disturbing element of his discourse. Even in the midst of peace talks, the paranoid Ameri-

46

cans were worried about Soviet machinations. As if the Premier's plane would be carrying any spying gear on it!

This was the very attitude that promoted the unparalleled arms race of the last four decades. Trust was the key to world peace. Without it, men would always be looking over their shoulders, always fearful that the other side was trying to unfairly gain the advantage.

As far as Graham was concerned, the time to set aside these childish paranoid fears was right now, before a new crisis once again brought the world to the brink of nuclear destruction. Since the Soviets appeared to be sincere with their desire to demilitarize their portion of the Arctic, the Americans could at the very least keep Polestar active as a gesture of international goodwill. For if this Arctic treaty indeed became reality, installations such as the one they currently occupied would eventually become as extinct as the great woolly mammoths that once walked these same frozen plains thousands of years ago. Certain of this fact, the Canadian yawned and discreetly excused himself. He headed for his bunk, lack of sleep and the toddy he had just consumed finally having caught up with him.

Three hours later, Graham was roused out of a sound sleep by a firm hand on his shoulder. Snapped instantly awake, the young ensign looked into the concerned face of Master Sergeant Jim Stanfield.

"Get up and throw on some clothes," the Yank whispered. "There's something you won't want to miss going on in the control room."

Not bothering to take the time to question the American, Graham wiped the sleep from his startled eyes and rose to dress himself. Minutes later, he was standing in the control center, along with some other

47

concerned technicians. All eyes were focused on the main display screen, where a single red star was visible directly over the North Pole. Glancing up to the large digital clock that was mounted above the screen, Graham spoke.

"I don't get it. If that's the correct time, why hasn't the *Flying Kremlin* progressed farther than that? I thought that they'd be flying almost directly above us by now."

"They most probably are," replied Jim Stanfield succinctly.

"Then what's that red star doing above the Pole?" continued the confused Canadian.

"That, my friend, is a Soviet Tupolev Tu-20, Bear-E reconnaissance plane," returned Stanfield. "We first tagged it a little over two hours ago, right before the *Flying Kremlin* began altering their flight plan."

Looking again to the giant display screen, Graham again queried. "What do you mean, altering their flight plan? Has something happened to the Premier's plane?"

Stanfield shook his head. "Right now, we just don't know. All we've got for certain is that approximately twenty minutes ago, the Ilyushin-76 carrying Premier Suratov left its prearranged cruising height of 42,650 feet, and began steadily descending. Since Polestar was scheduled to go off-line at this same time, Captain Schluter contacted Cheyenne Mountain and received permission to remain active, for as long as it took to get a firm lock on the Premier's plane. We thus remained briefly on-line, and what we subsequently learned shocked the dickens out of us. For the *Flying Kremlin* was located flying less than twenty-thousand feet off the ice pack's surface, and headed straight for us!

"Needless to say, with that Bear recon circling

nearby, we immediately went silent. What you're seeing now is being relayed to us by Thule."

"Maybe they're just having mechanical difficulties of some sort," offered the optimistic Canadian.

Nodding thoughtfully, Jim Stanfield pointed to the glassed-in balcony that directly faced the glowing display screen. "Though I seriously doubt that's the case. Right now those two are the only ones around here who most likely know what the hell is going on up there."

Looking up to the balcony, Graham spotted two seated officers. One of these bespectacled figures was Captain Carl Schluter. Sitting close beside him, his bald scalp shining in the bright track lighting, was the base commander, Colonel Oliver Paxton. With a red telephone handset cradled close to his ear, Paxton seemed to be in the midst of an animated conversation.

"I'll bet my pension that the old man is on the horn with CINCNORAD. He most probably wants to know if Polestar should go active or not."

Graham nodded, and with his eyes still glued to the glassed-in balcony, watched as Captain Schluter picked up a white telephone. Seconds later, the phone at the monitor console that lay directly beside Graham began ringing. An alert technician quickly answered it, and with his palm covering the phone's transmitter, began frantically scanning the lower portion of the control room. He halted his search when his gaze locked in on the gangly figure that stood beside the coffee machine.

"Hey Kowolski, the captain wants you on the double!" cried the seated technician.

Graham watched as Sergeant Vic Kowolski hurriedly made his way over to the console. The two had played chess together, and Graham had been somewhat surprised to learn that Kowolski had been born in the Soviet Union, though his parents had emigrated to the United States when he was but a youngster.

Kowolksi was the type of individual who always seemed to be in some sort of disciplinary trouble, yet he was on his best behavior as he took the telephone from the technician, listened to what the caller had to say, mumbled a brief reply, and hung up the receiver. As he addressed the airman who had called him over to the phone, Graham scooted over closer so that he could hear for himself what the Russian-born sergeant had to say.

"The colonel wants me to contact the Il-76. Can you get them for me, Smitty?"

"No trouble, Vic. Hang on a sec while I give them a ring."

Reaching up to activate his transmitter, the technician expertly dialed a large, black frequency knob, waited a second, and then turned to give Vic Kowolski a thumbs-up. Without hesitating, Kowolski picked up a lightweight headset and began speaking fluent Russian into its miniature transmitter. As he pressed the speakers to his ears to listen for a response, he somberly shook his head, and tried yet another burst of Russian into the microphone. He tried several more times before giving up and reaching for the intercom.

"It's useless, Captain. I can get through to them all right. But all they give me is some frantic, garbled crap saying that their radio is on the fritz. It certainly doesn't sound kosher to me, sir."

Listening to these words, Graham felt his gut turn sour. If Vic Kowolski was right and the Soviets were playing games with them, then what in the hell did they hope to gain by attempting such a foolish charade? Praying that this wasn't the case, the Canadian returned his glance to the glassed-in balcony, where

Polestar's bald-headed senior officer sat with the red phone cradled close to his ear, his somber stare locked on the central display screen, while their destinies hovered somewhere in the frigid skies above.

Chapter Three

During the early 1960's, engineers with the U.S. Department of Defense began blasting out a series of immense caverns inside the solid granite rock that made up Colorado's Cheyenne Mountain. Altogether fifteen separate buildings were constructed inside this subterranean netherworld, all of which were mounted on massive, steel-spring shock absorbers, that would hopefully allow the site to survive all but a direct hit in the event of a nuclear war. Once completed, the state-of-the-art complex became home to the North American Aerospace Defense Command, or NORAD as it was more commonly called.

The facilities' main job was to determine whether the Soviet Union was launching a surprise nuclear attack against the North American continent. NORAD did this by monitoring a variety of sophisticated sensors that ranged from satellites to ground-based radar stations. As the centerpiece of the entire U.S. strategic command and control system, NORAD had the task, if an attack was indeed determined to be forthcoming, of implementing a variety of preplanned retaliatory strikes, whose details were listed in the SIOP—the Pentagon's top-secret Single Integrated Operational Plan.

The individual responsible for making such a demanding decision was the installation's commander in chief. Currently holding the position of CINCNORAD was General Thomas Laird. Born and raised in a small farming community outside of Omaha, Nebraska, Laird was an early graduate of the Air Force Academy, where he quarterbacked the football team to an unprecedented national championship. Later, as a fighter pilot in Viet Nam, he won a wide assortment of decorations for valor, and, more importantly, the undying respect of his fellow officers and enlisted men. After being shot down over Da Nang during the Tet offensive, Laird was captured and taken prisoner by the Viet Cong. For six months he lived a miserable existence, subject to constant torture and starvation. Yet he never lost hope, and when the opportunity finally presented itself, he made good his escape, while carrying one of his less fortunate comrades on his back through miles of thick jungle and snaked-infested swampland.

With the war's conclusion, Laird moved on to Washington D.C., where he became involved with NORAD. One of the youngest generals in the history of the Air Force, Thomas Laird was appointed CINCNORAD on the anniversary of his forty-fifth birthday. For over a year now he had held this all-important position, though reliable rumor had it that he would once again soon be packing to return to Washington, this time as a full-fledged member of the Joint Chiefs of Staff.

Though such an appointment would certainly be the pinnacle of a relatively short but full military career, Laird found himself with little time to ponder his rapid rise to power. His current responsibilities as CINCNORAD demanded his total attention. This was especially the case this morning, as a potentially serious and somewhat puzzling incident was unfolding in the Arctic skies above Canada's Baffin Island. Here an Ilyushin I1-76 airliner carrying Soviet Premier Alexander Suratov had mysteriously departed from its prearranged flight plan. Last recorded at an altitude of less than 20,000 feet, the so-called *Flying Kremlin* had departed from its intended course to Ottawa, and was believed to be approaching the ultrasensitive, restricted airspace above Polestar, NORAD's newest DEW Line radar station. Such an unauthorized overflight could have serious consequences for NORAD's continued integrity, and Thomas Laird was taking this incident most seriously.

Currently positioned deep inside the Cheyenne Mountain facility, Laird was seated at his battle station, inside the glassed-in balcony of the central command post. Built into the wall before him was a huge, seventeen-by-seventeen-foot screen. Projected on to it was a polar view of the North American continent. With his intense, pale green stare locked on this map, Laird studied the small, blinking red star that slowly circled the vicinity of the North Pole.

"That Bear-E still bothers the hell out of me, Ben," grimly reflected CINCNORAD to his immediate subordinate, Brigadier General Benjamin Wagner. "If the *Flying Kremlin* was really having equipment problems, the Bear surely would have monitored their abrupt course change and attempted to contact the I1-76. But so far, we haven't heard a peep out of them."

"That's because this little course change is all part of a carefully planned scenario," offered Ben Wagner, whose silver-gray hair glistened in the muted green tones thrown off his computer display terminal. "It's all too obvious what the Reds are trying to pull off here, Tom."

54

"So you still think the Russkies are utilizing the I1-76 as a tickler?" retorted CINCNORAD.

"That's affirmative," answered Wagner. "We all know the Russians have been dying to find out what frequencies Polestar transmits on, ever since we first went on-line. Can you think of a more perfect probe than the *Flying Kremlin?* Assuming that we wouldn't dare question a Mayday coming from a plane carrying their Premier, the Reds are gambling that we'll turn on Polestar to track this so-called crippled aircraft, while meantime that Bear records the exact frequencies Polestar operates on. Then when it comes time to initiate a future attack, they'll know just how to jam our most sophisticated Arctic radar station."

CINCNORAD nodded. "Sounds convincing, Ben. But do you really think the publicity-shy Russkies would dare send the *Flying Kremlin* on such a mission? After all, I can't think of a much more high-profile flight than this one. Why every news service on the planet is covering it."

"All the more reason for them to think they can pull it off," Wagner shot back. He scanned the central display map and suddenly saw a pair of blue flashing lights become visible just off the northwestern coast of Greenland. "It looks like the ceiling has finally lifted in Thule, because there're those blessed Eagles we've been waiting for all morning!"

This hopeful statement was accented by the shrill, distinctive ring of a telephone. Briefly catching his subordinate's concerned stare, Thomas Laird reached down to the console and picked up the sole red handset.

"Yes, Mr. President," greeted CINCNORAD. ". . . I understand, sir. But if you'll just give us another fourteen minutes, we'll have this mystery solved once and for all. You see, those F-15's we've been waiting to launch have finally gotten airborne."

A worried expression crossed Thomas Laird's face as he intently listened to his Commander in Chief. "But Mr. President, what about that Bear recon platform that's still circling the Pole? We feel it's all too obvious that what we're witnessing is not a mechanical breakdown at all, but a deliberate attempt by the Russians to further probe our air-defense system."

Thomas Laird winced as the voice on the other line came through even stronger. There was defeat in CINCNORAD's hushed tone as he humbly replied.

"Yes, Mr. President. I understand your position. We'll do so at once."

As he hung up the receiver, Laird solemnly addressed his second-in-command. "Get back on the horn with Ollie Paxton, and tell him to crank up Polestar."

Looking on as disappointment registered on Benjamin Wagner's face, CINCNORAD grimly mumbled. "I hope to God the President is right. Because if this isn't a legitimate air emergency, the Russkies are about to reap a goddamned intelligence field day!"

The night that had just passed had been one of the longest of Ootah's young life. Kept awake by his father's worsening cough, both Ootah and his wife did everything they could to relieve the old man's discomfort. Extra fat was thrown on the lamp in an effort to sweat the evil spirit out of Nakusiak's diseased body. With the assistance of several fur blankets, his fever broke, yet the hacking cough that continued to bring blood to his lips seemed to further intensify. It had gotten so bad that it was difficult for the old man to even breathe properly.

Unable to get down any of the walrus meat, Nakusiak's strength continued to ebb. His cheeks and forehead were sallow, and it took supreme effort for him to sit up and relieve himself.

Remembering the sorrow that had crossed his heart when his mother had died, Ootah became desperate. In no mood for another burial, he racked his mind in an effort to come up with a cure. It was Akatingwah who suggested making a trip into Arctic Bay to bring back one of the white medicine men.

Ootah was seriously considering such a drastic move when Nakusiak forcefully intervened. Between violent fits of coughing he implored them to keep such a sorcerer far from their igloo.

"Please son!" he pleaded between gasps of air. "You mustn't dirty my soul now that I'm about to be visiting our ancestors. If I must die, let it be amongst my own people."

Ootah did not dare go against his father's iron will, and gracefully backed down, suggesting instead that he go and fetch Powhuktuk, the shaman. Nakusiak gave him his assent, and off Ootah went on this desperate mission of mercy.

It was a rare windless night. A myriad of stars twinkled in the sparkling-clear heavens, while on the distant horizon, the northern lights painted an ethereal canvas of spiraling, pulsating color. Taking these conditions as a good omen, Ootah roused his dogs and hitched up the sled. There were tears in Akatingwah's eyes as she bid him farewell before returning to the snowhouse to attend to Nakusiak.

Ootah only had to use his sinew whip but once, to turn the pack to the west, where Powhuktuk's snowhouse was located. His lead dog, Arnuk, seemed to sense his master's urgency, and pushed on his furry brethren with a maddening fierceness. Onward they raced over the ice pack, the knife-sharp runner's of the sled smoothly cutting through the surface of the frozen sea with a loud hiss.

Oddly enough, the shaman was fully dressed and seemed to be awaiting Ootah's arrival. With barely a word spoken between them, Powhuktuk shouldered his medicine bag and crawled beneath the blankets of the sled.

The trip back was a bit more strenuous. The dogs were tiring, and to make matters even worse, a headwind had developed. Forced to use the whip, Ootah sprinted beside the sled, to create as light a load as possible.

They arrived back at camp just as the first hint of dawn was coloring the eastern horizon. Akatingwah ran outside to greet them. Once again there were tears in her eyes as she explained Nakusiak's deteriorating condition.

Powhuktuk completely ignored her emotional state, and calmly went about his business. First the shaman removed a brightly painted mask from his bag. It had the features of a demon, and was designed to fit over Powhuktuk's head with the aid of a piece of sinew string. Next he pulled out a whalebone rattle, and a flat, hand-held drum that he began furiously beating.

Raising his deep voice to the heavens, the shaman sang out in prayer. All the time quickening his drumbeat, he circled the igloo three complete times before ducking through it's tunnel-like doorway.

Ootah and Akatingwah had been instructed to remain outdoors while the ceremony of healing was initiated. They passed the time by attending to the dogs. First they unhitched them. Then Ootah unsealed the cache and cut off several thick pieces of walrus meat. Hungry after their spirited journey, the dogs ate heartily before settling in behind their protective wall for a well-deserved rest.

Ootah was also beginning to feel the effects of their long sleepless night, and was just about to suggest to his wife that they curl up beneath the sled blanket, when a loud, rattling sound broke from the snowhouse. They turned toward this alien noise and caught sight of Powhuktuk, who had the mask over his head and was shaking the whalebone rattle with a furious intensity. Once again the shaman completely circled the igloo three times before halting beside the entranceway and abruptly silencing the rattle and pulling off his mask. Gazing out with wide eyes to the rapidly developing dawn, Powhuktuk cried out to the glowing heavens.

"Great Spirit, Nakusiak your son awaits the arrival of the fiery sled that will take him on his final journey. Tarry not, for this great hunter longs to return to the land of his ancestors."

Spreading out his arms overhead, the shaman let loose a bloodcurdling wail. So loud was this bansheelike scream, even the dogs were awakened from their deep slumber.

"Ootah, your father calls for you!" shouted Powhuktuk forcefully. "Go bid him farewell on this longest of trips from which no mortal returns."

Without a moment's hesitation, Ootah left his mate's side and headed straight for the interior of the snowhouse. He found his father lying peacefully beneath the covers of the sleeping pallet. Curled at his side, sound asleep, was his grandson.

Touched by this innocent scene, Ootah's expectations soared. Somehow Powhuktuk had performed yet another miracle, and Nakusiak would live! Yet any high hopes on his part were abruptly crushed when Ootah spotted the large pool of bright red blood that stained Nakusiak's lips, throat, and upper torso.

With the flickering flame of the soapstone lamp casting a somber shadow, Ootah kneeled down beside his dying father. No sooner did he reach this position, when Nakusiak's eyes popped open. So weak was the strained voice that followed, that Ootah had to bend his ear to his father's lips to hear him.

"Ootah, my son. You mustn't mourn my passing. For I go on a journey that I travel of my own choosing. Yet before I depart to rejoin the ancestors, you must promise me one thing."

Nakusiak halted a moment to clear his dry throat before continuing. "The bone amulet that I gave you, do you still have it, my son?"

Immediately grasping the sacred charm that hung from his neck, Ootah replied. "Of course I do, Father. Why I'll never take it off!"

Nakusiak managed a weak smile. "I knew that I could rely on you, my son. Now, remember our shared dream. And when the comet arrives in all its fiery glory, recollect the prophecy that the grandfathers handed down to the people at the very beginning of time. And perhaps the Great Spirit will intervene, and mankind will be spared."

With the conclusion of these words, Nakusiak was caught up in a fit of violent coughing. And as the blood poured down the corners of his cracked lips, the elder shut his eyes and initiated the first steps of his final journey.

Beside him, Ootah was strangely affected by his father's passing. No tears fell down his cheeks. Rather, he felt as if a great weight had been lifted from him. And it was in this spirit that he began making the burial arrangements.

Later that morning, not long after Nakusiak's corpse was deposited in a shallow grave at the outskirts of their camp, Ootah was drawn to the very edge of the pack ice. As he gazed up into the clear blue heavens, he felt a strange feeling overcome him, and for a brief, fleeting magical moment he touched upon the oneness that guides mankind's destiny. Suddenly no longer afraid of that final journey he, too, would have to eventually face, the Inuit scanned the vast Arctic sky, finally fixing his gaze on a thin white line that cut the heavens like a knife. No stranger to the vapor trails left in the wake of the white man's airplanes, he knew this track was lower than the others he had viewed, and somehow different.

Ootah was in the midst of contemplating what made this sky trail unique when the heavens exploded in a fireball of dazzling color. This blindingly bright shaft of light was followed by a deafening boom, that seemed to shake the very ice beneath him.

Mesmerized by the intense wheel of fire that seemed to be falling toward the earth, Ootah suddenly got an inspiration. Could this be the comet his father had warned of? And if it was, did this blast signal the end of the world that the grandfathers prophesied?

Trembling at this thought, Ootah brought his hand up to the smooth bone amulet that hung from his neck. He had sworn to Nakusiak that he would carry on the tradition handed down by his father's father. This was a great responsibility, and to insure that he didn't fail, he could do but one thing. With his eyes still locked on the smoking debris that continued to fall from the heavens in the distance, Ootah determined that he would initiate a holy pilgrimage to gather these remains and determine if they were indeed from the realm of the Great Spirit.

Chapter Four

Less than twenty-four hours after the USS *Defiance* returned to her home port, her captain was called to the base commander's office to explain their early arrival. Matt Colter had just completed this two-hour meeting, and as the car carrying him back to the *Defiance* returned to the docks, the blond-haired Annapolis grad pondered the rather tense conference that had just taken place.

During his past encounters with Admiral Allen Long, Colter had always found the distinguished, white-haired officer an open-minded, compassionate individual. It had been under Admiral Long's expert tutelage that Matt had adjusted to the rigors of his first command, and matured as both a naval officer and a human being. Yet for the first time ever, Matt had seen a different side to the admiral's personality. Cold and analytical, Long had proceeded as if it were Matt's fault the mission failed.

Quick to defend himself, Colter did his best to explain the reason why he was forced to cut their mission short. With the assistance of the ship's log, he described the three separate instances when their prototype surface-scanning Fathometer improperly interpreted the ice conditions topside, causing a trio of bone-jarring collisions. He even displayed a recently taken photograph of the *Defiance*'s rudder; it clearly showed the spot where a navigation beacon had been cleanly sheared off by the force of one of these violent confrontations with the pack ice.

Seemingly deaf to this certain proof, Admiral Long continued to probe Matt's motives for prematurely concluding the patrol. He even pulled out the transcript of the log of one of the *Defiance*'s earlier Arctic patrols. On that one Matt Colter had also hesitated to bring his command topside because of difficult ice conditions.

Such a move on Long's part angered the young captain. This past incident had been more than fully explained, and concerned an attempt by the *Defiance* to surface at the North Pole alongside a British weather station. Though their surface-scanning Fathometer had not failed on that day, in Colter's opinion, the polynya displayed topside had not been large enough to safely accommodate the *Defiance*. This was in direct contradiction to the observations of the weather station crew, who'd reported an opening more than sufficient for the three-hundred-foot-long vessel.

Matt struggled to control his gathering rage, and as calmly as possible reiterated his passionate feelings on the subject. As captain of the *Defiance*, he had been responsible for interpreting the data available to him. And in his opinion, the polynya that lay beside the weather station was just too narrow and jagged to attempt squeezing the *Defiance* into it.

"Since when is the captain of a US naval vessel allowed to be second-guessed by the civilian crew of a foreign weather station?" Matt Colter countered firmly. "As I said before, that open lead was just too tight, and I wasn't about to risk the ship on an ascent

I deemed a definite safety hazard."

Unable to contain himself, Matt forcefully continued. "The day I'm ordered to unnecessarily jeopardize the lives of my crew merely for the sake of adhering to a preplanned mission, that is the day I no longer want to be a part of this man's Navy!"

Sensing his upset, Admiral Long coolly replied. "Easy does it, Matt. As you well know, the well-being of our men is still the Navy's paramount concern. Yet the very nature of submarine duty is full of risks. Why every time you steam out of Long Island Sound you go in harm's way. Of course, these dangers are multiplied a hundredfold when dealing with Arctic operations.

"Don't forget, I've surfaced a sub at the Pole myself, and I'll be the first to admit I was scared as hell all the way topside. No one is questioning your bravery, Matt. But I've got to know if I can rely on the *Defiance* to carry out any mission that might be requested of it, should this Cold War we've been locked in for the last four decades ever heat up."

Matt Colter answered without a hint of hesitation. "Just give us equipment that can be depended upon and I'll take care of the rest, Admiral. If it has the slimmest chance of succeeding, the men of the *Defiance* will pull it off."

"You know, I believe you'll do just that," retorted the white-haired admiral with a sigh.

The tension was suddenly broken, and Long went on to consider Matt Colter's suggestion that the laser surface-scanning Fathometer be removed, and the old unit be reconnected. A compromise was eventually reached: an attempt would be made to repair the prototype device, while the original unit was to be readied as a backup. On this conciliatory note, the meeting was adjourned.

As the sub pens loomed in the distance, Matt decided that he had pleaded his case to the best of his ability. If command was going to officially censure him for his circumspect approach, then so be it. Yet it aggravated him that not once had the admiral mentioned condemning the one responsible for this meeting in the first place—the designer of the prototype surface-scanning Fathometer. As far as Matt was concerned, this was the individual who should be having his competency looked into, but he was thankful that he had received permission to get their old unit back on-line. Colter's attention was diverted as his driver braked the car to a halt before a central wharf. The young captain exited the vehicle and momentarily stood on the pier to admire the vessel floating before him.

Looking sleek and deadly, the USS *Defiance* sat low in the water, with barely half of its black, teardrop-shaped hull exposed. Gathered behind its tall sail were a group of three dungaree-clad sailors. One of these individuals wore a holstered pistol and alertly carried a combat shotgun. Anxious to return to the environment that he felt most familiar with, Matt Colter briefly scanned the dock site.

Parked in a nearby staging area were the support vehicles that were assisting with the current refit. A large, corrugated steel warehouse stood nearby, with the gray waters of the Thames River flowing in the background. It was a brisk late fall afternoon. The trees on the opposite bank had long since lost their leaves, and a sharp northerly wind hinted at the bitter, New England winter that would all too soon be upon them. Turning the collar of his light jacket up to meet these penetrating gusts, Matt gratefully strode forward to return to his floating home away from home.

Below deck in the *Defiance*'s wardroom, Lieutenant Commander Al Layman was contentedly nibbling away on a fresh cake donut when the sub's commanding officer entered the compartment. Seated at his usual place at the far end of the rectangularly shaped table, the XO noted Matt Colter's solemn expression and greeted him cautiously.

"How did it go, Skipper?"

Heavily seating himself at the head of the table, Matt replied. "The usual cock and bull, Al. As if I had anything to do with that damn Fathometer's failure."

From out of the nearby galley, an alert steward soundlessly appeared. He placed a cup of steaming hot black coffee and a platter of fresh donuts before the captain. Warming his hands on the side of his mug, Colter added.

"At least it seems I was able to get a portion of our case across. The admiral has given us permission to hook up the old ice machine as a backup."

While self-consciously wiping off the excess crumbs of powdered sugar that had gotten left behind in his thick mustache, the XO nodded. "That's certainly good news, Skipper. I'll get the chief on it at once."

As he jotted down a note on the half-filled legal pad resting on the table, Al Layman continued. "Speaking of that new-fangled Fathometer, we took on some support personnel soon after you left for your meeting. They're currently up in the sail trying to figure out what went wrong with the frigging thing."

Matt Colter seemed impressed with this revelation. "Well, I'll be. Command certainly doesn't seem to be dragging its feet on this one. I can't wait to hear what excuses they'll come up with to save the reputation of the pencil pusher responsible for dreaming up that device."

"I'm sure they'll be good ones," reflected the XO as

he reached into his pocket and removed a well-worn briar pipe and a pouch of tobacco. "I still think the laser was improperly calibrated. That would account for the discrepancy between the pictures of the ice conditions fed into our Nav system and those we actually ran into."

As the rich scent of vanilla- and rum-soaked tobacco filled the air, the captain responded. "But why in the hell do we even need such a system in the first place? Though they might take a bit more sweat and effort on the part of the crew, the old machines have been in service over three decades, and never once have I heard of one of those units failing."

"I guess there's no use trying to buck progress," the XO offered. "You must admit, when the bugs are finally worked out, having such a sophisticated system on board will certainly save a lot of time and worry on our part. Not only will the lasers accurately plot all available surface leads to the tenth of an inch, they'll determine the pack's precise thickness as well. And then all we have to do is sit back on our duffs while this data is incorporated into our Nav system, and look on as 'big brother' automatically handles the ascent from there."

"It still sounds like a pipe dream to me, Al. If this system works as planned, pretty soon a human crew won't be needed at all. Why risk lives when computers can handle the whole damn show?" Thoughtfully taking a sip of coffee, Matt Colter grinned. "I imagine many similar conversations filled the wardrooms of past warships when other radical changes were about to be incorporated into the fleet. I'll bet the sailors of a hundred years ago turned a skeptical eye on the introduction of fossil-fueled engines into ships and preferred sails."

"And don't forget the recent advent of the nuclear

reactor," added Al Layman. "If it wasn't for the vision and tenacity of Hyman Rickover, who knows if under-the-ice missions would even be possible today. No, Skipper, though it might take time to smooth out the kinks, I say it's impossible to ignore the advances technology brings our way."

Quietly absorbing this statement, Matt Colter worked on his coffee. He was a good halfway into the mug of strong brew when he again spoke.

"What do you have planned for your leave, Al?"

The XO replied while tamping down the tobacco in the bowl of his pipe. "Actually, this will be the perfect time for me to make good on that anniversary celebration I missed out on last week. I thought I'd surprise Donna and make a reservation at the inn on Nantucket where we spent our honeymoon."

"How long has it been now, Al?"

"Believe it or not, we're going on our eighth year, Skipper. Though in that time I've only been here twice to celebrate on the actual date of our anniversary.

"How about you? This would be the perfect opportunity for you to winterize your place in the White Mountains before the first big snows hit."

Matt Colter shook his head. "Afraid not, Al. You see, the last I heard, Kay and the kids were still living there. Seems she's got something going with the owner of the lodge she was selling her paintings at this summer, and she asked if it was okay to have the place for the rest of the season."

Conscious that he was treading on delicate ground, Al Layman carefully responded. "I didn't realize she had left Boston, Skipper. The last I heard, she had that great teaching position at Wellesley."

"So she did," reflected Colter. "But just like Kay, she goes and blows her tenure on a summertime fling. I pray this relationship works out for her, at the very least for the kids' sake."

The somber mood that had suddenly descended on the wardroom was broken by the arrival of a smiling, khaki-suited sailor carrying a half-filled duffel bag. Quick to note the no-nonsense looks on the faces of the ship's two most senior officers, Petty Officer First Class Stanley Roth sucked in his slightly bulging gut and stiffened to attention.

"Sorry to bother you, Captain. But you asked me earlier to give you an update on that sonar system's checkout before I took off, sir."

"That I did, Mr. Roth," returned Colter, instinctively putting personal concerns out of his mind. "But first off, how are you feeling? Did that medicine Pills prescribed for you do the job?"

The ship's senior sonar technician nodded. "I'm feeling much better, Captain. The fever's gone, and all I have left is a little discomfort in the lower left portion of my jaw."

"Good," replied Colter. "I hope you're still planning to see the base dentist."

"That I am, sir. In fact, I'm headed there right now. I talked it over with the guys, and they said if I didn't go to the clinic right away, I'd most likely put it off until the end of my leave. And that's not exactly something to look forward to, is it, sir?"

"No it isn't, Mr. Roth," answered the captain. "Get that problem looked after professionally and we can all rest easier on our next patrol. After all, I can't afford to have my best man in the sound shack down with any kind of ailment. Speaking of the devil, how did that equipment check out?"

Still basking in the warmth of the unexpected compliment his commanding officer had just given him, Stanley Roth quickly replied, "We're still showing a problem in the aft passive range-determination array,

Captain. I think it's merely a software glitch, sir. To find out for certain, I've got Seaman Warren running a complete program analysis."

"Very good," the captain nodded. "Make certain Warren lets the chief know if it's anything more serious than a software screwup. There's no telling how long we're in for, and if we've got a major problem, I'd like to get at it with all due haste."

"Captain, I'd be more than willing to do the rest of the check myself," the petty officer volunteered.

"I'd like nothing more than that, Mr. Roth. But have you forgotten about that appointment at the dental clinic? Have that tooth looked after, and then go out on the town and enjoy yourself for a night. Lord knows you've earned it. Besides, Seaman Warren seems like a capable enough fellow. Don't you agree, XO?"

Al Layman took the scarred bit of pipe out of his mouth and succinctly answered. "He'll do. So listen to your captain and hit the gangway, Roth."

"Yes, sir!" the petty officer snapped as he turned to exit the wardroom.

Enlivened by the likable sonar technician's visit, the XO stood. "Looks like I'd better get the show on the road myself, Skipper. The crew manifest is on your desk. Lieutenant Marshall is the current officer of the deck. On the way out, I'll make certain the chief gets the word on hooking up the old ice machine."

As Layman began gathering up his belongings, he remembered one last detail. "By the way, Skipper, you never did say how you were going to spend your leave."

Standing himself, Matt Colter answered. "Right now, it looks like I'll probably just hang around here for a while. I've got plenty of paperwork to get caught up on, and if I do get the hankering for some solid land under my feet and a little fresh air, maybe I'll go up to Mystic for a day."

"You do that," advised Al Layman firmly. "Because if there's anyone on board this ship who deserves some time to himself, it's you, Skipper."

"I don't know about that, XO. It seems to me you put in your fair share of overtime on this last patrol. So get out of here, and enjoy that second honeymoon!"

Mockingly saluting, the XO smiled and turned for his cabin. Alone now in the wardroom, Matt finished off his coffee and decided to take off for the ship's conning tower to see how the technicians were doing with the repair of the faulty surface-scanning Fathometer. To get to this portion of the *Defiance,* he exited through the forward hatchway. This put him in an equipment-packed passageway lined with stainless steel piping.

With a fluid ease, he passed by the locked radio room, picturing the state-of-the-art receivers and transmitters in this all-important compartment, equipment that allowed them almost instant contact with command even when deeply submerged. Next, he walked by the sonar room, or sound shack as it was affectionately called. The door to this room was open, and Colter could see Seaman Lester Warren hunched over one of the consoles. Though Warren was fairly new to the Navy, he was a self-proclaimed computer nerd, his fascination with such equipment having begun in grade school. A quick learner, the Texan had graduated first in his computer-science class while in basic training, and when it was learned that he had above average hearing, he was steered into the arcane art of sonar detection. So far he showed great promise, and with Petty Officer Roth's expert guidance, the youngster could have a bright career.

Confident that the sonarman could find the glitch Roth had suspected, the captain continued forward. This brought him into that spacious portion of the vessel where the sub's central control room and attack center were located. Several members of the crew were gathered around a console under the capable direction of the ship's current OOD, Lieutenant Don Marshall. The slightly built, red-headed Georgian was the *Defiance*'s full-time diving officer, and was not known for sartorial splendor. Yet in this instance the captain found Marshall dressed in a crisp pair of khakis, his perpetually loose shirt bottom neatly tucked into the sharply creased pants. Noting that the enlisted men working at the OOD's side were similarly dressed in fresh coveralls, Colter suspected that they had been anticipating a visit from the base commander, and had dressed this way to impress him.

Certainly not disappointed that his men were suddenly taking an interest in their outward appearances, the captain loudly cleared his throat to announce his presence.

"Good afternoon, gentlemen. I hope I'm not breaking in on anything important."

"Not at all, sir," Marshall replied in his deep southern drawl. "I was only going over the diving procedures with those seamen interested in qualifying during this tour."

"Well, don't let me keep you from continuing," returned Colter as he looked past the periscope well to the access hatch cut into the base of the sail. "Tell me, Lieutenant, the civilian engineers on board, are they still inside the sail working on that Fathometer?"

There was an unusual gleam in the OOD's eyes as he answered. "That they are, Captain. Shall I call them down for you?"

Colter shook his head. "That won't be necessary,

72

Lieutenant. I think under the circumstances it's better if I crawl up there unannounced."

"Whatever you say, sir. But it certainly won't be any bother for me to go up there and fetch 'em for you."

A bit puzzled by this reply, Colter turned to the sail. "You may return to your business, Mr. Marshall. I'm quite capable of handling this matter on my own."

The men's stares seemed to be following him as he ducked through the hatch and began to go up the narrow, steel-gauge ladder. Putting out of his mind the notion that his men were up to some sort of mischief, Colter made the climb up to the exposed bridge. A whiff of cool, fresh air, rich with the scent of the sea, met his nostrils, and in the distance he could just make out the sounds of muffled voices. In the hope that this repair team could explain precisely what had malfunctioned on the prototype Fathometer unit, he proceeded up the remaining rungs.

As Colter crawled through the final hatch, he viewed the backs of two workmen, busily digging through an exposed panel that was set near the bridge's latticed floor. Both were dressed in woolen hats and identical heavy, navy blue coveralls that had Naval Arctic Laboratory stenciled in white below their shoulder blades. It was evident that they were completely unaware of his presence, and Colter took advantage of his surprise appearance by going directly on the offensive.

"I hope one of you will be able to explain just what went wrong with that damn unit. If the pencil pusher who invented it only knew its malfunction almost cost the lives of one hundred seven men, he'd hopefully be more careful the next time. This is no laboratory experiment that we're running out here. It's reality of the harshest sort!"

"I doubt if you'll have to worry about another

failure," retorted one of the kneeling figures in an unnaturally high voice.

Only as this individual swiveled around and stood did Colter realize this technician wasn't a man as he had assumed, but a young woman, and a pretty one at that. With her dark, almond-shaped eyes locked onto his startled gaze, she took a step forward and added.

"You must be Captain Colter. I'm Dr. Laurie Lansing of the Naval Arctic lab, and I believe we just found the problem that caused the unit to malfunction. It seems that during installation, the lasers weren't calibrated properly."

"This is a hell of a time to figure that one out," snapped Colter. "That damn machine of yours was almost responsible for our deaths on three separate occasions."

"You have every reason to be upset," Dr. Lansing responded in a conciliatory tone. "I would feel the same way if our situations were reversed. But now that we know the problem, I'm certain it can be rectified."

Capping these words off with a brave smile, she removed her woolen hat and shook loose a long mop of silky black hair. This feature served to further enhance her natural beauty, and Matt Colter's wrath was temporarily quieted. Sensing this, Laurie Lansing continued.

"I know excuses are meaningless now, but this whole problem came into being when I was forced to miss the unit's final fine tuning. I pleaded with Admiral Long to hold off your sailing date, but he said it would be next to impossible to do such a thing for a mere double-check of the equipment. I prayed that the lasers were tuned properly, and when I heard about your close calls under the ice, I felt simply terrible."

74

Her sincerity was painfully real, and Matt Colter couldn't help but be placated. Yet he still found himself with a bone to pick.

"I appreciate your concern, Doctor. But how could the designer of this project allow us to go to sea without making absolutely certain the device was in perfect operating condition? He must have known the risks involved."

"He certainly did," replied Laurie Lansing somberly. "And believe me when I tell you that no one valued human life more than he did. For you see, he was my father, and it was his untimely death that kept me from making those final checks as he would have done."

Genuinely moved by her revelation, Matt Colter shook his head. "I'm sorry. I had no idea such a thing had taken place."

"You have nothing to apologize for, Captain. I guess I should just have been a bit more forceful in my appeal to the admiral to hold the *Defiance* in port a little longer. But with my father's sudden passing and all, I'm afraid that I didn't put up much of an argument."

"Understandably so," reasoned Matt Colter. "If anyone's to blame, it's the admiral for failing to heed your warnings. But that's water over the dam. We survived our confrontation with the ice pack, and now it appears we'll both be getting a second chance. How many hours will the repair effort take?"

"I should be able to give you a fully operational unit in approximately three more days. Most of the work will concern reprogramming the computer interface, though there was a bit of structural damage caused when the sail struck the ice. That must have been some impact."

"You don't know the half of it," observed Matt

Colter. "But fortunately the *Defiance* was built with just such punishment in mind. Though I wouldn't want to have to needlessly put my crew through such an experience again. We're going to be having enough nightmares about those collisions as it is."

Any response on Laurie Lansing's part was cut short by the shrill buzz of the sail's intercom unit. Quick to pick up the black handset, Matt Colter spoke into it.

"Captain here . . . Sure, Lieutenant, I'll be right down."

As he placed the receiver back in its cradle, Colter politely excused himself, then started to return below. Only when he was nearly halfway down the narrow ladder did he realize why the control room crew had appeared so dapper earlier. They had seen the type of woman who was working in the sail, and were doing their best to give her a good impression of them. Grinning at this thought, he jumped off the final two rungs, and expertly slid down the ladder's shiny steel handrails to the deck below.

Colter was surprised to find his XO waiting for him beside the fire-control panel. Al Layman looked serious, and the captain sensed trouble.

"What are you doing back here so soon, Al? I thought you'd be well on your way to Nantucket by now."

Meeting the captain's greeting with a somber scowl, the XO answered him directly. "I wish that was indeed the case, Skipper. But I bumped into the admiral's aide while I was in the Officer's Club making those reservations, and he dropped off this packet he was about to bring over to the *Defiance*. I'll bet my pension it's sailing orders."

As he handed Matt the sealed envelope, the XO added. "Thank the lord I didn't call Donna and let her

76

know about the trip I planned. One more heartbreak like that and it would have meant a divorce for certain."

Not paying this remark much attention, Colter tore open the envelope and removed several typed documents. After skimming the top sheet, he handed it to his second-in-command, commenting, "They're sailing orders all right. And it looks to me like Command wants us out of here as soon as we can restock our stores and get the men back from shore leave."

"Does it say where we're off to?" quizzed Al Layman.

Hastily reading the rest of the packet, the captain answered, "Looks like it's the Arctic again, my friend. Says here that we'll be getting additional orders while at sea."

"But the ice machine," protested the XO. "They can't send us up there again with one unit on the fritz and the other still inoperable."

Matt Colter replied while studying the packet's last sheet. "Command realizes that, and is authorizing us to continue the repairs while we're underway."

"They want us to take that civilian repair team to sea with us?" asked the XO incredulously.

"They sure do, Al. And you don't know the half of it. One of the members of that repair crew is one of the most gorgeous women I've ever laid eyes on."

Al Layman rubbed his forehead. "Oh, swell. A dame on board and more ice to boot. Perhaps you could convince the admiral to leave the woman behind where she belongs."

"I seriously doubt that, my friend," replied Colter with a sigh. "Because these orders aren't just coming down from COMSUBLANT. They're originating from no less a place than the White House!"

Approximately 2,100 miles northwest of the sub base at New London, Connecticut, lay the picturesque village of Banff. Situated on the far western border of the Canadian province of Alberta, Banff was cradled in a magnificent Rocky Mountain valley, that was a hiker's paradise in the summer and a skier's delight in the colder months of the year.

In addition to a variety of excellent hotels and resorts, Banff was also home to an Army cadet-training facility. Here in the brisk mountain air, young men and women prepared for a career in the military. Though this compound was usually closed down at summer's end, it was occasionally opened to accommodate branches of the Canadian armed forces that wished to train troops in the vicinity. This proved to be the case on a cool, crisp fall morning, as a group of twenty-two soldiers lay snug in their bunks catching the tail end of a sound night's sleep.

Oblivious to their contented snores, a pair of khaki-uniformed figures gathered at the head of the barracks. One of these individuals was tall and thin, with short brown hair and a creased, weather-worn face. The other was several inches shorter, with stocky build, smooth brown skin, and rather long, straight black hair. It proved to be the taller of the two who stepped forward. With the first light of dawn just visible through the window behind him, this man's voice boomed out deep and strong.

"Good morning, lads, rise and shine! I hope you enjoyed your little slumber party, because it's time to do your thing for God, Queen, and country. So out of those bunks boys, and look sharp. Because you're Arctic Rangers, the best damn soldiers in the northwoods!"

Looking out as his men began groggily stirring

from beneath their woolen blankets, Lieutenant Jack Redmond turned and briefly grinned as he caught the black, steady gaze of his second-in-command.

"Sergeant-Major Ano! Get this bunch of worthless scalawags off to the showers and then dressed and into the mess hall. I want them waiting for me on the parade ground in full battle gear by 0800. And then we'll soon enough see what Canada's best are made out of!"

Leaving the task of further motivating the young squad of soldiers to his capable Inuit subordinate, Jack Redmond smartly pivoted and left the barracks. Once outside, he hurriedly crossed the manicured parade ground. The pine-scented air was nippy, and just hinted at the frigid winter that would all too soon be upon them. Proof of this rapidly approaching season lay clearly visible on the lofty mountain tops that surrounded the valley, for the snow line was steadily working its way down the tree-covered slopes. While wondering if the section of wilderness he had chosen for that day's maneuvers was snowbound as yet, the forty-three-year-old veteran commando ducked into the adjoining mess hall.

Once inside this cavernous structure, Redmond headed straight for the cafeteria-style serving line. A single, potbellied cook stood behind the steam table.

"Good morning, Angus," greeted Jack Redmond. "I hope you had a pleasant enough sleep. What's for chow?"

"Red River cereal and hot cakes," replied the cook indifferently. His beard-stubbled chin was gray with several days' growth. "And have no fear, Jack Redmond, there's plenty of hot coffee, brewed extra strong just as you like it."

At this revelation, a warm smile painted the veteran soldier's face. "Bless you, Angus. I'll be taking the

79

lads on a bit of a hike today, and you're more than welcome to join us with your pipes."

Patting his stained, apron-covered belly, Angus McPherson thoughtfully answered. "So it's a bit of a hike you'll be taking, Jack Redmond. Though I would like a chance to work off a bit of this extra baggage, if I know you, you'll be taking your lads straight up Mount Rundle, and be back in time for tea."

Redmond replied while filling a white ceramic bowl full of hot cereal. "Not quite, Angus. I'll be taking the squad up through Simpson Pass to the Sunshine meadowlands. There we'll be doing some alpine climbing on the foothills beneath Mount Assiniboine."

"That's lovely land you've chosen," reflected the grizzled cook. "You wouldn't happen to know if the Sunshine gondola is operating as yet, would you, Jack?"

The veteran commando nodded. "As it so happens, I talked to the resort manager just yesterday to get clearance for our hike, and she mentioned that the gondola would be in operation all this week in preparation for ski season."

Satisfied that he would have a way down from the mountain should his legs give out, Angus winked. "Then it looks like you've got the services of one worn-out piper. I'll be out to join you on the parade grounds in my regimental kilts as soon as the boys have filled their bellies."

Sincerely happy to have the old-timer's company, Redmond added to his tray a platter of hotcakes and a large mug of black coffee. He sat himself down at a nearby table and immediately got to work on his breakfast.

Forty-five minutes later, he stood on the parade ground, his men smartly lined up before him. Dressed identically in snow-white fatigues, the squad wore backpacks. Unloaded M16 rifles were slung over the men's shoulders. While Sergeant-Major Ano initiated an intense inspection, a portly latecomer joined the ranks. Unlike his younger comrades, this individual wore gaily colored, red and black woolen kilts. He put the bagpipes he carried to work when Jack Redmond greeted him with a simple nod. To the spirited sounds of *Scotland the Brave,* the squad marched off to the bus that would take them to the trailhead.

The first portion of the hike took them through a thick wood of lodgepole pine and birch. The terrain here was relatively flat, with a swift-moving stream cascading on their left. To the melodious strains of such age-old pipe favorites as the "Highland Cradle Song," "Captain Orr-Ewing," "Culty's Wedding," and "Farewell to the Creeks," they made excellent time. Designed to set a marching regiment's pace and provide inspiration, the bagpipe tunes seemed as home here in the Canadian wilderness as they would back on the heather-covered meadows of Scotland.

The group stopped for a quick lunch of crusty french bread, cheddar cheese, and green apples at Simpson Pass. The weather was cooperating quite splendidly, and they munched away on their food under an almost cloudless blue sky. A gentle wind blew in from the west, while the temperature was so mild that the majority of the men were picnicking in their shirtsleeves.

After lunch, their hike took them up a gradually sloping trail. Unable to play his pipes on this portion of the path, Angus McPherson barely had enough wind to make the climb. Walking immediately behind the likable Scot, and taking up the rear of the pack was Jack Redmond.

Satisfied with their progress, the veteran commando was able to identify several species of passing wildlife. Fat black and white plumed magpies watched them from the branches of the pines, their characteristic long, graduated tails and squeaky voices quick to give them away. Ground squirrels were abundant, and once they startled a family of deer, who were innocently grazing on some green shrubbery at the edge of the trail.

Having grown up in nearby Kamloops, Redmond was most familiar with the rugged terrain they were passing through. Yet each time he ventured into such wilderness, he felt a new appreciation for its raw beauty. It had been his grandfather who'd originally given him his first lesson in woodsmanship. A grizzled logger, the old man had known the forest like a close friend, and much of his invaluable knowledge had been passed on to Jack during the frequent camping trips they took on the shores of Lake Okanagan. It was here the youngster had learned the names of the various plants and animals that abounded in this region. The impressionable lad had also heard many a frightening tale told around the fire-circle, such as that of the monstrous, serpentlike beast that supposedly lived deep in the lake's icy depths.

Twenty-five years ago, at the tender age of eighteen, Jack had enlisted in the Army. Never known for his ambition, he'd blossomed in the military's environment of vigorous physical activity and comradeship. Several tours had taken him to southern Germany, where he'd helped fulfill Canada's NATO obligation. In fact, it was in Germany that he'd met the only woman he'd ever really cared for. Gretchen was a willowy blonde, with a quick wit and a keen intellect. Unfortunately, the head-strong Canuck bachelor had feared a permanent commitment, and he'd lost his only love to a dashing Yank from California. Since that traumatic experience, he had remained aloof from the opposite sex, preferring instead to focus his energies solely on his military career.

In the 1980's, Canadians became increasingly concerned with the security of their borders. As the planet's third largest country in terms of available land space, Canada found itself in the awkward position of having more troops committed to the defense of central Europe than it did to its homeland. To rectify this shocking imbalance, attention began to focus on internal security.

Since much of the nation stretched above the Arctic Circle, special forces squadrons were created to patrol these vast frozen expanses of territory. These patrols became more and more important as the Arctic continued to be developed both commercially and strategically.

It was for such duty that Redmond's current outfit, the Arctic Rangers came into being. Comprised primarily of trained woodsmen and native Inuit, the Rangers were responsible for patrolling vast portions of northern territory, and were involved in search and rescue efforts and ecological enforcement as well.

To insure that his men could handle themselves in a variety of terrain and under differing climatic conditions, Redmond made sure their maneuvers took them to various regions of the country. Only recently they had stayed one month on isolated Ellesmere Island, Canada's northernmost territory. Almost directly adjoining the northern tip of Greenland, Ellesmere was a desolate spot that for the majority of the year was frozen over in ice and snow. Since the Rangers stay had been there in the closing days of summer, the weather conditions were a bit more tolerable. The Inuit members of the squad provided invaluable guidance, showing the men how to augment their dull canned diet with an assortment of nourishing local foods such as hare, caribou, and seal.

Jack Redmond couldn't help but be excited when his recent orders sent them packing for Banff. For these were practically the woods he grew up in, and spending the next couple of weeks exploring the surrounding countryside was like a trip back to the days of his childhood. This especially seemed to be the case when a trail they had been steadily following upward passed by the side of a huge granite mountain that had recently lost a good portion of its bulk to a major rockslide. As a lad, Jack had played in similar debris, and he would never forget the many hours he'd spent climbing amongst the rocks, looking for gold and other treasures.

As they came upon a portion of the trail that had been covered by this slide, the squad was forced to pick its way around the fractured rock. Briefly halting before doing so, Angus McPherson pulled out a handkerchief to wipe his soaked brow.

"My lordy, Jack, I guess I'm in worse shape that I ever imagined," observed the Scotsman between gasps of breath. "Why just look at your boys up there, climbing onward like this was nothing but a sunday stroll through Stanley Park. Why there was a time not so long ago when I could easily have kept up with those lads and then some."

Stopping also to catch his breath, Redmond took a swig out of his canteen, before offering it to his portly hiking companion. "I know what you mean, Angus. Because I'm beginning to feel those additional years as well."

"Come off it, Jack Redmond," countered the Scotsman. "Why you're looking just as fit today as you were twenty years ago when we first met outside the town of Lahr in the Black Forest."

The veteran commando shook his head. "Thanks for the well-meaning compliment, Angus, but this old body's logged quite a few kilometers since then. Why I've got pains in places I never knew existed before."

Looking up the rock-strewn trail as the last of the squad disappeared into the tree line, Angus voiced himself. "I hope Sunshine Village isn't much further. These old legs have about had it."

Jack checked the position of the sun overhead before responding. "It's not much longer now, Angus. Just think, you'll be sitting in the lodge cooling your thirst with an ice-cold frosty one, while I'm still out on the trail with my boys. I'm beginning to seriously think about leaving this field work to younger, more capable individuals, like Sergeant-Major Ano."

"Ah, that one's as cool and no-nonsense as they come," observed Angus. "During the whole time I've known him, never once have I heard him crack a joke or even laugh for that matter. Does the chap ever have a light moment?"

"Not very often," answered Redmond. "Though there's no one better with the men than Cliff Ano. He gained their respect from the very beginning, and that is the whole secret of successful command. From what little he's told me of his upbringing, I pretty well understand his serious outlook on life. Growing up in an Inuit family that still followed the old ways and lived off the land, he didn't have much time for childhood fun. When other kids were playing with toys and watching cartoons on television, he was out on the hunt with his father, or helping his mother repair and make clothing.

"I'll tell you one thing though. If there was one person on this planet who I wouldn't mind being stranded in the Arctic with, it would be Cliff Ano.

85

That fellow is a survivor, pure and simple."

Taking a moment to stow away his canteen, Redmond added, "Well, we'd better be pushing on. Can you make it, Angus?"

"Can I make it?" mocked the Scotsman. "Why I was only needing my second wind. Come on, Jack Redmond. There's some life left in these old bones yet."

To prove his point, he put the reed mouthpiece of his pipe between his lips, and as he began picking his way through the rubble, the mournful notes of "Donald Blue" vibrated through the crisp mountain air.

It took them another hour to reach the trail's summit. This put them above the tree line, on a gently sloping plateau filled to the horizon with stunted pines, weatherworn granite escarpments, and acre upon acre of lush green heather. Spots of snow covered much of this meadowland, yet the mild temperature was more like that of summer than late fall.

With the surrounding mountain peaks providing an inspirational backdrop, the squad took a brief break. Removing their forty-pound packs, the men stretched their cramped muscles and munched away on chocolate-coated granola bars and oranges.

Anxious for a proper rest, Angus McPherson scanned this new landscape and soon spotted just what he had been searching for — a tightly stretched, elevated cable that had a chair swinging beneath it. Forty-five minutes later, the Scotsman was actually on this lift, comfortably on his way to the lodge at Sunshine Village.

With a good four hours of sunlight left, Jack Redmond directed his squad in the opposite direction. Still traversing a high Alpine meadow, they passed through a valley dotted with several crystal-clear lakes. From this point onward, a single narrow footpath had been cut through the heather, its gentle meander crossing the broad valley and disappearing in the direction of several distant, snow-covered peaks. The loftiest of these summits was a triangularly shaped formation that looked much like the Swiss Matterhorn. Known as Assiniboine, this was the mountain for which the provincial park they were about to enter was named.

They passed by a cairn indicating that they had just entered the province of British Columbia. Jack Redmond had walked this same trail as a teenager, and once again he felt right at home in this breathtaking wilderness valley that had changed little over the years.

To give the men a better feel for the land, he sent them off on the trail alone, at five-minute intervals. While waiting for the squad to thoroughly disperse, he passed his time working on his log, and sharing some advanced pointers in the demanding science of orienteering. A little over sixty minutes later, he hit the footpath himself.

Their goal was Assiniboine Pass. Here they would set up an overnight bivouac, before continuing on to the mountain itself early the next morning. As last man on the trail, Redmond would most likely be arriving at this campsite well after dusk. Yet fortunately, the sky remained unusually clear, and because a full moon was scheduled to rise that evening, he figured he should have more than enough illumination to guide him by.

So as to not lag too far behind, he set himself a moderately stiff pace. The muscles in his calves were tight after the climb up from Simpson Pass, and the relatively level terrain he was now following was most welcome.

The one thing he found himself missing as he crossed through the meadows of lush heather was the sound of the Scotsman's bagpipes. Surely this was the type of countryside in which the stirring music of the pipes could be most appreciated.

Subconsciously whistling, "Scotland the Brave," Redmond thought of Angus McPherson. The affable army cook had been a long-time friend and confidant. They'd been together on two tours of duty in Germany, and had managed to get into their fair share of trouble along the way.

The son of an immigrant sheepherder from Edinburgh, Angus was brought to Canada as a teenager. His family settled in the Cypress Hills area of Saskatchewan, and it was while on a buying trip to Regina that he decided to run off and join the armed forces.

With his parents long dead in their graves, Angus had no other family but the army. Soon to be faced with mandatory retirement, he planned to start a small restaurant near the Currie Barracks in Calgary. Destined to be one of his best patrons, Jack Redmond was forced to temporarily halt his improvised whistling version of "Bonnie Dundee" when the footpath began ascending up a fairly steep ridge.

A series of switchbacks led him steadily upward. Conscious of the alien, forty pounds he carried on his back, he had to make a total effort to keep from halting before he reached the summit. Lungs wheezing and leg and back muscles protesting with cramping pain, he pushed himself to the very limits of his endurance. He was able to continue on only by resorting to a trick his grandfather had long ago taught him. When in the midst of a steep, steady climb, it was best to focus one's complete attention on a tiny portion of the trail approximately a meter ahead. This allowed one to establish a constant speed, and not be distracted or discouraged by the passing scenery.

Redmond's pulse was madly pounding away in his chest as he turned up the final switchback. Briefly eyeing the flattened summit above, he initiated one last major effort. Step by tedious step he proceeded, until his goal was at long last attained after a final, agonizing burst of expended energy.

Crouching down in an effort to regather his breath, Redmond wiped his soaked brow with the back of his hand and peered out to scan the ridge he had just traversed. From this elevated height he could follow the narrow footpath all the way back to the top of the Sunshine chair lift, where they had dropped off Angus. Knowing the Scotsman's love for alcohol, he could imagine him at the resort's lounge, pouring down an ice-cold dark ale.

More than happy to satisfy his growing thirst with a swig of water, Jack was in the process of reaching down for his canteen when he realized with a start that he wasn't alone. His pulse once again quickened as he slowly turned and set startled eyes on a young grizzly cub contentedly grazing less than a dozen meters distant.

No stranger to encountering bears in the wild, Redmond immediately contemplated his options. Since a cub was not likely to initiate an unprovoked attack, his best move would be to get out of the area as quietly and quickly as possible. Forgetting all about his sore legs and back, he stood and began to make his way across the summit's broad plateau. The cub seemed completely unaware of the mortal's presence, and his apprehensions already easing, Jack hurried across a tiny, trickling stream.

It was as he cut through a copse of stunted evergreens that he spotted yet another bear. This mammoth brown beast was obviously the mother, and because of a sudden shift in the wind, she had already gotten the human's scent. Cursing his misfortune, Jack started to go for the rifle slung over his shoulder. But since Rangers carried no bullets while on maneuvers, it would be useless except as a bludgeon.

As the adult grizzly scanned the portion of the plateau that lay downwind, Redmond was thankful for the bear's poor eyesight. With his white fatigues, he would be hard to spot as long as he didn't make any quick, jerky moves.

The possibility of sliding back into the thin thicket of trees crossed his mind, but the evergreens would provide little cover and were much too fragile to climb. Even if a climbable tree were available to him, a bear could follow him up into the branches just as easily as it could run him down on an open field. That left him with but three options. He could furtively slink off and pray that the grizzly failed to spot him, directly confront the beast and attempt to scare it away, or — the third alternative was probably the safest bet, but was surely the most difficult to do — he could lie down, cover his pulse, and play dead.

Because the beast had yet to locate him, Jack decided to try to soundlessly slip away through the thicket of trees that lay behind him. Not daring to completely turn around, he took a shaky step backward. He followed this with another and could actually feel a tree limb scrape up against the back of his leg as a muted, high-pitched grunt caused a sickening heaviness to form in his stomach. Breathlessly turning his head, he peered through the limbs and had his worst fears realized — the cub was suddenly galloping straight for him!

Sandwiched between the two bears as he was, and certain that the curious offspring would all too soon give him away, Jack did the only prudent thing left to do. He dropped to the ground, gathered himself up into a tight fetal ball, and began praying in earnest.

He was well into his second Hail Mary, when the cub reached his side. The beast sniffed his prone body from head to toe, and Jack was positive that his pounding heart was going to pop right out of his chest.

His terror further intensified when the air vibrated with a deep, throaty roar. Daring to open one of his eyes, he focused in on a horrifying sight that would stay with him for all eternity. For standing directly before him, less than a half-dozen meters away, was the mother grizzly, her huge brown frame fully erect, her red eyes locked directly on him. He snapped his eyes shut as the bear let loose with another deafening roar, and seconds later, the beast was upon him.

It was the smell that gave the adult away. Its heavy musky odor sickened Jack, and as he fought back a rush of nauseous bile, he felt a series of hard poking jabs to his back. Another series of blows were centered on his legs, and when the bear's cold nose actually touched the back of his exposed neck, the Arctic Ranger lost control of his bowels.

Fighting the natural instinct to get up and run like hell, Jack desperately tried to center his thoughts. Never one to easily frighten, his panic filled him with a sickening dread, and for the second time in his life, he prepared to meet his maker. Past experiences suddenly flashed in his mind's eye as clearly as if they were being projected on a picture screen, and he instantly relived his first brush with death almost ten years ago. He was assigned to a tank batallion in the Black Forest, and a noxious engine fire and a stuck turret hatch claimed the lives of two of the tank's four-man crew. Miraculously, Jack had been one of those pulled alive from the smoking wreck, though it took two full days of cardiovascular treatment to bring him back to consciousness.

Had his luck finally run out? Certain that it had, the commando took another series of blows to his back and neck, and was just about to cry out in utter desperation, when a distant, somewhat familiar chopping sound diverted his attention. The bear seemed to be distracted by this constantly increasing noise also, and as it temporarily backed away from its strange find, Jack was filled with a wave of new hope. His expectations further heightened as the throaty grinding roar intensified to a point where he was able to identify this sound as belonging to an approaching helicopter!

Still fearful to break out of his fetal ball, or even open his eyes for that matter, Jack knew his prayers were answered when a powerful, amplified voice boomed down from the heavens.

"Lieutenant Jack Redmond?"

Wondering if this wasn't some sort of hallucination, Jack gathered the nerve to peer upward, and his gaze focused on a wondrous sight, a hovering Huey helicopter.

"Are you all right, Lieutenant?" quizzed the resonant voice.

Somehow Jack was able to move one of his arms and signal that he was, indeed, still amongst the living. And at this sign, the helicopter landed on the plateau to a swirling, ear-splitting gust of blowing debris.

Soon afterward, the Huey was once again airborne, this time with an additional passenger in its hold.

"Lieutenant Redmond, I still think it's a miracle you weren't even scratched by that grizzly. When we first spotted the bear on top of you, we thought you were a goner for certain."

His nerves somewhat settled by the flask of brandy he had just consumed, Jack replied in a cracked voice, "You and me both, pardner. May I ask what brought you out to this godforsaken valley in the first place?"

Having to repeat this question to be heard over the whine of the spinning rotors, Jack listened intently as the jumpsuited airman explained their mission.

"Actually, we were sent out here from Calgary to look for you, Lieutenant. Seems you're wanted back at the Currie Barracks in a real hurry. Command's sending in a Sikorsky to bring in the rest of your squad."

"Any idea what this is all about?" quizzed the breathless Ranger.

Momentarily hesitating, the airman shouted, "Though this is all mere scuttlebutt, rumor has it that it's all tied in with the recent disappearance of the Soviet Premier's plane somewhere over the Arctic."

"The disappearance of what?" repeated Jack, his tone filled with disbelief.

Scooting over, the airman cupped his mouth with his hands and spoke right into Jack's ear. "Premier Alexander Suratov's plane has gone down somewhere over Baffin Island, sir. And we believe your squad has been called in to be one of the units sent up there to find out what in hell happened to it."

Shocked by this sobering revelation, Jack Redmond caught the airman's glance and knew in an instant that this was no joke. Diverting his gaze to the nearby Plexiglas porthole, Redmond absorbed this astounding disclosure, all the while taking in the quickly passing terrain, his encounter with the grizzly all but stripped from his mind.

Chapter Five

Thirty million years ago, an event of cataclysmic proportions tore apart the heart of central Asia. At this time the continent split in half latitudinally, causing the earth's crust to buckle and creating a voluminous fissure more than a thousand miles long, thirty miles wide, and as much as three miles deep. Over a period of thousands of years, this chasm filled with the runoff from the surrounding mountains and it was in this manner that Siberia's Lake Baikal was born.

As Admiral Mikhail Kharkov stood on the windswept ledge gazing out to the lake, he attempted to mentally visualize these great physical forces at work. The white-haired veteran knew that though erosion had filled in a portion of the original fissure, Baikal was still the world's largest and deepest freshwater body. And as such was home to hundreds of species of plants and wildlife that were indigenous to this portion of the earth only.

Thus, in this very special part of the Motherland, Kharkov had decided to locate his dacha. Though the great responsibilities of his lofty position in the government kept him sequestered in Moscow or visiting naval bases for most of the year, those rare free weekends and cherished vacations sent him packing for the four-hour plane flight that would bring him to his beloved wilderness home.

Unusual though it was, official State business had brought him to the nearby city of Irkutsk only three days ago. At that time he had participated in an unprecedented meeting of the thirteen members of the ruling Politburo. This conference had several purposes. Because of the growing importance of the vast reaches of Siberia to the Soviet Union's future economic development, the Party was determined to pay this region the respect it deserved. As a fitting way of reminding their hardworking Siberian comrades that they were not being snubbed by the major power centers that lay west of the Urals, this forum was inaugurated. Here problems unique to the region could be discussed in a relaxed, informal atmosphere.

Since vast tracts of undeveloped land still lay to the north, plans were unveiled that included the establishment of over a dozen new cities. Many of these population centers were to be situated above the Arctic Circle, and would be created to help extract from the earth the copious amounts of oil and mineral wealth that lay buried beneath the permafrost.

It had been their Premier, Alexander Suratov, who had personally chaired this portion of the conference. Born in the Siberian town of Yakutsk, on the banks of the Lena River, Suratov considered this meeting a second homecoming. In fact, his entire family flew down from Yakutsk to be with this vibrant, popular leader as he opened the meeting with a sumptuous cocktail party, that would be the talk of the town for months to come.

Suratov used this reception to announce to the world his plans to travel to Ottawa, Canada in two days' time. Here together with the Canadian Prime

Minister and the President of the United States, he would be participating in a surprise summit, whose purpose was the signing of an Arctic demilitarization treaty. Of course, Mikhail Kharkov had known about this summit for some time now, and disgustedly shook his head at the mere thought of the tragic series of events that were destined to follow.

Mikhail and his supporters had vainly tried to convince the Premier to cancel this hastily conceived meeting of the three heads of state. But Suratov had turned a deaf ear to their pleas, and now had been forced to pay the ultimate price for his stubborn folly. For the plane carrying Alexander Suratov had never made it to Ottawa at all, but was last seen dropping from the radar screens somewhere over Canada's Baffin Island.

With a shocked world still waiting for the wreckage of the *Flying Kremlin* to be found, Mikhail had canceled his plans to fly back to Moscow and had instead returned to his cherished dacha. His wilderness retreat had already done him good, for his previously confused thoughts were now crisply focused. Reaware of his purpose, he had called to his dacha three fellow Politburo members who had also remained in Irkutsk. This all-important meeting would take place that afternoon, and its outcome could very well determine the future direction the Motherland would next follow. Anxious to see how his vision would be shared, Kharkhov peered skyward when a sharp, staccato cry sounded from the heavens.

At seventy-six years of age, Kharkov still marveled at the wonders of nature as he spotted an immense golden eagle soaring on the thermals less than twenty-five meters above him. The massive bird of prey was in the process of intently scanning the lake bluffs below for food, and for a fleeting second seemed to directly meet the admiral's admiring gaze. Then with the subtlest of movements of its rudderlike tail, the eagle canted hard to the left to resume its perpetual hunt over another section of the bluffs.

Stirred by this encounter, Mikhail gazed down upon that portion of the lake that was visible before him. A single fishing boat could be seen bobbing on the surging, steel blue waters. Having sailed these same seas in just such a sturdy vessel before, he wondered if its crew had been fortunate enough to hook into a school of omul, that native whitefish whose sweet flesh was venerated throughout the Motherland. Or perhaps they were after the giant Baikal sturgeon; a species that was once on the brink of extinction, it had recently made a remarkable comeback. Mikhail had a personal interest in this last species of fish, as a full kilogram of fresh caviar made from its roe currently sat in his refrigerator awaiting his guest's consumption.

Suddenly aware of the fact that he had only taken the time for a cup of tea for breakfast, Mikhail briefly scanned the eastern horizon. In the far distance, a mass of threatening dark clouds had gathered over the range of snow-clad mountains that formed the shoreline of this portion of the lake. Since the winds were continuing to gust from this direction, the veteran mariner assumed it was only a matter of time before the storm front headed their way. Baikal was notorious for such storms. They often swept across the lake creating turbulent breakers, many as large and as dangerous as those he had encountered on the open seas.

In over five decades of active naval service, Mikhail had weathered many a storm in his time. Once in the Atlantic, they had skirted a hurricane, and the heavy cruiser he had been commanding had almost had its

97

spine broken by the ensuing swells, some of which swept all the way over the elevated bridge. Yet in all his years, never had he been so terrified as when he'd found himself caught up in a sudden storm alone on Lake Baikal in a small sailboat. Just as furious as those of the hurricane, the waves of the lake smashed into his sturdy wooden vessel, carrying off the mast, and half of the small cabin as well. He only kept from being washed overboard by tying himself to the helm, and even then it was a struggle merely to keep from choking to death on the solid walls of water that were being constantly swept his way. From that day onward Mikhail had a new respect for the lake that had conveyed him to the very portals of death yet had spared him to sail its waters again in the future.

A sudden cool gust of wind ruffled his thin white hair, and Mikhail decided it was time to turn for home before the squall was upon him. He followed a narrow earthen footpath that led away from the bluffs and into a section of thick primeval forest. Called taiga by the Siberians, this wood was made up of towering cedars, spruce, birch, and several varieties of larch.

The harsh, resonant caw of a raven greeted him as he continued down the trail. His stride was as brisk as ever, and he was thankful for the superb health that had kept him as far away as possible from doctors and clinics.

As he climbed over a fallen birch trunk, he directed his gaze to the clearing where he had spotted a fox less than an hour ago. Of course, the elusive red-coated creature was long gone, yet this sighting only further proved that portion of taiga was as full of life as it had been a hundred years ago. Since arriving at his dacha, Mikhail had already spotted several elk, some deer, and even a pack of marauding wolves that had tried to bite its way into his supply shed only last night. Recently, a large black bear was seen in the vicinity. Mikhail was content to stay as far away as possible from such a dangerous, unpredictable predator.

The crash of cascading water sounded in the distance, and he was soon standing beside the stream from which this racket eminated. Its current was swift, its meander was determined by assortments of various-sized rocks that had been swept down from the surrounding mountains. As the clear water smashed white upon the largest of these boulders, Mikhail squatted down, dipped his cupped hands into the icy current, and brought a cool, refreshing drink to his parched lips. Tastier than the costliest of bottled mineral waters, this sparkling liquid quenched his thirst perfectly.

It was as he rubbed his wet hands over his face that he spotted a series of prints etched in the moist mud of the stream bank beside him. This characteristic track belonged to a fairly small animal that left behind a series of five distinct paw prints. Mikhail couldn't help but wonder if it didn't belong to a Barguzin sable. Like the giant Baikal sturgeon, this animal had also been hunted to the point of extinction, and was finally being seen in good-sized numbers once again.

His wife Anna certainly had an appreciation of this weasel-like mammal. She had been after him for years to buy her a full-length sable coat. Finally, on the eve of their twenty-fifth wedding anniversary, he withdrew a small fortune and fulfilled her dream. As it turned out, it had been one of the best investments he had ever made. Not only was it a truly magnificent garment, it was practical as well, for the thick fur countered even the harshest of Moscow winters.

Disappointed that the tracks seemed to disappear at this point, Mikhail stood and searched the underbrush. He had a great-uncle who was once a fur trapper, and remembered his stories about the first organized exploration of this portion of Siberia. This took place over three hundred years ago. At that time it had been the Stroganovs who sent a Cossack army, under the leadership of Yermak, to breach the Urals and search for Siberian "soft gold," or as it was better known, sable pelts. These cossacks were a rough, brutal bunch, who often terrorized the native inhabitants of the area into paying them tributes in furs.

When the sable population was finally exhausted, the newcomers turned to Lake Baikal itself for a new source of riches. They found it in the huge herds of seals that made the lake their home, and fish such as the giant sturgeon. Barely saved from extinction, these species were only now once again flourishing, to a point where harvesting controlled numbers could finally be allowed.

Since it was apparent the animal that had left the tracks behind on the stream bank was not going to show itself, Mikhail decided to resume his hike. A series of large, flat rocks provided a convenient bridge, so the robust old-timer crossed the gurgling creek and once more found himself on the footpath.

The clean fresh air was like a tonic, and he lengthened his stride, his long legs feeling limber and fit. Back in Moscow, he hardly ever got a chance to walk like this. Not only was his schedule a busy one, with hardly a free minute in his entire fourteen-hour day, but the city itself was hardly conducive to this type of exercise. Diesel-belching trucks and buses tainted the air, while the jostling masses that crowded the sidewalks barely gave one a meter of free space of his own. Parks such as Gorky were lovely enough places, though on a decent day, they too were crowded with families and individuals seeking a moment of pastoral peace inside the capital's bustling confines.

Mikhail often fantasized on how it would be to live out here in the wilderness permanently. He'd fish, hike, and even clear some land to plant a vegetable garden. He'd often thought about doing such things while at sea. A career sailor spent precious few hours on solid land. This was especially the case when one's active career spanned five decades. Thus he'd promised himself that as soon as he was given a steady desk job, he'd look into purchasing a country dacha of his very own.

His great-uncle had suggested that he look into the Lake Baikal region. So, without even seeing the property, he bought the dacha from the family of a deceased shipmate. The house itself was only three years old, and from the very first time that he flew over the area on the way to the Irkutsk airport, he knew that he wouldn't be disappointed.

Located outside the village of Jelancy, some sixty kilometers northeast of Irkutsk, the dacha turned out to be everything that he had dreamed about. Built entirely of local timber, the six-room cabin had all the comforts of their Moscow apartment including a fully outfitted kitchen and an indoor bathroom. What made it unique were its cathedral ceilings, massive stone fireplace, and of course the magnificent forest it was situated in.

Mikhail had discovered the trail that he was currently following by sheer accident, on the very first day of their arrival at the dacha, nearly ten years ago. Leaving Anna to clean house, he'd struck out for the woods with his walking stick and trusty compass in hand. Since the lake was evidently some distance east of them, he'd pointed himself in that direction and had spotted the bare outline of a trail invitingly beckoning inside the adjoining tree line. Even though this path snaked through the thick taiga, its general direction remained eastward, and Mikhail was determined to follow it to the very end.

He was out on the trail for almost a half hour, when he encountered the stream that he had just crossed. Halting briefly to admire this brook, he pushed on and soon came to the bluffs and what was to turn out to be his very own private balcony, allowing him a magnificent vista of the lake.

He was so excited with his breathtaking discovery that he dragged Anna out there that same afternoon. She was equally enthused, and later that week they set up some deck chairs on the bluffs to admire the lake in relative comfort. And now a decade later, to find oneself every bit as inspired by this same vista only went to prove its beauty.

While wondering if he'd have the time to escort his guests to the overlook, Mikhail passed by a startled ground squirrel and climbed up a small rise that brought him to a grove of particularly ancient cedars. Like a group of stately elders, these giant conifers were the senior statesmen of the taiga, having grown here for centuries. A good majority of the trunks were so thick it would take the combined reaches of three fully grown men to encircle one of their lower trunks.

The very character of the forest seemed to change here. Because of the lofty branches that cut out most of the direct sunlight, ground cover was almost non-existent. In its place was an occasional clump of giant clover or a moss-covered boulder. The very air was hushed and still as Mikhail silently cut through the grove, as reverently as one of the faithful on the way to Mass.

He was in the process of passing through a stand of young birch trees when the air filled with the alien chopping sound of an approaching helicopter. With his gaze now drawn to the heavens, he was afforded a brief view of the vehicle responsible for this noise as it zoomed over from the southwest. The dark green chopper had an elongated boxcarlike fuselage that had a series of circular viewing ports cut into its sides and a bright red, five-pointed star emblazoned on its tail. Quick to identify it as a Mil Mi-8, the veteran was suddenly conscious of the late hour.

"I'll bet you anything my guests are aboard that vehicle," observed Mikhail to the wind. "Some host I'm going to turn out to be, when I'm not even there to welcome them to my very own home!"

A new sense of urgency hastened his step as he pushed on down the pathway. Five minutes later, he anxiously broke out of the treeline and entered a wide, spacious clearing. In the center of this clover-filled tract was a cozy log cabin, that had a plume of gray smoke contentedly pouring from its stone chimney. Parked beside the dacha, appearing like a beast from another world, was the helicopter that he had spotted earlier.

A tall erect figure wearing the light gray greatcoat and cap of a Soviet Army officer suddenly broke from the opposite woods that stood beside the Mi-8. This solid individual sported massive shoulders, and Mikhail was able to immediately identify him.

"Ivan, my friend!" shouted Mikhail.

General Ivan Zarusk heard this salutation and raised his own gravelly voice in greeting. "So there you are, Misha. Anna thought a bear might have gotten you, so I volunteered to lead the rescue party."

The two met with a warm hug.

"Actually, I was just enjoying some of this wonderful fresh air," added Zarusk, the Motherland's Minister of Defense. "Your grounds are as delightful as I remembered them during my last visit."

"And that was over two years ago," reflected Mikhail.

Ivan shook his head. "Has it really been that long, Misha? Where does time fly to, old friend?"

"At least you can watch it pass in the faces of those spirited grandchildren of yours," observed Mikhail. "And how is Sasha?"

"As fat and sassy as ever. She sends her love, and her regrets to Anna for not being able to accept your gracious invitation to stay with you during the conference. Right now, she's being the typical grandmother, babysitting and spoiling the children rotten while their parents are on vacation in Odessa."

Mikhail grinned. "Anna sincerely missed her, but I'm glad she's keeping herself busy."

Taking his guest by his arm, Mikhail led him toward the dacha, his tone turning serious. "So tell me, my friend, did our two respected colleagues from the Politburo join you on this visit?"

Ivan Zarusk nodded. "That they did, Misha. While Anna was in the process of giving them the grand tour, I stepped out here to regather myself. Comrade Kasimov is as stubborn and obstinate as ever. During our short flight from Irkutsk, it was all I could do to keep from grabbing him by that scrawny neck of his and beating some sense into him."

Mikhail stifled a chuckle. "I'm glad you were able to contain yourself, Ivan. Otherwise our little session here would have been doomed before it even started."

"I still say we're merely wasting our breath with that one," the general muttered bitterly. "Though Comrade Tichvin is another story. Our esteemed Minister of the Interior seems to be a bit more receptive. Why, on the limo ride to the heliport he actually asked me if I thought it possible for the *Flying Kremlin* to have been downed by some sort of missile."

"You don't say," observed Mikhail, his eyes wide with interest. "And may I ask how you answered him?"

"Misha, I merely advised him that until we recovered the airliner's cockpit voice recorder, we have to be open to a variety of possibilities."

Mikhail Kharkov made certain to meet his old friend's penetrating glance before replying. "That's indeed most interesting, comrade. For him to have even mentioned such a thing is an excellent sign."

"But even if we were able to win him over, that still makes us a vote short," protested Ivan.

"Come now, my friend. Have you no faith in my oratorical skills? Whatever you might say, Yuri Kasimov is still a reasonable man, and as such, there's always the chance that we'll be able to win him over."

Shrugging his massive shoulders, the Minister of Defense sighed. "I only wish that I could be so optimistic."

As they stood by the dacha's front door, Mikhail affectionately patted his old friend on the back. "Relax, Ivan Andreivich, and leave all the worry to me. Besides, I was able to purvey you a very special treat for this occasion. Do you remember your last visit here, when you ate all the appetizers and spoiled your appetite for dinner?"

The Defense Minister's eyes gleamed. "I certainly hope it's Baikal caviar you're talking about, Misha. To my taste, there's no finer delicacy in all the world."

"So we've noticed," reflected Mikhail with a grin as he turned the door handle and gestured for his guest to enter.

Ivan Zarusk did so, and led the way into a warm, spacious hallway. Adding his coat and cap to the two that already hung there, the seventy-one-year-old Defense Minister uncovered a uniform filled with dozens of colorful campaign ribbons and other decorations, all proudly displayed on a solid, muscular chest. With his thick head of black hair and bushy eyebrows to match, it was easy to see why he was often mistaken for a man twenty years his junior.

In vast contrast, his host's snow-white hair and brows were more characteristic of a man in his seventies. In decent shape himself, Mikhail Kharkov had firm legs and shoulders, though his bulging waistline was a by-product of too much time spent behind his desk and, of course, his wife's excellent cooking. Out of uniform, as he was, in gray slacks, white shirt, and a black cardigan sweater, the Admiral of the Fleet of the Soviet Union looked like a typical retiree. Yet this was as far as the likeness went. For this was no gentle grandfather, but a cold, calculating bureaucrat who had survived both Stalin's purges and the Great Patriotic War, and had since fought his way to prominence, until today he was one of the most powerful individuals on the entire globe. Yet to totally consolidate his hard-earned position, he still needed the support of the two of the individuals who awaited him inside the adjoining den.

With Ivan Zarusk at his side, Mikhail, led them into the dacha's central room. Here under a lofty cathedral ceiling was a collection of comfortable furniture, set around the den's dominant feature, a massive, flagstone fireplace. Gathered around the roaring fire were three seated individuals. At their host's entrance, two of these figures alertly stood. Both were dressed in identical black suits, white shirts, and red ties.

First to step forward and offer his handshake was Minister of the Interior Dmitri Tichvin, who sported a shiny bald scalp and wore an ever-present pair of wire-rimmed glasses over his bulbous nose.

"Good afternoon, Admiral," he said politely. "We were just getting the history of your wonderful dacha from your wife, and I must admit I'm quite jealous. You have a very special place here, Comrade Kharkov."

"Why, thank you for saying so," returned Mikhail as he reached out to accept the cool hand of the figure who stood behind the Minister of the Interior.

Clearly the shortest individual in the room, Yuri Kasimov seemed out of place amongst the tall, big-shouldered men who surrounded him. Of slight build, with longish black hair and a pasty-skinned, pock-mark-scarred face, the beady-eyed professional bureaucrat nervously cleared his throat before expressing himself.

"Hello, Admiral. Thank you for the kind invitation."

"Not at all" replied Mikhail Kharkov. "In fact, all of you deserve my gratitude for taking time out from your busy schedules. You honor me with your presence. The past twenty-four-hour period has been a most demanding one. This is a sad moment for the Motherland. Alexander Suratov was well known and was liked by each of us in this room. His tragic loss will be greatly mourned for many years to come. Yet before we return to the helm of power, to chart our country's future course, there's something extremely important I need to share with every one of you. Before I do so, however, I insist that you join me in some refreshments."

Taking this as her cue, Anna Kharkov rose from the fireside chair she had been occupying. A pert, buxom woman, who wore her advanced years well, Anna played the role of the perfect hostess, as she addressed them.

"I know it's not much, but please eat and drink to your heart's content, and don't hesitate to ask for seconds."

Looking up toward the hallway, she clapped her hands twice and firmly commanded. "Tanya, you may serve now!"

This was all that was needed to be said to bring forth a pink-uniformed maid. Her long, straight, black hair and dark, almond-shaped eyes betrayed her heritage as local Yakhut as she shyly pushed a large silver serving cart into the room's center. Attractively displayed on the top tray were a wide variety of delicacies, including smoked salmon from the nearby Lena, Kamchatka crab meat, sliced tongue, herring, and a mound of glistening black caviar. A basket of assorted breads accompanied this selection.

Anna Kharkov took a second to make certain that all was in order. Only when she was completely satisfied did she take the young maid by the hand and lead her out of the room.

Alone now with only his guests, Mikhail was quick to fulfill his duties as host. "Though these are black, confusing days for the Motherland, life still goes on. Come, let's refresh ourselves. And then there will be plenty of time to discuss the serious matter that brings us together."

Bending down to reach the cart's bottom shelf, he picked up a sterling silver tea server, and placed it on the nearby coffee table, where four porcelain cups and matching saucers sat. Then, from the serving cart he removed a heavy, cut-crystal decanter, that was filled with a deep, amber-colored liquid.

"Comrades, please let me pour each of you some tea. And to further take the chill off, I'll be including a taste of excellent Ukrainian cognac in your cups. Meanwhile, don't be shy. Grab a plate and help yourselves to some food."

While the Admiral of the Fleet expertly prepared the drinks, his three guests gathered around the serving cart. It proved to be General Zarusk who got the ball rolling by picking up a china plate and a serving spoon, and digging into the mound of caviar.

"It's been much too long since I've tasted the roe of a real Baikal sturgeon," revealed the Minister of Defense. "If neither one of you have ever had this pleasure before, my, are you in for the treat of a lifetime. For such caviar simply melts in your mouth!"

Following his enthusiastic lead, both Dmitri Tichvin and Yuri Kasimov picked up plates of their own. As the three men proceeded to fill them, their white-haired host finished filling the last of the cups, and ambled over to see how his guests were doing.

"Ah, excellent," reflected Mikhail. "It seems that this afternoon everyone has an appetite as ravenous as my own."

After choosing several slices of smoked salmon, some crab meat, and a good-sized spoonful of caviar, Mikhail tore off a heel of crusty pumpernickel and then joined his three colleagues on the large sofa that sat in front of the fireplace. A moment of silence followed us they dug into their food. Yet this quiet was all too soon broken by the spirited voice of Ivan Zarusk.

"Didn't I tell you that this particular caviar is the finest to grace the earth? Why its flavor is as delicate as any I've ever tasted. So tell me, Admiral, since this species of sturgeon is on the official endangered species list, were you forced to go to a poacher to purchase it?"

An angry scowl suddenly tightened Mikhail's brow. "General Zarusk, are you accusing me of abetting a known criminal act?" The angry look was all too soon

109

replaced by a warm smile. "No, comrades. You can enjoy your caviar knowing that it wasn't obtained on the black market. In actuality, the Baikal sturgeon has been making somewhat of a remarkable comeback as of late. So healthy is its present population, the conservationists have opened portions of the lake to limited fishing."

"How very fortunate for us," added the Defense Minister, as he prepared to bite into a piece of caviar-coated black bread.

Waiting until he had thoroughly chewed and swallowed the tongue sandwich he had prepared for himself, Dmitri Tichvin matter-of-factly observed. "The Baikal sturgeon is only one of the many success stories in this field. All over the Soviet Union, species that were once on the brink of extinction are thriving once again. This is truly something that each citizen of the Rodina can be proud of, because to lose the last of a species is to lose it for all time."

Suddenly inspired, Mikhail picked up his cup in a toast. "To the citizens of the Motherland. Long may they live in peace and prosperity."

As his guests responded to this toast by also lifting their cups to their lips, Mikhail added. "And to the Motherland itself. From its parched deserts to its frozen tundras; from the vast grain fields of the steppes to the thick, resource-rich taiga—surely we live in the greatest, most diverse nation ever to grace the face of this earth!"

"Here, here!" added Ivan Zarusk, who drained his cup. As his colleagues did likewise, Mikhail made the rounds to refill the cups this time only utilizing the deep golden liquid that was stored inside the cut-crystal decanter.

Their appetites further stimulated by the powerful cognac, the four Politburo members cleaned their plates. Only the Defense Minister returned for seconds, quickly polishing off the remainder of the caviar. With filled bellies, the men sat around the crackling fireplace. Once again their host refilled their cups, yet this time instead of reseating himself he remained standing.

Turning to briefly poke the burning logs, Mikhail slowly pivoted to address his guests, the roaring fire now directly behind him. "We've refreshed ourselves with the by-products of our land's natural bounty, and now it's time to get to the heart of the matter that prompted this gathering. For today we face a threat just as dangerous as the crazed hordes of Fascist Germany. Like the Nazis, this foe will not rest until the entire Rodina is under its greedy control.

"Capitalism is this opponent's name. It's a subtle evil, that works its way slowly into our people's souls until they ultimately lose sight of their socialistic direction. Like a cancer, it has only one cure—cut it out completely before a malignancy develops for which there is no cure.

"Unfortunately, it has taken the loss of one of the Motherland's most beloved sons to present us with an unprecedented opportunity to strike the proponents of capitalism a fatal blow. All of us knew Alexander Suratov to be a compassionate man, who wanted peace and plenty for his people above all else. Our beloved Premier was in the process of conveying his message to the leaders of Canada and the United States when the hand of fate intervened to abruptly cut his mission short.

"Yet what exactly took place in those frigid Arctic skies to doom this mission? Was it merely a mechanical fault that sent the *Flying Kremlin* crashing into the ice pack, or was an outside force responsible? If you'll just bear with me, comrades, I think that I can provide you with irrefutable proof that will support the latter of these two conjectures."

Halting at this point, Mikhail caught Ivan Zarusk's steel gray gaze. Without betraying himself, the Defense Minister gave his host the barest of supportive nods. As he briefly scanned the faces of his other guests, Mikhail found Dmitri Tichvin's expression filled with thoughtful contemplation, while a look of bored indifference etched the pockmarked face of Yuri Kasimov. Focusing his energies on this individual, Mikhail passionately continued.

"The Ilyushin Il-76 airliner known as the *Flying Kremlin* was one of the most checked-over planes ever to fly. Sporting a spotless service record, the Premier's personal jet had only recently had its four Soloviev two-shaft turbofan engines overhauled. To insure that this overhaul was a successful one, the plane was recently flown on a cross-country jaunt from Petropavlovsk to Leningrad, to insure the integrity of all of its sophisticated components. I myself saw the results of this test flight, and can assure you that the *Flying Kremlin* was as mechanically safe as a human-made machine can be.

"Besides having a variety of redundant systems, the aircraft was piloted by Stanislaus Kossovo, a decorated veteran, with more flying hours than any other active pilot in the Air Force. Together with a hand-picked crew of seven, Kossovo was well equipped to handle any emergency that might befall.

"Yet in the unlikely event that a mechanical failure did occur, then one puzzling question still remains. Why was this seasoned crew unable to broadcast even a single distress call? The *Flying Kremlin* carried no less than five separate communication systems. Several of these circuits were EMP hardened, that would allow them to transmit even in the event of a nuclear war."

"Perhaps this unlikely emergency that you just mentioned occurred so quickly that Kossovo didn't even have time to transmit a Mayday," offered Dmitri Tichvin.

Mikhail ingested this thought and answered after the briefest of pauses. "Since such a possibility crossed my mind also, I discussed it with our esteemed Defense Minister earlier. General Zarusk, why don't you share with our comrades here your expert opinion on this matter?"

Without bothering to stand, Ivan wasted no time responding. "There are several reasons why the scenario you mentioned isn't plausible, Comrade Tichvin. The first centers around the Bear-E reconnaissance plane that we had circling the North Pole as the Il-76 penetrated Canadian air space. This AWACS platform was fitted with the latest in rapid digital processing, over the horizon radars, and was assigned with a single mission in mind—to monitor each and every kilometer of the *Flying Kremlin*'s flight. As you may very well know, such AWACS platforms are extremely sophisticated and can track dozens of separate airborne targets at a single time. With this fact in mind, I immediately contacted the commander of this flight the second we learned the Premier's plane had dropped from their screen. I have since seen the crews documentation. These tapes show that a full twenty minutes passed between the moment the Il-76 initially dropped from its normal cruising altitude of 13,000 meters, until its disappearance altogether."

"I don't follow you, General," interrupted Yuri Kasimov.

"My heavens, comrade, don't you realize what such a thing means!" shouted Ivan Zarusk excitedly. "If a mechanical malfunction had indeed occurred, Captain Kossovo would have had an entire twenty minutes to inform us of it!"

"You mentioned a change of altitude, General. Is such a thing unusual?" continued Kasimov.

A bit flustered by the scrawny bureaucrat's continued probing, the general spoke more sharply. "Why of course it is, comrade! Though every flight deviates in altitude a few hundred meters or so, the *Flying Kremlin* fell over 6,500 meters with no explanation whatsoever."

"Maybe it was the weather," offered Dmitri Tichvin.

Conscious of the Defense Minister's impatience when it came to dealing with civilians, Mikhail Kharkov interceded. "That's out of the question, comrade. The skies were perfectly clear in the area, with not even a single storm front. These meteorological observations were subsequently corroborated by photos relayed to us by the cosmonauts aboard the Salyut space station, Red Flag. Incidentally, the *Flying Kremlin* was sent skyward from Irkutsk several minutes earlier than planned, so that the space station would be in a position to monitor the Il-76 as it crossed the North Pole."

Though Dmitri Tichvin seemed to be impressed with this surprise revelation, Yuri Kasimov impatiently stirred.

"I still don't get it," complained the pockmarked bureaucrat. "If it wasn't a mechanical problem or the weather that took the *Flying Kremlin* down, just what did?"

Waiting for this very question, Mikhail Kharkov pivoted and took a step aside. He was now facing the blank wall, directly adjoining the fireplace. With an outstretched hand, he triggered a recessed switch that

114

had been hidden in the flagstone of the hearth, and as a result of his touch, the wall board lifted up, revealing a large cabinet. An assortment of electronics gear was stored there. With a deft movement of his hand, Kharkov switched on a good-sized television monitor, whose picture screen filled with a polar projection map of the entire Arctic region.

With the assistance of a telescoping pointer, the admiral singled out an elongated island, to the immediate west of Greenland. "As you very well know, comrades, this is Baffin Island. It is somewhere on this frozen landmass that the remains of the *Flying Kremlin* are thought to lie. Though almost every informed citizen of the Motherland, and of the world for that matter, is aware of this previously insignificant piece of ice-covered permafrost from the newspapers and news broadcasts of late, what they don't know about are the top-secret, NORAD installations that litter this same island. The newest and most sophisticated of these installations is called Polestar, and is located here, on the extreme northern tip of the island, directly east of the tiny outpost of Arctic Bay.

"We have known about Polestar for some time now. From its very inception, our Intelligence analysts suspected it of being a major element of the West's so-called Strategic Defense Initiative. Built in total disregard of the latest ABM treaty, Polestar is believed to incorporate a sophisticated array of scrambling devices, that are designed to interfere with the delicate navigational systems of our ICBM, bomber, and cruise missile forces.

"Both the Bear recon plane and the Salyut reported that contrary to prior practices, Polestar briefly went active on two separate occasions. The first burst was monitored seconds before the *Flying Kremlin* made its mysterious, unauthorized change of altitude. While

115

the second burst occurred almost at the very moment the Il-76 disappeared from our radar screens altogether."

"Are you saying that it was Star Wars that was responsible for the death of Alexander Suratov?" quizzed Yuri Kasimov.

Though he was bothered by the bureaucrat's skeptical tone, Mikhail Kharkov took a deep breath and held his ground. "Yes, Comrade Kasimov, I am indirectly. For, you see, another vital item that the newspapers and television reports didn't mention that two American F-15 Eagle fighters were scrambled from Thule at the very same time Polestar was going active. Thus while this so-called early warning radar installation was in fact interfering with the *Flying Kremlin*'s sensitive navigation and communication's systems, the Eagle interceptors were provided a target that was little challenge for their Phoenix air-to-air missiles. And mind you, comrades, all of these clever Yankee machinations were intended to take place with the whole world totally ignorant of their guilt!"

"Such a thing must not be allowed to happen!" cried Ivan Zarusk, who excitedly stood and in the process knocked over his teacup. "We've caught the Imperialist pigs with their hands in the proverbial cookie jar, and it's now up to us to revenge our beloved Premier's passing and in the process guarantee that his death was not in vain."

Disgustedly shaking his head at this outburst of emotion, Yuri Kasimov coolly put in, "I imagine that the next thing you'll be asking from us is our support in ordering an immediate nuclear retaliatory strike against the West to set the record straight."

"And what's wrong with that?" countered the red-faced Defense Minister. "Here the Imperialists have been caught in a clear-cut case of cold-blooded murder and Comrade Kasimov doesn't even want to retaliate!"

"I didn't say that!" the usually mild-mannered bureaucrat said forcefully. "I'd be the first to support such a strike, if you could supply me with some concrete proof of the West's guilt."

"I agree!" added Dmitri Tichvin. "A nuclear strike is serious business. Yet if the Americans were indeed directly responsible for the downing of the *Flying Kremlin,* we have no choice but to teach them a lesson they'll never forget."

All the time breathlessly watching this spirited exchange, Mikhail Kharkov could hardly believe what he was hearing. Sensing that he had his two naive colleagues right where he wanted them, the battle-wise veteran returned the focus of their discussion back to the Arctic map, as he tapped the end of the pointer up against the monitor's glass screen.

"Then what would you say, comrades, if I could get you that indisputable proof?" Mikhail questioned boldly. "Because I happen to know almost precisely where that evidence currently lies. All that we have to do now is find the Il-76's cockpit voice recorder, or as it is more commonly called, its black box. And it so happens the cosmonauts in our Salyut space station have already picked up this device's ultrasonic homing signal, on the ice directly adjoining the northern coast of Baffin Island. So all that remains to be done is to go up there and grab it. Then we merely have to analyze its digital tape; that holds a detailed account of every single second of that flight, from its lift-off in Irkutsk, to the plane's final moments. And if it's indeed learned that an American missile was responsible for taking the *Flying Kremlin* down, can I at the very least count on having your support in the planning and carrying out of a proper retaliatory attack?"

117

"Why, of course!" returned the two bureaucrats almost simultaneously.

Fighting to control his joy, Admiral of the Fleet Mikhail Kharkov turned his glance on his old friend, Ivan Zarusk. A wide smirk etched the Defense Minister's face, and Mikhail couldn't help but smile in this moment of triumph.

Chapter Six

It was late into the night before the USS *Defiance* was ready to set sail. A cool, penetrating breeze blew in from the north as two uniformed figures stood on the vessel's exposed sail. The taller one pulled from his lips the pipe he had been smoking, and called out to a bearded dockhand below.

"Release number one!"

As the last line connecting the *Defiance* to the docks was freed, the XO addressed his next command to the bridge's black plastic, intercom handset. "All back two-thirds."

A frothing patch of agitated seawater formed astern and the sub's black hull began inching its way into the Thames River. Al Layman relayed another order into the intercom, and as the propeller shaft reversed the direction of its rotation, the vessel began to head for the open sea.

"Well, Skipper, seems we're not the only ones working late tonight. Looks like the men and women over at Electric Boat are getting in a little overtime themselves."

"That's nothing unusual," returned Matt Colter, as he scanned the brightly lit, industrial complex that hugged the waterfront on this portion of the Thames.

"With all the new orders the Navy's throwing their way, EB never shuts down nowadays. And even then, their backlog of past-due product is growing."

"That's what we get for having only two company's geared to produce submarines," observed the XO.

The blinding flare of a welder's torch lit the black night, and the *Defiance* silently surged past the mammoth marine construction facility, where its own keel had been laid over fifteen years ago.

"By the way Al, did you ever get ahold of your wife?" queried Matt Colter.

"Sure did, Skipper," replied the XO, who paused a second to put a flame to the tobacco in his pipe's bowl. "Even got to see her for a whole quarter of an hour back in the officers' club. She looked great. That aerobic's class she's been attending has done wonders for her."

"I hope you didn't spill the beans on that second honeymoon you were planning."

"For once in my life I was able to keep this big trap of mine shut," observed the XO. "Otherwise, that anniversary celebration could have been our last. Now, I only pray Donna doesn't get wind of the fact I've got another woman shacked up in my quarters here on the *Defiance*."

"Like a good Navy wife, she'd understand, Al. I hope you were able to make our guest comfortable."

The XO thoughtfully exhaled a long ribbon of fragrant smoke from his nostrils before responding. "At least Ms. Lansing didn't seem to be carrying any hair curlers or blow dryers on board. With the eager assistance of Lieutenant Marshall, Chief Sandusky, and several assorted gawking seamen, we were able to accommodate her. For a dame, that one sure travels light. She seemed to be carrying along more technical gear than personal belongings."

"I don't like having a woman on board any more than you, Al. But if she's able to get that newfangled surface-scanning Fathometer working like it should, it'll be well worth the hassle she's causing. Besides, Dr. Lansing seems to be definitely low profile. She'll do her work and hopefully stay well out of the way of the men."

"I sure hope so, Skipper. Because even without a lot of makeup and provocative clothing, the doctor seems to exude plenty of good old-fashioned sex appeal."

The captain grunted. "So I've noticed, XO. So I've noticed."

A contemplative silence followed, and all too soon they were leaving the lights of Connecticut behind them and entering the black waters of Block Island Sound. It was as the sub's rounded bow bit into the first Atlantic swell that a sudden voice sounded over the intercom speaker.

"Captain, we have a surface contact on radar, bearing one-four-zero. Range five and a half miles and closing."

The lights of this ship could barely be seen in the distance. Matt Colter spoke into the intercom handset. "Helmsman, come port to one-one-zero true."

As the bow of the *Defiance* swung left, Colter stretched his arms and yawned. "I'll leave the *Defiance* in your capable hands, Al. When we reach thirty fathoms, submerge and set your course for Nantucket Shoals, speed twenty knots."

"So it looks like I'll get out to Nantucket this evening after all," reflected the XO, as he watched the captain turn for the hatch leading to the ship's interior.

Exhausted after the full day of last-minute preparations, Matt Colter climbed down the steep, steel ladder, heading below. With practiced ease he passed through a narrow, water-tight hatch and stepped down into the control room.

Lit by an ethereal red light designed to protect the crew's night vision, the control room was hushed, a serious atmosphere prevailing. Trying not to break this spell, Colter briefly glanced at the helmsman, who sat strapped to his padded chair, the airplane-type steering column gripped firmly in hand. Mounted before this alert seaman was a compass repeater, their exact course clearly displayed in a dimly glowing, digital readout screen.

Behind the helmsman was the ship's diving station. Here Chief Sandusky passed the time sipping a mug of coffee, while waiting for the inevitable order that would cause him to trigger the ballast mechanisms and send the *Defiance* plunging down into the silent depths below.

Before heading on to his cabin, Colter took a moment to visit the station that was set immediately aft of the diving console. Silently picking his way through the equipment-packed deck, the captain caught sight of the glowing, green fluorescent display of the radar screen. Projected on this monitor was a portion of the coastline they had long since left behind them, and a single blinking contact that was situated off their starboard bow.

Matt Colter firmly addressed the young seaman who was perched beside this screen. "Make certain to inform Lieutenant Commander Layman the moment that contact changes its course."

"Aye, aye, sir," shot back the alert sailor. "As it appears now, our closest point of approach will be three miles."

The captain nodded. "Good. I want to keep it that way. Any idea what type of vessel it might be?"

Ever ready to impress his commanding officer, the

seaman retorted. "Looks like a fishing trawler, sir."

"If that's the case, let's just hope they don't have any nets in the water. We certainly wouldn't want to get snagged."

His gaze still glued to the radar monitor, the young seaman cleared his throat and dared to put forth a single question. "Sir, is it true that we're headed back for the ice?"

The astounding speed with which Navy scuttlebutt spread never failed to impress Colter. He cautiously answered, "I'll be officially announcing our destination tomorrow, sailor. But in the meantime, if I were you, I'd keep those woolen sweaters and long johns handy."

The radar operator grinned. "I'll do that, Captain."

Having affectionately patted the young sailor on the back, Colter turned for his quarters. It had been a long tiring day. The unexpected sailing orders had caught everyone by complete surprise, himself most of all. It had taken a combined effort to get the *Defiance* once again ready for the sea. The restocking of their limited food supply was a primary concern. Yet because they had just returned a week earlier than anticipated, their larders hadn't been totally empty. Since their reactor didn't need to be refueled for at least another year, Colter next concentrated on tracking down those crew members who had already left the ship to be with their friends or families. While phone calls, and even messengers, were used to track down these errant seamen, Matt turned to yet another major concern—the surface-scanning Fathometers. No matter how you looked at it, the *Defiance* would soon be on its way to the frozen Arctic without either of its Fathometers in working order.

Hopefully, this deficiency would be rectified in three days' time. Yet Matt was still hesitant to rely on the prototype system. Regardless of the fact that Laurie Lansing was aboard to insure that the device was functioning properly, his gut feeling warned him to be extra cautious this time around. At the first sign of trouble, he intended to switch over to the old unit; the chief engineer had promised it would also be operational in three more days. Of course, by that time he'd most probably have the rest of his orders and know precisely what their mission was.

Unexpected patrols such as the one they were on were a headache to coordinate, but they were exciting. Usually designed with a definite purpose in mind, such missions were far more invigorating than dull sea trials and predictable maneuvers with the fleet. Because Dr. Lansing had been ordered to sea with them, it was evident that the orders he'd soon be receiving would have something to do with an ascent to the surface of the polar ice cap.

Remembering his all too recent meeting in New London, Colter wondered if the admiral had known about this mission all along. Could this then be the reason why Long had proceeded to vehemently question Matt about his decision to return a week early? It would also explain why he had resurrected the incident concerning Matt's reluctance to surface beside the English weather station, over a year ago. It was evident that Command was afraid he had lost his nerve, and wouldn't be fit to lead the next mission under the ice they already had in mind for him!

Bravado and recklessness were two vastly different terms that were sometimes confused. This was especially true when a careless act, carried out with total disregard for human life, reaped successful consequences. Wars were full of such incidents. Yet Matt Colter was not about to risk his ship and crew merely to show that he was made out of the right stuff. To

124

him, human life was sacred, and shouldn't be needlessly wasted if a legitimate threat existed.

The brand of coward stung every man. Even more so those who'd chosen to be officers in the military. There was a thin line between responsibility for carrying out the order of the day and the obligation to look after the welfare of those entrusted to one's command. For Matt Colter, the choice had been obvious. He had been unwilling to compromise his ideals, and stood behind his decisions one hundred percent. The mere fact that he had once again been sent to sea proved that the powers that be had accepted his judgment, and that his choice had been the correct one.

Satisfied with this realization, Colter stepped through the hatchway that led to officers' country. The wardroom table was empty as he turned to his left and entered his cramped private domain.

It seemed that he had just fallen asleep, when his cabin filled with the resonant sound of the diving klaxon. Briefly opening his weary eyes, he stared out into the pitch black confines of his stateroom, and instinctively felt the angle of the deck alter as the *Defiance* took on ballast and dipped its spherical bow beneath the surging Atlantic. Confident of his crew's ability to safely run the ship in his absence, Matt Colter yawned and almost instantly fell back into a sound dreamless sleep.

Meanwhile, on the deck immediately below, Petty Officer First Class Stanley Roth sat in the crew's mess room, gingerly spooning down a bowl of oatmeal. At the same table, his shipmate Brian MacMillan was also in the midst of a meal. Yet unlike the sonar technician, Mac as he was known to the crew, was well into a four-course steak dinner. Wolfing down his chow like he hadn't eaten for a week, Mac started with a bowl of onion soup and a tossed salad. Once this was consumed, he began working on a plate filled to capacity with a juicy T-bone steak, fried potatoes, and an ear of steamed white corn.

His mouth still filled with partially chewed meat, the curly, blond-haired torpedoman gulped down a sip of milk and addressed his dining companion. "Are you sure you don't want to try a bite of this steak, Stan? For once in his life, Cooky prepared it good and rare like a steak ought to be."

Stanley Roth wearily downed another spoonful of oatmeal before replying. "I'll take a rain check, Mac. This tooth of mine is still a bit sensitive."

"But I thought you were going to see the base dentist today?" quizzed the torpedoman in between bites of potato.

Stanley disgustedly threw down his spoon and cautiously rubbed the lower left side of his jaw. "I did, Mac."

"Well if that's the case, why can't you have a real supper?" queried the puzzled seaman.

Reaching into his pocket, Stanley removed a folded sheet of prescription paper, and attempted to read from it. "The doc says I have a deep peridontal pocket on the distal of my left mandibular first bicuspid."

"Sounds fatal," reflected the torpedoman as he went to work on his corn. He proceeded to polish off half the ear before adding. "Now, in English, what the hell type of ailment is that?"

Stan Roth seemed utterly frustrated. "How the hell should I know, Mac? I'm no jaw breaker!"

Sensing the degree of his shipmate's distress, the torpedoman put down his partially eaten cob. "Easy, Stan. I'm not purposely trying to aggravate you. I only wanted to know what that dentist did for your toothache."

After a series of calming breaths, the sonar technician replied. "First off, I should have walked right out of there the moment I entered that clinic, because there wasn't a soul in the waiting room. Some scrawny nurse had me put what seemed like my whole life's history on a form and then led me into the back room. We must have surprised the hell of that jaw breaker, because we caught him red-handed, putting golf balls into one of those electronic gadgets that simulate a golf hole.

"He must have been right out of dental school, because not only did he look as innocent as a choir boy, he had pimples as well. But that's beside the point, because the next thing I know he's got me in the chair and that's when the fun really began."

"Did he use the drill?" quizzed the wide-eyed torpedoman who had temporarily abandoned his silverware.

Stanley shook his head. "No, he only poked around a bit with some sort of probe. Then, after scraping off a bit of tartar, he treated the gum with some horrible-tasting medicine and dismissed me with a warning to brush and floss after every meal or I'd lose that tooth for sure." While carefully rubbing his lower jaw, Stan added. "Right now, I'm beginning to wonder if he shouldn't have pulled it right there. At least it still wouldn't be bothering me."

Compassion etched his dining companion's face, as Brian picked up knife and fork and responded while cutting up the remainder of the T-bone. "I don't know about that, Stan. The pain has got to go away sometime, and why lose a perfectly good tooth if you don't have to."

"Jesus, Mac, I've had this damn toothache for over two weeks now, and it's really starting to get to me! Why I can't even get down a cup of hot coffee without it killing me."

"Now that's serious," retorted the torpedoman between bites of meat. "Say, didn't those painkillers Pills gave you last week do some good?"

Stanley pushed away his bowl of half-eaten oatmeal and replied. "Sure, they took away the ache for a while, but in the process they left me so doped up I couldn't even stand my normal watch. And when they eventually wore off, I was stuck with that same damn throbbing pain all over again."

"My friend, I really do have compassion for you," offered Mac as he cleaned off his plate, mopped up the remaining juices with a piece of bread, and reached for a big slice of apple pie.

Sickened by this sight, Stanley retorted. "At least your compassion hasn't spoiled your appetite any. Christ, Mac, you're worse than a pig!"

Not taking this remark seriously, the torpedoman attempted to change the subject. "Lighten up, Roth. That toothache will go away, and you'll be right back here wolfing down the chow with the best of 'em. But until then, you've got to get your mind onto something other than what ails you. Otherwise, you're going to wig right on out of here."

"I'm afraid that sounds a lot easier to do than it actually is, Mac."

"I don't know about that, Stan. You haven't by any chance seen the latest addition to the *Defiance*'s crew as yet, have you?"

As Roth shook his head indicating he hadn't, his grinning shipmate glibly continued. "Well you'd better prepare yourself, sailor, because one look at that face and body and you'll forget all about that damn toothache of yours."

"What the hell are you talking about, Mac?"

"I'm talking about a young, good-looking dame, living right here inside this very same hull, along with you, me, and the rest of the boys!"

"Aw, come off it, Mac. What kind of sucker do you think I am? Everyone knows that the US Navy doesn't allow women aboard it's submarines while they're on patrol."

"Are you calling me a liar, Roth? Or perhaps you don't think I have enough experience to know the difference between a man and a woman when I see one. Because I'm telling you we've got a female on board this submarine, and a stone fox at that!"

Though still thinking this all a mind game, Stanley couldn't help but be impressed by his shipmate's sincerity. "So the *Defiance* has a woman on board. I guess next you'll be telling me she's been assigned to share the crew's berthing facilities."

The torpedoman snickered. "Very funny, Stan. Actually, from what I heard from the chief, she's staying in Lieutenant Commander Layman's cabin. The XO's moved in with lieutenants Marshall and Sanger."

With the sudden realization that this wasn't a joke after all, Stanley further probed. "Is this female you're talking about in the Navy?"

Mac was all business as he answered. "Again it was the chief who explained that she's some civilian hotshot with the Naval Arctic's lab. Seems she was sent on the *Defiance* to have a look at that surface-scanning Fathometer that was almost responsible for deep-sixing us back under the ice. Since she barely had time to look at the unit before we were ordered back to sea, and since scuttlebutt has it we're returning to the ice once again, she was sent along to repair it while we're on the way."

"Well, I'll be," reflected the senior sonar technician. "I thought the crew looked a bit more dapper than their normal grubby selves when I boarded late this afternoon."

A sudden thought entered MacMillian's mind and his eyes widened. "Say Stanley, isn't that new Fathometer somehow tied in with your sonar gear?"

"As a matter of fact, it is. Why do you ask, Mac?"

A bit more excitedly, the blond-haired torpedoman answered. "Because that means she'll most likely be working in the sound shack. Damn, you lucky stiff! Say, Stan, if her duty does send her into the sonar room, and your toothache gets too bad, just call the forward torpedo room and I'll be happy to fill in for you."

"I'll bet you would," remarked Roth. He couldn't wait to see this mysterious woman his shipmate was raving about so, and he suddenly realized that since they'd been talking about her, his tooth had miraculously stopped throbbing.

While sailors throughout the three-hundred-foot vessel were immersed in similar discussions concerning the latest addition to the crew, the woman responsible for this scuttlebutt sat in her cramped, Spartan quarters in officer's country. Laurie Lansing had been so busy organizing her technical materials, she was just now finding the time to sit back and reflect on more personal concerns. Though she was certainly no stranger to submarines, and had even gone to sea on one before, this would be her first overnight stay on such a craft. Thus her perspective was completely different on this occasion.

The cabin she found herself in was just about the same size as the roomette of a train. It had a similar Pullman-type washbasin that folded up into the wall when not in use. The rest of the furnishings consisted of a built-in bunk, beneath which was a clothing locker, a small desk and chair, and a mounted bookshelf. Even though cramped, it would allow her space to work in peace, and would give her some semblance of privacy. This last feature was most appreciated, considering that she was the only female in a crew of 107 men. Though she didn't foresee any problems developing in this respect, it was nevertheless somewhat comforting to have a solid door to shut behind her when she desired to be alone.

Were it not for the digital knot indicator and Fathometer mounted in front of the bunk, she would have found it hard to believe they were currently three-hundred feet beneath the Atlantic, clipping away at a steady twenty knots. Except for a slight tilting sensation that had followed the triggering of the dive klaxon, there'd been absolutely no sensation of movement or instability, though this hadn't been the case when they were still traveling on the surface. The keelless vessel had incessantly rolled in the endless ocean swells, and for a while there Laurie had thought she might vomit. Fortunately, she had been too busy organizing her work materials to pay her nausea much attention, and it soon passed.

Though she had originally intended to try to turn in early, she found herself wide awake. Making the most of this restlessness, she seated herself at the desk, took out a legal pad and pen, and began organizing her work schedule.

With the able help of her assistant, she'd been able to work on the recalibration of the laser almost right up to the moment of departure. Since this procedure would require the *Defiance* to be on the surface, it would have to be completed long before they reached the ice. Because of the excellent progress they had already made, only a couple of hours more work in the sail would be needed. Earlier, when she had informed Captain Colter of this fact, his relief was most noticeable. Submariners, especially those in the nuclear-powered navy, tended to shy away from surface

131

travel whenever possible. They preferred instead the safety and anonymity of the black, cold depths in which their vessels were initially designed to operate.

Once the work in the sail was completed, the majority of Laurie's time would be spent in the sonar room. Here a spare console had been reserved for her, where she could initiate the time-consuming task of programming the surface-scanning Fathometer to interact with the *Defiance*'s navigation system. When this job was completed, the mere punch of a button would automatically guide the submarine upward into an opening in the ice of sufficient size and width to accommodate the vessel.

Because of the newness of the software involved in this program, Laurie didn't really know what problems she might be facing in the next couple of days. Thus she was greatly relieved when the captain informed her that he was having the sub's old surface-scanning unit reconnected, to be used as a backup if needed. Such devices were primitive when compared to the new unit, but crudely effective all the same.

Thirty years ago, Laurie's father, Dr. Frank Lansing, had been involved in the development of this equipment. In reality, it was but an inverted Fathometer, mounted on a submarine's topside instead of in its keel. As the sound signals this Fathometer projected echoed off the ice above, a device sketched the ice cover's actual thickness and shape, and then printed out a profile on an eight-inch piece of graph paper, right in the control room. Utilizing this cross section, it was then up to the captain to find an open lead large enough for his vessel and then to surface in it.

Frank Lansing had worked three decades on improving this device. For the past five years, Laurie had been actively involved with his tireless effort, and at long last an actual working unit had been placed inside the USS *Defiance*. As fate would have it, her father did not live long enough to see his dream fulfilled. Now it was up to her to insure that his life's work was not in vain.

This was a great responsibility, and one that Laurie did not take lightly. Her life, and the lives of one-hundred and seven others, were on the line, for the slightest miscalculation could prove fatal. Only last week, the *Defiance* had participated in three harrowing collisions with the pack ice. By the grace of God, a submerged ridge hadn't ripped the submarine's hull open like a can opener.

The *Defiance* had been given a reprieve, and in this respite Laurie had one last chance to clear her father's name. She could not afford to fail this time around.

Setting the pad she'd been scribbling on down on the desk, Laurie glanced at the photograph she had propped up on the nearby bookshelf. She hadn't seen this particular picture in years, then had found it stuck between the pages of one of her father's journals, the one she had been skimming through earlier in the day.

Laurie remembered this snapshot well, for it had been taken on her twenty-first birthday. Having just graduated from MIT summa cum laude the month before, she'd been presented with a very special present—a trip to the Virgin Islands. This was to be her first visit to the Caribbean, and the photograph showed her and her father decked out in bathing suits on the deserted, white-sand beach of St. John's exclusive Turtle Bay resort. These were happy, carefree days, and the spirit of them was conveyed in their joyous expressions.

Though this trip took place over eight years ago, Laurie would never forget how very special it had been. After four years of grueling school work, doing nothing all day but eating, swimming, and sunbathing was a welcome change of pace.

The seawater was warm and crystal clear. Decked out in mask, snorkel, and fins she explored a seemingly untouched realm. A coral reef lay right off the central beach, and it attracted many brightly colored species of tropical fish and marine life. Her favorites were the giant turtles for which the area was known, and the graceful, strangely shaped stingrays.

Her father accompanied her on these underwater excursions, and afterwards, over beachside lunch or dinner, they compared notes. It was during these sessions that a new understanding developed between them. For the first time ever, Laurie felt like his equal. No longer merely daddy's little girl. At twenty-one years of age, with four years of college behind her, she was an adult, well on her way to choosing her particular path in life.

It was during one of the dinners they shared, while the full moon rose in all its magnificence over the adjoining bay, that the subject of Laurie's mother came up. Since she'd died in a plane crash when Laurie was only five years old, she had always been a shadowy, enigmatic character. A nanny had taken her place, and Laurie had grown up with little knowledge of the woman from whom she'd inherited her tall, shapely figure, dark eyes, long, black silky hair, and, as she was soon to learn, her probing, keen intellect.

Her father had always been hesitant to talk about his first and only wife. In fact, there was only one photograph of her in the entire house, and this was but an informal framed snapshot placed on the mantel over the fireplace.

With his tongue loosened by several powerful rum cocktails, he did finally open his soul to Laurie, however. For the first time she was told that her mother had been an up and coming anthropologist, whose expertise centered on the native peoples living above the Arctic Circle. Her travels took her to such far-off, exotic locations as Norway, Finland, and Siberia. In them she studied the natives' religious rites, with a particular focus on their musical traditions. While she was on a field trip in Northern Alaska, the small plane she had been flying was lost in a violent snow storm. Her body was never recovered, and for many years Laurie's father lived with the slim hope that his wife was really not dead. He even made several futile trips up into Brooks Range to investigate, but each time came back with his hopes crushed.

Laurie found it remarkable that in all the years that followed her father had been able to keep so much to himself. He had to have been full of pain, yet heedless of his personal concerns, he'd dedicated himself to his young daughter's development and to his career.

And somehow he seemed to always find time for Laurie. While growing up, she looked upon him as her best friend, always there with a smile and an interesting story to tell. When she was ready for school, she was sent to the very best available. Science and mathematics always came easiest to her, and for as long as she could remember, her goal was to be a famous scientist like her father.

Through the years, her natural good looks didn't go unnoticed by members of the opposite sex. In high school, she had her fair share of dates, but for the most part she found those boys boring and vain. Of course, there was always the natural inclination to compare them to her father. And in every instance, none came close to matching Dr. Frank Lansing in brains, charm, or force of personality.

Her social life was almost nil in college. She was much too busy mastering the challenging principles

135

of applied physics or probing into the intricacies of advanced engineering. During summer vacations, she went to work for her father in the Naval Arctic Lab. Because of the strategic importance of the Arctic Ocean, the US Navy was interested in knowing all it could about the region's unique physical makeup. Surprisingly little past research had been done in this area, and her father's lab was helping to coordinate this new effort.

Advances in technology were changing the character of Arctic research. Exciting new inventions such as the laser-guided surface-scanning Fathometer were finally coming out of the test stage and being applied to actual, operational hardware.

To Laurie, there could be no more exciting field than this. Though she had several other attractive offers, there was never much doubt in her mind as to the direction of her graduate curriculum, and finally, with a doctorate in advanced Arctic studies in hand, she applied for a position on her father's staff. She was instantly accepted, and spent the next five years assisting her father develop what one senior admiral in the Pentagon called "the most significant advancement in under-the-ice technology since the advent of the nuclear reactor."

All their hard work came to fruition six months ago, when the US Navy notified the lab that it was accepting one of the laser-guided Fathometers to test on an actual sub. After the briefest of celebrations, they went to work preparing an operational system. Because they had to meet a sailing deadline, they had little time to tarry. Fourteen-hour work days were not uncommon, and a day off was almost unheard of. Yet during the entire six-month period, never once did Laurie hear one of the staff voice a complaint. For they really believed in the project, and were willing to sacrifice their personal lives to insure its success.

Of course, no one was as dedicated to this effort as Dr. Frank Lansing. Going to the extreme of setting up a cot in the lab, he worked tirelessly for hours on end. It was a chore for Laurie to even get him to break for meals, and several times she actually had to drag him away from his work in order to get some decent food into his system.

Two weeks before their deadline was upon them, her father moved into the lab permanently. It was at this point that the hundreds of hours of hard work began to show in his eyes and general physical appearance. He seemed to be uncharacteristically slovenly, and it was obviously an effort for him to drag his tired, bent body around the laboratory. Several times he complained of attacks of what he called heartburn, but whenever Laurie advised that he should see his physician, he inevitably changed the subject.

She knew now that she should have been firmer with him about seeking medical treatment. Yet her work schedule was equally as intense, and when it came time to begin installing the Fathometer into the *Defiance,* it was all she could do to find the time to take care of her own personal concerns.

On the morning of the day the installation was to be completed, Laurie found herself on her way to the docks to personally supervise the final calibration of the scanning lasers. Since her father wished to be on the scene also, she stopped at the lab to pick him up. It was a brisk, clear autumn day, and as she expectantly pulled up to the three-story brick building where their offices were located, she spotted a pair of police cars parked immediately in front of the entranceway. Not really giving these vehicles much thought, she entered the central foyer and encountered two policemen intently interrogating Will Harper, one of the project's senior technicians. It only took one look at Will's face for her to know that there had been some sort of tragedy. But little was Laurie prepared for what she was soon to learn, when the bearded scientist took her aside and with tear-stained eyes explained the grim discovery he'd made that morning.

Also on his way to the *Defiance,* Harper had stopped off at the lab first to pick up a program manual. Once inside, he'd decided to see if the project's director needed a lift to the docks. Poking his head into Frank Lansing's office, he found the white-haired researcher slumped over his desk. At first Will Harper assumed that Lansing had only fallen asleep. But as he took a step inside, he realized that their venerated director was no longer breathing. Harper called 911, and then began a frenzied attempt at pulmonary resuscitation. His efforts were futile. Ten minutes later the paramedics arrived and pronounced Dr. Frank Lansing dead from an apparent heart attack.

Laurie's initial reaction was one of shocked disbelief. She demanded that she be taken to the hospital where her father's body had been transferred. And only when she had personally viewed his corpse did cold reality suddenly sink in. Numbed into speechlessness, she sat in the morgue and contemplated her loss, and for the first time in her relatively young life tasted the bitter fruit of real loneliness.

Tears clouded Laurie Lansing's eyes as she sighed heavily and tore her gaze away from the photograph that had triggered these intense memories. Absentmindedly scanning the cramped cabin of her current submerged home, she could only wonder what her father would have to say about her present duty. Surely he'd be immensely proud of her. In his earlier days, Frank Lansing had spent many months at a time beneath the world's oceans, while in the midst of a variety of experiments designed to enhance the nation's fledgling nuclear submarine fleet. Yet the culmination of his long, selfless career wouldn't be attained until his most cherished project went operational. And it was up to Laurie to insure that it did.

The throbbing hum of a muted turbine sounded in the distance. Other than this barely audible noise, there was no hint of the true nature of her current means of transport. There was no shifting of the deck, no feeling of movement, as the 4,600-ton nuclear-powered attack sub cut through the icy Atlantic depths at a steady twenty knots of forward speed. Truly this craft was an incredible engineering feat, and to be a part of a project intended to make such a technological marvel even better was a stimulus to the twenty-nine-year-old research engineer.

Chapter Seven

The view from the Antonov An-22 airliner was a limited one. Since it had crossed the Ural Mountains just south of the Siberian city of Vorkuta, the weather had progressively worsened. Even at its present cruising altitude of 12,500 meters, the sky was filled with nothing but roiling, black storm clouds. Accompanying this front were stiff northerly head winds, and because of the resulting turbulence, the pilot had long ago activated the seatbelt sign.

Peering out the rounded viewing port, Admiral of the Fleet Mikhail Kharkov looked out to the stormy skies and tried his best to ignore the mad, shaking vibration of the plane's fuselage. Thankfully, he wouldn't be in this bumpy, unstable craft much longer. For his immediate destination, Murmansk airport, was less than twenty-five kilometers distant.

Encountering an air pocket, the massive An-22 suddenly lost altitude, and Mikhail found himself tightly gripping his seat's armrests as the plane sickeningly plunged downward. To the grinding roar of its four dual-propped Kuznetsov turboprop engines, the mammoth transport vehicle strained to stabilize itself. Somehow it did so, yet Mikhail couldn't help but wonder how the plane's frame was able to stay in one piece.

The largest aircraft in the world apart from the American C-5A, the An-22 was a marvel of Soviet engineering. Not only could it carry a squad of T-62 battle tanks in its lower hold, but up to 100,000 kilograms of freight and 29 passengers as well.

Currently seated in the passenger cabin situated immediately aft of the flight deck, Mikhail Kharkov knew that he was very fortunate to get this lift. The route from Irkutsk to Murmansk was not a popular one, and nonstop flights were few and far between. Originally having taken off from Vladivostok, the An-22 had subsequently been diverted to an unscheduled stop in Irkutsk by a single call from General Ivan Zarusk. Though the spirited Defense Minister would have liked to join Mikhail on this trip, affairs of state had sent him packing back to Moscow, along with Dmitri Tichvin and Yuri Kasimov.

Just thinking about his old friend caused a grin to lighten Mikhail's face. They went back a long time together, and their shared exploits could fill a good-sized novel. Of course, the latest chapter of this book had only recently been concluded. Like a pair of slick black marketeers, they had exploited the two naive bureaucrats right in Mikhail's own living room. Afterward, Ivan had briefly pulled Mikhail aside and congratulated him on his superb performance. Then after promising to celebrate in style once the rest of their mission was successfully completed, they'd joined their guests for the short helicopter ride back to the Irkutsk airport. Here Mikhail left the others to initiate his current journey.

Again the An-22 plunged downward in a sickening, gut-wrenching free-fall and the Admiral of the Fleet of the Soviet Union silently cursed the weatherfront responsible for this turbulence. Knowing now why

141

he'd not joined the air force, the white-haired veteran diverted his gaze to the forward portion of the cabin. There the only other passenger, an Aeroflot flight attendant, was somehow able to sleep through all this terrible weather.

Mikhail had never liked to fly, and doubted if he ever would, no matter how many times he was airborne. There was something about not being at the controls himself, not understanding the systems involved, that bothered him. It felt uncomfortable to have one's life in the hands of a complete stranger, no matter how many flight hours he might have logged.

Mikhail never experienced such anxieties when he was traveling by sea. Even when not personally at the helm he felt secure, for a ship's fate was shared by its entire crew. Very seldom could the loss of a vessel be pinned on one man, though ultimately the captain was always the one held responsible.

The world's oceans were his second home, and even though pleasant memories of his recently concluded hike to the shores of Lake Baikal were fresh in his mind, he was glad to be going back to sea. When his wife Anna heard of his intention, she'd cornered him while he was in the bedroom hurriedly packing and had fully vented herself.

"What do you mean, you're going back to sea again? Don't you realize you're a seventy-six-year-old man? And besides, Misha, you've got other responsibilities now. Leave the operational side of your job to younger, more fit individuals. An old man like you will only get in the way."

Mikhail had been anticipating such a reaction, and did his best to dispel her apprehensions. While still continuing to fill up his dusty duffel bag, he countered, "You're right, my dearest. It's a young man's world out there. But sometimes us old-timer's are needed as counselors, to share our hard-earned experience, gained by sweat and toil and many years in the field. Besides, I'll be gone less than a week. And I promise you, once this patrol is completed, I'll hang up my duffel bag for good."

This last statement served its purpose, and realizing that it was useless to fight him, Anna pushed him out of the way and completed the packing herself.

As it so happened, he hadn't been lying to her about quitting the sea for good. There would be much to do upon his return, and he would have no time for the operational side of the Fleet. This would be left in the capable hands of the officers and enlisted men of the Soviet Navy, men who would be instrumental in helping him consolidate the glorious worldwide Socialistic state that would shortly unite all men in brotherhood.

Merely thinking about the realization of his goal caused shivers to run up and down his spine. At long last, the time for dreaming was over. Action was the order of the day, as the world anxiously perched on the verge of a brave new beginning.

It wasn't mere whim that was calling him to Murmansk. Rather, it was the *Sierra* Class nuclear-powered attack submarine, *Neva*. Less than a year old, the *Neva* was a state-of-the-art vessel, especially designed for under-the-ice operations. Mikhail had been at the Gorky shipyards and had participated in the sub's launching. Yet never did he dream then that one day in the near future he'd be boarding the *Neva* himself, to lead it on the most important mission of his long career.

As the enormous airliner that was carrying him to his destiny shook in a violent windshear, Mikhail reached into the breast pocket of his uniform and briefly touched the case holding the steel-jacketed cassette tape that would play a key role in their rapidly unraveling plot. The *Neva* must get him and this tape to the northern coast of Baffin Island with due haste.

From what he knew of this submarine's captain, there was no better officer in the entire Soviet fleet to accomplish this task. Sergei Markova was young and aggressive. The talented son of a decorated war hero, he had been groomed since birth for his present position. Graduating first in his class at Leningrad's Frunze Naval Academy, Markova had gained Mikhail's attention while he was attending postgraduate courses at the A. A. Grechko Academy. Acting as a silent patron, Mikhail had made certain that the young officer's first active assignment had been on one of the Motherland's newest attack subs. As Mikhail expected, Markova distinguished himself as an officer who could be relied upon, and quickly moved up the ranks.

In an unprecedented five years' time, Sergei Markova was a full captain. As one of the youngest, most intelligent commanding officers in the submarine force, it was only natural that he be given the newest, most technologically advanced attack vessel in the fleet. Powered by two pressurized water-cooled nuclear reactors, the *Neva* was built for speed and endurance. The sub's primary operational area was the Barents, Kara, and Laptev Seas, and of course, the Arctic Ocean. Here the *Neva* accomplished several diverse missions—from escorting the mammoth *Typhoon* class ballistic missile-carrying submarines to patrolling clandestinely. Several of these latter types of missions involved surfacing in the pack ice while in unfriendly waters, and not once had Markova failed to fulfill his orders.

The young captain was said to have nerves of steel, and this was just the type of individual the Admiral of the Fleet was looking for. Mikhail was not deceiving himself into believing this was going to be an easy mission. For they would be going deep into enemy territory, surfacing in frozen, uncharted waters, and then searching for an object that was as insignificant as the proverbial needle in a haystack.

The risks were great, yet, if successful, this mission could very well signal a turning point in world history. As significant as the glorious October Revolution, the outcome of this upcoming patrol could mean the difference between another century of Soviet mediocrity or the final fulfillment of Lenin's prophetic vision of a world united in equality and brotherhood. Thus, Mikhail couldn't even begin to ponder the possibility of failure. For the future of the Motherland, he had to succeed!

A slight change in the An-22's cabin pressure signaled that the airplane had at long last begun its descent into Murmansk. As the veteran mariner yawned to clear his blocked eardrums, he was thrown violently forward, and then shaken from side to side, by the worst turbulence yet encountered. The entire fuselage vibrated with an unnatural intensity, and as the overhead bins began snapping open, even the soundly sleeping attendant was roused from his slumber.

Mikhail tightly gripped the armrests of his chair, and looked on as the door to the flight deck suddenly popped open. Like a sailor on a three-day drunk, out stumbled the airplane's senior pilot. A look of concern was on his weathered face as he struggled to make his way down the aisle of the constantly rocking plane.

"Shouldn't you be buckled up snugly in your seat, Captain, in anticipation of our landing?" Mikhail asked tensely.

The senior pilot held on tightly to the chair beside that of his distinguished passenger as he replied "I'm afraid I've got some rather distressing news for you, Admiral. I don't have to tell you what the weather's like up here. But down in Murmansk, there's a regular blizzard blowing. This storm is so bad the airport there has just closed down until further notice. It looks like we'll be diverting to Severodvinsk. And if we're lucky, maybe we'll get there before this storm does."

Not believing what he was hearing, Mikhail firmly retorted. "We are not going to Severodvinsk, Captain! If I have to fly this plane myself, we're going to land in Murmansk as planned."

"But the airport's closed!" the pilot pleaded, holding on for dear life as the plane suddenly canted hard on its left side. "We're barely holding together up here at ten thousand meters. Down below, it will be even worse."

"I don't care if there's a full-fledged hurricane down there, Captain. The security of the Motherland hinges on my reaching Murmansk before the next tide changes."

"But that's impossible!" protested the red-faced pilot.

"So was the defense of Stalingrad," barked the determined mariner. "There will be no deviations from our flight plan, comrade. As Admiral of the Fleet of the Soviet Union, I order you to land this aircraft at the Murmansk airport right now! Do I make myself absolutely clear, Captain?"

Obviously outranked the grim-faced pilot could only shrug his thin shoulders. "All right, Admiral. If that's what you want, that's what you'll get. It's your funeral. To tell you the truth, in this line of work, I never expected to live past forty anyway."

Like a punch-drunk boxer, the pilot proceeded to return to the flight deck, while Mikhail Kharkov took a deep, full breath to regain his composure. The veteran mariner had come too far to be delayed now, and neither a cowardly pilot nor a tempest from hell itself would keep him from attaining his goal.

The storm hit Murmansk right at the start of the late afternoon rush hour. Already overcrowded with trucks, buses, and automobiles, the icy streets were gridlocked. In this weather, the expedient commuter moved by foot, though even this means of transport had its hazards. Blinded by blowing snow, and forced to pick their way around the already gathering drifts, thousands of scurrying pedestrians left their places of work and madly scrambled to get home before the snow made even walking impossible.

When Sergei Markova and his six-year-old daughter Sasha left their apartment, only a few scattered flurries were falling. By the time they had finished their shopping, the blizzard had struck in all its fury. Fortunately, Sergei's wife had made them bundle up properly before leaving home. An avid follower of the weather forecast, Lara had been anticipating this storm, and though it had hit earlier than expected, she'd made certain her family was sufficiently clothed.

With his right hand holding the large mesh bag in which their recently purchased treasures were stored, the thirty-seven-year-old submarine captain prepared to leave the bakery, their last stop of the day. Comfortably dressed in a red nylon, down-filled ski jacket that he had picked up while on shore leave in Gdansk, Sergei turned to see what was keeping his daughter. As he expected, the precocious youngster was still standing beside a bakery rack, munching away on a freshly baked cookie. She looked like a little marshmallow in her long white fur coat with the matching hat, mittens, and boots, and her proud father couldn't help but grin as he called out to his only child.

"Come now, Sasha. It's time that we got going. We've been gone long enough, and Mommy's going to be worried. Besides, you don't want to miss Uncle Viktor and Aunt Tanya's visit, do you?"

Eyeing the rack of freshly baked cookies that had just come out of the oven, the youngster excitedly replied. "Oh, Poppy, can't I have just one cookie before I go? They're my very favorites!"

Lev, the white-haired baker, heard this request and briefly caught Sergei's gaze and winked. Without another word said, he put several of the cookies in a small sack, bent over, and handed them to Sasha, who was one of his favorite customers.

"Here you go. Now be a good girl and give the package to your father so that he can put it in his parcel."

"But I want one now!" the stubborn six-year-old demanded.

The potbellied baker had five children of his own so he knew how to deal with her. "You've already had two whole cookies, young lady. And with supper time rapidly approaching, you won't have any room for that cake that your father just bought you for dessert."

Having already forgotten about this anticipated treat, Sasha weighed the likeable baker's words. Then with the brown paper sack holding the cookies clutched tightly in one mittened hand, she bid the baker farewell.

"Goodbye, Comrade Lev. Thank you for the cookies."

As he guided the youngster to her father's side, the baker responded. "And goodbye to you, Sasha Markova. Enjoy your treats and don't eat too much and get a bellyache."

Admiring the manner in which the red-cheeked proprietor handled his headstrong daughter, Sergei safely stashed away Sasha's prized cookies and addressed the portly figure who had baked them. "Good day to you, Comrade Petrofsky. And thank you again for taking such good care of my family while I'm out at sea."

"Nonsense, Captain," retorted the baker. "It's you who deserve all the thanks. All of us can sleep just a bit more soundly at night knowing that our shores are protected from the advance of any enemy."

The two men exchanged a warm handshake as a howling gust of wind sounded from outside the glassed-in storefront. Through the steamed-up windows, the blowing blanket of snow that accompanied these gusts could be seen.

"Are you sure you don't want me to give you a lift home, Captain?" the baker offered. "My truck is parked right in the back lot."

Sergei Markova shook his head. "That's most kind of you, Comrade. But I imagine that the going will be just as fast on foot. And besides, we don't have far to go, and my wife made absolutely certain that we were dressed warmly enough for a polar expedition."

The baker chuckled at this and escorted them to the door.

"Walk carefully, my friends," he said as he opened the door and watched them duck out into the thickly falling snow.

Outside, Sergei found the brisk air invigorating. His daughter seemed oblivious to the cold, and was already scraping the snow off the bakery's window ledge and compacting it in a tight ball.

"Let's have a snowball fight, Poppy!"

Before he could answer her, she let loose the powdery snowball that struck Sergei on his right thigh.

"Now hold on a minute, young lady!" he responded, practically shouting to be heard over the howling wind. "Since I'm carrying all the packages, I can't defend myself. You could at least wait until we get home and I stash away our goodies. Then I'll take you on."

"All right!" Sasha screamed, glee in her voice.

With his daughter's mittened hand firmly in his own, Sergei began to make his way down the snow-covered sidewalk. Though crowded with bundled pedestrians, this thoroughfare was much more easy to travel than the icy street to their left. Anyway the snarled roadway was bottlenecked with bumper-to-bumper traffic.

As fortune would have it, their route took them downwind. This fact, plus their wise choice of clothing, made the frigid Arctic storm all the more bearable.

While taking a shortcut through Revolution Park, Sergei was forced to carry his daughter in his free arm. This was necessary since many of the drifts he was soon trudging through were several meters thick and would have all but buried a standing Sasha.

Halfway through the park, they stopped to watch a team of hockey players at work on one of the many frozen lakes situated in it. Such a sport was serious business in the Soviet north, and not even a howling blizzard could keep the players from their daily practice.

It was while watching them work out on the ice that Sergei thought he heard an alien whining roar through the constant howling gusts. This high-pitched racket could easily have come from a low-flying airplane, on its way to the nearby Murmansk airport. But Sergei dismissed this thought as pure nonsense. Not even Aeroflot, or the devil himself, would be flying on such a stormy, windswept afternoon. It wasn't possible to scan the sky in such a storm so the naval officer turned to complete the short, five-minute hike home.

Inside the warm lobby of their building, Sergei and Sasha were met by the apartment's vigilant duty woman. Olga Rybinsk took her position as concierge seriously, and since she lived in the building, she knew her fellow tenant's comings and goings better than the KGB.

Because Sergei's duties kept him away from home for a good six months out of every year, he was glad to have the services of such a watch lady. There could be no better home security force than Olga Rybinsk, for no criminal in his right mind would dare incur the feisty septuagenarian's wrath. The submariner couldn't help but notice how the old lady's eyes lit up when Sasha went dashing into the entry hall.

"Well, if it isn't the snow princess herself," the adoring duty woman exclaimed. "Were you out there building a snow castle, Sasha?"

"Poppy wouldn't let me," the youngster answered as she studiously wiped the snow from her boots. "You see, we went shopping, and so we have to put away our purchases before we can go back out to the park and play."

As the duty woman helped Sasha remove her mittens, she firmly commented. "Those fingers of yours are as cold as icicles, young lady! You'd better rest a while indoors and warm up properly first. This snow will be around for a long time to come, and it will be

151

much more fun to play in once the winds stop. Besides, you don't want to go out and play while you've got company in your apartment, do you?"

Sasha's eyes widened. "I bet it's Uncle Viktor and Aunt Tanya! I do hope they remembered to bring along my birthday present."

The duty woman looked up and caught Sergei's glance. "Comrade Belenko and his wife arrived here approximately a quarter of an hour ago, Captain. According to your instructions, I allowed them to go up to the apartment without first calling your wife."

Sergei nodded. "Thank you, Olga. Let's just pray that I don't get in trouble for being late to my own party."

"I believe that the Belenkos said something about being a half-hour early," the duty woman stated efficiently. "Seems they anticipated this storm and left their place before the rush hour started."

Conscious that Olga Rybinsk would have made a marvelous intelligence officer, Sergei smiled. "Then perhaps my guests will forgive me after all. Stay warm, and have a nice evening, Comrade."

With this, Sergei followed his daughter up a twisting flight of stairs. Though the building had an elevator, it hadn't worked properly since it was installed. By the time he reached the seventh floor, he was wheezing and his brow was matted with sweat. In contrast, Sasha, hardly affected by the climb, merrily skipped down the corridor and burst through their apartment's front door. With leaden limbs, his sack swinging at his side, Sergei followed in her wake.

Inside the apartment, Peter Ilyich Tchaikovsky's Nutcracker Suite was blaring forth from the radio's speakers. As Sergei identified the particular movement as the "Waltz of the Flowers," he scanned the combination dining room/den, and found it vacant.

152

A roaring fire burned in the fireplace, however, and the nearby coffee table held several platters of mixed appetizers. Yet there was still no hint of his wife's presence or his guests'.

Only when a characteristic high-pitched voice sounded from the enclosed kitchen did Sergei realize where they could most likely be found.

"Oh Uncle Viktor, Aunt Tanya, it's wonderful!" exclaimed Sasha.

The mesh bag he continued to drag along at his side seemed to have gained in weight as Sergei headed toward the kitchen. As he had assumed, it was in this cramped, linoleum-lined cubicle that the entire party had chosen to gather.

He first spotted his pert, redheaded wife Lara standing beside the sink. At her feet, Sasha sat comfortably on the floor, already absorbed in the toy doll she had just been given.

"She's got several additional outfits as well," observed Tanya Belenko. "We got you the ski suit, some formal wear, and bathing gear."

As the svelte blonde bent down to show Sasha where these outfits were stored, Sergei Markova announced his presence by loudly clearing his throat. It proved to be his wife who spotted him first.

"Well, look what the wind blew in. I hope you don't mind, but we started the party without you."

"So I've noticed," replied Sergei as he swung the mesh carrying bag onto the counter. After accepting a kiss from Lara, he turned to the tall, black-haired man standing by the refrigerator.

"Hello, Senior Lieutenant. Glad you could make it."

Any guise of formality was dispeled as Sergei picked his way across the room and warmly hugged his co-worker.

"Greetings to you, Captain," replied Viktor Belenko. "That's some storm that's brewing outside, huh, my friend?"

"It certainly is," answered Sergei, who was about the same height as his swarthy second-in-command, but fair-skinned and blond. "Why it was an effort just to keep Sasha from being blown away."

"That's not true!" shouted the six-year-old from the kitchen floor. "Come see what Aunt Tanya and Uncle Viktor have given me, Poppy. It's a Barbuski doll!"

As Sergei bent down to take a look at this present, he planted a kiss on Tanya Belenko's cheek.

"We've got to stop meeting like this, Captain," whispered Tanya with a provocative wink. "People will talk."

"Let them. I'm not shy," retorted Sergei playfully, as he examined the lifelike doll Sasha was already expertly dressing in ski coat and boots.

"That's a marvelous gift, little princess," he observed. "Why she almost looks real. Now why don't you gather everything up and take your Barbuski off to your room before one of us grown-ups steps on something."

"Come on, Sasha dear. I'll help you," offered Tanya.

As they began picking up the various articles of realistic, miniature clothing and the colorful paper in which the present had been wrapped, Sergei stood and rejoined Viktor.

"It looks like Sasha certainly has something to keep her out of trouble for the rest of the evening. Thanks for remembering her, comrade."

"The pleasure's ours, Sergei. After all, we've known Sasha since she was an infant, and we like to think of her as our own flesh and blood."

Sergei smiled. "We're very lucky to have friends

154

such as you and Tanya. So what do you say to a drink to seal our bond?"

"I thought you'd never ask," Viktor replied.

Beside them, Lara Markova was in the process of emptying the mesh sack her husband had just brought in. Most of the items she took from it were bottles of liquor. Lara counted three liters of Georgian champagne, two of Ukrainian potato vodka, and a bottle of French cognac. She also exhumed four loaves of crusty bread, a package of assorted fruit tarts, Sasha's prized cookies, cake, and several tins of Beluga caviar. As she turned the empty sack upside down and shook it as if expecting something else to fall out, she commented.

"Do you mean to say that you've been gone over two hours, and this is all you were able to bring back? Why this isn't even half the items I put down on the list. Where's the milk, the chicken, and the fresh fruit I needed? Why our guests will positively starve!"

Already breaking the seal of one of the vodka bottles, Sergei made a vain attempt to defend himself. "In anticipation of this snowstorm that's upon us, I think every single *babushka* in Murmansk was out this morning hoarding food. The milk and poultry counters were bare by the time I got to them. And the only fresh fruit available was a load of rotting Cuban mangoes."

"Well, I see that you had a bit more luck at the liquor store," Lara wisely observed, as she set four clean glasses on the crowded counter. "And where in the world did you ever find real Beluga caviar? I thought all of it was being exported for hard currency."

A gleam sparkled in Sergei's eyes. "Sometimes being an officer in the People's Navy does have its benefits, my dear wife. Old man Litvak, the fellow who runs the Red Star liquor store was a naval commander himself during the Great Patriotic War. Though I've heard his exaggerated exploits told time and again, I bit my tongue and listened as he took me back to the time he single-handedly ran a Nazi blockade to successfully land a shipment of food badly needed by the starving citizens of Leningrad. After he finished this narrative, I humbly asked if he knew where a current-day naval captain could find a special party treat to share with his wife and a small group of friends. Not only did he come up with the caviar, but that bottle of Napoleonic cognac as well."

"I'll have to remember that next time I'm out shopping," reflected Viktor Belenko.

To this, Sergei shook his head. "Sorry, Senior Lieutenant. It only works for captains." There was a wide grin on Sergei's face as he filled up the glasses and proposed the first toast. "To good friends, warm homes, and to peace in the Motherland!"

While each of the women took but a sip of the powerful potato vodka, their husbands each downed an entire glassful. Grabbing the rest of the bottle, Sergei beckoned Viktor to join him in the den.

With their glasses again filled, they settled down in the large, upholstered couch that sat beside the blazing fireplace. From the mounted radio speakers, Tchaikovsky's soulful Symphony No. 5 in E minor began unraveling. Such a thoughtful piece of music proved to be the perfect background as the two submariners sipped their drinks and stared into the crackling embers.

"Your Lara seems very happy," reflected Viktor. "And little Sasha is as adorable as ever. You are a very lucky man, Sergei Markova."

"I don't know about that, Viktor Ilyich. That sexy wife of yours is the type of woman a man dreams of."

156

Viktor looked introspective. "I guess that we're both very fortunate in our own ways, my friend. Has this week gone as quickly for you as it has for me?"

Sergei rolled his eyes up and responded. "I'll say. The hours are just flying by, and all too soon we'll be packing our bags and returning to the *Neva*. Speaking of the devil, weren't you going to put a call into our esteemed michman this morning?"

The senior lieutenant grunted. "That I did, comrade. Ustreka sends his regards and was able to give me a fairly comprehensive update on the state of our refit. As we expected, the SS-N-15 nuclear-tipped antisubmarine missiles are the only weapons that have yet to be delivered. Other than that, we seem to have a full complement of torpedoes and decoys. Our food larders have also been restocked, though Ustreka mentioned that much of the fresh produce and fruit is little more than garbage. The michman also reported that a supply of Arctic outerwear arrived late last night. In the same locker with this clothing were a dozen Kalaishnikov assault rifles, several portable mortars, and a large supply of ammunition and grenades."

"You don't say," returned Sergei Markova "I don't remember requesting such specialized gear. Do you, Viktor?"

Shaking his head that he didn't, the senior lieutenant continued. "Since this delivery didn't show on the ship's manifest, the michman was prepared to turn it away, when our good friend the Zampolit intervened. It seems that Comrade Zinyagin knew all about the shipment, for he personally signed the receipt invoice."

"Now that is strange," observed Sergei as he reached for the bottle to refill their glasses. "I must remember to ask our dear Political Officer about this when I meet with him at the end of the week."

"I still think Konstantin Zinyagin is a snake," disgustedly spat Viktor. "That man can't be trusted for a single minute. Some keeper of morale, when he's instigated the majority of personnel problems we encounter on the *Neva*."

"Now Viktor, is that any way to talk about out beloved Zampolit? After all, the Party puts such individuals on board each and every Soviet warship merely to direct the crew's ideological indoctrination."

"Like hell they do, Sergei. You know as well as I that officers such as Konstantin Zinyagin are there for one purpose only, to act as Party spies."

Any response on Sergei Markova's part was cut short by the arrival of his wife.

"Just like I told you, Tanya. I knew that they'd be talking shop," observed Lara, as she placed a platter of caviar down on the coffee table.

Following with two half-filled glasses and an open bottle of champagne, Tanya Belenko took this opportunity to get her own two kopecks in. "It never fails, does it, Lara? Leave these two alone for more than ten seconds and they can't wait to talk about that damn submarine of theirs. I don't understand it. When they're out on patrol, they always tell us how during every spare moment, their thoughts are of us, yet when they finally get home, what do they do in their spare time but talk about that infernal boat."

Sergei realized the truth in this statement and held up his hands. "You're right, ladies. This is certainly no time for talk of work. So what do you say to getting this party rolling? Has anyone tried that caviar yet?"

Lara's face filled with an ecstatic expression. "I can't tell a lie. We both gave it a try in the kitchen, and are you two in for a special treat. Why should such a delicacy be only reserved for rich foreigners? Such a policy is a national disgrace."

As the conversation turned to the wisdom of bartering away national treasures such as Beluga caviar for the hard currency it brought, the telephone began to ring. Lara was in the process of turning for the bedroom phone when the ringing abruptly stopped, to be replaced by the shrill voice of their daughter.

"Poppy, it's for you!"

These unexpected words hit Sergei like a blow to the stomach. Briefly catching the concerned stares of his guests, he put down his glass, excused himself, and headed for the bedroom.

Several minutes passed before he returned. It only took one look at his sullen face to know he would be the bearer of bad news.

"I don't believe it," said Sergei with a heavy sigh, "but I just got off the phone with Admiral of the Fleet Kharkov. And not only has he just landed in Murmansk, he wants—immediately—to meet us at the docks, where we're to have the *Neva* ready for sea at the next change of tide!"

A moment of constrained silence followed as the navymen's wives exchanged disappointed glances while the tragic conclusion of Tchaikovsky's Fifth symphony rang out appropriately in the background.

Chapter Eight

Lieutenant Jack Redmond sat in the jumpseat of the Canadian Forces CP-140, Aurora long-range patrol aircraft. The muted whine of the plane's four turboprop engines produced an almost hypnotic effect on the exhausted, forty-three-year-old Arctic Ranger, and he briefly closed his eyes to take advantage of this rare moment of free time.

The past twenty-four hour period had been a most hectic one. It had all started innocently enough, with what was to be a routine overnight bivouac in the foothills surrounding Mount Assiniboine. With Angus McPherson accompanying them a good portion of the way with his melodious bagpipes, they had proceeded up into the Sunshine meadowlands without incident. Of course, this atmosphere of normalcy had changed the moment Jack had had his terrifying encounter with the two grizzlies. Yet the hand of fate had miraculously intervened in the form of the Canadian Forces helicopter that had literally rescued Redmond from the jaws of death and whisked him off to nearby Calgary.

It was at Calgary's Currie Barracks that he learned why the chopper had been sent for him in the first place. In yet another isolated corner of the world's third largest nation, a plane carrying Soviet Premier Alexander Suratov had presumably crashed. To make certain of this, and hopefully to locate the plane's black box which would explain to the world the reason for this tragedy, Jack Redmond and his crack squad of Rangers were to be sent northward to far-off Baffin Island.

Most anxious to undertake this demanding mission, Jack waited as the rest of his squad arrived at the barracks. They flew in aboard a lumbering Boeing Chinook helicopter. This same vehicle whisked them off to the Calgary airport, where a chartered jet was waiting to convey them on a one and a half hour flight almost due northward, to the town of Yellowknife, in the Northwest Territories. It was here that the Arctic Rangers had their permanent headquarters.

Once at their home base, they hurriedly gathered together the gear they would need. This included six snowmobiles that could each carry up to four men, special Arctic clothing, food, ammunition, and a directional finder with which to home in on the missing cockpit voice recorder. As soon as this assortment of equipment was gathered together, their present means of transportation arrived to carry them off to Baffin Island.

Jack Redmond was no stranger to the prop-driven Aurora aircraft they had been flying in for the last two hours. These reliable planes were used by Canadians to patrol their vast Arctic frontier. Loaded with state-of-the-art surveillance gear, eighteen long-range Auroras covered that immense frozen wasteland. And it was a difficult, demanding task. Yet if Canada was serious about extending its sovereignty to the portion of North America above the Arctic Circle, such patrols were vital.

"Excuse me, Lieutenant Redmond." The voice came from the front of the cockpit. "We've spotted the *Louis St. Laurent.*"

These words were all that was needed to break Jack from his light slumber. Quickly wiping the sleep from his weary eyes, he unbuckled his seat belt and carefully edged his way forward, to the front portion of the flight deck. As he settled in between the two pilots, the uniformed figure seated to his left pointed out the cockpit's window and continued.

"There she is now."

Gazing in the direction in which the pilot was pointing, Jack spotted a single, black-hulled vessel, barely two-hundred feet from stem to stern, seemingly locked in a solid sheet of frozen ice. Though a thick column of gray smoke poured from its dual stacks, the ship didn't appear to be moving and Redmond observed, "It doesn't appear that they're making much progress. Exactly where are they, Captain?"

"That's the Barrow Strait they're trying to transit," returned the pilot. "They're currently in between Somerset and Cornwallis islands, but I'm afraid that's about as far east as they're going to be able to go. That ice looks way beyond their capability."

Redmond shook his head. "Looks like we can't be counting on the Coast Guard to give us any help. I still find it hard to believe that we don't even have an icebreaker capable of operating in this portion of the Arctic all year round."

"I hear you, Lieutenant," retorted the pilot. "With all those millions we waste on our NATO obligation to defend Germany, we can't even come up with the funds to protect our own coastline. Ottawa's still fighting over committing the resources needed to build the Polar 8 icebreaker. With one hundred thousand horsepower engines and a specially fortified

162

bow, such a ship would smash through that ice below quick enough. Eh?"

"I think we should build those nuclear submarines," the copilot put in. "I've got a brother based on the *Onondaga* in Halifax, and he says the amount of trespassing that's going on beneath these waters is positively criminal. The Soviets, Yanks, and even the Brits, carry on up here like it was their own territory. Yet if we had a fleet of nuclear submarines, it would be a different story. Then we could block off the choke points, and keep these seas one hundred percent Canadian like they should be."

Jack Redmond turned to the young copilot. "Does the *Onondaga* do much under-the-ice work?"

While slightly enriching the fuel mixture, the copilot answered. "They'd certainly like to, but they can't. As you know, all three of our subs are diesel-electrics. Since they're dependent on their batteries while traveling submerged, prolonged patrols under the ice are just too dangerous."

Jack Redmond thoughtfully reflected. "I realize it would be enormously expensive, but a nuclear submarine would sure suit our needs right now. All one would have to do is cruise under the frozen waters of Lancaster Sound and pop up in an open lead. Then me and my lads could crawl out of the hold and take it from there."

"Who needs a blooming submarine when we can do the job for you in a fraction of the time it would take the Navy to get you to Baffin," the pilot retorted with a proud smirk. "In fact, if you hold tight, we can have you there in just under an hour."

Redmond met this offer with an enthusiastic thumbs-up, and looked on as the pilot turned the steering yoke and the Aurora smoothly banked to the right. The compass read due east as the Ranger returned to his jumpseat. No sooner had he rebuckled his seatbelt than the door to the flight cabin popped open. With an excited gleam in his eyes, a short, jumpsuit-clad airman entered and wasted no time expressing himself.

"I believe I've got it, Captain! I started picking it up right after you made that last course change."

Not having the slightest idea what the sensor operator was talking about, the pilot was quick to intervene. "Now hold on, lad. Just take a deep breath and tell us just what it is that's got you so riled."

Suddenly realizing the reason for the pilot's confusion, the airman paused and then explained himself. "It's the homing beacon, sir. I was warming up the directional receiver in preparation for our arrival at the suspected crash site, when much to my amazement, I began getting the faintest of returns on bearing zero-nine-zero. At first I didn't think much of it, but when we turned on that course ourselves and the signal began steadily increasing in strength, I knew we were on to something. I know it's still a bit early, Captain, but I'm almost positive it's the black box."

This last revelation caused Jack Redmond's eyes to open wide with wonder, and he anxiously questioned. "Were you able to get a definite fix on this signal, airman?"

The sensor operator turned to directly address the Ranger. "Though it's still hard to pinpoint exactly, it seems to be emanating from the north end of the Brodeur Peninsula, on Baffin Island's northwestern tip."

Jack Redmond leaned forward expectantly. "That's it all right. Why I'll bet my pension on it. The last radar sighting NORAD had on the Premier's plane was right over that same portion of coastline. How close can you drop us, Captain?"

Busy studying his cockpit's own radar screen, the pilot hesitated a moment before answering. "Under normal circumstances, with our heated ski/wheel landing system, we could deliver you practically anywhere on the ice, but I'm afraid that's not going to be the case this afternoon. It looks like we've got a hell of a nasty storm moving south over Lancaster Sound even as we speak."

"How about giving that landing strip at the new Polestar DEW line station a try, Captain?" the copilot suggested. "It's on the Brodeur Peninsula and less than a dozen kilometers from the coastline."

"Sounds good to me," Jack Redmond said.

With his eyes still peeled to the radar screen, the pilot responded. "Why don't we give them a call and see what the weather conditions are like down there. Because from this vantage point, even Polestar doesn't look too promising."

It was the copilot who looked up the DEW line station's special radio frequency and punched it into their digital transmitter. Seconds later, a small green light lit up on the console, and the pilot himself picked up the microphone and spoke into it with his deep, bass voice.

"Polestar One, this is Canadian Air Defense flight zero-one-alpha requesting emergency landing clearance. Over."

As the pilot released the transmit button that was recessed into the microphone, nothing but a throaty blast of static boomed forth from the cabin's elevated speakers. Once again the pilot repeated his request. This time the static was undercut by the distant, scratchy voice of a man.

"CAD flight zero-one-alpha, this is Polestar One. How do you copy? Over."

"I'm afraid the signals a little weak, Polestar," returned the pilot.

"CAD flight zero-one-alpha, please switch to frequency zulu-foxtrot-bravo. Over."

As the copilot punched in this new frequency, the pilot of the Aurora once more addressed the DEW line station. This time the response that filtered in through the cockpit's speakers was crisp and clear.

"What can we do for you, CAD zero-one-alpha?"

"We're requesting emergency landing clearance, Polestar," replied the pilot.

"Though we'd love the company down here, I'm going to have to deny that request, zero-one-alpha. You could say that we've got a bit of a blizzard smacking into us at the moment. Wind gusts are up to eighty five miles per hour, with blowing snow, a minus forty degree wind chill and visibility nil."

As the captain turned his head and caught Jack Redmond's concerned stare, he again spoke into the microphone. "Are you absolutely certain we can't land a plane down there, Polestar? We're on a mission of the utmost priority."

"CAD zero-one-alpha," returned the amplified voiced, "not only do we currently have white-out conditions prevailing, but the wind's blowing so hard the base commander won't even allow an emergency response team outdoors to assess any storm damages we might already have sustained. I suggest you come back in a day or two when this thing finally blows over."

"We copy that, Polestar. Perhaps we'll take you up on that invitation. This is CAD zero-one-alpha, signing off."

The pilot hung up the microphone and pivoted to address Jack Redmond. "I thought that this might be the case, Lieutenant. During this morning's weather briefing, I saw the low-pressure front responsible for this storm developing over Ellesmere Island. Unfortunately, it seems to have crossed Lancaster Sound sooner than anticipated, making a landing at Polestar out of the question."

Not about to be perturbed by this news, the Ranger responded. "Well, if you can't drop us off at Polestar, where can you land?"

It proved to be the copilot who answered this. "Arctic Bay still looks clear, Captain. If we crank this crate up, maybe we can get there before the storm does."

"Is that okay with you, Lieutenant?" the pilot asked. "Though that won't put you right on the Brodeur Peninsula, if we can, indeed, get into Arctic Bay, that will only leave you about eighty kilometers from where that homing signal is believed to be originating."

"That's a lot shorter hike than walking in from Yellowknife," returned Jack Redmond "You just get us into Arctic Bay, Captain, and leave the rest to us"

"You've got it, Lieutenant," snapped the pilot, as he opened the throttles wide.

The grinding whine of the Aurora's four turboprops roared in response, and Jack Redmond excused himself to let his sergeant-major in on their destination. He exited the flight deck, crossed through the equipment-packed sensor bay, and ducked through a narrow doorway.

This brought him into a spacious cabin that stretched all the way from the forward portion of the wings to the plane's tail. The majority of his twenty-three-man squad sat strapped to the fold-down chairs that lined the cabin. Most were asleep, though a spirited poker game was under way on the floor. His sergeant-major could be seen in the tail-end portion of the cabin, where their equipment was stored. Cliff

Ano, totally absorbed with the snowmobile engine he was in the process of repairing, failed to see Redmond enter and begin picking his way down the bare steel walkway.

As he passed by the poker players, Jack lightly greeted the four pure-bred Inuits who made up the game. "Who's got all the luck this afternoon, gentlemen?"

"Corporal Eviki as usual," returned the mustached soldier seated closest to Redmond. "I still say he deals off the bottom."

The long-haired Ranger seated opposite this individual shot back forcefully. "Watch your tongue, Private. Before you accuse a man of cheating, you'd better make certain to have the evidence!"

Quick to sense the start of trouble, Redmond intervened. "Now that's enough out of both of you! Either cool it right now, or kiss those cards goodbye."

"I was only making a joke," offered the mustached private who'd made the initial accusation. "What are you so damn sensitive about, Eviki?"

"You and your damn jokes," reflected the long-haired corporal disgustedly. "Someday one of your wisecracks is going to get you in real trouble."

As the men turned back to their card game, Redmond continued on to the cabin's rear. It was obvious that his men were frustrated and tired after their long day of air travel. An eighty-kilometer forced march over the ice in blizzard conditions would all too soon channel their frustration into a struggle for survival. Of this fact Jack Redmond was certain.

The plane shook in a sudden pocket of turbulence, and Redmond was forced to reach out to one of the exposed ribs of the fuselage in order to steady himself. More rough air was encountered, causing one of the snowmobiles to slip from its mount and lurch violently forward. Only the lightning-quick reaction of his sergeant-major kept the streamlined, fiberglass vehicle from breaking loose altogether and slamming into the seated card players.

"Let me give you a hand with that," offered Redmond, as he hurriedly made his way over to his second-in-commands side.

Together they lifted up the tracked snowmobile and placed it back in it's mount. Only when the vehicle was securely in place did the sergeant-major respond.

"We can't afford to lose one of these snowcats, especially if our search leads us onto the pack ice."

"I'm afraid it's going to do just that," returned Redmond. "I just came back from the flight deck, and it appears we've got our first solid lead on the location of that cockpit voice recorder. A faint ultrasonic homing signal was picked up somewhere on the north face of the Brodeur Peninsula."

"Excellent!" replied Cliff Ano. "If the Aurora can get us in close enough, then we may not even have to use these damn machines."

Jack Redmond shook his head. "It's not going to be so easy, my friend. Under normal circumstances the pilot could have done just that, but blizzard conditions have made such a landing impossible. In fact, we'll be very fortunate even to make it to Arctic Bay."

"So we'll be going in from there," observed the sergeant-major grimly. "I should have expected such a thing all along."

"Why the long face?" queried Redmond. "If it was my birthplace we were headed for, I'd be thrilled."

Cliff Ano heavily sighed. "It's apparent that you've never been to Arctic Bay, Lieutenant. Especially under the conditions in which I came into the world."

The Inuit lowered his voice to a bare whisper and continued. "It was a full year before I was conceived

169

that my parents were moved up to Arctic Bay by the RCMP. Before that, my people lived near Rankin Inlet, on Hudson Bay. They were trappers, who had hunted in that area for many generations. Faced with the need of settling vast regions of unpopulated territory to the north, the government offered my mother, father, aunts, and uncles a chance to live in a virgin wilderness on Baffin Island. Since the beaver and muskrat that once flourished in Hudson Bay had been thinned to a point of extinction, my people agreed to a twelve-month trial stay in this new land.

"Little were they prepared for the type of existence that awaited them on Baffin Island. It was almost one thousand miles closer to the Pole than our ancestral lands, and the frigid climate of the island caused nothing but sickness and despair. The beaver and muskrat the government officials had promised they'd find here didn't exist. They proved to be a lie fabricated by some insensitive bureaucrat in Ottawa. And when the supplies that had also been promised to them failed to materialize, my people had no choice but to learn to hunt new game such as the caribou and the seal. Such knowledge is not easy to come by. And in the many months it took them to master the skill of bringing down such game, many starved.

"When the year was up, the elders petitioned the RCMP to return them to the south. But the government had no intention of disrupting this vital settlement, and explained that such a thing would be impossible. Unable to get off the island themselves, my people were stuck in an alien, unfriendly place of long, bitter winters, and summer's that passed like a fleeting dream. It was in such a land that I was born."

Little prepared for such a lengthy narrative from close-lipped Cliff Ano, Jack Redmond grunted. "No wonder you're not exactly thrilled with our current destination. Do you still have people living in Arctic Bay?"

"Though my parents are both long in their graves, I believe my father's brother and his family still live there. I'm not certain though, for I haven't been back since I left for school over fifteen years ago."

"Then I don't suppose you'd remember the terrain we'll be facing as we take off from Arctic Bay for the northern coastline of the Brodeur Peninsula?" queried Redmond.

Cliff Ano's face broke out in the slightest of grins. "It hasn't been that long, Lieutenant. As a matter of fact, I remember making this same trip several times as a teenager. There were some Inuit on the peninsula who had long ago left all civilization behind to live off the land like their ancestors did. My father wanted me to see such wise people firsthand, and learn their ways. I did, and will be eternally grateful for this invaluable lesson in the real science of survival on the ice.

"Now as to the terrain we'll be facing . . . The most direct route from Arctic Bay will take us over Admiralty Inlet. This narrow tongue of water empties directly into Lancaster Sound and is over two hundred kilometers long. Depending upon weather conditions, we should find it solidly frozen by this time of the year. Thus, except for an occasional pressure ridge or open lead, our going there should be swift.

"The peninsula itself is another story. Formed out of solid granite, it's home to treacherous crevasses and deep, unforgiving rifts. Bloodthirsty polar bears also abound here, and more than one Inuit horror story tells of the huge packs of marauding wolves that make this desolate land their home."

"Sounds like just another ordinary mission for the Arctic Rangers," offered Jack Redmond, who was

171

forced to reach out for one of the snowmobiles to steady himself as the airplane violently shuddered in a sudden gust of turbulence.

"It's certainly nothing that we can't handle," reflected the Inuit. "Though for the peninsula portion of our journey, it would sure be nice to have a first-rate dog team leading us onward. For some uncanny reason, a good sled dog can sense a lurking crevasse, long before an unwary man in a snowcat can."

"Do you think such a team would be available?" questioned Jack Redmond.

"For our sake, I sure hope so, Lieutenant. Otherwise, this is going to be the longest eighty kilometers of our lives — and the most dangerous."

Captain Matt Colter was up bright and early, and after a quick breakfast of half a grapefruit, oatmeal, and coffee, he initiated his customary morning walk through of the ship. He began this tour in the engineering spaces that filled the sub's aft portion.

Almost directly amidships, he entered a narrow, forty-foot-long passageway, completely lined with steel tubing. He smelled the familiar waxlike scent of warm polyethylene, and could hear the barest of throbbing noises coming from the padded deck beneath him. Halting in the center of this passageway, he kneeled down and lifted up a circular metallic cover that exposed a thick, heavy, leaden glass viewing port set flush with the decking.

Almost twenty feet below him he could now view the heart of the *Defiance*'s propulsion unit, its nuclear reactor. Lit by a pulsating, golden glow, the sealed reactor vessel contained a vast grid of uranium plates, and was filled with water so highly pressurized it could not boil. Control rods kept nuclear fission from

172

occurring until the reactor went on line. At that time the rods were slowly removed, and as the uranium-235 fuel elements began interacting, the unit went critical.

To achieve propulsion, the hot pressurized, contaminated water was pumped through a series of heat exchangers. Here a second loop of uncontaminated water absorbed this heat, which turned to steam, that subsequently spun the turbines producing both power to drive the ship and the electricity needed to operate the rest of its systems.

Continually amazed by the efficiency of such a relatively simple propulsion system, Colter closed the viewing port, stood, and continued to make his way aft into the maneuvering room. The sign above the hatch he was soon stepping through read Defiance Power and Light. Inside this all-important portion of the ship, three seamen sat before a massive console filled with dozens of complicated gauges, digital read-out counters, switches, and dials. The senior of these individuals was responsible for monitoring the power level of the reactor itself. He did so by keeping a close watch on the gauges showing the temperature of the water flowing out of the containment vessel, its pressure, and its velocity. To influence these factors, he merely had to trigger a compact pistol switch that was directly connected to the control rods. Beside him, his two shipmates kept a close watch on gauges showing the state of the sub's electrical and propulsion systems.

Standing in the compartment's shadows, sipping on a mug of coffee and intently watching his men at work, was Lieutenant Peter Frystak, the ship's engineering officer. The six-foot, solidly built officer had originally studied architecture while at UCLA, but became fascinated with nuclear physics while enrolled in the universities NROTC program. To pursue this interest further, he'd chose to fulfill his active service obligation on submarines.

"Good morning, Captain," Frystak's eyes never seemed to leave the bank of instruments displayed before him. "Can I get you a cup of coffee?"

Matt Colter walked over to the engineering officer's side and responded. "No thanks, Pete. I already had today's caffeine fix. And besides, I'm trying to cut back."

"Good luck," returned the UCLA grad. "Because it seems this ship runs on nothing but uranium-235 fuel and piping-hot java."

Colter grinned. "Isn't that the truth. How's she running this morning, Lieutenant?"

Frystak made a brief entry in his log before answering, "Smooth as can be, Captain. Old man Rickover would be proud."

"I'm sure he would," reflected Colter, in deference to Admiral Hyman Rickover, the visionary father of the nuclear navy. "From the very beginning, Rickover's standards were the very highest, and we were extremely fortunate to inherit them. By the way, what's the scenario for this afternoon's drill?"

Frystak lowered his voice to a whisper. "I'm going to simulate a steam leak in the main condenser. Then throw in a fire in the auxilliary turbine unit, to keep the boys honest."

"Interesting combination," observed Colter. "I'm anxious to see how they'll handle themselves."

"You never do know, do you, Captain?"

"That's what these surprise drills are all about, Lieutenant. Let's just continue to pray that real emergencies are few and far between."

Finally diverting his eyes from the maneuvering panel, Frystak caught his commanding officer's direct glance. "Especially when we're under the ice, Captain. Since the first step in countering the majority of emergency situations is an immediate order to stand by to surface, a solid covering of ice above you kind of cuts down on your alternatives."

"That it does, Lieutenant," replied Colter with a sigh. "But that's the unique challenge of Arctic operations."

"During yesterday's briefing, you mentioned that the orders you just received from COMSUBLANT were going to put the *Defiance* on the surface of the ice for a good portion of this patrol. Can that new-fangled surface-scanning Fathometer really be relied upon to get us topside safely, Captain?"

Since Frystak had been along on the *Defiance*'s last cruise, and still had bruises on his back to show for the trio of bone-jarring collisions with the ice, Colter knew where his skepticism was coming from. Thus the captain answered him as directly as possible.

"Our civilian guest has been working sixteen-hour shifts since we left New London to make certain that the system is one hundred percent operational. But I still have nightmares about those collisions, and I'll feel a hell of a lot better when I know the chief's finally got the old unit on line as a backup if needed."

The engineering officer grunted. "Not taking anything away from Dr. Lansing, but I've got a gut feeling that says it will be. Let's just hope I'm dead wrong with this one. But regardless, any luck with those volunteers for the surface party when we finally do get up to Baffin?"

"You'd be surprised at the excellent response," answered Colter. "Though I don't seem to recall seeing your name, Lieutenant Frystak."

The UCLA grad grimaced. "Sorry Captain, but I'm a Southern Californian. This old blood is too thin to stand up to the kind of numbing temperatures we'll be encountering topside."

Colter smiled. "I understand, Lieutenant. Though even if you wanted to go along, I wouldn't have let you. I need you right here, at the helm of Defiance Power and Light."

Checking his watch, the captain added. "Now I'd better get moving along. Good luck with that drill."

As Matt Colter left maneuvering, he continued aft into that cavernous section of the ship reserved for its massive turbines. Bright fluorescent lights illuminated the heavy gray machinery needed to convert the steam pressure into actual knots of propulsion. A single spinning shaft bisected the room, leading to a complex series of seals that directly connected it to the twin, contra-rotating propellers. Surprisingly quiet, the engine room was spotlessly clean, yet two seamen were busy with rags and mops to insure it stayed that way.

Satisfied that all appeared well, the captain retraced his steps, cutting back through maneuvering, over the reactor vessel, and into a passageway dominated by a single ladder. By climbing up this ladder he would gain entry to the officer's wardroom, his own cabin, and the adjoining control room. Yet before returning to these familiar environs, he continued forward on the lower level. This brought him directly into the crew's mess hall.

A dozen men currently sat in this large compartment that served as a combination dining room, rec hall, and library. Several were playing cards, while others were gathered at various tables working away on breakfast. The scents of freshly perked coffee and frying bacon met Colter's nostrils as he halted beside a booth holding Petty Officer First Class Stanley Roth.

"Good morning, Mr. Roth. How are you feeling?"

The ship's senior sonar technician was far from his usual self, and he rather unenthusiastically answered, "I'm doing pretty good, Captain. At least I can get my oatmeal down this morning."

"So that tooth is still bothering you. I thought you were going to see the base dentist and get it taken care of."

"I did," snapped the petty officer, "And to tell you the truth, that visit really didn't amount to a hell of a lot. If you ask me, the doc would have rather been out on the golf course. He scraped and poked around a bit, and then dismissed me with a warning to brush and floss after every meal or I'd lose my tooth for sure. And here I've been conscientiously brushing and flossing ever since, and the damn thing is still throbbing."

"Sounds like he should have pulled it right there. Is the pain interfering with your work in sonar?"

"Not really, sir. I guess I'm finally getting used to it."

Colter could tell that the technician wasn't being honest with him. "No one should have to live with constant pain. I want you to see Pharmacist Mate Krommer right after chow. There has to be something he can do for you."

Stanley Roth looked glum as he laid down his spoon. "I know what Pills is going to do, Captain. He'll look inside my mouth, take my temperature, then my pulse, and hand me a bottle of those damn painkillers. Though they help a bit, I can't go around doped up all day."

"Ask him to prescribe a less potent drug," advised Colter. "He's certainly got plenty to choose from in the ship's pharmacy, and one of them has got to do the trick until you get that tooth taken out."

"I never thought I'd look forward to the day when

I'd get a tooth pulled, but now I know better. Thanks for your concern, Captain. And don't worry. I'll survive."

"I'm sure you will," returned Colter. He patted the petty officer on the shoulder and then continued on through the mess hall.

He was about to pass by the galley when a familiar voice broke on his right. "Hello, Captain. Can I fix you up a plate? Just pulled some fresh buttermilk hotcakes off the griddle, and the bacon's nice and crisp just as you like it."

Stepping forward to greet him was Petty Officer Howard Mallott, the sub's head cook, his perpetual smile cutting his bespectacled face. The hefty brown-haired, ten-year veteran was second-generation Navy. His father had been the head steward on the battleship *New Jersey,* and it was because of his exciting war tales that Howard had enlisted right after his high-school graduation.

"I'm afraid that I'm going to have to pass up that enticing offer, Mr. Mallott," Colter responded as he touched his waistline. "Your culinary magic has already been responsible for too many of these spare pounds."

"Well, make certain to bring your appetite along at lunchtime, Captain. I'm serving your favorite — roast turkey, mashed potatoes, cranberries, and broccoli casserole, with apple pie à la mode for dessert."

"Thanks for the warning, Mr. Mallott. Now I'll be certain to walk through the ship another time around just to burn up some of these excess calories."

The jovial cook waved him away. "Nonsense, Captain. You look just as fit today as you did in your Annapolis photo. Now this gut is another story."

As the senior cook playfully patted his own bulging stomach, Colter excused himself to get on with his

178

tour. Briefly glancing into the galley itself, the captain found its relatively small space clean and neat. This said a lot for Petty Officer Mallott, whose responsibility was a heavy one.

One hundred and seven men put away a lot of chow in the course of a typical two-month patrol. Yet all meals came out of this single cramped galley. With the help of three assistants, Mallott served three complete meals a day along with a variety of light snacks in between.

US submarines have always been known for the excellence of their chow, and Howard Mallott kept this proud tradition alive. With the flair of a gourmet chef, he carefully supervised the preparation of each and every menu. Because the very nature of underwater duty was in itself boring, meal times on the *Defiance* were looked to as a welcomed break from the humdrum routine. After a tasty fried chicken dinner with all the trimmings, or even hamburgers and french fries, the crew felt refreshed and ready to return to their duty slots.

Matt Colter passed by the larders where the majority of food was stored. In these jampacked lockers, the ingredients for over 18,000 meals were stowed away. That in itself took the patience of a saint, and Petty Officer Mallott supervised this complicated procedure after personally purchasing the ingredients from the base supply officer.

Realizing that they were very fortunate to have such a dedicated individual aboard, Colter left the galley, transitted a narrow passageway, and passed by the main bunkroom. Forty-eight enlisted men called this portion of the *Defiance* home. To make the best use of the vessel's limited space, the bunks were stacked in tiers four high. Each of these separate spaces had a curtain that could be drawn to provide privacy, along with individual ventilation fans and reading lights. Like the officer's quarters, clothing lockers were situated beneath each foam-rubber mattress. The room was only partially filled by the sleeping sailors that had stood the midnight to 4 A.M. watch, or as it was more commonly known, the midwatch. Not wishing to disturb them, the captain continued on through a double-wide hatch and ducked into the forward torpedo room.

This compartment also contained living space for thirty individuals. Yet its predominate feature were four, twenty-one-inch-wide, bronze breech doors, from which the sub's various weapons and decoys would be launched. Currently gathered around the torpedo loading rack was a group of three sailors. Leading them in the dissection of a Mk48 Mod 1 torpedo was Lieutenant David Sanger, the weapon's officer.

"Is this one of the new fish, Lieutenant?" the captain asked.

The balding weapons' officer backed away from the torpedo, wiped his receding forehead dry of sweat, and succinctly answered. "That it is, sir."

"How do they look so far?" continued Colter.

Sanger shook his head. "This is only the third one we've had a chance to examine, Captain. Though the other two checked out, we've got three more to go after this one."

Colter knew that when it came to new reloads, any weapons' officer worth his salt scrupulously inspected each torpedo to double-check it for defects. David Sanger had only been with him on two previous patrols, yet in each instance he'd proved to be a hard-working perfectionist, who took his all-important job most seriously.

"Well, I can rest a bit more easily knowing that if

we need 'em, these fish will be ready to bite when the time comes. Keep up the good work, Lieutenant."

Briefly looking up to examine the mattresses that were situated on the upper casing of the torpedo rack, Matt Colter ducked through the double-thick hatchway. Outside the torpedo room, a ladder conveyed him upward into a passageway that directly adjoined the control room. It was here that he laid his eyes on a closed door that had a sign reading, Sound Shack tacked on its length. Below this wooden placard was a fist-sized decal showing the hammer and sickle insignia of the Soviet Union with a thick red diagonal line drawn over it. Though he was overdue in the control room, Colter approached this doorway, turned its latch, and entered.

Inside the sonar room were a series of three individual consoles, each separated by an acoustic barrier. At the position closest to the door, Seaman Lester Warren sat hunched over his monitor screen. A pair of bulky headphones covered the Texan's ears, while his eyes were riveted on the repeater screen. The console beside him was vacant, though the station on the far side was not. Seated here in dark blue, Navy-issue coveralls was Dr. Laurie Lansing.

Matt Colter walked soundlessly past the sonar technician and positioned himself immediately beside the black-haired civilian.

"Hello," he said softly. "You're certainly up with the chickens this morning."

The scientist finished typing a complex series of digits into the data bank before pushing away from the keyboard and answering. "Actually, I haven't gone to bed yet."

Colter seemed astounded by this revelation, "Does everyone at the Arctic lab take their work so seriously?"

"Only those of us who have a point to prove," retorted Laurie. Then she yawned and stretched her cramped limbs.

Matt Colter found himself admiring her soft features and the dark eyes that didn't seem to show a hint of fatigue. "Seriously, Doctor, I know you want to get your Fathometer on line, but aren't you pushing yourself a little too hard? At least break for a couple of hours of shut-eye. This console will be waiting for your return. And being properly rested, you've a lot better chance of not making a foolish mistake."

"Don't worry, Captain. I know what I'm doing. And besides, another couple of hours' work and my job will be completed."

"I'm glad to hear that," said Colter. "Otherwise, you'd most probably keep working until you just dropped to the deck. How are your quarters, by the way? I'm sorry I couldn't get by here sooner to ask, but the past couple of days have been hectic for all of us."

"No apologies are necessary, Captain. My cabin is most satisfactory, and the crew has been most helpful, what little I've seen of them. Lately, I've been going right from my cabin to the officer's wardroom to grab a bite to eat, and then straight over here."

"Once you've completed the reprogramming and gotten a little rest, I'd be honored if you'd join me on a proper tour of the *Defiance*. Besides, from what I gather, the crew's even got money riding on when you'll finally be making an appearance."

The scientist blushed. "I sure wouldn't want to let them down, now would I, Captain?"

"Not if you know what's good for you," returned Colter with a wink. "Now, don't hesitate to call out if you need anything—and get some rest!"

As he exited the sound shack, Colter found himself

thinking about the warm smile she had flashed his way as he'd excused himself to get on with his duty. She was certainly a hard worker, and there could be no doubting the sincerity of her intentions. Realizing that they'd soon know the results of her efforts, he transitted a cable-lined passageway, and entered the familiar confines of the control room.

Lieutenant Commander Al Layman was waiting for him at the chart table, "Morning, Skipper. Did you sleep in this morning?"

"Afraid not, Al. Just spent a little longer on my morning walk through than usual."

"I hope you found everything shipshape."

Still thinking about the scientist's smile, Colter absentmindedly replied. "Everything was fine, Al."

The XO knew his commanding officer well, and noting the distant look in Colter's eyes, saw that his full attention was elsewhere.

"We can go over those charts another time, Skipper. There's nothing here that can't wait until later."

Only then did Matt Colter realize how far his thoughts had been drifting. Such a thing could be dangerous in times of crisis, and he instantly regained control of himself.

"There's no reason for that, XO. You can carry on."

"If you say so, Skipper," replied Layman as he pulled his pipe from his pocket and placed its bit between his lips unlit. He then reached down and switched on the light to the chart table.

Clearly displayed beneath the clear Plexiglas of the table was a polar projection chart of the eastern portion of North America. Utilizing a blue crayon, Al Layman marked a small x in the sea halfway between the extreme northern point of Labrador and the southern coast of Greenland.

"As you can see, Skipper, we're well on our way to the Davis Strait by now. We've currently got Labrador's Cape Chidley off our port bow, and Greenland's Cape Farewell to our starboard."

"We must have gotten a little help from the Labrador Current," observed Colter. "We're doing much better than I had anticipated. Any ice above us as yet?"

"As of two hours ago, the sea was clear, Skipper. But that could be a whole different story now. If I remember correctly, this is about where we spotted the first floes on our last visit."

"Seems like just the other day," reflected Colter. "How about taking us up to periscope depth and having a look around?"

"My pleasure, Skipper."

As the XO relayed the orders that brought the *Defiance* up from the black depths, Matt Colter stepped up on the low steel platform that lay beside the plotting table. Only when the digital depth gauge reached sixty-five feet did the captain take over.

"Up periscope!" he barked.

An alert seaman hit the release switch, and to a loud hiss of pressurized hydraulic oil one of the two eight-inch-thick, steel cylinders that hung before Colter began sliding upward. Several drops of water ran down the cylinder's barrel from its overhead fitting, as an eyepiece and a pair of folded handles emerged from the well. Bending over slightly, the captain snapped down the hinged handles and nestled his eyes up into the periscope's rubberized lens coupling.

The direct light was at first so intense that it stung Colter's eyes. The sky was a brilliant, deep blue, and as a wave of greenish seawater slapped up over the lens, Matt spotted several disturbingly familiar formations floating on the distant horizon. By merely

184

increasing the magnification of the lens tenfold, these pure-white crystalline objects seemed to jump forward and a sudden heaviness formed in Colter's gut. For the monstrous icebergs meant only one thing, from this point onward, if something went wrong in the black depths below, the *Defiance* could no longer rely on the sea's surface for a safe haven. Very much aware of this unsettling fact, Matt Colter sighed heavily and, like Arctic explorers for centuries past, consigned his fate to the spirits of the frozen sea.

Chapter Nine

Barely three hours after Captain Sergei Markova and his senior lieutenant got the unexpected call that sent them sprinting from Sergei's Murmansk apartment, the *Neva* was steaming out of its sub pen at Polyarny. With barely enough time to change from their civilian clothing, the two senior officers coordinated the rushed departure that brought the last of the *Neva*'s eighty-five crew members on board with only twenty minutes to spare before the mooring lines were loosed.

Still not certain where they were ultimately headed, Sergei followed the orders that had him chart a course into the Barents Sea, between the island of Svalbard and Franz Josef land. Authorized to travel at its top speed of forty two knots, the *Neva*'s progress was swift, and twenty-four hours after the vessel set sail, it had attained the edge of the Arctic ice pack.

From the vessel's highly automated attack center, Sergei Markova made certain that there was plenty of spare room between the top of the *Neva*'s stubby sail and the deepest of the inverted ice ridges. Only when he was confident that such a safe depth had been attained did he look to his watch, and then address his second-in-command, who was standing at the nearby plotting table.

"It looks like it's just about time to be off to the wardroom, Viktor Ilyich."

"But what should we do about our course?" countered the puzzled senior lieutenant. "We've completed the first leg of our transit, and still find ourselves without a clear-cut destination."

"Patience, Viktor. I'm certain that's why Admiral Kharkov called this conference in the first place."

"So the old fox is finally going to emerge from his den," observed Viktor Ilyich Belenko. "I can't believe that we've been at sea a whole twenty-four hours and he hasn't shown himself even once."

"It's obvious that our esteemed Admiral of the Fleet hasn't merely been pining away in my quarters with a servere case of seasickness," offered Sergei. "Our Zampolit has been bringing him a constant stream of dispatches and charts ever since we left port."

The senior lieutenant smirked. "I bet Konstantin Zinyagin hasn't worked so hard since basic training. Why from what I understand, our Political Officer even brings the admiral his meals!"

"It's about time Zinyagin did his fair share of work around here, Viktor. But that's immaterial. Now, shall we go see what this great mystery is all about?"

As Viktor beckoned him to lead the way, Sergei Markova crisply exited the hushed attack center and headed toward the aft portion of the one-hundred-and-ten-meter-long vessel. The narrow passageway that they were soon transitting was lined with storage lockers and snaking, stainless steel cables. To the muted whine of the *Neva*'s single shaft, geared steam turbines throbbing in the distance, they passed by the locked radio room and ducked through a double-thick hatch that brought them to their desired destination.

187

The officer's wardroom consisted of a large oval-shaped mahogany table around which eight upholstered chairs were placed. The haunting strains of Borodin's "In the Steppes of Central Asia" emanated from the mounted stereo speakers and the two senior officers seated themselves at the vacant table. Sergei Markova's customary place was at the head, yet because of the high rank of their special guest, protocol guided him to take the seat directly opposite this position. Viktor Belenko sat down on his right and cautiously whispered.

"I tell you, Sergei, I don't like what's going on here one bit. To me, it has all the trappings of a conspiracy."

The captain responded, also taking extra care to keep his voice low. "Your fears are noted, comrade. But I still find them completely groundless. For what kind of conspiracy can take place on a ship when its two senior officers aren't even involved?"

"Admiral of the Fleet Kharkov is not the type of man to take lightly," warned Viktor. "And you mustn't underestimate our Zampolit. Konstantin Zinyagin might not be much of a sailor, but he's sly and crafty and that's a dangerous combination."

Sergei shook his head. "I still think you're making a mountain out of a molehill."

A prophetic tone flavored the senior lieutenant's voice as he replied. "I hope you're right, comrade. But in this instance, my instincts tell me otherwise."

Dismissing his subordinate's unfounded suspicions as mere paranoia, Sergei Markova once again checked his watch. With a minute to go until the meeting was scheduled to begin, he glanced up at the colorful mural that hung on the wall before him. This expertly rendered painting showed one small portion of the river for which his command was named. Entitled

188

The Neva at Spring, the mural displayed that section of the river lying immediately east of the city of Leningrad. Here the Neva cut through a tract of wild marshland.

As it so happened, Sergei had visited this exact same spot several years before, while he was a cadet at Leningrad's Frunze Naval Academy. Having been born and raised near the Black Sea resort city of Odessa, this trip to Leningrad proved to be his first visit to the north. He found himself particularly fascinated by the swamps and marshes that Peter the Great had first tried to tame almost three centuries ago, and made an effort to get out into the countryside whenever possible. One fair day in May, Sergei's wanderings had brought him to the same section of riverbank that currently graced the wardroom's wall. On that magical morning, he'd been able to view the same magnificent landscape that had inspired the mural's creator. He'd seen the swirling blue current, the stunted birches that hugged the Neva's wide banks, and the immense fields of blooming red poppies that filled the landscape with their vibrant color. He had been sincerely touched by this inspirational vista, and when he'd come across the exact same scene gracing the wardroom of his first command almost a decade later, Sergei had taken this as an excellent omen.

So far, the vessel had not let him down. The *Neva* was a submariner's dream. Packed with the most advanced equipment the Motherland had to offer, and manned by an experienced, handpicked crew, the *Neva* proved herself time after time to be a first-rate warship. And thus it was only fitting that she be named after the great river that brought life to the people of Leningrad.

Sergei's ponderings were abruptly broken by the arrival of the ship's Zampolit. Konstantin Zinyagin strode into the wardroom with all the self-important airs of an Oriental potentate. With his dark, bushy brows, beady eyes, clipped mustache, and short, pointed beard, he resembled Socialism's great founder, Vladimir Ilyich Lenin. Yet this was as far as the physical similarity went, for the Political Officer was not only the smallest man on the *Neva,* but the plumpest as well. As he placed the assortment of rolled-up charts he held in his pudgy hands down on the table, the Zampolit stepped aside and stiffened his portly frame to attention. Seconds later, Admiral of the Fleet Kharkov emerged from the aft hatchway.

In vast contrast to Konstantin Zinyagin, Mikhail Kharkov was tall, trim, and aristocratic. Only his snow-white hair gave away his advanced years as he acknowledged the two senior officers with an alert nod.

"Good morning, Captain Markova, Senior Lieutenant Belenko," greeted the admiral. "Please join me for some tea and then we can get on with the briefing."

Impatiently looking over at the Zampolit, Mikhail Kharkov implored. "The tea, Comrade Zinyagin!"

"Of course," stuttered the Zampolit. Then he clapped his hands twice.

This signal brought forth a white-coated steward carrying a silver tray holding four cups of tea and a platter of sweet rolls. Only when this steward pivoted and disappeared back into the passageway did the admiral seat himself at the head of the table, clear his throat, and continue.

"First off, I'd like to take this opportunity to personally thank you for giving up your cabin, Captain Markova. These old bones have found your cot quite comfortable, and the privacy of your stateroom has provided a most conducive work environment."

190

"Your thanks are not needed, Admiral," returned Sergei Markova. "It is an honor to have you aboard, and the best that the *Neva* has to offer is yours, sir."

"You are a most gracious host, Captain," replied the white-haired veteran. "Having captained a submarine, I realize how awkward such an unexpected visit can be. I do hope that you haven't been too inconvenienced."

Sergei briefly caught Viktor's curious gaze before responding. "Actually, I'm using the extra bunk in Senior Lieutenant Belenko's cabin. As long as he can put up with my snoring, I should get along just fine."

"Excellent." The Admiral of the Fleet reached out for his teacup and thoughtfully stirred the amber-colored liquid. "I must admit that these past twenty-four hours have been quite stimulating. Though I've seen precious little of the submarine, I can't get over how smoothly things are run around here. This efficiency is only one of the reasons why the *Neva* has been selected from all the vessels in the fleet for this all-important mission."

As he took a sip of his tea, the veteran introspectively grinned. "Thirty-three years ago, when I had the honor of taking the first nuclear-powered *November* Class submarine to sea, vessels such as the *Neva* were but a dream. But through an unprecedented effort, our brilliant engineers somehow made this dream come true, and in ships such as this one, the fantasy has been realized.

"Because of the great advances of the last three decades, I can reveal the details of our present mission with full confidence that our difficult goal can be achieved. For the *Neva* has been picked to undertake a perilous journey deep into the frozen waters of the enemy. It is a mission in which failure of any sort can't be accepted, as the future security of the Motherland rests in our hands!"

Noting that he had his audience's rapt attention, Mikhail Kharkov continued. "Two days ago, the plane carrying our beloved Premier, Alexander Suratov, disappeared off the northern coast of Baffin Island. The Bear-E recon plane that was sent up to monitor the *Flying Kremlin* on its flight to Ottawa, watched the Il-76 drop off its radar screens. No further contact of any type was established with the *Flying Kremlin,* and it is presumed to have crashed with the subsequent loss of all aboard. Now the question is, was this tragedy the result of a mechanical failure, or was another party responsible for the death of our great leader?

"According to the instructions of our Defense Minister, General Ivan Zarusk, I initiated an immediate investigation in an effort to answer this question, and the facts I soon uncovered were shocking. Fifteen minutes before the Il-76 dropped from the radar screens a final time, a flight of two American F-15 Eagles took off from Thule, Greenland, with afterburners fully engaged. At this same time, a top-secret NORAD radar installation known as Polestar was monitored directing a powerful beam of electronic interference toward the *Flying Kremlin.* It is my supposition that this activity was not an innocent probe, but signaled a deliberate attempt by both the Americans and the Canadians to jam the Il-76's sensors, while the F-15's proceeded to blast our aircraft out of the skies with a Phoenix air-to-air missile."

"Why, that's incredible!" dared Viktor Belenko. "Wouldn't such a thing be a direct act of war?"

The admiral sneered sardonically. "It certainly would, Senior Lieutenant. But before we can answer this act of cold-blooded murder with a suitable response, the members of the Politburo have asked me

192

to provide them with concrete evidence proving it was a willful act of Imperialist aggression that sent the *Flying Kremlin* plummeting down to the frozen ice-fields below. And with the *Neva*'s invaluable help, I intend to do just that."

The veteran only had to snap his fingers a single time to get Konstantin Zinyagin into action. With sweat rolling down his flushed forehead, the stocky Zampolit unfolded one of the charts he had brought along, and spread it out on the table. Both of the submarine's senior officers recognized this map as an exact twin of the polar projection currently gracing the *Neva*'s chart table.

After consuming a mouthful of tea, the admiral continued. "If I'm not mistaken, taking into account the course which I relayed to you at the beginning of our journey, and the fact that we have been traveling at flank speed, our current position should be somewhere between Svalbard and Franz Josef Land. If we continued on this same course, in another twenty hours or so, we'd be transitting directly beneath the North Pole. Long before we reach the Pole, it is my intention that the *Neva* turn toward Cape Morris Jesup and the Lincoln Sea. Here we will penetrate the Nares Strait between the western coast of Greenland and Ellesmere Island. Utilizing such a direct route, we will enter Baffin Bay and be in perfect position to access the frozen waters of Lancaster Sound."

"Excuse me, Admiral," interrupted Sergei Markova. "But I question the wisdom of using the route you just mentioned. The Nares Strait is not only extremely narrow with treacherous currents, it is also littered with American and Canadian SOSUS arrays. Such undersea hydrophones will surely pick up the *Neva* as we initiate our transit. Wouldn't it be more prudent to approach Lancaster Sound from the other direction, by way of the M'Clure Straits?"

Quick to support Sergei was his senior lieutenant. "I agree with the captain. Three months ago, the *Neva* attempted to penetrate the Nares Strait and enter the waters of Baffin Bay undetected. After carefully skirting the known SOSUS station at Alert, off the northeastern coast of Ellesmere Island, we activated our anechoic masking system and cautiously continued southward. Yet for all our circumspection, waiting for us as we entered Baffin basin was a US Navy P-3 Orion that was able to tag us with an active sonobuoy on its very first pass. Surely this indicates that no matter how stealthily we might travel, the Nares Strait's SOSUS line will be able to pick us up."

"I appreciate the wise feedback, comrades," Admiral Kharkov responded. "And under normal circumstances, I wouldn't hesitate to heed your excellent advice. But we currently find ourselves in a situation where time is of the essence. For it's imperative that we reach Lancaster Sound with all due haste."

"But the American's will be waiting for us," repeated Viktor.

"To hell with the Americans!" exclaimed Mikhail Kharkov passionately. "I don't give a damn if their SOSUS line does indeed pick us up, for we'll be in and out of there long before the pathetic Imperialists will be able to react to our presence."

Again the admiral snapped his fingers, and in instant response, Konstantin Zinyagin once more unfolded another chart. This one was of a meteorological variety, and as the two senior submariners looked on, Mikhail Kharkov was quick to explain it.

"Please note the series of tight circular lines that are located off the northern coast of Baffin Island. This unique pattern is indicative of an intense low-pressure

194

system. The chart that you see before you was compiled from data relayed to the *Neva* by way of the Salyut space station, Red Flag. It is less than three hours old, and shows a storm of great magnitude, currently stalled over the waters of Lancaster Sound. Since it appears that this powerful system will be influencing the region for at least forty-eight more hours, we can forget about the threat of encountering any type of observation from above. No airman in his right mind would brave such a blizzard. And concerning the possibility of meeting up with a surface vessel, I think this photo speaks for itself."

Quick to take the hint, the Zampolit uncovered a large glossy, black and white photograph and handed it to Sergei Markova. As Belenko leaned over to take a look at the picture, the Admiral of the Fleet continued his narrative.

"What you are now seeing has also been relayed to us by Red Flag; I took the liberty of bringing it along with me from Murmansk Fleet headquarters. Taken two days ago, it shows the Canadian Coast Guard cutter, *Louis St. Laurent,* hopelessly trapped in the ice to the west of Lancaster Sound. This pitifully weak icebreaker is the only ship in the entire Imperialist fleet that could possibly give us any trouble. And unless the spring thaw comes six months early this year, the *Neva* won't have to worry about sharing these waters with a boatload of crazed Canucks."

As he placed the photograph back on the wardroom table, Sergei Markova voiced himself. "This is all rather fascinating, Admiral. But I still don't understand why it's so urgent for us to get into the waters of Lancaster Sound."

"Of course you don't, Captain," Kharkov answered. "But if you'll hear me out a bit longer, all your confusion will soon be gone."

Pushing his chair back and standing at this point, the white-haired veteran continued, his voice strong with conviction. "Taking it for granted that the *Neva* will successfully reach Lancaster Sound in the minimum amount of time, I will need five members of the crew. These men have got to be tough enough to take an inordinate amount of physical punishment, and they must have resolute characters. They will be outfitted with special Arctic survival gear that has already been brought onto the ship, and will leave the Neva under my command, once the vessel has surfaced in a suitable polynya.

"At this point I will utilize a directional homing device to locate the *Flying Kremlin*'s cockpit voice recorder, or, as it is more commonly known, its black box. Such an instrument contains a specially constructed cassette tape on which a full account of the flight is recorded. Hopefully this black box can be located before its battery pack runs low, and the ultrasonic beacon it continually projects stops transmitting. The Salyut space station Red Flag has already picked up this signal, and has definitely traced its origin to somewhere on the northern shore of Baffin Island. Unfortunately, these were the most accurate coordinates that could be relayed to us."

"How long before this battery is scheduled to fail?" questioned Sergei.

Glad to see that the captain was following him, the admiral replied. "The best estimate gives us another seventy-two hours before the transmissions stop."

"Then no wonder it's so important we get there with such haste," reflected Viktor Belenko.

"Precisely, comrade," responded Mikhail Kharkov, as a hint of gathering excitement flavored his tone. "If the fates are with us, then the black box will be successfully retrieved. And once it's conveyed back to the *Neva,* I will be able to complete an almost-instant analysis of the tape's composition by using the ship's computer and a special software program that is currently locked in my cabin's safe. Within minutes, we'll soon enough know the true nature of the disaster that led to our Premier's tragic passing. And if it's indeed learned that a Yankee missile was responsible for the *Flying Kremlin's* demise, then the *Neva's* next mission will be one of pure revenge!"

These last words rang out with a threatening intensity, and as the *Neva's* two senior officers shared the briefest of concerned glances, the wardroom's intercom rang. Without hesitating, Viktor Belenko reached out for the nearby plastic handset.

"Senior Lieutenant, here . . . Why of course, Chief. You may stand down from flank speed at once. I'll join you in the engine room to assess the situation."

No sooner did Viktor hang up the handset than Admiral Kharkov exploded with rage. "How dare you cut the *Neva's* speed! Haven't you been listening to a single thing I've said?"

Barely paying this outburst any attention, Viktor stood and directly addressed Sergei Markova. "That was Chief Engineer Koslov, Captain. It seems we've got a problem in the engine room. The main seal to the propeller shaft is leaking."

Immediately standing himself, Sergei quickly backed up his subordinate's decision. "You acted correctly by allowing the chief to cut our speed, Senior Lieutenant. If this leak is a serious one, and we ignore it, this mission may well be over long before it's even started. Come on, comrade, let's get down there and inspect the damages."

As the two officers rushed off toward the aft portion of the boat, Admiral of the Fleet Mikhail Kharkov vainly tried to control his rising frustration.

Directly meeting the empty look projected from the Political Officer's beady eyes, the white-haired veteran vented his anger.

"Well don't just stand there like a complete moron, Comrade Zinyagin! Show me the quickest route to the engine room. And for the Motherland's sake, don't tarry! Why, this entire operation could be in jeopardy!"

Thusly motivated, the Zampolit led Mikhail Kharkov through the aft hatchway. The sweat was pouring off his forehead as he tried his best to lengthen his short stride. Yet try as he could to quicken his pace, the seventy-six-year-old veteran remained glued to his heels as Konstantin Zinyagin sprinted down a narrow passageway and began to descend a steep ladder. His palms were so wet that once his grasp faltered, and as the ladder's steel rung slipped out of his right fingers, he found himself hanging precariously by his left hand only.

"Can't you do anything right, you uncoordinated idiot!" screamed the Admiral of the Fleet from above.

Desperately flailing out with his free hand to steady himself, the Political Officer's grasp made contact with a vacant rung, and with his heart pounding away in his chest, he hung to it for a moment to regather his nerve. Yet a furious command all too soon had him resuming his downward climb.

"Move it, you fool! Or so help me, I'll climb right over you!"

By the time they reached the engine room, Konstantin Zinyagin feared that he might keel over from a coronary. The out-of-shape Zampolit's wheezing breaths were pained and irregular, while a tight knot had gathered in the left portion of his chest.

Completely oblivious to the Political Officer's condition, Admiral Kharkov expertly surveyed the chaotic scene before him. All of the action was focused on the extreme aft section of the compartment, where the end of the propeller shaft penetrated the hull. Here a geyser of water shot through the air. A half-dozen soaked seamen were gathered beside the shaft and the excess water was already well over their ankles.

On the catwalk beside these sailors, Captain Markova and his senior lieutenant could be seen. Both of these officers had flashlights in hand, and were angling the narrow beams of their battery-powered torches on the area of the hull where the faulty seal was located.

"Get those bilge pumps working, Chief!" cried Sergei Markova forcefully.

One of the seamen who had been gathered on the deck below the captain waved in response to this command. He was a barrel-chested, giant of a man, with bulging biceps and a short spiky crewcut. Ignoring the soaking that he was getting, the Chief turned around to head for the emergency pump activation switch. Yet as he pivoted, he lost his footing and fell awkwardly to the soaked deck with a splash. When he didn't immediately pick himself up out of the water, Admiral Kharkov sensed that he could have had the wind knocked out of him. In such a compromising position, lying in the water as the chief was, a common injury could become most serious, yet his shipmates had turned their attention back to the leaking seal and seemed completely ignorant of their comrade's plight.

It was like a scene from a nightmare: the Admiral of the Fleet screamed out to the sailors, but the constantly spraying water effectively veiled his shouts of warning. Prepared to pull the downed seaman off the deck himself, Kharkov was just about to intervene when the *Neva's* captain bolted over the catwalk he had been standing on. With long, fluid strides Sergei Markova sloshed over the wet deck, reached the injured seaman's side, and bent down to assist him.

The fallen man was soon sitting up on his own, rubbing the side of his head, and coughing up the water he had swallowed. Not stopping to celebrate this fact, the young captain, who was now thoroughly soaked, turned his attention back to the leak.

"Try backing up the shaft, Viktor!" screamed Markova to his senior lieutenant. "Perhaps that will plug the seal."

The admiral breathlessly watched as the *Neva's* second-in-command sprinted over to the annunciator. Seconds later, the shaft began spinning in reverse, and as the sub's huge propeller bit into the surrounding seawater, the *Neva* shook wildly and trembled with such force that Mikhail Kharkov had to reach out to a nearby bulkhead to steady himself.

Cowering at the admiral's side, the Zampolit looked at the veteran mariner, his eyes filled with horror, and somehow found the words to express his worst fears. "And to think that all this is happening while we're under the ice. We'll never be able to get to surface again!"

Kharkov was all set to slap some sense into the cowardly Political Officer when a torrent of water exploded from the still-spinning shaft. This geyser shot through the air like a tidal wave, and with his own uniform now thoroughly soaked, Admiral Mikhail Kharkov sensed that something was seriously wrong. The roar of the spinning propeller rose to an almost deafening crescendo, and with the hull still wildly vibrating around him, the white-haired veteran found his own gut tightening with fear. For the first time since the closing days of the Great War, when an exploding Nazi depth charge almost sent his command to the bottom, he prepared himself for a painful but quick, watery death.

It was at that exact moment the leak sealed itself. With the sound of spraying water suddenly absent, Captain Sergei Markova's voice rang out clear and true.

"Stop the shaft, Viktor!"

As the senior lieutenant faithfully carried out this directive, the mad vibration finally halted. Noting that only a small trickle of water was now seeping through the seal, Kharkov listened as the *Neva*'s captain cried out forcefully.

"All ahead two-thirds, Viktor. She'll hold now, I can just feel it!"

Once more the shaft began rotating. Yet this time as it started rapidly spinning, the trickle of leaking water stopped flowing completely. As the young captain had said, the seal had indeed held—the crisis was over!

Exhaling a grateful breath of relief, Admiral of the Fleet Mikhail Kharkov looked down to the man responsible for their salvation. Sergei Markova stood on the still partially flooded deck, his blue-eyed stare locked on the spinning shaft. With his wet blond hair slicked back off his forehead, the captain looked strikingly handsome, like a movie actor playing out a scene in a remarkably accurate set.

A sudden feeling of pride swelled in the old warrior's chest. He had picked Sergei Markova to be a winner when the man was but a cadet in postgraduate school. As a secret patron, Mikhail had guided the young officer's career from its very start, and he had been an instrumental force in getting Markova his current command. Certain now that he had picked the right man for the all-important mission that faced them, the white-haired veteran turned to head for his cabin and a change of clothing.

Chapter Ten

The storm struck Arctic Bay soon after the Aurora CP-140 aircraft carrying Lieutenant Jack Redmond and his squad of Rangers landed at the settlement's primitive airport. With the gathering winds already beginning to strengthen in velocity, the commandoes hurriedly unpacked their gear. As Jack Redmond supervised this effort, his sergeant-major rushed into the adjoining town to see about getting the services of a dog team and sled to lead them across the ice fields.

The Rangers were in the process of carefully carrying their six snowmobiles out of the plane's cargo bay and down onto the windswept tarmac when a short, powerfully built figure approached them. Dressed in a heavy, down-filled parka and wearing a distinctive dark blue hat, this individual climbed up into the plane's rear cabin and quickly cornered the squad's commanding officer.

"Excuse me, sir. You must be Jack Redmond. I'm Lieutenant Bill Elliot, the local representative of the Royal Canadian Mounted Police. Welcome to Arctic Bay."

Redmond accepted the Mountie's firm handshake and replied. "Thank you, Lieutenant Elliot. Looks like we got here just in time to beat this storm. Eh?"

"You certainly did," returned the Mountie. "From what I understand, it's going to be a real bad one. In fact, if this Aurora doesn't get airborne in a hurry, they'll be staying right here for at least the next thirty-six hours. May I ask what your exact plans are? The telephone briefing I got was a bit sketchy."

With the wind howling in the background, and his men scurrying around them to unload the supplies, Redmond answered. "We're off for the northern portion of the Brodeur Peninsula. Seems Ottawa feels the plane carrying the Soviet Premier could have gone down here, and we've been dispatched to search for any debris that would prove it did. We're particularly interested in finding the aircraft's cockpit voice recorder."

"Sounds like you've certainly got your work cut out for you," reflected the Mountie. "Where do you plan on staying until the blizzard passes? We can't offer much in the way of accommodations here, but I think the school gymnasium could be outfitted with enough mattresses to hold you and your men."

Jack Redmond shook his head. "That won't be necessary, Lieutenant. You see, we'll be leaving for the Brodeur Peninsula within the hour."

A look of total disbelief came to the Mountie's face. "You can't be serious! Perhaps you didn't understand, but we've got a nasty low-pressure system moving in from Lancaster Sound even as we speak. Not far north of here, the winds have already been clocked at over sixty miles per hour, meaning plenty of blowing snow and temperatures well below minus thirty degrees."

"I understand all too well, Lieutenant Elliot. But our orders don't allow us the luxury of waiting for this blizzard to vent itself. We have no alternative but to proceed as directed."

The Mountie still seemed flustered by what he was hearing. "Good lord, man, this is ridiculous! This storm has all the makings of a killer, and it's sheer lunacy to challenge it. Wouldn't it be wise to first give your commander a call and inform him of the situation up here before needlessly putting your lives on the line?"

"I sincerely wish I could do just that, Lieutenant. But my current orders come right from the Prime Minister's office, and I'm not about to call Ottawa to give them a blooming weather report! No, my friend. I've been instructed to get up there as quickly as possible, and I intend to do just that."

Easing off, the Mountie reflected. "Perhaps the Prime Minister has reason to believe there could be some survivors up there, though this is certainly the first I've heard of it."

"Who can say?" retorted Redmond, softening his tone a bit. "But orders are orders, and as Arctic Rangers, my men are prepared to take on just about anything that Mother Nature can throw our way. Thanks for your concern, Lieutenant, and now if you'll excuse me, I'd better give the lads some help with the rest of the gear. Otherwise, this plane crew is going to be stuck up here longer than they had anticipated."

"May God be with you," offered the Mountie, who continued on to the flight deck, leaving Redmond free to assist four of his men as they unloaded the last of the snowmobiles. Outside the plane's rather comfortable cabin, frigid air swirled with a breathtaking intensity. Snow flurries were already beginning to fall as a line of dark, low-lying clouds gathered on the northern horizon.

"Corporal Eviki, have the men start loading up the snowcats with our supplies!" Redmond shouted over the howling wind. "Divide the food and ammunition up equally. That way if we lose a vehicle, the others will keep us going."

As the Inuit got on with this task, Redmond was forced to pull up the collar of his parka when a bitingly cold blast of stinging air hit him full in the face. His exposed cheeks and forehead felt as if they had been slapped, and Redmond momentarily considered the Mountie's words of warning. Yet his ponderings were brief for a voice cried out from the direction of the airplane.

"This is the last of our gear, Lieutenant!"

The soldier responsible for this revelation jumped down onto the runway with two white nylon backpacks in hand. He was followed by Bill Elliot of the RCMP.

"Lieutenant Redmond, you're going to have to clear your men from the area," directed the Mountie. "The crew of the Aurora is going to try to get their bird skyward."

Signaling that he understood, Redmond informed his men of the air crew's intentions. As soon as the squad gathered together beside the corrugated steel Jamesway hut that served as the airport's main terminal, the first of the plane's engines was started. Three others turned over in quick succession, their grinding roar all but swallowed by the howling wind.

By this time the snow was falling so heavily that Jack Redmond had to pull down his protective goggles in order to watch the plane taxi out to the ice-covered runway. The pilot of the Aurora, obviously wasting as little time as possible, opened up the throttles and the aircraft lunged forward. It seemed to take forever for it to pick up speed. In fact, the plane was well over halfway down the runway's length before its wheels finally parted from the icy pavement. Though a particularly violent downdraft sent the lumbering vehicle abruptly back to the earth, it's stubborn crew fought off the elements and with a roaring whine the plane seemed to leap off the runway and soar into the cloud-filled heavens. Seconds later, it had disappeared.

"That was cutting it too close for comfort," observed the relieved Mountie. "Now are you certain you won't reconsider and at least wait until the brunt of this storm passes."

Jack Redmond responded by cupping his hands around his mouth and calling out forcefully. "All right you shirkers, mount 'em up! We've got us some traveling to do!"

The Mountie could only shrug his shoulders, as Redmond issued a crisp salute and turned for the lead snowmobile. With a practiced eye, the senior commando double-checked the gear that had been stored inside the locker located beneath the vehicle's one-piece, molded-plastic seat. He counted four M16 rifles, a dozen clips of spare ammunition, a carton of field rations, a compact butane stove, and several tightly rolled, heavy woolen blankets. Satisfied that all looked in order, he slammed down the seat, locked it in place, and checked the dashboard-mounted fuel gauge. Finding the tank barely three-quarters of the way full, he turned and shouted.

"Corporal Eviki, you'd better top off these tanks until they're overfull! It's going to be a long way until we reach the next service station."

While his alert subordinate sprinted off to the adjoining hangar to find a gas can, Jack Redmond inspected the storage compartments of the five remaining snowcats. Each of the vehicles were packed almost exactly like his own, except for the last one in line. Instead of spare food or ammunition, this one

207

held a single elongated crate. Inside this padded carton was a battery-powered directional receiver. Such a device would be needed once they reached their ultimate destination and began the search for the black box.

The sudden barking of dogs drew Redmond's attention. He looked up and expectantly scanned the compound. The blowing snow made visibility poor. Yet as the barking grew progressively louder, he viewed the dim outline of a team of harnessed huskies headed toward him. Like a ghostly apparition, the dogs momentarily disappeared in a veil of thick, white snowflakes, only to reappear again, this time with a sled clearly visible behind them. Standing on the runners of this sled was a single figure clad in a fur parka. With an expert snap of his wrist, he utilized a long, rawhide whip to motivate the team, whose frantic pace further quickened.

It had been a long time since Jack Redmond had seen such a team in action. During his childhood, dogsleds were a common sight, particularly in the wintertime. The arrival of the gasoline-powered snowmobile had signaled the doom of such a means of transportation, and today the sleds were all but obsolescent.

Memories of his childhood rose in his consciousness, and a grin painted Redmond's face as the sled pulled to a halt beside him. The dogs whined with excitement as the team's driver stepped off the sled. Only when the man pulled back his fur-covered hood and removed his goggles did Redmond identify this previously mysterious personage as his sergeant-major.

"Sorry it took so long, Lieutenant. But it took a bit of convincing to get my uncle to part with his dogs."

"I'm surprised he gave them up, especially to a

nephew he hasn't seen in almost fifteen years," Redmond replied while inspecting the sled. It was of fairly modern construction, with a pair of razor-sharp, steel runners and an elongated, wooden-slat storage compartment.

"I'm afraid the price was pretty stiff though," Cliff Ano added. "Not only did I have to promise to bring the team back in decent shape, I had to swear that if anything happened to them, I'd come up to Arctic Bay on my leave time and work for my uncle until the debt was repaid. Talk about driving a hard bargain!"

Redmond chuckled. "By the way, that's some parka you're wearing."

"That's compliments of my aunt," returned the Inuit. "It's my oldest cousin's actually. Made out of caribou hide on the outside, with a sealskin lining. One thing for certain, it's a lot warmer than the Army-issue parka I had to trade for it."

Redmond peered out to the roiling line of dark clouds blowing in from the north. "It looks like you're going to need that parka, Sergeant-Major. This storm has got all the brewings of a full-force blizzard."

"The dogs don't seem to mind it," the Inuit commented as he replaced his glasses and pulled up his hood. "What's the matter, Lieutenant, are you starting to have second doubts about taking off now?"

"I'd be a liar if I told you such a thought hadn't crossed my mind, Sergeant-Major. The trip we're about to undertake is going to be hazardous enough even without this damn storm."

Not used to hearing his senior officer so readily express his fears, Cliff Ano interjected, "Things could be worse, Lieutenant. My uncle tells me he was out on the Brodeur Peninsula a little less than three weeks ago, and even then Admiralty Inlet was frozen as solid as a hockey rink. Though we might have a few snowdrifts to contend with, at least that portion of our trip should go smoothly."

"I hope to God that you're right, Sergeant-Major — and that we haven't bitten off more than we can chew."

The Inuit seemed surprised by such a statement. "Come now, Lieutenant. Have you already forgotten that we're Arctic Rangers, the best damn soldiers in the northland? Why no task is impossible for Canada's best!"

Redmond's grin was a sarcastic one. "Thanks for the pep talk, Sergeant-Major. And with that said, how about getting this bunch of ragtag malcontents on the road?"

As he fit on the white ski mask he had stuffed into his parka's pocket, Jack Redmond turned to check on the status of his squad. The majority of the men were huddled behind the Jamesway hut, using its rounded south face as a windbreak. Corporal Eviki was in the process of gassing up the last of the snowcats, and seeing this, Redmond boomed out loudly.

"Gentlemen, it's show time! Mount up, and get those engines purring! We'll be forming a single line behind the sergeant-major. The going might be slow, but it's a hell of a lot better than dropping off into an open lead of water. So keep your formation tight, and hit those sirens the second you run into any trouble. Otherwise we might never be able to find you again. Do I make myself absolutely clear?"

Looking like heavy-handed ghosts in their white parkas and snow pants, the squad sprinted out to their individual vehicles. One by one the ignitions were triggered, and for a second the high-pitched whines of six engines rose above the incessant roar of the wind. Yet the howling gusts all too soon took precedence as the drivers shifted their vehicles into gear and followed the dogsled out of the compound and into the swirling wall of snow that lay beyond.

Petty Officer First Class Stanley Roth was at his wit's end. As the headphone-clad senior sonar technician sat at the console with dozens of dials staring back at him, he found his thoughts were far away from his current duties. That throbbing, never-ending pain in his tooth was so unbearable he felt as if the entire top of his head was going to erupt.

Hardly paying the least bit of attention to the conglomeration of sounds being conveyed through his headphones, Roth reached into his breast pocket and removed a single plastic vial. Inside this small container were a dozen pills. For a fleeting second, he toyed with the idea of popping open the vial and swallowing one of the tablets. The powerful narcotic they contained had already successfully dulled his pounding ache a number of times. Yet in each instance it had inevitably left him drained, irritable, and groggy. And besides, only a few hours later the pain would be back in all its excruciating glory!

One and a half days ago, Roth had taken his captain's advice and had visited sickbay. Pharmacist Mate Charles Krommer had been anticipating his visit and, after initiating a cursory examination, had prescribed the mildest pain killer in his medicine chest. With the greatest of expectations, Stanley swallowed one of these pills and went off to work. Forty-five minutes later, he was found slumped over his console, in the midst of a sound sleep that took him over ten hours to snap out of. Upon awakening, the conscientious sonar operator swore that he would somehow learn to live with the pain and would stay as far away from the pills as possible.

"Damn it!" cursed Stanley to himself as he rubbed his throbbing left jaw and resolutely stuffed the unopened vial back into his pocket.

Desperate to escape from his agony, he attempted to refocus his thoughts on his work. He sat up straight in his chair, and turned up the volume gain to his headphones a full notch. The distinctive whining crack of fracturing sea ice met his ears, and he closed his eyes in an attempt to visualize the monumental forces at work on the surface to create such a racket. Unfortunately at about this same moment an excruciating, piercing spasm of pain flared up the left side of his jaw leaving him trembling in pure agony. It was then he realized that he had had enough.

Roth reached out for the nearby intercom handset and made two quick calls. The first one sent his replacement, Seaman Lester Warren, scrambling from his bunk. The second call pulled Pharmacist Mate Charles Krommer away from a poker game that he had been in the midst of.

"I don't give a damn if you are on a hot streak, Krommer," the desperate sonar technician said forcefully. "As God is my witness, you're going to do something about this friggin' tooth right now!"

Stanley Roth had to wait for his breathless replacement to arrive before storming off to meet the perplexed pharmacist mate in the *Defiance*'s sickbay. This infrequently patronized portion of the ship contained a complete operating theater, including a dental chair. Though any number of complicated surgeries could be performed here, the crew of 107 physically fit young men rarely came down with anything more serious than a cold or the flu, so the pharmacist's mate's main responsibility was to monitor the radiation badges each crewman wore to insure that his exposure was kept to a minimum.

"Now are you certain you want to go through with this, Roth?" quizzed Charles Krommer as he changed into his gown and scrubbed up. "I'm warning you, I'm not a licensed jaw breaker."

"Of course, I'm positive!" Roth retorted passionately. "I'm telling you, Charlie, this tooth of mine is just killing me. I've got to do something drastic or I'm going to go stark raving bonkers!"

Quick to sense the extent of his patient's upset, the medic attempted to calm the senior sonar technician by adopting his best chairside manner. "Easy does it, Stan. Just settle down into the chair and relax. Though I've never actually extracted a tooth before, I've seen it done in the clinic a number of times and it didn't look all that difficult. So just hang in there, buddy, and check out the scenery while I make a quick consultation."

Stanley Roth took a series of deep breaths, and following the medic's advice let his stare wander to the series of cutouts taped to the wall before him. Starting on Miss January, he attempted to lose himself in the buxom, sensuous centerfolds that had been put up to give a whole new dimension to the field of dentistry.

With the sonar technician thusly occupied, Pharmacist Mate Charles Krommer nervously picked up a manual entitled, *The U.S. Navy Guide to Emergency Dental Surgery*. The St. Louis native had expectations of becoming a full-fledged M.D. one day in the future. His plan was to enroll in premedical studies at St. Louis University, where he also hoped to attend med school. To finance such an expensive endeavor, he'd enlisted in the Navy's college plan.

After completing basic in San Diego, Krommer had been accepted into the Fleet medical program. He completed an intensive six-month course in which he learned a full range of skills including first aid, phar-

213

macology, radiology, and elemental surgical techniques. For an entire week, he worked as an assistant in a dental clinic, where he acquired knowledge of such basics as treating an abscess and how to temporarily fill a cavity. Yet actually taking out a tooth was a whole different ball game, and he couldn't keep his hand from shaking slightly as he turned to the chapter marked, "Extraction."

With the help of a fold-out diagram of the mouth, he identified the suspect tooth as being the lower left mandibular first bicuspid. He breathed a sigh of relief upon noting that this particular tooth had only a single root, and decided since it was slightly loose already, it shouldn't be that difficult to remove. On the next page he found a list of the items he would need to facilitate his efforts. They included Xylocaine, a dental syringe and needle, a straight elevator to remove the gum from the bone around the tooth, a lower universal anterior forceps, and a dozen or more four-by-four cotton sponges. Only when he was armed with these items did he turn his attention back to his patient.

"Well Stanley, here it goes. I want you to open wide and turn your head slightly to the right."

The sonar technician willfully obeyed these simple instructions, and Charles Krommer initiated step number one—the administration of the anesthetic. With the syringe, he proceeded to inject that portion of the gum that surrounded the tooth. As a kid, needles had always scared the dickens out of the pharmacist's mate, and he found himself more frightened than his patient as he carried out this far from pleasant task.

A wide, relieved smile turned the corners of the medic's mouth as he pulled the empty syringe out and his patient awkwardly mumbled. "Hey, Charlie, it finally stopped hurting!"

A bit more confidently, Krommer proceeded, according to the manual, to take the straight elevator and remove the gingival tissue from the tooth. He then utilized the lower anterior universal forceps, clamping it securely to the tooth. Taking a deep breath, he yanked on the forceps with a slight rotating upward movement, and, unbelievably, the tooth came right out of its socket! Before he could cry out in triumph, the blood started flowing. Here the cotton gauze sponges came into play. After instructing his patient to bite down on them, Krommer waited. In approximately five minutes the bleeding would stop, hopefully. Only then would his first venture into the fascinating world of oral surgery be completed.

Back in the sound shack, Seaman Lester Warren was completely oblivious to the historic operation that had just been concluded in the *Defiance*'s sick bay. Though his prayers were certainly with Petty Officer Roth, he had no time to let his thoughts wander. For the myriad of wondrous sounds that were currently streaming into the headphones were unlike any he had ever heard before. The Texan was able to identify the distinctive crackling cries of shrimp, the tremulous, vibrating barks of several species of seal, and the high-pitched clicks and mournful moans of a herd of passing narwhal.

Since this was only Warren's second Arctic cruise, many of these noises were still new to him. Under Stanley Roth's expert guidance, his last patrol in these waters had been a great learning experience, and today Lester readily applied his knowledge during his colleague's conspicuous absence.

By and far the dominant noise presently passing through the sub's hydrophones was the grinding, fracturing sound of the ice topside. This raucous racket was an overriding presence and was unique in its intensity. Try as he could, Lester had a difficult time visualizing what this sea of constantly shifting ice must look like. Back home in San Antonio, Texas, the winters were fairly mild. An ice storm occasionally paid them a visit, but this was definitely an exception to the norm. During his entire childhood, he could only remember it snowing a handful of times. Yet in each instance, he'd been one of the first kids out in the powdery white precipitation, making a snowman or having a snowball fight.

Lester was looking forward to the moment when the *Defiance* would surface in an open lead in the ice. At that time he planned to ask the XO for permission to go topside and check out this winter wonderland with his own eyes. Perhaps if he got lucky, he might even get a glimpse of a polar bear or a real live Eskimo! Then he'd certainly have something special to share with the folks back home during his next leave.

He would never forget the last time the *Defiance* attempted surfacing in these same frozen seas. He had been stationed at the very same console during the ascent, and had actually been thrown from his seat when the sub's sail smashed into a solid wall of impenetrable ice. Fortunately, he hadn't been injured during this unexpected collision, though several of his shipmates had.

For the last couple of days, a civilian technician had been industriously working at the sound shack's spare computer terminal to insure that such an accident never again occurred. Dr. Laurie Lansing was one of the hardest-working women Warren had ever met. She was also one of the brightest.

During much of the time, they were the only ones in the sonar compartment, and since both of them had a sincere interest in computers, it was only natural that they discuss their shared passion at coffee breaks.

When his shipmates learned of this fact, they immediately began pestering Warren to tell them all about their newest passenger. Their incessant questions mostly had to do with her personal life, her marital status, and her exact measurements. Quick to dismiss such immature queries, Lester couldn't understand what the guys were making such a ridiculous fuss about. Big deal if Dr. Lansing was a good-looking lady. She had her job to do just like the rest of them, and deserved her fair share of respect. And this certainly included not gawking at her as if she were some sort of sex goddess.

Lansing's absence from the sound shack this morning probably meant that she had finally finished the project she had been working on. Either that or she had finally collapsed from sheer exhaustion. Because nobody on board the *Defiance* had worked as hard as she had these last couple of days.

Hoping that her laser-guided surface-scanning Fathometer would function properly this time around, Lester directed his attention back to the grinding noise of the ice pack. Like an original musical score, the natural sounds being conveyed into his headphones were unlike any other on this planet. When combined with the unique cries of the sealife that roamed these frigid depths, a macabre symphony resulted, the likes of which his friends back in San Antonio could never begin to fathom.

In a nearby portion of this same frozen sea, a symphony of a vastly different nature was being appreciated by yet another submariner. Captain Sergei Markova had only recently returned to the stateroom

217

he was currently sharing with the *Neva*'s senior lieutenant. Having been up the entire night supervising the transit of the narrow strait through which they were traveling, he gratefully crawled into his temporary bunk to catch a few hours' sleep.

To properly unwind after his twelve-hour duty stint, Sergei pulled out his prized Sony Walkman. Purchased in Viet Nam, while he was assigned to a *Victor* class attack sub stationed at Cam Rahn Bay, the portable cassette player had already provided him with hundreds of hours of musical pleasure. Thanks to its miniature headphones, he could enjoy his favorite composers without having to worry about disturbing his shipmates.

By pure chance, the young captain reached into his bag of cassettes and selected Tchaikovsky's Fifth Symphony. It was only as he lay back on his bunk and the first movement began unraveling that he remembered where he had heard this soulful selection last. It had been at his apartment in Murmansk, less than four days ago. This thought unleashed a flood of fond memories that seemed to have taken place in another lifetime.

He had spent a marvelous afternoon with his daughter Sasha. Dressed to the hilt in preparation for the storm that would soon be upon them, they'd made the round of the local stores. With their precious purchases in hand, they walked home in the thickly blowing snow. Once back at the apartment they were greeted by their guests, Viktor and Tanya Belenko. It had been while Viktor and Sergei sat before the fireplace that Peter Ilyich Tchaikovsky's Symphony No. 5 in E minor began blaring forth from the room's mounted radio speakers. Over drinks and appetizers, and the continually developing music, they had all joked, told stories, and relaxed in a casual atmosphere as alien to that of the *Neva* as day is to night.

The symphony was just reaching its spirited conclusion when the fateful phone call that was to put an abrupt end to their party came. Could Sergei ever forget the look of pained disappointment that painted the face of his dear wife as he revealed that call's grim purpose? Viktor's beautiful wife had been equally shocked, and when Sasha had learned that her Poppy was leaving for the sea once again, her tears had been instantaneous.

As it turned out, Sergei had had little time to share their frustrations. He'd been too busy packing his clothes and mentally formulating the long list of tasks that would have to be taken care of before the *Neva* was able to put to sea as ordered. He last glimpsed his beloved family as he sprinted out the lobby doors to Viktor's waiting automobile. Even the duty woman seemed to have tears in her eyes as Sasha ran up to the frosted windows to wave one last goodbye.

From that point on, Sergei's official military duties had occupied him completely. Yet the chance playing of one of the loveliest pieces of music ever written had unlocked precious memories, and Sergei's heart was suddenly heavy, with a loneliness only a sailor could understand, as his heavy eyelids closed and he surrendered to his exhaustion.

He awoke an hour and a half later when a firm hand shook his shoulder. Reaching up to remove the headphones—he had fallen asleep with them on—Sergei looked up into the concerned face of his senior lieutenant.

"I'm sorry to have had to awaken you, comrade, but we've picked up something on sonar that I know you'll be interested in."

The captain replied while sitting up and wiping the sleep from his eyes. "I bet it's an active sonobuoy from a Yankee P-3 Orion. I knew they'd tag us the moment we exited the Nares Strait."

Viktor Belenko shook his head. "I'm afraid your hunch is wrong this time, old friend. For what we've discovered in the waters before us is not a mere sono-buoy but another submarine!"

This revelation hit Sergei with a jolt, and he was suddenly wide awake. "You don't say, Viktor. Any idea as to its nationality? And have they realized they're not alone as yet?"

An excited gleam flashed in Viktor's eyes as he answered, "The computer shows a forty-seven percent probability that this contact is an American *Sturgeon* class vessel. They're apparently traveling northward in a hell of a hurry, and it appears that they have no idea we're out here."

"Wonderful!" exclaimed Sergei, who stood and hastily threw on his coveralls. "Let's sound general quarters and see just what it is that our enemy is doing in these waters."

"I've already taken the liberty of sending the men to their battle stations, comrade. Admiral of the Fleet Kharkov is anxiously waiting for us in the attack center."

"Then we'd better be quick and join that old fox before he takes out the Yankees with a torpedo salvo," Sergei jested, as he beckoned his subordinate to lead the way to the *Neva*'s control room.

A hushed, tense atmosphere prevailed in the attack center as the vessel's two senior officers hurriedly entered and made their way to the sonar console. Here they joined Admiral Kharkov and the *Neva*'s Zampolit.

It proved to be the white-haired veteran who anxiously greeted the newcomers. "Ah, it's about time, Captain. It appears that we've caught ourselves an unwary Imperialist *Sturgeon* all right. The probability is now up to sixty-eight percent."

With his eyes glued to the repeater screen that showed the vessel's sound signature as a line of quivering light, Sergei Markova thoughtfully observed, "This is most unusual, comrades. It's very rare to catch the overly cautious Americans at a sprint speed such as this. One can't help but wonder where they're off to in such a hurry."

"Why that's only too apparent," offered Konstantin Zinyagin, as he patted his sweating jowls dry with a handkerchief. "The *Sturgeon* is obviously bound for the frozen waters of Lancaster Sound, just like we are."

"The Zampolit's observations are correct," concurred Mikhail Kharkov. "For it's to their advantage to retrieve the *Flying Kremlin*'s black box before anyone else does and reveals to the world the real cause of our beloved Premier's tragic passing."

"Sounds logical to me," reflected the senior lieutenant.

His glance still riveted on the flashing repeater screen, Sergei cautiously spoke. "Though this indeed might be the case, we must make certain to keep our minds open. Perhaps they've only been sent up into Baffin Bay to check on the contact that their SOSUS line picked up as we entered the Nares Strait."

"But why travel at such an extreme velocity?" countered the alert white-haired veteran. "At their current speed, their passive sensors will be all but useless except for listening to the crackling ice above and an occasional passing whale below. No, Captain, I tell you that the Imperialists are on a mission of a much greater magnitude. And to insure that they don't succeed, the *Neva* must intervene."

"And just how do you propose to do such a thing?"

questioned Sergei.

Mikhail Kharkov was quick to respond. "Though a well-placed torpedo would be the most logical solution, there's yet another way open to us, one that doesn't have such bellicose overtones. I say, ram them."

Sergei Markova was clearly astounded by this suggestion. "I strongly disagree, Admiral. It's much too early to determine the Sturgeon's exact mission. By intervening at this time, the *Neva* could very possibly be guilty of a flagrant overreaction that many might look at as a direct act of war."

"And what do you call shooting down the *Flying Kremlin,* Captain?" bitterly retorted the Admiral of the Fleet. "The Imperialists are the ones who started this whole thing. And now it's time to begin evening the score."

While considering these belligerent words, Sergei queried the seated sonar operator. "What's the contact's range, Chief Magadan?"

The technician efficiently addressed his keyboard and as his monitor screen flashed alive, crisply answered. "They've just broken the fifteen kilometer threshold, sir. At their current speed, intercept will be in another eighteen minutes."

"Why that still leaves us with plenty of time to set up the ambush," observed the admiral, a hint of impatience flavoring his tone. "Come to your senses, Captain, and take advantage of this one in a million opportunity that the fates have so kindly brought our way."

Quite aware that Mikhail Kharkov could easily try to pull rank on him if he so desired, Sergei decided upon a compromise. "Bring us down to loiter speed, Senior Lieutenant. Activate all stealth systems, and prepare the ship for a collision."

"Then you're going to go ahead with it?" queried the expectant admiral.

Sergei hesitated a moment before responding. "Though I'm still not totally convinced the Americans have been sent here for the same purpose we were sent, circumspection forces me to keep our options open. If the *Sturgeon* is indeed headed for Lancaster Sound, she will be altering course shortly, just as we were about to do when we first picked them up. If such a course change does in fact occur, then the *Neva* will close in at once to stop the Americans long before they're able to further interfere with our mission."

Relieved by what he was hearing, the Admiral of the Fleet grinned. "I knew that the Motherland could count on you, Captain Markova. You are a credit to your uniform."

Ignoring this superfluous remark, Sergei addressed his senior lieutenant. "Prepare a proper intercept vector should the American's course turn westward, Viktor. A glancing blow of our bow directed at the stern portion of the Sturgeon should cause enough damage in their engine room to send them topside for repairs."

As Viktor Belenko turned to the chart table, the Admiral of the Fleet beckoned Sergei to join him at the vacant weapon's console.

"Something tells me you've had experience in carrying out such an unorthodox maneuver before, Captain. If I remember correctly, at the conclusion of the *Neva*'s second patrol you returned to Polyarny with a peculiar dent in your ship's reinforced bow. I believe your log mentioned something about striking an uncharted coral reef while cruising deep below the Mediterranean south of Mallorca. At the time I read your report, two things immediately came to mind. The first was that to my knowledge coral is not indigenous

223

to that portion of the Mediterranean. And the second, I couldn't help but remember the *New York Times* clipping I had just received telling of an American 688 class submarine that had been involved in a serious underwater collision with an unidentified object in these same waters. I believe that poor 688 had to be towed back to the US navy base at Sicily afterward. Some say it was a miracle it was even able to ascend after it had been so violently struck. Now I wonder what on earth could have hit them like that?"

As he patiently awaited a response, Kharkov studied the face of the young captain much as a father would his son's. Unable to escape the veteran's clever trap, Sergei managed the barest of smiles.

"Such an incident is certainly news to me, Admiral. Although who knows, maybe it wasn't a reef that we struck after all."

"No, comrade, perhaps it wasn't." The white-haired veteran couldn't help but respect the young officer's coolness under fire.

"The contact is cutting its forward speed!" It was the voice of the excited sonar operator.

Quick to return to the console, both Sergei Markova and Mikhail Kharkov studied the repeater screen. The electronic line showing the contact's screw turns had evened out dramatically, and it was obvious that the sub had substantially cut its forward velocity.

"Maybe they've spotted us," offered the Zampolit, who had vigilantly remained at the sonar operator's side.

"I don't see how they could," returned the captain. "Right now the *Neva*'s practically dead in the water. With our stealth system in operation, they would have to go active to even have a chance of locating us. And with our anechoic tiles in place, there's a good chance even that tactic wouldn't be fruitful."

"Maybe they've known our position all along, and have only been playing with us," the paranoid Political Officer said.

Sergei looked out to the repeater screen and replied, "That's even more unlikely, Comrade Zinyagin. If you ask me, I say that within the next sixty seconds the Yankee skipper is going to reveal his intentions once and for all."

Barely a half minute later, this prophetic remark came true when the sonar operator pressed his headphones tightly over his ears and then called out loudly for all to clearly hear, "They're changing course, Captain! The new bearing is two-six-zero."

"Why that's almost due west!" exclaimed the admiral. "I told you they'd be headed for Lancaster Sound."

"It looks like they're after the black box all right," observed the ship's captain as he thoughtfully stroked his square chin. "Senior Lieutenant, put that intercept vector into the navigation computer right now. Those Yankee bastards don't realize it as yet, but they've come as close to spoiling our mission as they're going to get!"

"And this Dr. Lansing is that portion of the ship we fondly call Defiance Power and Light. You just saw the reactor compartment. This is where it's controlled from, and where the resulting energy is transformed into steam to turn our propellers and electricity to run almost everything else."

Matt Colter stepped aside and beckoned his attractive guest to enter the maneuvering room before him. Laurie Lansing readily did so, and soon found herself in a relatively cramped compartment dominated by a massive console filled with dozens of gauges, switches, and dials. Three seated figures were responsible for monitoring these instruments, though the newcomer's entrance momentarily diverted their attention from them.

Quick to bring the three back in line was the deep, firm voice that emanated from the room's shadows. "What the hell's the matter with you guys? Get your eyes back on the instruments where they belong or you bums will never qualify!"

As his men instantly complied, the tall, dark, solidly built figure of Lieutenant Frystak stepped forward to greet his guests. "Good morning, Captain. And I presume that this is Dr. Lansing?"

"You presume right," replied the civilian as she accepted the officer's warm handshake. "I'm sorry about the interruption."

"Lieutenant Frystak and his men here are the guys I rely on to keep the heart of this ship pumping," said the captain. "And speaking of the devil, so far you've given me everything I've asked for and then some, Lieutenant."

Frystak affectionately patted a nearby instrument panel. "It's all in a day's work, Captain. We were able to survive our little disaster drill and keep on line even as we reacted to that simulated steam leak in the main condenser and the fire in the auxilliary turbine unit."

"So I noticed," returned the captain. "You and your men deserve a hearty job well done."

Frystak humbly nodded. "Thanks, Captain. And by the way Dr. Lansing, how is your work progressing?"

Laurie instantly liked the straightforward engineering officer, who reminded her of a college schoolmate. "We'll know for sure soon enough, once the captain gives the order to surface. As of this moment, all the installation and reprogramming have been completed. Now begins the hard part, the waiting."

"Any new system is going to have its bugs," reflected Frystak. "If the theory's correct, you'll get it right eventually." .

"I hope a lot sooner than that," retorted Laurie.

Matt Colter grinned. "If Lieutenant Frystak and his men can keep these engines purring away as they have been, you'll have that chance soon enough, Doctor. Now, how about having a look at the engine room? I'm sure the men there won't mind a little company, will they, Lieutenant?"

Well aware of the crew's undying curiosity whenever the subject of their civilian passenger came up, Frystak responded. "I don't think they'll mind at all, Captain. Shall I ring the chief and let him know that you're coming?"

Shaking his head that this wouldn't be necessary, Colter escorted his guest through the aft hatchway. This brought them directly into the engine room. The cavernous compartment was brightly lit, and Laurie could clearly view the massive gray turbines and the vessel's single propeller shaft. Though the size of the equipment was impressive, its quietness was even more so.

"I thought it would be a lot noisier in here, Captain. And with all this heavy machinery crowded together like it is, what would happen if something went wrong with one of the machines buried on the bottom of all that gear?"

Matt Colter was quick with an answer. "Practically every piece of heavy machinery you see before you can be hoisted out with a block and tackle and subsequently repaired. From the *Nautilus* onward, this was a feature each one of our nuclear subs was designed around. I've seen the wooden scale models myself, that were built showing each piece of equipment and every square inch of piping in this compartment. Such mock-ups were constructed to make certain that no piece of equipment was inaccessible."

By this time, a small group of grease-stained sailors had realized they had company. As they did their best to tidy themselves up, they hesitantly approached the newcomers. Leading this group forward was a potbellied, crew-cut sailor wearing a filthy white T-shirt.

"Good morning to ya', Captain," the first man said as he hitched up his trousers and tucked in the tail of his T-shirt.

Noting that the chief and his crew were unusually quiet and reserved, Matt Colter proceeded with the introductions. "Dr. Lansing, I'd like you to meet Chief Engineer Joe Cunnetto and the best bunch of grease monkeys in the entire US Navy."

Only after he was certain his palms were clean did the chief shyly step forward and offer his hand. "Me and the boys would like to welcome you aboard the *Defiance*, Doc Lansing. Please feel free to visit anytime, day or night, that you get the hankering."

"Why thank you, Chief," Laurie responded. Then she pointed toward the compartment's aft bulkhead. "Do you mind if I take a look at the way the shaft penetrates the hull? I've always wondered what type of seals you utilized to keep the sea out."

Genuinely surprised by this request, Chief Cunnetto beamed proudly. "Why of course, Doc. I'd love to show you."

His men were gathered in a tight group close behind the chief, and when Cunnetto pivoted he practically tripped right over them. "Don't you good-for-nothings have some work to do? At the very least you could give a guy a little breathing room," the chief complained.

Matt Colter fought to hold back his laughter as the

228

sailors proceeded to trip over each other while they attempted to disperse. Yet the captain's moment of levity was abruptly cut short by a piercing, high-pitched warbling tone, whose distinctive sound filled Colter with instant dread.

"It's the collision alarm!" cried the chief at the top of his lungs. "To your stations, men!"

Madly grabbing out for the nearest intercom hand-set, the captain took in the frantic words of the *Defiance*'s current OOD, Lieutenant David Sanger.

"It's another submarine, Captain! It came up on us from out of nowhere and—"

The OOD's report was cut short by a bone-jarring collision that sent Matt Colter crashing hard to the deck. A deafening, screeching noise filled the engine room as the lights blinked off and the *Defiance* canted hard on to its left side. Blindly groping out in the darkness for something solid to hold on to, Colter slid hard into a prone figure pinned up against the iron railing that lined that portion of the elevated catwalk. As he tightly gripped this figure's lean torso in an effort to keep from sliding off the passageway altogether and go slamming into the machinery stored below, an unfamiliar perfumed scent met his nostrils. And in that instant he realized that his savior was none other than Dr. Laurie Lansing.

Loosening his grip a bit, Colter knew he could do absolutely nothing until the hull stabilized and he could safely stand. Yet he did manage to whisper some words of encouragement to the woman he found himself so desperately clinging to.

"Hang in there, Doctor. This ship's built tough and we're not licked just yet."

As if to emphasize these words, the emergency lights popped on, and the first thing Matt Colter's eyes were able to focus on was the pale, terror-filled face of his civilian passenger. Doing his best to control his own panic, the captain managed a brave smile.

"At least we've still got lights," he said. "That means that our power system is still on line. Now if only our hull stayed in one piece."

The sickening sound of rushing water met his practiced ears, and Colter's gut tightened. The deck having finally stabilized beneath them, the captain painfully got to his knees and struggled to stand erect. Bruised but still in one piece, he helped the civilian to stand.

Behind them, the deep voice of Chief Cunnetto rose strong and firm. "It looks like the port circ pump has busted loose, men, and we're taking in water. Get those bilge pumps going, Hardesty! And you, Mulroney, quit cowering like a baby and go get a tarp to cover the pump casing motor with, or it'll be completely ruined!"

Imagining similar scenes occurring throughout the *Defiance,* the ship's captain felt a new self-confidence. At long last, the thousands of hours of endless practice drills would finally pay off as the men reacted to save the ship by pure rote.

With one eye on the geyser that was erupting out of the left side of the engine room, Colter limped over to the intercom.

"Control room, this is the captain. Do you have a damage report as yet?"

There was a long pause that was eventually broken by a breathless, high-pitched voice. "This is Ensign Mitchell, sir. Lieutenant Sanger is being treated for a bad gash he suffered on his forehead, and I've taken over as OOD until the XO shows up."

Ensign Ed Mitchell was the ship's supply officer and was fresh out of sub school. Far from being a seasoned veteran, the ship's junior-most officer was suddenly being cast into a starring role.

"What do you hear from the other stations, Ensign?" queried the anxious captain.

"It looks like we rode out the collision in one piece, sir. Though we're still waiting to hear from the engine room where the majority of the blow was taken."

The supply officer's report was met by a long sigh of relief on Colter's part. "Well you're hearing from the engine room right now, Ensign. It appears that we've lost our port circ pump, and we're taking in a lot of water. I don't think the bilge pumps are going to be able to handle this flooding, so I'm ordering an emergency surface."

"But the ice, Captain," the confused supply officer responded.

Just as Mitchell was about to continue, another individual replaced him at the microphone. The voice Colter now heard was steady and most familiar.

"Skipper, it's the XO. Sorry about the delay in getting up here, but I had to stop and do a little first-aid work while picking my way to the bridge from the wardroom."

"Anything serious?" questioned the captain.

"Just some nasty cuts and bruises, Skipper. They'll live. What about you? And what's this I hear about us taking in water?"

With his glance locked on the frantic efforts of the chief and his men as they tried to stem the rush of flooding water, Matt Colter barked into the intercom. "It's the port circ pump, Al. The chief's on it now, but it's flooding pretty badly and I suggest an immediate emergency ascent."

"Skipper, as of ten minutes ago, we had a pretty thick sheet of ice above us. Even if we did take her up, there's no telling how close the nearest lead would be."

Redirecting his gaze to take in the nearby figure of Dr. Lansing, Colter responded. "This is as good a time as any to give that new laser Fathometer a try, Al."

"Can't do, Skipper. The Nav computers are still out, and without them that device is useless."

"Well, crank up the old ice machine, and pray that there's some open water close by. I'll be up to join you as soon as I let the chief in on what we intend to do. And then I'm going to want to know what in the hell it was that hit us."

Briefly catching Laurie Lansing's worried stare, Matt Colter rushed down into the engine room's flooded confines as the fight to save the *Defiance* began in earnest.

Chapter Eleven

The Arctic Rangers' course took them to the northwest, out of the small community of Arctic Bay and over the frozen waters of Admiralty Inlet. Because of the constantly blowing snow, visibility was poor, and they were forced to travel at a minimum speed in order to keep the convoy of six snowmobiles and the single dogsled within sight of each other.

Hunched down over the steering wheel of the second vehicle in line, Jack Redmond did his best to stay as close to the rear runners of the lead sled as possible. Considering his relative inexperience, his sergeant-major was doing an excellent job keeping the dogs moving. Yet even then the snowcats that followed progressed at only a fraction of the speed they were capable of attaining.

So far, this cautious approach had saved them from certain disaster on two separate occasions. The first of these incidents took place as they were traveling over a particularly smooth portion of the frozen inlet. Though the blizzard was still blowing in all its fury, the going here was fast, and they were able to clip along at a good ten kilometers per hour.

Redmond was mentally calculating that if they could keep up this pace for the rest of the journey they could be at their intended destination in another eight hours. He had initially anticipated a journey of twice this duration. Yet he knew better than to get his hopes up, for the portion of the trip that took them over solid ground was still to come. Here they would have to contend not only with ice and snow but with dangerous crevasses and other geological irregularities.

The senior commando was in the midst of such a pondering when the sled before him unexpectedly ground to a halt. Reacting as quickly as possible, Redmond released the throttle and hit the hand brake. An uncontrolled skid followed, during which time his snowcat missed striking the edge of the sled by only a few centimeters. Sheer instinct had made him steer into the skid, and after an anxious few moments the brakes had finally held.

His limbs were still trembling as he carefully opened up the throttle and returned to the lead sled's side. He found Cliff Ano standing beside the dogs and peering out into the veil of white that lay before them.

"I don't like it, Lieutenant. The dogs have gotten real skittish lately, and it's an effort just to keep them moving," observed the heavily bundled Inuit.

Shouting to be heard over the wind, Redmond replied. "Maybe they're just tired."

His sergeant-major shook his head. "It's not that, Lieutenant. They seem to be consciously holding themselves back. I think there's open water up ahead."

"Well, there's only one way to see if that's the case," returned the senior commando. He pivoted and shouted to the driver of the snowcat parked immediately behind them. "Corporal Eviki, I want you to scout ahead on foot. Go out about a quarter of a kilometer, and be extra cautious as there's a chance there's open water somewhere ahead of us. Take Private Etah with you, just in case you run into any trouble. And watch your compass reading so that you can find your way back!"

As the two full-blooded Inuit climbed off the snow-cat and began their exploratory trek, Redmond made a hasty examination of the rest of the squad. Since the majority of them were also Inuit, the raw elements really didn't bother them that much. Their army-issue clothing was first rate, and they were certainly no strangers to such a snow squall. Utilizing the line of tracked vehicles as a windbreak, they gathered together with their backs to the powerful gusts. Several of them even managed to light up cigarettes.

Jack Redmond was toying with the idea of setting up the receiver to see if they could pick up the homing beacon as yet when the two scouts arrived back at camp. With white tendrils of breath streaming from his nose and mouth, Corporal Jim Eviki revealed the outcome of their short search.

"There's water out there sure enough, Lieutenant. It's less than an eighth of a kilometer ahead, and seems to stretch for a good distance."

"So your dogs were right." Redmond turned to his sergeant-major.

"But my uncle was wrong," retorted Cliff Ano. "He seemed to think the inlet would remain solidly frozen until the spring thaw."

"Go easy on him, Sergeant-Major," advised Redmond. "After all, it was his team that saved our necks. Besides, it's common knowledge any frozen body of water up here is subject to open leads, no matter how cold the temperature might get."

"Where do we go from here?" questioned the corporal.

Redmond answered firmly. "We go north, and skirt the open water until we come across some solid footing."

As it turned out, they were forced to travel for two more hours in this direction before finding the type of flat, icy terrain that allowed them to continue on their original course. Here their pace once again quickened, though the dogs took it upon themselves to institute yet another abrupt change in direction as they approached the western shore of the inlet.

Steering hard to the left to follow the sled, Redmond soon saw for himself why the dogs had turned this way. For a ridge had formed in this portion of the ice, and if they had remained on their original course, they would have smacked right into it.

Ever thankful to have such a reliable, intuitive team leading the way, Redmond and his men completed their transit of the inlet when they came to an icy, boulder-strewn shoreline. In the shelter of these rocks they broke for lunch.

Over a hot thermos of tea, Redmond conferred with his second in command. "Well, we're almost halfway there, Sergeant-Major."

"But this is where the going gets tough," returned the Inuit. "Once we pick our way over these rocks, there's a valley on the other side that practically splits the peninsula in half. Uncle says we'll do best by following this ravine all the way to Lancaster Sound. He warned us to be on the lookout for open crevasses here. And it's also wise to remember that this area is known for its high concentration of polar bears and wolves."

"It's not the wildlife that scares me," observed Redmond. "Is it my imagination, or has this storm further intensified since we stopped here?"

Dreamily gazing out at the frozen expanse of water they had just crossed, Cliff Ano thoughtfully replied, "This is the type of weather my ancestors greeted with open arms. Because such extreme conditions made hunting impossible, they passed the time snuggled warmly in their snowhouses, telling stories, chewing away on frozen meat, and waiting for the clouds to vent themselves."

"Sounds enticing," said Redmond. "But duty calls. Shall we get on with it, Sergeant-Major?"

Hurriedly finishing off their tea, the two commandoes ordered their men to break camp. With little level ground to follow, they were forced to pick up their snowmobiles and carry them over the rocky terrain. Cliff Ano was able to manage his lightweight sled all on his own, while his harnessed dogs noisily followed at his heels.

Because of the slippery footing, their progress was slow. Frequent rest stops were needed because of the great weight of their equipment. And none of the twenty-four commandoes was disappointed when they finally reached the valley they had been searching for.

With the dogsled once again taking the lead, the Arctic Rangers began their way northward. Though the snow was deep here, visibility was somewhat better. Redmond attributed this welcome fact to the mountainous spine that lay to their left and acted as a partial windbreak.

Able to safely increase the distance between the vehicles at this point, the column twisted its way down the valley's snow-covered floor. They had accomplished over an hour's worth of uninterrupted travel when Cliff Ano held up his right hand and pulled his sled to a halt. Quick to go to his side was Jack Redmond.

"What's the matter, Sergeant-Major?"

The Inuit answered while carefully scanning the surrounding foothills. "The dogs are acting up again, Lieutenant."

"Could it be a crevasse?" quizzed Redmond.

"I doubt it," returned the Inuit. "The footing here is fairly firm and this section of the valley appears to be geologically stable."

It was at that moment that a high-pitched, mournful cry sounded in the distance. This brought an immediate response from the dogs in the sled team. They began barking and yelping.

"Wolves!" exclaimed Cliff Ano. "And they're close."

Jack Redmond surveyed the nearby hills. "Should we break out the rifles?"

"They wouldn't dare bother us while we're still moving," the Inuit answered. "Although when we bed down for the night, it's another story."

Several additional banshee-like cries resonated through the frigid air and Redmond commented. "Let's get the hell out of here, Sergeant-Major. This place gives me the creeps."

With a single crack of his whip, the Inuit got his team moving. Following in a straight line behind him were the six snowcats, their engines constantly sputtering and whining.

Minutes later, as they rounded a broad bend, Cliff Ano once more held up his hand and halted the caravan. Yet this time as Redmond joined his subordinate, one look at the conglomeration of beasts that had gathered on the floor of the valley before them told him the reason for this abrupt stop.

Approximately one-quarter of a kilometer away, was a large herd of musk oxen. Jack Redmond had once seen such beasts in a zoo, but this was his first sighting of them in the wild. Their long, glossy fur blowing in the still breeze, and their characteristic curved horns appearing much like those of a cape buffalo, they seemed to be standing in a straight line, shoulder to shoulder and flank to flank. A single large bull was slightly forward of the bunch, his attention locked on some sort of disturbance taking place along the ridge of broken rock on the west side of the valley. It proved to be Cliff Ano who pointed to this ridge and explained precisely what was occurring.

"There are wolves over there. The musk oxen have formed a defensive formation and are awaiting an attack."

"Those brutes must weigh well over six hundred pounds each, and the points of their horns look razor sharp. Do the wolves even stand a chance?" questioned Redmond.

The Inuit's eyes glistened. "The wolves might be smaller physically, but they're patient and opportunistic. What they'll attempt to do is get behind one of the charging musk oxen and cut it off from the herd. Another favorite tactic is to sprint into a momentary opening and snatch a calf."

The sled dogs began yelping madly when a pack of over a dozen gray wolves trotted out from behind the rock-strewn ravine where they had been gathered. Ignoring this racket, the shaggy predators began slowly closing in on the herd. The lead bull bellowed in response to this movement, and the musk oxen shifted their positions, gathering in a roughly symmetrical formation, the calves and yearlings wedged in between the adults.

The wall of outward-pointed horns looked formidable, yet this didn't appear to intimidate the wolves, who continued creeping forward with short, furtive steps. When they finally attacked, it was with such

239

swiftness that Jack Redmond nearly missed it. It all started with a feint by several of the largest wolves. When the dominant bull charged forward to repulse them, the rest of the wolf pack darted into the herd with a snarling, lightninglike ferocity. To a chorus of growls and bellows, the valley floor erupted in a primal struggle for survival. And when the blowing snow cleared, the wolves could be seen trotting off triumphantly, dragging a young yearling in their viselike jaws.

"And only the strong shall survive," reflected Jack Redmond as he watched the wolfpack disappear behind the ridge to initiate their blood feast. Well aware that this basic law of nature applied to them as well, the senior commando silently lifted his hand and beckoned his men forward to continue their mission.

Less than a hundred miles north of this wilderness valley, the crew of the *Sierra* class attack submarine were in the midst of a jubilant celebration. The festivities were particularly joyous in the sub's wardroom, where a bottle of Ukrainian champagne was being passed around compliments of Admiral of the Fleet Kharkov.

"And here's to our brave captain, who made this great victory possible!" toasted the white-haired veteran. "To your health, Sergei Markova, and to that of your family."

"Here, here," added Viktor Belenko as he put his glass to his lips and sipped on the slightly sweet, effervescent beverage. As an old friend of the *Neva*'s captain, Viktor knew that Sergei Markova was not the type of fellow who liked the limelight. Thus, to put his blushing comrade at ease, the senior lieutenant stood to propose a countertoast.

"And here's to Admiral of the Fleet Mikhail Kharkov. For decades you have selflessly served the Motherland, and it is largely because of your visionary efforts that vessels such as the *Neva* exist. May health and happiness be with you always!"

This flowery toast served its purpose as all eyes shifted to the head of the table. The old-timer was grinning from ear to ear as the *Neva*'s Zampolit asked, "Admiral, do you really think that little love tap of ours was enough to put the Imperialist warship out of commission?"

"Love tap, comrade?" Kharkov repeated incredulously. "I would say it was a little more than that, Comrade Zinyagin. Since it appears that our blow caught the *Sturgeon* squarely in its engine room, I'd say it will take a miracle just for the Yankees to get to the surface, let alone continue with their mission. Don't you agree, Captain?"

Sergei Markova hesitated a moment before answering. "It's readily apparent that we hit them with enough force to cause severe internal damage. Yet their hull remained intact, and since the Americans build a sturdy vessel with an assortment of redundant systems, I'd say it's still too early to definitely count them out."

"Come now, Captain. Aren't you being a bit of a pessimist? We hit them square in the stern, and at last report they were just lying there dead in the water."

The admiral's remarks did little to change Sergei's mind. "If I know the scrappy Americans, they're just taking a moment to lick their wounds. With a bit of luck and a lot of hard work, they'll get their vessel operational once more. And this time there will be revenge in their hearts."

"Then maybe we'd better go back and finish them off with a couple of torpedoes," the concerned Political Officer suggested.

"Nonsense!" barked Mikhail Kharkov. "We've wasted enough valuable time on this crippled vessel, and now a greater mission calls us onward. At our present course and rate of speed, we should be at the northern edge of the Brodeur Peninsula within the next two hours. Then all we have to do is ascend to the surface, activate the homing receiver, triangulate a fix, and march out to retrieve the device whose analysis will change the very world as we now know it. At long last the workers of the planet will be freed, and all men will share equally in the one, great Socialistic state that will follow. Just think of it, comrades, the glorious dreams of the Motherland's founding fathers will at long last be realized!"

An excited murmur rose from the admiral's captive audience. All lifted up their glasses to drink to this day's coming. Yet two of those present at the table, and were conspicuously somber. Both Sergei Markova and Viktor Belenko knew that their mission still had a long way to go. Beyond the fact that they would soon have to be surfacing in dangerous pack-ice conditions to search for a device that could be in any number of remote places, the two senior officers shared a single concern. Regardless of what the admiral had said, the American *Sturgeon* class submarine was still a very real threat. Though slow to anger, once their ire was provoked, the United States Navy was no force to take lightly. Of this fact, they were certain!

Beneath another portion of the frozen sea, the men of the USS *Defiance* valiantly fought to bring their ship back from the threshold of destruction. This tireless effort was particularly intense in the ship's control room, where Captain Matt Colter and his

Executive Officer huddled over a normally insignificant console located behind the chart table. This device was designed around a rotating drum onto which a piece of graph paper was continually fed. Onto this paper a hissing stylus drew a jagged pattern which was activated as a pulse of intense sound energy directed upward to the surface. A thin black line meant open water above. Yet for the last half hour, the only pattern visible was an agitated vertical series, meaning the presence of pack ice topside.

"I don't like the way this looks, Al," whispered the captain. "The majority of this ice is at least ten feet thick, with some of those inverted ridges extending thirty feet or more."

"The odds are we've got to come across an opening eventually, Skipper. After all, this isn't the frigging North Pole."

The captain sighed. "It might as well be as far as the *Defiance* is concerned. With half our power plant shut down because of that busted circ pump, we'll be fortunate to crawl out of here by spring."

"Our luck's going to change, Skipper, just you watch. We'll find a nice wide polynya, and the chief and his men will have that pump fixed in no time flat. And then we can go after the Red bastards responsible for almost giving us the deep six."

"Let's just start off by finding some open water," the captain suggested.

As Colter stood up to stretch his back, he spotted Laurie Lansing standing beside the chart table, intently watching them.

"Feeling better, Doctor?" greeted Colter.

The civilian meekly nodded. "I guess so, Captain. You know, I've never been so scared in my life."

"I know what you mean," returned Colter. "I wish I could say that you get used to it, but I'd be a liar if I did. Oh, and by the way, thanks for being in the proverbial right place at the right time back in the engine room. If you weren't there for me to grab onto, there's no telling what would 'have happened if I missed that handrail."

"I'm just glad to help out in any way that I can, Captain. Though I certainly wish your men would hurry up and get that Nav computer back on line. I can't tell you how frustrating it is for me to stand here and watch you relying on a piece of outdated equipment designed over thirty years ago. With the laser scanners in operation, surely we would have found a polynya by now."

"Skipper, I think we might be on to something," interrupted the XO.

Both Matt Colter and Laurie Lansing arrived at the ice machine in time to see a thin solid line flow off the head of the stylus.

"It's an open lead all right," observed the civilian. "And a big one at that."

"All stop!" ordered the captain firmly. "Prepare to surface."

Back in the ship's engine room, this command was met with a sigh of relief. No one was happier that Chief Joe Cunnetto, as the roar of venting ballast sent the now lightened vessel ballooning toward the surface. There was no secret that there was ice topside, and the tension was thick as the chief prayed that the opening the Skipper had picked was large enough for the *Defiance* to safely fit in.

Another blast of ballast sounded in the distance and this time the boat seemed to leap upward. This alien sensation all too soon passed, to be replaced by the shrill ringing of the nearby intercom.

"Chief here . . . You bet, Captain. We'll have that pump fixed in less than six hours, or I'll personally donate all my retirement to the Navy scholarship fund. . . . I'll do that, Captain. And don't forget to get some fresh air for me."

As he hung up the handset, the portly chief turned to address his motley bunch of assistants. "All right, you shirkers, the time for fun and games is over. We're on the surface now, and there's work to be done. So let's get on with it!"

A relieved cheer broke from his shipmates' lips as they gratefully rolled up their sleeves and turned to begin the repairs. The damaged pump was a vital piece of machinery that was responsible for circulating the water necessary to turn the blades of the ship's turbines. To get to it, their first task was to remove the storage lockers, wires, and pipes that were set above the pump. Then a block and tackle would be rigged to hoist up the motor itself. After that was done the real repairs would begin.

The clatter of tools was music to the chief's ears, as he climbed down to give his men a hand. For he had promised the captain that he would have the job completed in six hours' time, and to Joe Cunnetto, his word wasn't something he gave lightly.

While the engine-room crew industriously immersed themselves in their work, three parka-clad figures climbed up into the vessel's exposed sail. They were met by a shrieking, frigid wind that sent tiny spears of flying ice whipping through the air with near lethal velocity. Turning their backs to these howling gusts, the trio focused their gazes on the surrounding landscape. For as far as they could see stretched a solid white line of hummocked icehills and contorted pressure ridges. The only clear water visible was that which surrounded the *Defiance*. With barely enough room to fit another similar-sized vessel at their side, the polynya was just beginning to ice over.

For the ice was far from a static environment, and the constant deep-throated grinding noise that rose beyond that of the wind was proof that the ice pack was in constant motion.

Shivering in the bitter cold, Lieutenant Commander Al Layman said, "Damn, and I thought Buffalo was cold!"

"What do you mean, cold?" countered Matt Colter as he bent down to check the thermometer. "Why it's only twenty-five degrees below zero, and it's not even winter yet!"

Turning his attention to the figure at his other side, the captain queried. "What do you think of your first view of the ice, Dr. Lansing?"

She had to practically scream to be heard over the howling wind. "It's incredibly beautiful and threatening all at the same time."

"That it is," agreed Matt Colter, who added, "It's hard to think of the Arctic as a desert, but as you well know it's one of the driest regions on the planet, with a total yearly precipitation of less than ten inches. From what I understand, it's because such cold air can carry little moisture."

"You're absolutely correct," returned the scientist. "Back in the lab, we tried to create these extreme conditions artificially, and though we could handle the temperature, we had a lot of trouble simulating the ice. The Arctic pack ice is extremely hard because the salt has had time to drain out of it."

"I can personally vouch for that," replied Colter. "You should have seen how the ice sheared the welded navigational beacon right off our rudder during our last encounter with it. The thing looked like it had been surgically cut off."

A high-pitched whine suddenly sounded behind them, and the XO turned to identify this noise. "Here comes the receiver, Skipper. I sure hope it holds together in this wind and all."

The thick, whiplike antenna rose upward from the interior portion of the sail. Matt Colter looked up and saw it wildly quivering in the powerful gusts.

"She'll hold, all right. I just hope we're close enough to that black box to pick up its homing signal. Otherwise, we could be up here for God knows how long."

"Not me, Skipper," returned the XO. "If it's all right with you, I'd like permission to go below before my mustache drops off. Even with all these layers of clothing, I'm freezing!"

The captain was quick to consent. "I think I've taken enough punishment myself. Will you join us, Doctor?"

Laurie Lansing's teeth were chattering so badly that she didn't even bother to respond, but merely turned for the ladder that would convey her back to the blessed warmth of the ship's interior.

Five minutes later, Matt Colter was in the process of making the rounds of the control room with a steaming hot mug of coffee in hand, when he received word that the engine-room crew had begun hoisting up the damaged pump. It wasn't long afterward that the compartment filled with a distant, deep-throated booming noise that sounded much like the report of an exploding artillery shell. When this mysterious sound continued, Colter hurriedly threw on his parka and once again climbed up into the exposed sail.

He was greeted by a familiar blast of frigid air, and as he turned his back to it, his gaze locked in on the surrounding ice pack and he couldn't help but gasp at what he saw there. The ice seemed to have moved at least twenty yards closer to the *Defiance* since his last trip topside!

Another explosive crack sounded in the distance, this time with an even greater intensity. A grating, shrieking moan followed, and Colter realized that what he was hearing was the sound of the ever-shifting pack ice as it gradually closed in on them. There were many reports of ships trapped in such ice. Some of the vessels were locked in for months, while the less fortunate ones had their hulls crushed by the immense forces at work.

Because of the unique nature of the *Defiance's* design, all Colter had to do was give a single order to send the sub plunging into the relative safety of the depths. But this would mean forcing the engine-room crew to halt their repair effort and then having them resecure the loose equipment. This would leave them with only half their propulsion system on line. And since there was no telling when the next polynya would be encountered, the sub could be in such a crippled state for an indefinite length of time.

Yet if he didn't order them to submerge, could Chief Cunnetto and his men finish their work before the surrounding ice had the *Defiance* in its fatal grip? It was a gamble either way he looked at it, and Colter struggled to summon the wisdom to make the correct decision. So deep were his ponderings that he didn't even notice when someone joined him on the sail.

"The noise is getting pretty bad inside the ship, Skipper," observed the XO. "Is it coming from the ice?"

Colter nodded and pointed toward the open water off their starboard bow. "It appears the lead is slowly closing. There's a pressure ridge over there that only formed in the last couple of minutes. It's obvious that this entire section of ice is under tremendous pressure, and I don't like the idea of having the *Defiance* stuck smack in the middle of it."

"Shall I inform the chief to halt work and secure the engine room, Skipper? We can be under this stuff in a couple of minutes flat."

A deafening, high-pitched shriek rose above the constant howl of the gusting wind, and Colter had to practically scream at the top of his lungs to be heard. "I hate to do it to them, but I don't think we have much of a choice right now. Under the circumstances, I think it's best if I run down there and tell them myself."

"You do that, Skipper. I'll tough it out, and keep an eye on things from up here."

With a fluid ease, Colter climbed down the sail's internal ladder, ducked into the control room, and began to make his way aft, without even bothering to take off his parka. Inside the ship, the noise of the fracturing ice was further amplified, and the deck was beginning to vibrate with the resulting shockwaves. This vibration intensified as the captain rushed into the engine room and approached the potbellied, T-shirted figure, working on the damaged pump with a large wrench.

"Chief, I'm afraid I'm going to have to order you to suspend your repair effort. The lead we picked to surface in is rapidly closing in on us, and I have no choice but to take us under."

"So that's what all that infernal noise is about," observed the grease-stained chief engineer. "And here I thought it was the hordes of hell playing a little Arctic lullaby on the *Defiance*'s hull. I'll have this gear stashed and secured in five minutes, sir."

"Thanks, Chief," returned the captain as he turned to head for the control room.

Noting that there wasn't the merest hint of complaint in the chief's response, even though his work was now to be doubled, Colter passed through maneuvering and climbed up to the deck above. It was as he hurriedly crossed through the wardroom that he realized the noise of the fracturing ice could no longer be heard. This fact was most apparent as he climbed back up to the sail and was met only by the incessant howling of the wind and the excited voice of his XO.

"It stopped, Skipper!"

"So I've noticed, Al. It looks to me like those pressure ridges have diminished some."

"They have, Skipper. And not only that, the ice actually seems to be receding."

Colter looked out to the ever-widening channel of open water that surrounded them and cursed angrily. "Damn it! And I just got through telling the chief to close up shop."

"You never know, Skipper. The ice might just start moving in once again."

Colter considered this observation and shook his head. "I don't think so, Al. As far as I'm concerned, this polynya is as good as any other. So I'm going to call the chief and have them start up again."

"Whatever you say, Skipper. I'll get him on the horn for you."

As the XO bent over and fumbled for the handset with his mittened hands, Matt Colter stared out at the ice pack. Nothing was as dangerous as a captain who had trouble making up his mind. This was the quickest way to lose a crew's confidence, and once this occurred, a successful command was all but impossible.

Yet an officer also had to be open to the constantly changing variables that influenced a decision, and had to be unafraid to change his mind when new facts were presented to him. Thus, Matt Colter had few reservations as he closely cupped the intercom to his lips and informed the Chief to resume the repair effort.

During this entire sequence of events, the two senior officers were all but oblivious to the industrious efforts of the vessel's radio man. Locked deep within the bowels of the *Defiance,* behind an acoustically padded, sealed doorway, Petty Officer Jules Thornton was about to initiate his second consecutive duty shift. Though a junior rating was all set to relieve him, Thornton would have none of it. Well aware of the unique nature of their mission, the Chicago native wanted to spend as much time as possible monitoring the recently activated receiver.

This process was especially important now that they were on the surface. At long last the antenna had been fully extended, and he could begin listening for the homing beacon that had sent them up to these frozen waters.

Because the cockpit voice recorder they had been sent to retrieve was Soviet in origin, there was still some question as to the exact frequency it would be transmitting on. Thus Thornton was forced to monitor a wide variety of channels in the hope that the proper one would eventually be chanced upon.

With a pair of bulky headphones covering his ears, the senior radioman hunched over his console. As he routinely flipped through the frequency selection knob, he closed his eyes in order to focus his attention solely on the static-filled signals that were being sucked into the receiver.

For as long as he could remember, radios had always fascinated him. As a Cub Scout he had built his own crystal set, and by his eighteenth birthday Jules was a licensed ham operator. To further follow his fascination, he got a job at an FM radio station based in Glenview, Illinois. There he could indulge himself to his heart's content on a wide variety of excellent equipment, the upkeep of which was his responsibility.

It was during a radio interview that he met a commander stationed at the nearby Glenview Naval Air Station. Already looking for additional challenge, Jules followed up on the officer's invitation and visited the base on his first day off. As it turned out, the sophisticated radio gear he was soon introduced to was the type of equipment he had always dreamed about. And a week later he had enlisted, and was soon in basic training.

Jules picked submarine duty because communications were such a vital part of such a warship's operations. The very nature of seawater refracted and diffracted the majority of radio signals sent into it. Since only signals of a very low frequency could penetrate the depths, the systems were geared to utilize these. To cover depths of up to fifty feet, the VLF—very low frequency—bands were put into use, while deeper operations necessitated the use of the ELF (extra low frequency) channels. Since submarines desired to initiate their patrols as deep as possible to avoid detection, these latter ELF bands were ideal. Yet there was one major problem: such frequencies transmitted data at a very slow rate, with some three-letter codes taking up to fifteen minutes to go from sender to receiver.

In addition to land-based communications, the submarine could also be contacted by TACAMO, take charge and move out, a Lockheed EC-13OA aircraft that served as an airborne relay station. In the wake of such a plane trailed a six-and-a-half-mile-long antenna that could broadcast on a variety of wave lengths. Communications buoys were yet another method of establishing contact, and could be dropped from a passing ship or a suitably equipped aircraft.

While in Navy radio school, Jules learned about an experimental system that could someday revolutionize his chosen field. This technology used blue-green lasers to penetrate the ocean's depths. Such a communications system was dependent upon a considerable power source, and it was hoped that this problem could be solved by basing the transmitters on land and using a space-based satellite to reflect the signal back down into the sea.

Though his current duty didn't involve any such exotic, high-tech machinery, it was stimulating nonetheless. For somewhere on the surrounding icepack, lay the wreckage of a plane that had been carrying the Premier of the Soviet Union. And the key to finding this debris was the emergency signal being broadcast from that aircraft's black box. The entire world was anxiously waiting for this device to be recovered and analyzed so that the cause of this tragic crash could be determined. Jules was quite aware of the importance of his present assignment, and applied himself diligently.

It was on a pure hunch that the twenty-four-year-old petty officer switched the dial over to the ultra-high frequency bands. Such a channel was infrequently used, especially by emergency equipment. Yet knowing the Russians' paranoia when it came to such matters, Thornton figured it would be just like them to assign such a band to the cockpit voice recorder's transmitter.

A throaty blast of static immediately met his ears, and as he reached out to activate several filters that he had available to him, a barely audible, high-pitched tone arose from the clutter. Unlike any signal that he had ever received before, the alien tone seemed to pulsate with a throbbing regularity, and he was certain that it was man-made and not an atmospheric anomaly. Jules Thornton's pulse quickened as he urgently accessed his computer to determine from which direction the signal was emanating.

While the senior radioman initiated this task, his commanding officer was in the nearby control room, an intercom handset snuggled up to his ear and a wide smile turning the corners of his mouth.

"Why that's fantastic news, Chief. You and your men are going to get a commendation for this, I promise you. How soon until we can start up both turbines? . . . Are you certain that's all the time you need? . . . Why of course I'm anxious to get underway, even if the ice has quit closing in on us. Thanks again, Chief, and pass on a job well done to your men."

Matt Colter hung up the handset and directly addressed his XO. "They've done the impossible yet again, Al. The chief promises full power in another ten minutes."

"You've got to be kidding, Skipper!" retorted the astonished XO. "Why that means they've pulled it off a whole two hours ahead of schedule, and their preliminary estimate was far from a conservative one."

The captain shook his head. "I hope to God it's no joke, but that's what the chief says and I'm not about to call him a liar. Prepare the boat to dive, Mr. Layman. We've got us a little business to settle with a certain Russkie submarine crew."

"With pleasure, Skipper," snapped the XO, as he turned to relay this directive to the ship's diving officer.

Matt Colter was on his way to the plotting table to chart the most logical intercept course, when a sudden disturbance diverted his attention. In the process of sprinting through the aft hatchway was a single ecstatic figure, whom the captain recognized as being their normally reserved senior radio man.

"I've done it, Captain!" cried Jules Thornton excitedly. "I've located the black box!"

This surprise revelation was all it took to grab the undivided attention of all the men who heard it. Relishing the spotlight, the radio operator added, "Those paranoid bastards are transmitting on ultra-high frequency, yet I got 'em all the same."

"For God's sake, where man?" shouted the captain.

Somewhat sobered by this firm query, Jules Thornton managed a deep calming breath and matter-of-factly responded. "I've locked the homing beacon on bearing two-two-zero, sir. Its relative rough range is approximately eighty miles."

With these figures in mind, Colter looked down to the chart that was spread out before him. Bearing two-two-zero lay to their southwest, and a course in that direction would take them to the northern coast of Baffin Island's Brodeur Peninsula. Confident that their quarry could most likely be found in these very same waters, Matt Colter barked out to his XO.

"Make our course two-two-zero, Mr. Layman. And get the chief engineer on the horn — let him know that we're going to call his bluff. It's going to be a cold day in hell before Ivan gets another cheap shot at the USS *Defiance*. That I can assure you!"

Chapter Twelve

The first hint that something was wrong came just after they fed the dogs their evening meal. Instead of burrowing into the snow and resting at this point, the agitated huskies restlessly yanked on their canvas tethers and yelped incessantly. Cliff Ano was the first of the Arctic Rangers to notice this unusual behavior.

The commandoes had been chowing down themselves, in the snowhouse they had hastily built on the floor of the windswept valley. Because of the continuing inclement weather and the unstable nature of the terrain they were crossing, their progress was much slower than anticipated. Exhausted by the constant detours they were forced to take, and hindered by the rapidly falling twilight, the Rangers had decided to bed down for the night and get a fresh start in the morning.

The sergeant-major had just crawled out of the sturdy, snow-block igloo to relieve himself when he heard the barking dogs and walked over to investigate. Even with his presence, they failed to calm down, and the Inuit intently scanned the icy ridge of snow-covered rocks that surrounded their bivouac. Through the bare light of dusk, his keen glance spotted no visible trespassers, yet his instincts warned otherwise.

Quick to return to the igloo, he approached Jack Redmond and discreetly commented. "The dogs are barking up a storm, Lieutenant. I think that we could have some uninvited visitors outside."

Putting down the tin cup filled with the tea he had been sipping, Redmond curtly queried. "Wolves?"

The sergeant-major nodded. "Could be. Yet if that's the case, our dogs won't stand a chance. And don't forget my deal with my uncle."

Redmond grinned. "I doubt if you'd let me, Sergeant-Major. What do you propose we do to scare 'em off?"

Ano briefly checked the room, taking in the other commandoes as they finished their rations and sipped their drinks. Several exhausted soldiers had already turned in for the night.

"I'd like to reconnoiter the perimeter of our camp," answered the Inuit. "Though I'd sure hate to go out there without someone watching my back."

"You got it," Redmond retorted. He silently rose to put on his gear.

From their cache of supplies he removed two powerful, waterproof flashlights and a pair of M16 assault rifles. Only after he was certain both weapons were loaded with full clips did he hand one to the Inuit and beckon Ano to join him outside.

The huskies were still barking up a storm as the two commandoes assembled in front of the igloo. The dark gray sky had just a hint of light in it as the Inuit spoke, just loud enough to be heard over the gusting wind.

"I'm going to start behind the dogs and follow the ridge around to the floor of the valley. If there's a pack of wolves on the prowl, they'll most likely be

257

found somewhere along the way."

"I'll follow about ten meters behind you, Sergeant-Major. If these guys are as hungry as that bunch we encountered earlier in the day, its going to take at least a full clip to put the fear of god into those buggers."

The Inuit flashed Redmond a thumbs-up and turned to begin his reconnoiter. With a fluid ease he scrambled up the ridge of rock that lined this portion of the valley and deftly proceeded down the icy ledge. As he passed behind the tethered huskies, he switched on his flashlight and aimed its narrow beam at the ground below.

Halfway between their campsite and the valley's floor, the ridge widened into a large clearing. At first the Rangers had chosen this site to build their igloo in, but Cliff had pointed out the danger of an avalanche of rocks from above. As he now crossed this flat expanse, his torch picked out a series of large animal tracks in the deep powdery snow. They were freshly deposited and immense in size, and the Inuit didn't need to see anymore to know what was disturbing the dogs so.

Moments later, Jack Redmond joined him in the clearing. His torch clearly illuminating his discovery, Ano firmly whispered, "It's Tornarsuk. My ancestors called him the one who gives power, but we know him by a different name—polar bear."

Redmond's gut tightened. "What in the hell is a bear doing out in this weather? I thought they'd be in their dens by now."

The Inuit was quick with a response. "One can't generalize when Tornarsuk is involved, Lieutenant. Though a good majority might be in hibernation at this time, others are still putting on fat to sustain them until spring. While some won't even bother to den at all."

"Do you think he'll bother us?" queried Redmond.

"Chances are he's already scented our dogs. That means he won't rest until he's checked out the possibilities firsthand."

"Tied to their tethers like they are, they won't stand a chance," said Redmond.

"Not only that, after he finishes off the dogs, he'll most likely come after us," added the Inuit all too seriously.

A pained expression crossed Jack Redmond's face. "I've had my fair share of bear troubles this week, Sergeant-Major. Any ideas on how we can solve our problem? I don't know about you, but I've had enough of this damn wind. And besides, I was looking forward to snuggling up in my blanket and cutting some z's."

While waiting for some sort of response, Redmond noted that the Inuit's glance had suddenly shifted. As Cliff Ano's narrow gaze centered on that portion of the clearing directly behind his commanding officer, Redmond sensed the approach of trouble.

"Your prayers have just been answered, Lieutenant," managed the Inuit in the barest of whispers. "Just stay cool and don't make any sudden moves."

Redmond's pulse quickened as he whispered back. "Is it the bear?"

The Inuit nodded that it was and smoothly flicked off the safety of his rifle. Then in one smooth movement he pushed Jack Redmond aside and let loose a deafening volley of gunfire. By the time Redmond regained his balance and pivotted to put his own weapon into play, Cliff Ano had squeezed off the last 5.56mm bullet of his thirty-round clip.

It only took one look at the mammoth, blood-stained body lying motionlessly at the edge of the clearing less than ten yards away for Redmond to lower the sights of his rifle. The polar bear lay fully extended, as if the Inuit had caught it while it was in the midst of a charge. It was at least twelve feet tall, its sinewy muscles still twitching in the last throes of death.

"Sweet Jesus!" managed Redmond as he slowly approached the bear and viewed its deadly razor-sharp claws.

"I'm sorry I had to ruin the pelt," offered the Inuit coolly. "An experienced hunter can take Tornarsuk out with a single shot to the head, thus insuring that the skin will be free from bullet holes."

While yanking out his commando knife, the Inuit added, "Ever have a fresh polar bear steak, Lieutenant? Though it might taste a bit strong to you at first, you'll soon enough get used to it. I guarantee you, our dogs are certainly going to be in for a feast this evening. Why tomorrow they'll be strong enough to pull the sled all the way to Lancaster Sound and back without even stopping to catch their breaths!"

Ootah's search for the fiery comet he'd seen falling from the sky on the day of his father's death took him far up the coastline. With Akatingwah and their son riding on the sled that Ootah had originally built for Nakusiak, they began this pilgrimage. Fortunately, they still had walrus meat left over from his last kill, so they could travel without the time-consuming chore of stopping to hunt.

Arnuk, his lead dog, seemed to sense the importance of this journey, and led the pack onward with untiring effort. Still not certain what, if anything, they'd find at the end of this trek, Ootah chose their course by dead reckoning. Perpetually etched in his mind's eye was the fiery exploding wheel he had watched soar through the dawn sky, and the resonant, ear-splitting boom that had shaken even the pack ice beneath him. Thus, he needed no white man's compass to lead them onward.

The fractured ice made their progress slow, and whenever Ootah's doubts clouded this mission's purpose, he had only to touch the bone amulet that hung from his neck. Carved by the hands of Anoteelik, his grandfather, this sacred charm inspired Ootah to push on. For how could he ever forget the horrifying nightmare he had shared with Nakusiak? During this dream, his mother had journeyed from the land of the dead to warn of the great evil that would soon be upon them. Surely this vision was a presentiment of things to come, for Nakusiak's body was still warm in his grave when the very sign he had warned of filled the dawn sky with a fiery brilliance.

The tales of the grandfathers told of this very same event. And if the time of prophecy was indeed upon them, it was now up to Ootah to appease the great evil that had fallen from the sky and been subsequently released in the frozen land of the people. This responsibility was a great one, and Ootah did not take it lightly. For to fail meant utter calamity, as the land would be cleansed with fire and the people would be no more.

Try as he could, Ootah had valiantly tried to keep his thoughts pure ones. But he was only a man, and as such was subject to the weaknesses that each and every member of his species shared.

Consigning himself to do his best, Ootah relentlessly pushed his team further up the coastline. A vicious wind began blowing in from the north, and when a line of black clouds began gathering on the horizon, he knew that a storm would soon be upon them. A moment of indecision followed, in which Ootah was caught between halting and immediately building a snowhouse, or continuing on to reach his mysterious goal. As the fates would have it, it was Arnuk's incessant barking that convinced Ootah to push the sled onto the ridge of the next ice hummock. With the storm continuing to develop on his left, he looked out onto a massive snow-covered plateau located at the very edge of the frozen sea. Scattered throughout this plain were thousands of bits of fire-charred debris. And at that moment, Ootah knew that his pilgrimage was over.

Their first priority was to build a snowhouse. Ootah, Akatingwah and their son joined in to help with the construction of this domed structure in which they would ride out the rapidly advancing storm. Ootah planned to begin his exploration of the debris field that surrounded them as soon as the igloo was completed. Yet no sooner was the last rectangular block in place than the blizzard was upon them.

Rushing outside, Ootah began to work on a windbreak for his dogs. The snow was falling thickly by this time, and as he hurried to complete building this protective barrier, it was Arnuk's mad yelping that convinced him to temporarily abandon his efforts and see what was upsetting his lead huskie so.

Ootah loosened Arnuk's tether and the dog went dashing out onto the plain. The snow was falling so heavily that Ootah lost sight of the huskie in a matter of seconds. Yet knowing full well that Arnuk would not run away like this on a mere whim, Ootah reluctantly trudged out into the gathering drifts to see where the dog had run.

The howling gusts penetrated even his double-thick caribou fur parka, and Ootah was set to abandon his quest when Arnuk came bounding through the snow. After briefly nuzzling his master's legs, Arnuk once again turned away from the campsite. Yet this time the huskie proceeded at such a pace that Ootah could readily follow him.

After climbing up a jagged ice-filled ridge, the Inuit was in the process of questioning his dogs' sanity when the alien flash of a blinking light suddenly caught his attention. Emanating from the opposite base of the ridge he had just scaled, this flickering light had an intense reddish glow to it, and easily cut through the falling snowflakes. Arnuk could be seen furiously pawing into the adjoining drift, and Ootah decided that this mysterious object certainly deserved a closer look.

Paying little attention to the bone-chilling winds, the Inuit slid down the ridge and approached the blindingly bright light that continued flashing in short staccato blasts. With Arnuk's help, Ootah merely had to kneel down and lift the now-uncovered object out of the drift it had been buried in.

It was shaped like a small box, and considering its size was surprisingly heavy. Its four sides were painted jet black. The flashing red light was mounted firmly on its lid. A warm glow emanated from its interior, and could be felt even through Ootah's thick fur mittens. Anxious to see what it contained, the Inuit decided to carry it back to the igloo to share this amazing discovery with Akatingwah.

The trip back proved a bit more difficult. The snowdrifts were rapidly forming, and the bitter winds were gusting with such velocity that it was a chore just to remain standing. With Arnuk leading the way, Ootah lowered his head and plowed forward, his newly found treasure locked firmly in a tight grasp.

With great relief he crawled back into the snow-house. Arnuk was not about to be denied, and followed him inside. Before Akatingwah could shoo the dog away, her attention was drawn to the strange object her husband had placed beside the igloo's flickering soapstone lamp. The intense flashing red light hurt her eyes at first, and as she shielded her gaze from its blindingly bright radiance, she spoke out in protest.

"What in the world is that thing, Ootah? Get it out of here this instant before it blinds all of us!"

Their young son Arno was instantly infatuated with his father's find, and sprinted over to its side. Yet much to the youngster's dismay, his mother pulled him away and carried him off to the sleeping rack, where she proceeded to tuck him beneath the furs.

Only when she was certain that her son was properly protected did Akatingwah again turn her wrath on Ootah. "Did you hear me, husband? I said get that infernal thing out of here this instant!"

A wondrous gleam filled Ootah's eyes as he looked down at his find, and he replied, "Why in heaven's name should I do that, Akatingwah? Don't you see, this is the object of my quest!"

"Nonsense," returned his mate. "Whatever it is, it's a creation of the devil, and must be disposed of immediately before it brings heartache to us all."

To prove his wife wrong, Ootah crawled up to his discovery and gently stroked its smooth black sides. "This is no demonic creation, Akatingwah. It's a sign from the Great Spirit, the one my father warned of before he began his final journey. Come wife, touch it yourself and feel how it pulsates with a warmth that needs no flame in order for it to glow."

"That's the fire of hell that burns inside of it," warned Akatingwah.

Ootah calmly shook his head. "I beg to differ with you, dear wife. For what you see before you is the heart of the comet, sent to us from the Great Spirit to warn of the time of prophecy. We must treat this heavenly messenger well, and burn offerings to it, for the fate of the people is in its divine hands."

"You're beginning to sound more like Powhuktuk the shaman," offered Akatingwah disgustedly.

Ootah held up the bone amulet that hung from a piece of sinew string around his neck. "Perhaps the spirit of the shaman has possessed me, dear wife. This amulet that my father transferred to me on his death bed was carved by the hand of his own father. Anoteelik was a great shaman of the people; no miracle was too great for him. It is said that once my grandfather took off to capture Tornarsuk armed only with his sacred rattle, and seven days after leaving his snowhouse he returned with the body of the dead demon, who had taken the form of a huge polar bear. Upon further examination, it was found that the bear hadn't suffered a single flesh wound. Now what do you suppose it was that took the beast down?"

As Akatingwah shook her head that she didn't know, Ootah continued. "I'll tell you what it was, dear wife. It was the power of the Great Spirit acting through its earthly vassal that was responsible for slaying the beast. And now I too have a direct channel to this all powerful source, because of this amulet I wear!"

Akatingwah seemed upset by this revelation, and, while shielding her eyes from the flashing beacon, worriedly sat down on the edge of the sleeping platform. "Surely this does not sound like my husband. What ever happened to Ootah the hunter?"

His eyes still locked on the blinking red strobe, while thoughtfully fondling the bone amulet, Ootah passionately answered. "The pursuer of game has become the hunter of souls, and at long last I now know my destiny!"

Hardly believing what she was hearing, Akatingwah vainly pleaded, "Please, dear husband, take this infernal object that you dragged in from the snow and drop it into the depths of the frozen sea. Listen to the pleas of my heart, and know that it will only bring tragedy!"

Deaf to her words, Ootah directed his supplications solely toward the incessantly flashing light. "Welcome, Great Spirit, to the humble home of this neophyte shaman. You have been called here to fulfill the prophecy of the grandfathers. The time of trial is upon us, and to insure a favorable judgment, the people's vision must be spotlessly clean. For already the red demon approaches, and it will be our petitions alone that will send this beast back to the cold depths from which it struggles to emerge!"

Akatingwah could only look on in horror as her husband's eyes rolled up into his head and Ootah slipped into the deepest of trances. Fighting the urge to grab the alien blinking object herself and then dispose of it, she consoled herself by reaching out for her son. Hugging her beloved offspring close to her full breasts, the Inuit closed her eyes and prayed for the evil spell to pass. While in the distance, the mad shrieking howl of the wind signaled that the brunt of the blizzard was now upon them.

"Captain Markova, we have just reached the coordinates relayed to us by the cosmonauts on the Red Flag. Will we be surfacing now?"

The *Neva*'s commanding officer had been seated at the wardroom table with several of his crew when this news was personally delivered by the michman. After putting down the tea he had been sipping, Sergei anxiously responded.

"Why of course, Comrade Ustreka. Please let the senior lieutenant know I'll personally join him in the attack center to supervise this ascent."

"I'll do so at once, sir," snapped the Michman as he smartly pivoted to convey this message.

As Sergei Markova pushed back his chair and stood, the white-haired figure at the head of the table did likewise.

"I hope you don't mind if I join you, Captain?" queried Mikhail Kharkov. "This is a historic moment, and I'd like the honor of witnessing it first-hand."

"I don't mind at all," replied Sergei. "Surfacing in the ice is always an adventure, and I'm certain that you won't be bored."

"So I remember," reflected the Admiral of the Fleet, who addressed his next remark to the individual still seated at the table. "Well, Comrade Zampo-lit, aren't you interested in joining us? I'm sure that piece of cake will be waiting for you once we're on the surface."

Having been totally absorbed in the tasty poppy-seed cake the steward had just served him, Konstantin Zinyagin looked up and blushed. With his mouth still full, he awkwardly stood and began brushing the crumbs from his clipped mustache and beard.

Mikhail Kharkov shook his head in disgust and followed the captain out of the wardroom, the still-chewing Political Officer close on his heels. They were halfway down the passageway when the *Neva* banked violently over onto its side. The force of this unexpected turn was so great that both Sergei and his distinguished guest were forced to reach out for the handrail to keep from falling. Behind them, the Zampolit's reactions were a bit slower, and the Political Officer went sprawling to the deck, where he landed squarely on his backside.

Not bothering to give Zinyagin the least bit of attention, the admiral quickly said, "What in the hell was that all about, Captain?"

Sergei held back his answer until the *Neva*'s deck was stable once more. "I guess such tactics hadn't been perfected when you took the first Victor up to the ice, Admiral. Such a turn is standard procedure when looking for a polynya in which to surface. Most likely we just passed beneath such an opening, and the senior lieutenant ordered this abrupt course change so that we wouldn't miss it."

By the time they began to make their way down the passageway once again, the Zampolit had picked himself up. While rubbing his bruised rear end, the pained Political Officer did his best to continue on also.

Once in the attack center, they joined the *Neva*'s senior lieutenant as he stood beside the periscope well.

"What have you got, Comrade Belenko?" questioned Sergei.

The senior lieutenant was quick to answer. "We just passed beneath what looks to be a fairly good-sized lead, Captain. The ice was thick to this point, and I thought it best if we didn't pass this polynya up knowing our present coordinates and all."

"You decided correctly, comrade," returned the captain.

"We've got thin ice above us," observed the seaman responsible for monitoring the surface-scanning Fathometer.

"All stop!" barked Sergei. "Bring us up to thirty meters."

The loud whirring growl of the ballast pumps activating filled the hushed compartment. This was followed by the sound of water flowing back into the tanks as the diving officer attempted to control the rate of ascent of the now-lightened vessel.

"Secure flooding. Thirty meters, Captain," said the diving officer.

"Up scope," ordered Markova.

There was a loud hiss and the hydraulically controlled periscope lifted up from its well. Sergei pulled down the hinged grips and peered through the rubberized viewing coupling.

Behind the captain, Mikhail Kharkov softly addressed the *Neva*'s second in command. "What in the world does he hope to see down here? We're still a good ten meters away from periscope depth."

"That we are, Admiral," offered Viktor. "But you'd be surprised what these new lenses can pick up while still submerged. Actually, all the captain is trying to do is locate any inverted ice ridges that the Fathometer may have missed."

"Looks good from this angle," observed Sergei as he backed away from the lens. "Down scope. Bring us up to twenty meters, Comrade diving officer. But do it gently, my friend, just as you'd caress your lover."

This remark was intended to help break the strained atmosphere inside the compartment as the ballast pumps once again whirred alive.

"Twenty-five meters," noted the diving officer.

"We've still got thin ice above," added the Fathometer operator.

"Twenty meters and still rising," said the diving officer a bit tensely. Then, "We seem to have hit a strong current of colder water and I can't hold her!"

This revelation was followed by the distraught cries of the seaman assigned to the Fathometer. "Heavy ice, Captain! We're drifting out of the polynya!"

"Flood emergency!" commanded the captain.

To a blast of highly pressurized air the ballast tanks opened to the sea. Yet this order was given a fraction of a second too late, and the *Neva* smashed into the ice pack above with a deafening, bone-jarring concussion. Once again the Zampolit found himself thrown to the deck, yet this time he was not alone; several of his shipmates joined him along with an assortment of loose gear.

As the lights blinked off then on again, the frantic diving officer could be heard screaming, "Blow negative to the mark!"

The tons of seawater that the *Neva* had just taken on in its vain attempt to keep from striking the ice were vented, but not in time to keep the vessel from spiraling down into the black depths.

"One-hundred and fifty meters and still falling," observed the sweating diving officer.

At a depth of two hundred meters the *Neva*'s welded steel hull began groaning as the ship approached its crush threshold. At two hundred and fifty meters this sickening, rending sound intensified prompting the ship's Zampolit to cry out in panic.

"Can't you do anything to save us, Captain?"

Knowing full well that it was out of his hands, Sergei Markova briefly caught the resolute stare of his white-haired passenger. Mikhail Kharkov appeared cool as ice as he turned toward the whimpering Political Officer and disgustedly spat out.

"Shut up, Comrade Zinyagin!"

It wasn't until a depth of three hundred and twenty meters that the *Neva* quit falling. There were no shouts of celebration, no cries of joy. Only the firm voice of the vessel's captain as he barked out commandingly.

"Take her back up, Comrade Diving Officer. And this time we'll anticipate that inversion current and we'll break through to the surface as we intended!"

Chapter Thirteen

Petty Officer First Class Stanley Roth was like a man reborn. Since his successful oral surgery, the constant pain that had left him listless and irritable for days on end was gone. And with this change for the better came an entirely new outlook on life.

Though his gum was still sore where the tooth had been removed, he could drink down a mug of hot coffee without having to howl out in agony. And for the first time in weeks, he actually slept for an entire six-hour stretch without resorting to a narcotic stupor to do so.

There was an expectant smile on his lips as he pranced down the passageway that led to the sound shack. It had been much too long since he'd really looked forward to going to work, and he felt like a wide-eyed recruit again.

Inside the padded door of the sonar compartment he found Seaman Lester Warren hunched over his console. The youngster was totally absorbed in his current scan, and didn't even realize that his relief had arrived.

"Good afternoon, Seaman Warren. And how are you on this glorious day at fifty fathoms?"

Not certain who it was that was greeting him, the

Texan looked up from the repeater screen and had to do a double take when he spotted the grinning petty officer.

"Is that really you, Mr. Roth? Why you look like your old self once again."

"Why I didn't know that it showed," Stanley jested, then added. "Now I remember how it felt when I was a freshman and had my cherry popped by the hottest cheerleader in school. Why I feel absolutely wonderful!"

Unable to share the petty officer's enthusiasm, Lester turned back to his screen. Stanley Roth could see that something was bothering the kid, and he gently touched him on his shoulder.

"What's with the long face, Les? Life's too short to be taken so seriously."

The Texan replied while studying the repeater screen. "I'm just doing my job, sir."

"Oh, cut the crap, Les. What the hell is bothering you?"

The frustrated seaman emotionally vented himself without taking his eyes off the monitor. "It's that bogey, sir, and the way they were able to sneak up on us without me even knowing they were out there. Why if lady luck wasn't with us, we all could have been killed!"

"Easy, kid," prompted the veteran. "Ours is far from a perfected art, and these things happen from time to time."

"Tell that to the XO," retorted the distraught seaman. "Lieutenant Commander Layman came down here and really read me the riot act after those cowardly bastards rammed us. Yet when I played him back the tapes, he had to admit that with all the natural commotion going on in the water around us, even he had a hard time identifying Ivan's signature."

Stanley shook his head. "It's this damn ice, Les. The way it's always fracturing and cracking, the *Queen Mary* could be on our tail and we'd never know the difference. So relax kid, and look on the bright side. The *Defiance* survived Ivan's best blow to the chops, and now that we've got all of our turbines back on line, it'll soon be our turn to even the score. That's the way it works in this game."

The junior seaman seemed unaffected by these words of wisdom, and Roth sighed heavily. "You damn kids today take life so seriously. Nobody's perfect, and no machine is either."

Realizing that he was wasting his breath, the veteran walked over to the adjoining console and seated himself. It felt as if he had just returned to work from a long vacation. While absorbing the familiar sights and smells, he activated his repeater screen and clipped on his headphones.

He initiated his scan by isolating the hydrophones set into the upper portion of their bow. As Roth had expected, he was immediately greeted by the gut-wrenching sounds of the ice. No matter how hard he tried to filter them out, they still prevailed. When one nearby floe fractured, it sounded like the explosive crack of a rifle shot. A passing ice ridge expressed the monumental pressure it was under by groaning loudly and sounding like the rusty hinge of a gate. And yet another ridge surrendered, and could be heard buckling under with a high-pitched squeal of protest.

Well aware of the great difficulty of picking out a man-made sound signature in this maelstrom of white noise, Stanley readjusted his scan to take in that portion of the sea that lay beneath them. As soon as he completed this connection, his headphones filled with a mournful, high-pitched cry that was followed by a sharp series of resonant clicks and whistles. From several different directions this call was answered, and the senior sonar technician mentally visualized the graceful creatures responsible for this distinctive racket.

Because of their current position in the waters of Lancaster Sound, these undersea mammals were either the white-skinned beluga whale or its legendary cousin, the narwhal. The males of this latter species were known for the long spiraling ivory tusk that pierced their upper lip on the left side of the jaw; it could extend foward for as much as ten feet. Once selling for up to twenty times their weight in gold, these tusks were treasured in medieval Europe where they were ground up and utilized as an aphrodisiac or the filler for a magical amulet.

Stanley had once read a *National Geographic* article that described these creatures in detail. He had been surprised to learn that scientists were still confused as to the reason such tusks were needed. It used to be believed that the narwhals used these appendages to stir up the seafloor for food. But the tusks themselves were hollow for most of their length and could easily be broken. The going theory was that they played some sort of sexual role, though Stanley couldn't begin to theorize on what this might be.

Beyond the singing whales, a herd of seals could be heard harshly barking. While an assemblage of shrimp chattered away in the distance like a bunch of hyperactive castanets. To the veteran sonar operator, all of these sounds were like old friends. This would be his twelfth Arctic patrol, and during many a long lonely duty segment, the noises of the ice pack and of the creatures that lived there were his only company.

As he scanned the *Defiance*'s baffles, that sound absorbent cone that lay immediately aft of their spinning propellors, Stanley realized that his colleague was still seated before his console.

"Jesus Les, don't you even want to grab some chow, or at least a cup of joe? You've been at this for a straight four-hour clip, and I'm more than capable of handling it on my own."

The determined Texan replied without taking his eyes off the repeater screen. "If it's all right with you, I'd like to hang around a little longer. Maybe with both of us listening, Ivan will finally give himself away."

"Suit yourself," returned Stanley. "Though all the overtime in the world isn't going to make up for the fact that Ivan was able to use a combination of stealth and the natural ambient noises of these waters to land a crisp right jab to the *Defiance*'s kisser. No matter how many ears we had listening for their approach, chances are they still would have been able to get within punching distance."

"All I'm waiting for is just one damn chance to even the score," muttered the Texan. "Just one damn chance!"

The young technician was obviously not the type of person who accepted failure easily, and Roth knew that the best way to let him vent his frustrations was to let him work them out. After a couple more hours in front of the repeater screen, his growling stomach and sore back would send him packing.

Stanley was in the process of isolating the hydrophones mounted into the very tip of the ship's spherical bow, when he heard a series of distant crashing sounds that were followed by a muted, throbbing whine that was disturbingly familiar. His shipmate also heard this alien racket and shouted out excitingly.

"Do you hear that, Stanley? It sounds like the commotion the *Defiance* made when we slammed into the ice on our last patrol!"

This acute observation hit home, and Roth was able to identify the pulsating whine that followed the initial clamor. "Jesus Christ, you hit the nail right on the head, Les. That's a friggin' ballast pump! Hang in there, my friend. You wanted a chance for revenge, and if I know the Skipper, you're about to get your wish."

Admiral of the Fleet Mikhail Kharkov was absolutely certain he had picked the right man for the difficult job at hand as he watched the *Neva*'s young captain in action. Faced with a variety of calamities ranging from an unexpected collision with the ice to an unscheduled dive to depths that tested the very integrity of their hull, Sergei Markova remained absolutely cool under fire. Not even stopping to wipe the sweat from his brow, the *Neva*'s commanding officer barked out the orders that would once again send the vessel topside to meet the challenge of the ice.

Persistence was a quality Mikhail greatly respected. It was his great uncle who'd given him his first lesson in that all-important virtue. They had been hiking beside the wooded shores of Lake Baikal at the time, and had come across one of the many hot springs in the area. As his adult guide ripped off his clothes and invited Mikhail to join him in the steaming water, Mikhail humbly admitted that he didn't know how to swim.

"That makes not a bit of difference," instructed

his great-uncle as he immersed himself in the torrid pool. "Jump right in and you'll learn soon enough."

Mikhail did just that, yet since he neglected to close his mouth, the youngster almost drowned in the process. His great-uncle pulled him out, and though Mikhail was more than content to forget all about this swimming lesson, his guardian would have no part of it.

"You must jump back in at once, Misha," wisely directed the grizzled trapper. "Otherwise one bad experience might cause you never again to enter the water."

With a bit more circumspection, Mikhail took the old-timer's advice and jumped back into the pool, this time making absolutely certain to keep his mouth closed. And less than a half hour later, the youngster was actually swimming all on his own.

Throughout his career, Mikhail remembered this invaluable lesson. He utilized it time and again, especially during the traumatic years of the Great War. Battle brought out both the best and worst qualities in men. And even the bravest soldier's nerves were put to the test each time he went into harm's way.

After returning from his first wartime submarine patrol, common sense would have had him ask for a transfer to the surface fleet at once. For their vessels were not of the best quality, and the exploding Nazi depth charges put a fear in a sailor's soul that none would ever forget. Yet with his great-uncle's words in mind, he returned to the undersea world and came back from his second patrol with his first confirmed kill—a fully loaded German troop transport.

Now to watch the *Neva*'s brave young captain at work brought a satisfied grin to the white-haired veteran's cracked lips. Not about to let adversity get in the way of his mission's success, Sergei Markova hunched over the extended periscope and called out firmly.

"Looks good from this angle. What's our depth, comrade diving officer?"

"Thirty meters," replied a tense, high-pitched voice.

As he backed away from the scope, the captain added. "Now this time the *Neva* will be anticipating that cold current, and will be more than prepared to counter it. Bring us up, comrade, as gently as if your own mother were on top of our sail."

A muted surging hum filled the attack center as the ballast pumps were activated. As the now-lightened sub began to rise, the diving officer reversed the ballast process to insure that the ship was heavy enough to meet the temperature inversion that had sent them shooting upward like a rocket last time.

"We're at eighteen meters, and holding, Captain," he proudly observed.

"Keep her right there, Comrade," ordered the captain. "At this depth we should be just above that current and we'll be able to drift right under the polynya."

As Sergei returned to the periscope well, he peered inside the lens coupling and eagerly called out. "Come here, Admiral. I'd like you to take a look at something."

Surprised by this request, Mikhail Kharkov proceeded to have a look through the lens. An expanse of startlingly clear water met his eyes. This was in itself astonishing, since most of the world's oceans would appear pitch black at this depth. The veteran mariner was struck with wonder when a translucent, rainbow-colored blob gracefully floated by. One look at this creature's long, flowing tentacles and Mikhail was able to identify it as a jellyfish.

"Well, I'll be," reflected the admiral as he backed away from the scope. "So we're not so alone in these frozen waters after all."

"We certainly aren't," returned Sergei Markova. "And from the clarity of the water and the amount of light visible, I'd say if there is ice above us, it should be thin enough for us to smash through with our sail. Shall we give it a try, Admiral?"

Not about to tell the captain otherwise, Mikhail beckoned him to get on with it and Sergei snapped into action.

"Down scope. Bring us up ever so gently. And don't worry about that current. We're well above it as the jellyfish that surround us seem to be just hanging there motionless."

The ballast pumps again activated and the diving officer anxiously reported. "Fifteen meters."

"Thin ice above," observed the seaman assigned to monitor the surface-scanning Fathometer.

"We're close, comrades. So very close," said the captain. "Stop the pumps!"

The muted hum of venting ballast suddenly ceased, to be followed by a barely perceptible bumping sensation.

"Our sail's up against the ice pack!" exclaimed the captain. "Now it's time to break on through. Lighten those tanks."

The diving officer once again activated the ballast pumps. The familiar throbbing hum returned, yet even with this increase in positive buoyancy, the ice remained immovable.

Mikhail Kharkov watched as the captain thoughtfully walked over toward the diving console.

"That's enough, comrade. You can stop pumping

now since it's evident this ice is a bit more dense than we assumed."

It was at this point that the ship's Zampolit stepped out of the shadowy corner in which he had been perched. "What are we to do now, Captain? Shall we go and find a more suitable polynya?"

"And why in Lenin's name should we go and do a thing like that, Comrade Zinyagin?" returned the captain. "It's foolish to waste all this effort just because of a little tough ice. And besides, have you already forgotten that it's to this very sector duty calls us."

"But how are we to get topside if the ice blocks our way?" continued the puzzled Political Officer.

Sergei Markova grinned. "I guess we'll just have to go and smash our way through. Flood her down, comrade diving officer. But only ten meters or so. Then lighten our load, and we'll see what kind of icebreaker the *Neva* makes."

Unable to hide his unease, the Zampolit sighed heavily. As he removed his handkerchief to mop his dripping wet jowls, he returned to his corner to brace himself for that inevitable collision that would soon be coming.

A carefully monitored surge of onrushing seawater brought the submarine down another ten meters in depth. Then with a single turn of his wrist, the diving officer vented this additional ballast and the now lightened vessel drifted upward.

There was a loud crack and for a moment the deck below quivered and trembled. Yet the *Neva* still found itself beneath the dome of solid ice.

"So it's going to take a little more muscle," observed the captain. "Take us down fifteen meters, and this time blow the main ballast. With a couple of hundred tons of additional positive buoyancy, the

Neva will smash on through that ice like a fist through a plate-glass window."

Though stimulated by the young captain's vigor, Mikhail Kharkov knew that such a procedure was not without its dangers. The encompassing ice could be thicker than they anticipated, and even if their specially reinforced sail could take the resulting collision, their fragile rudder might not. And there was always the ever-present threat of encountering an inverted spike of ice that could pierce the *Neva*'s hull and send them all to their watery doom. Yet such were the risks of Arctic operations. And since the completion of their mission depended upon a successful ascent, they had few alternatives, other than gambling on locating another polynya close by.

For the first time in years, Kharkov felt his gut tighten with dread. And only then did he realize what a sheltered existence he had been living as a landlocked bureaucrat. As a sailor, fear had been a constant companion. Though infrequently acknowledged, it showed itself every time a storm at sea was encountered, or enemy waters were attained. At such times even the most decorated individuals felt that dreaded twinge deep in their bellies as they prepared for one more brush with mortality.

Men such as their current Zampolit were less tolerant of that horror, and expressed their anxieties openly. As a commanding officer, Mikhail had learned to control his emotions. For fear was contagious, and a subordinate only had to see it on his captain's face to lose whatever courage he might have summoned up to that point.

A prime example of an officer who appeared to be in perfect control was Sergei Markova. As Mikhail had noted while watching him in action in the flooding engine room, the *Neva*'s young captain met even the direst of emergencies with a cool acceptance. His confident, level-headed demeanor was especially evident now as he stood behind the diving console. Except for the ship's Zampolit, the crew seemed to mirror their captain's state. Even Mikhail was under the man's spell, and he found himself consciously holding back questions he wouldn't hesitate to ask if another was at the helm.

The sound of rushing seawater broke the veteran mariner's ponderings, and he reached out to steady himself as the *Neva* began slowly drifting downward. Expecting to next hear the surging roar of the main ballast tanks being vented, Mikhail found himself with the distinct impression that something was not right here. Seconds later, this presentiment was confirmed by the frantic voice of the sonar operator.

"We've got an unidentified submerged contact, bearing zero-eight-zero, Captain! From the racket it's making, it's headed toward us with a bone in its teeth."

"Belay that order to blow the main tanks!" directed Sergei Markova. "Senior Lieutenant, what's the best course available to see us out of this trap?"

Before Viktor Belenko could answer, the Admiral of the Fleet found himself crying out in protest. "You can't be serious, Captain? This is no time to be fainthearted. If this vessel is the Yankee Sturgeon that we paid our respects to earlier, now is the time to finish them off for good."

This remark was given some substance by the sonar operator's next report. "The computer shows a seventy-three percent probability that this contact is an American *Sturgeon* class submarine, Captain."

"We've got clear water ahead of us on course three-four-zero, Captain," offered the senior lieutenant firmly.

"That's the coward's way!" spat the white-haired veteran. "If we stand a chance of successfully completing this mission, we must make our stand here and now. Flood those torpedo tubes, Captain Markova, and rid the seas of this Imperialist menace once and for all!"

For one brief confusing moment, Sergei Markova found himself vacillating between two drastically different choices. Under normal circumstances, he would not hesitate to send the *Neva* running for the cover of open water. The alternative was to launch a torpedo attack. In his relatively short but full career, he had never before given such a drastic order. As a veteran cold-warrior, he was well aware of how much one could get away with before crossing that thin line leading to the unthinkable — a global nuclear exchange.

A set of unwritten rules existed that regulated the degree of escalation in the undersea realm. Each side probed deep into the other's territory, and even such potentially dangerous practices as ramming were unofficially condoned. Yet an actual torpedo attack was definitely out of the question.

"The contact continues on course, and is reaching our offensive threshold, Captain," reported the sonar operator.

"For the sake of the Motherland, launch those torpedoes, Captain! Don't you see? We have no other choice in this matter."

Sergei turned to directly face Kharkov as the white-haired veteran continued his impassioned plea. "I realize such an attack is unprecedented in this time of fragile peace, Captain. But the moment the Imperialists shot down the *Flying Kremlin,* a new and violent stage of this so-called cold war came into being.

"Don't forget about that squadron of F-15 Eagles we monitored closing in on our Il-76 with their afterburners ignited. And how can you ignore the disruptive electronic interference sent skyward from their Polestar DEW line installation? The Soviet Union might have lost a beloved leader in the dastardly missile attack that followed, but I can guarantee you that we haven't lost our resolve. So for the sake of Alexander Suratov's memory, now is the time to start evening the score. And once the black box is ours you'll realize the validity of these words, and the whole world will cry out for justice!"

"Captain, the contact has entered our defensive zone," interrupted the unemotional sonar operator. "From this point onward, the *Neva* is well within the range of the Sturgeon's Mk-48 torpedoes."

"Shall I initiate immediate evasive maneuvers, Captain?" quizzed the concerned senior lieutenant. "A launch by the Sturgeon now would most likely prove fatal."

His gaze still locked on the distinguished face of the Admiral of the Fleet, Sergei felt the old-timer will him onward, and the young officer reluctantly nodded.

"There will be no evasive maneuvers, Senior Lieutenant, until we first launch a salvo of our own," declared the captain. "Such a drastic decision is necessitated by a single concern. As long as that Sturgeon remains in these waters, our ultimate mission is compromised. So we have no choice but to eliminate it."

A relieved grin broke upon Mikhail Kharkov's face as he listened to the young captain call out forcefully.

"Prepare tubes one and three for firing. Sonar, we're going to need a sonic interface between the

285

target's signature and those warheads. And for our very lives, make it a secure one!"

Helping tag the suspected Soviet submarine as it attempted to smash its way through the ice, was just the kind of thing that Seaman Lester Warren needed to snap him out of his doldrums. A new spirit of self-confidence infused the junior sonar technician as this contact was confirmed and the *Defiance* moved in to intercept it.

Any thoughts of abandoning his console to fill his empty stomach were far from the Texan's mind. Instead he was very content to remain right at his duty station, with his veteran shipmate manning the terminal on his right.

Since initially picking up the enemies' signature, they had monitored them making yet another futile attempt to smash their way to the surface. Currently headed downward for what appeared to be one last effort, the Russians had just taken on additional ballast. Even at a range of thirty miles, this distinctive racket was clearly audible.

One of the unusual features of under-ice operations was the manner in which such signatures traveled. Because the sound waves were reflected upward by the seabed and downward by the ice cover, man-made signatures could be heard for a great distance. This would be particularly significant if the ambient sounds of the ice itself could be filtered out. Yet since this was extremely difficult to achieve, Warren was quite content to receive startlingly clear readings at their present range.

They were rapidly approaching the point where the *Defiance* could initiate a torpedo attack if it so desired. Though Lester Warren thought such a response was more than appropriate considering the scare Ivan had given them, it was Captain Colter's decision. However, anxious to know if this was indeed the course they would next take, Warren sat forward expectantly when Stan Roth hung up the intercom handset on which he had been talking.

"You'll never guess who I just got off the horn with, Les? That was none other than Lieutenant Commander Layman, and he wanted to personally convey to you a job well done."

Though this was certainly better than another censure, the Texan still found such a remark unnecessary. "That's all very well and good, Stanley. But what did he say about the Russkies? Are we going to take them out, or what?"

Noting his shipmate's impatience, Stanley Roth snickered. "My, aren't you the eager one. Since when did you become such a hawk?"

"To tell you the truth, Stan, I always thought I had a pretty good understanding of the Soviet people. They impressed me as a levelheaded sort, who wanted peace just as much as we did. But my opinion abruptly changed the moment they rammed us."

"I hear you, Les. And you'll be happy to know that the captain happens to feel likewise. In fact, the XO just told me to lock Ivan's sound signature into the Mk-48's in tubes one through three."

"All right! We're finally going to play hardball," exclaimed the Texan as he watched his shipmate hit the switches that would feed the Russian sub's sound signature directly into the computers mounted inside their torpedoes.

Yet as the reality of this bold new step sunk in, Lester's tone suddenly revealed concern. "Do you think this will mean war, Stan?"

287

Only after he had successfully completed the interface did the senior technician answer. "That's hard to say, Les. But where I'm sitting, the prospects for detente sure don't look very promising."

This statement was punctuated by a distant muted whirring sound that flowed into their headphones from the direction of their target. In all his years of service, Stanley Roth had only heard this distinctive racket during sea trials with the fleet. Yet this certainly wasn't an exercise. A look of pure disbelief came on the veteran's face as he cried out in horror.

"Holy Mother Mary, Ivan just launched a broadside at us!"

Listening on in sheer terror as the signatures of two separate torpedoes filtered in through his headphones, Lester Warren found that his worst nightmare had at long last been realized—they were at war!

The frantic call from the sound shack caught Captain Matt Colter and his XO huddled around the plotting table.

"Damn it!" cursed Colter. "I should have known this Ivan would be the type to shoot first and ask questions later. Let's return the favor. Lieutenant Sanger, hit 'em with tubes one, two, and three. Then release our MOSS Mk-70 decoy out of tube number four."

"You got it, Captain," answered the alert weapons' officer as he punched the buttons of the ship's Mark 101A fire-control system.

Seconds later, the sound of four exploding blasts of compressed air filled the control room with a resonant roar. The deck beneath them quivered as the now-empty tubes began filling with water to

288

compensate for the great weight they had just lost.

"All four weapon's running straight and true," observed the breathless weapons' officer.

"Then let's get the hell out of here!" yelled Colter. "Take her down deep and quick, Mr. Marshall. I want to leave a knuckle in the water that those Red torpedoes will never be able to follow."

As the muted whining sound of the turbines engaging filled the control room, the *Defiance* seemed to lurch forward in a sudden burst of speed. The helmsmen made the most of this additional momentum, and the 5,000-ton vessel canted hard on its side and initiated a tight, spiraling dive into the black depths below. With all the grace of a jet fighter, the sub made a corkscrew maneuver that left a hissing vortex of agitated seawater in the ship's baffles.

"Five hundred feet," observed the diving officer coolly.

Tightly gripping the rail behind the chart table, Matt Colter absorbed this information. His practiced gaze scanned the compartment, and he watched how the crew fought to keep their balance as the deck violently tilted from side to side. The g-forces proportionally increased to a point where loose objects such as unsecured coffee mugs and rulers began crashing to the deck.

The digital knot indicator that lay mounted on the forward bulkhead before the harness-constrained helmsmen registered twenty-one knots. Yet the turbines were just getting warmed up and before this maneuver was over they would be shooting through the water at a speed of over twice their present one.

"Seven-hundred and fifty feet," said the diving officer.

The boat canted hard on its left side and seemed to momentarily shudder as it penetrated a depth to which few other man-made vessels could safely hope to venture. As the hull began to groan in protest of the great water pressure it now encountered, Colter looked over and caught the concerned gaze of his XO.

"Well, Mr. Layman, do you think we shook those Red fish yet?"

The XO answered directly. "I'd say there's a damn good chance that we did, Skipper. We're getting awfully close to our depth threshold, and now might be a good time to pull out of this dive and see what's behind us."

Almost to punctuate this response the diving officer dryly called out, "Nine-hundred feet."

Colter held back his reply until the depth gauge read an even thousand. "Helmsmen, pull her up and hold us at nine-hundred and ninety feet. Make your new course one-six-zero."

Glancing up at the knot indicator, the captain disgustedly called out to his XO. "Damn it, Al! Get on the horn to the chief and tell him to get the lead out of this old lady's pants. We need at least forty knots, and we need it now!"

As the XO alertly nodded and picked up the nearest handset, Colter addressed his next remarks to the quartermaster. "Mr. Lawrence, patch in the sound shack with our overhead speakers, and activate the remote pickup."

This allowed the captain to talk directly to the sonar room, with the response filtering back through the public address system for all inside the control room to clearly hear.

"Mr. Roth, this is the captain. Do you read me?"

"I hear you, sir," returned the tense voice of the senior sonar technician.

Noting this tension, Colter responded. "Good.

290

Now take a deep breath and tell me, did that little knuckle we left behind do the trick?"

Stanley Roth's voice remained strained as he responded. "It looks like our decoy took care of one of 'em, Captain. Yet the other one wasn't so easily fooled and is still on our tail. Range is thirty-thousand yards and starting to close."

"Damn!" cursed Colter, whose eyes flashed to the knot counter. "Where's that additional speed, XO?"

With the intercom handset still cradled up against his ear, Al Layman could only hunch his shoulders as the digital indicator seemed to remain locked on thirty-five knots.

"Helmsman, swing us around to bearing one-zero-zero. And make it crisp!"

The captain's forceful directive was met by such a sharp turn to port, the loose material that had already been deposited on the deck careened across the floor. Forced to further tighten his grip to keep from being flung to the deck himself, Matt Colter locked his gaze on the speed counter. His glance seemed to narrow as the indicator suddenly rose one, two and three complete knots.

"That's more like it!" cried the captain. "Yet since it's doubtful we can outrun that damn fish, we're going to have to lose it another way. Planesman, bring us up to a depth of three-hundred feet and do it quickly."

As the seated seaman responsible for operating the ship's two, sail-mounted planes yanked back on his airplane-type steering column, the bow angled sharply upward. This change of course caused those sailors not having the luxury of stabilizing seat harnesses to grasp some support to keep from being flung backward.

Matt Colter gripped a rail. With the sweating

palms of his hands rubbed raw by the tubular steel his grip had locked onto, the captain watched as the depth gauge passed the six-hundred-foot mark. Doing his best to ignore the excruciating pain that shot up his wrists, Colter queried.

"Mr. Roth, what's that torpedo doing?"

An awkward moment of silence forced the captain to repeat his question. It was now met by a stuttering response from the mounted speakers.

"Uh, sorry about that, sir. But I'm afraid the news is still grim. The fish is coming up with us, and has now closed the gap to eighteen thousand yards."

Instinctively, Colter's gaze went to the digital speed counter. It registered a blistering forty-three knots, and since any additional speed on their part was highly unlikely, the captain held back on venting his fury on the chief engineer.

"We're approaching three hundred feet, Captain," observed the diving officer.

"Torpedo's still closing, sir," added the intense voice of Stan Roth. "Range is now down to twelve thousand yards."

Matt Colter caught his XO's somber stare. The two senior officers seemed to be attempting to silently read each other's thoughts when a sudden flash of inspiration gleamed in the captain's eyes.

"The damn ice!" reflected Colter fervently. "We'll head right on up to the surface, and then plow back down into the depths. And if we're lucky, that torpedo will breach and smack right into that everloving ice!"

The barest of grins broke out on the XO's previously worried face, and this was all that Colter needed to convince him to put his hastily conceived plan into action.

"Mr. Marshall, we're going to go all the way up to

one hundred feet before flooding the tanks and going back down to crush depth. I know it's going to be a hell of a roller-coaster ride, but if the Lord is with us, this one should do the trick."

As the diving officer prepared to implement this highly complicated and dangerous maneuver, the two occupants of the ship's sonar compartment remained anxiously glued to their consoles. With their headphones tightly clipped to their ears and their stares locked to the flashing repeater screens, both Stanley Roth and Lester Warren waited for what seemed to be inevitable.

"It doesn't look good," quietly observed the concerned young Texan to his partner. "That fish can't be less than eight thousand yards off our tail."

"I'm afraid it's more like seven, and closing in with each passing second," returned Roth grimly.

"Maybe it will run out of fuel," offered Lester. "It can't keep on going like that forever."

The veteran sonar technician shook his head. "Don't underestimate those Russkie engineers, Les. They build 'em tough and with plenty of staying power."

As the menacing whine of the approaching torpedo continued to fill his headphones, the Texan took a deep breath and prepared himself for the worst. "Well, if it does catch up with us, I hope we won't go down without taking some Reds with us."

This pessimistic remark was met by a passionate response. "Don't even think that way, kid! The *Defiance* ain't licked just yet. You'll see. Why the old man is probably cooking something up even as we speak."

With this said, the steep angle of ascent that had forced them to tightly grasp the edges of their consoles to keep from sliding backward, abruptly evened out. For a few fleeting seconds, the *Defiance* ran level in the water before initiating a sickening, gut-wrenching plunge downward. Now it was all that they could do to keep from being cut in half by their consoles as the ship began yet another incredibly steep, spiraling dive.

Struggling to keep his headphones securely clamped over his ears, Stanley Roth listened intently for the manner in which their pursuer reacted to this precipitous maneuver. At first the torpedo's distinctive signature was completely lost in the sudden turbulence left in the *Defiance*'s wake. It seemed to take an eternity for their baffles to clear, yet when they eventually did, the sound that met his ears brought forth an exclamation flavored by sheer joy.

"It's still moving away from us! If it doesn't turn soon, it's going to leap right out of the water."

Suddenly remembering the unique nature of the seas beneath which they were currently traveling, Stanley made the right connection. "Why that's it! The Skipper took us on this roller-coaster ride so it would do just that!"

Still not certain what his shipmate was carrying on about, Lester made the mistake of turning up his volume gain a full notch just as a thundering explosion sounded above them. His eardrums painfully reverberating under the force of this sonic lashing, he ripped off his headphones. Yet instead of sympathy, his shipmate greeted him with a wide, beaming smile and a hearty pat on the back.

"We did it, Les! I told you the Skipper would see us out of this fix."

"What in the hell happened?" queried the dazed junior technician.

Realizing the extent of his shipmate's confusion, Stanley wasted no time explaining. "Don't you understand, Les? Captain Colter had it planned from the very start. By sending us up almost to the surface, and then abruptly ordering the *Defiance* back down, he caused that Russkie torpedo to smack right into the ice. The old man's a genius, pure and simple!"

Lester Warren listened to these spirited remarks, his ears still ringing in pain. Quite willing to forget about his own agony and join in the celebration, the Texan became puzzled when his colleague anxiously returned to his console to initiate yet another intensive scan of the surrounding waters.

"What in the hell is that all about, Stanley? With that fish gone, and the other one still chasing our decoy, we're surely in the clear."

The veteran held back his response until his scan located what he had been searching for. "You seem to have forgotten the *Defiance* wasn't the only sub under attack, Tex. Go ahead and isolate the bow hydrophone array, port side."

As Lester gingerly replaced his headphones and reached forward to address his keyboard, Stanley Roth added.

"Ah, now this is sweet music to my ears, if I ever heard any. Because if you think the *Defiance* was just on a hectic roller-coaster ride, wait until you hear what Ivan's in the midst of. Why that sub is cutting up the sea something fierce, with our three ever-loving torpedoes smack on its tail!"

"Captain Markova, for the sake of my poor wife and three young children, you must do something! Why, we're all going to die!"

As the Zampolit's shrill pleas filled the previously hushed attack center, Admiral of the Fleet Mikhail

Kharkov reacted swiftly. Oblivious to the steeply canted, vibrating deck beneath him, the white-haired veteran crossed the entire length of the compartment and slapped the cowering Political Officer full on the cheek.

"Now that's enough of your pathetic whining, Comrade Zampolit!" the fuming veteran chided. "You're a disgrace to both the Fleet and the Party, and I will have no more of this. Do you understand, comrade?"

Sobered by this surprise blow, the still-whimpering Political Officer managed a tear-stained reply. "I'm sorry, Admiral. It's just that I can't bear the idea of my poor Katrina being such a young widow."

"And don't you think each one of us feels the same way about our loved ones?" countered the admiral. "This is no way for a naval warrior to act, comrade. Especially when there's still a very good chance we'll yet escape this attack."

The deck rolled hard to the right, and as Kharkov reached out to stabilize himself, the seated sonar operator called out dryly. "The three torpedoes continue their approach, Captain. The range of the lead weapon is now down to a thousand meters."

From the corner of the attack center directly opposite Mikhail Kharkov, the *Neva*'s Captain absorbed this observation with a pained grimace. Beside him, his senior lieutenant did likewise.

"It's obvious that these diversionary tactics are worthless," reflected Viktor Belenko somberly. "The American Mark 48's are quicker than we had anticipated, and even the *Neva*'s great speed won't be enough to outrun them."

Sergei Markova knew very well that his old friend was right. Even though the *Neva*'s turbines were spewing out an incredible forty-eight knots of forward speed, the trio of persistent torpedoes continued their relentless pursuit.

When it didn't appear that their great speed would save them, Markova tried sending the *Neva* deep into the sea's depths. Yet even a well-defined thermocline failed to fool the Mark 48's, who were programmed to home in on the vessel's acoustic signature.

Finally the captain decided, if they couldn't outrun or outdive these persistent weapons, only one course remained open to them. Somehow Sergei would have to get the *Neva* in a position where he could order the power plant shut down. Then, once the mad, grinding wash of their propeller spun to a halt, the torpedoes would no longer have a target to home in on and the chase would be over.

As the frustrated young captain stared down at the bathymetric chart of the sound they currently sailed beneath, Viktor Belenko offered yet another desperate proposal.

"Perhaps we should try launching another decoy, Sergei. Even if it is the last one we carry."

"What's the use?" the captain sighed. "The others were useless. Why should this one be any different?"

"That doesn't sound like the Sergei Markova I know," retorted the senior lieutenant. "I realize the other decoys only served to temporarily divert the Mark 48's, but at least there's a slim chance this one will do better. And even if it doesn't, at the very least we'll have a few minutes reprise to come up with something better. Otherwise, my friend, our fate is all but sealed."

Still intently gazing at the chart, Sergei smashed his fist down onto the table's Plexiglas top.

"Damn!" he cursed. "If only we could buy enough time to successfully scram our reactor. That's the

297

only thing that would save us."

"Torpedo range is down to eight hundred meters, Captain," said the sonar operator.

This grim observation was followed by the strained voice of the *Neva's* diving officer. "We've attained a depth of seventy-five meters, Captain, and are presently running out of water. Shall I proceed with another dive? For the surface-scanning Fathometer shows a nasty-looking inverted ice ridge above that could be a problem shortly."

This innocent remark registered in Sergei's mind, and he was all set to order yet another plunge into deeper waters when an idea suddenly came to him.

"Comrade diving officer, is this inverted ridge that you speak of large enough to shelter a vessel the size of the *Neva?*"

Not certain of what the captain was getting at, the diving officer answered. "Most definitely, Captain. It's one of the largest and thickest I've seen so far, and extends downward well over forty meters."

"Then that's it!" exclaimed Sergei. "We'll launch our last decoy, then as the Mark 48's give it their usual brief chase, we'll ascend into the cover of this ridge, scram our reactor, and when the American torpedoes reinitiate pursuit, they'll be unable to find us because of the ice!"

Hurriedly crossing the attack center's length to join the captain was Mikhail Kharkov. "Why that's a brilliant plan, comrade! Yet we mustn't tarry, for time is of the essence."

With the invaluable assistance of Viktor Belenko, Sergei Markova's unorthodox maneuver was put into action. In a growling, swirling rush, the *Neva's* last remaining decoy was launched. Soon afterward, the trio of attacking torpedoes were fooled into checking this new vibrant signature out for themselves.

Though this deception would only be a temporary one, it gave the *Sierra* class submarine time to drastically cut its forward speed, level out, and begin the intricate process of inching its way upward until it was nestled beneath the shelter of the inverted ice ridge.

No sooner had the sub's reinforced sail delicately touched up against the roof of this barrier than the three torpedoes realized the decoy was not their intended prey. With a whining vengeance, they turned back toward the *Neva's* last known coordinates and attempted to seek out the vessel that they had been sent to destroy. It was fate alone that allowed the Mark 48's sensitive acoustic sensors the opportunity of getting one last fix on the *Neva's* propellor wash seconds before its turbines were deactivated and its reactor scrammed. Knowing now where the true enemy lay, the torpedoes streaked upward to complete their mission.

Guided solely by acoustic sound waves, the Mark 48's took the quickest route to their target's last known fix. Ignoring the fact that the signature suddenly stopped transmitting, the torpedoes surged forward in their final attack run. The trio of weapons impacted almost simultaneously. A blindingly bright, ear-splitting detonation followed, during which time over three-thousand pounds of high-density TORPEX explosives bit into the solid wall of ice the warheads had mistakenly run into.

On the surface, this massive blast was hardly noticeable. As the incessantly howling wind scarred the pack ice smooth with trillions of bits of flying razor-sharp ice pellets, a sudden fracture formed on the ridge's surface. Immense in size, this rift was fed by the tremendous heat of the explosion that had just occurred a few meters below. As this fracture continued to widen, it eventually tore apart the entire ridge itself with a grinding, gut-wrenching crack. With the ice now open to the sea below, an immense, black-hulled vessel popped up from the depths to fill this sudden gap. And in just such an unlikely manner, the *Sierra* class nuclear submarine *Neva* came to rest on the ice-encrusted surface of Lancaster Sound.

Chapter Fourteen

The Arctic dawn broke dull and gray. As the Rangers scrambled from their igloo, they were met by a shrieking gust of frigid wind that provided instant proof the storm had yet to pass. The snow had continued to fall during the night, and many of the drifts were waist high or better. It proved to be an effort just to locate two of the snowcats, though the dogs fared better because of the protective berm the soldiers had built for them.

With his snow goggles already covered by a translucent coating of frost, Lieutenant Jack Redmond did his best to break camp with all due haste.

"Sergeant-Major! Forget about exhuming those buried snowcats and get up there on that ridge with the directional receiver. Take Corporal Eviki with you, and see if we're close enough to pick up that homing signal as yet. I'll take care of everything else."

As Cliff Ano crisply saluted and pivoted to begin this task, Redmond turned for the staging area where their vehicles had been parked. Several of the men were there, digging into the snow drifts in an effort to find the two missing snowmobiles. Joining in with a collapsible shovel, the senior commando

301

motivated his men to do their utmost.

"Come on, lads! It's got to be down here some-where. The sooner we get moving again, the closer we'll be getting to this mission's conclusion. And I'll personally guarantee a week in Hawaii if we should manage to pull this thing off."

This last remark was all that was needed to inspire his men to really put their backs into their work. And minutes later, the first of the snowcats was reached. As the other vehicle was also uncovered, Redmond helped his men remove the excess snow. With a collective grunt, they lifted up the ice-encrusted snowmobiles and transferred them out of the thick drifts.

The breathtaking cold made their labor all the more difficult, and it was a supreme effort merely to get the vehicles in line and ready for travel. While supervising this job, Redmond shouted out to his men.

"Do any of you know how to hookup that dog-sled? The sergeant-major should be back shortly, and I'd like to be ready to take off as soon as he does so."

A young, mustached Inuit private, who had been busy scraping the frost off the windshields, was quick to respond. "I think I can do it, Lieutenant. Though I never had a team of my own, I helped my grandfather harness his team when I was a kid."

"Then get to it, Private!" screamed Redmond, who turned to duck back inside the snowhouse to make certain all the supplies had been removed.

Ignoring the empty ration cans that lay scattered on the igloo's floor, Redmond pocketed a compass that had been dropped. He also found a dog-eared girlie magazine, that had been absentmindedly stuffed in between two snowblocks. This was obviously a treasured piece of literature, for its pages were worn and wrinkled. The weathered commando couldn't help flipping through its pages and was surprised to find that the scantily clad models were entirely Oriental. The centerfold was a gorgeous creature with long dark hair and a huge, firm bosom. For the first time that morning he was unmindful of the constant bitter cold. Yet his reverie was brief, as he was joined by his breathless sergeant-major.

"We've got it, Lieutenant! The signal's coming in loud and strong. It can't be more than a couple of kilometers to the northwest of here."

Quickly snapped back to thoughts of his duty, Redmond stuffed the magazine into the folds of his parka and met his subordinate's excited glance.

"Good job, Sergeant-Major. But are you certain that this particular signal is the one we're searching for?"

"Absolutely, sir," snapped the Inuit. "Just like Command said, we found it on the high-frequency band, only seconds after we set up the receiver. It's got to be that black box. What else could it possibly be?"

"For the squad's sake, I hope you're correct, my friend. Because this rotten weather has been more physically demanding than I anticipated, and I don't think either the men or our equipment can take much more of it."

A determined expression came to the Inuit's face. "Don't underrate us, Lieutenant. We might not look like much, but I guarantee you my boys can take a whole lot more punishment than this. Why, for an Inuit, this is nothing but a Sunday walk in the park."

Jack Redmond slyly grinned. "I was hoping that

you'd say that, Sergeant-Major. So let's get the lads on the go, and wrap up this assignment once and for all."

The Inuit flashed Redmond a hearty thumbs-up and led the way through the igloo's tunnel. Outside they were met by gusting wind, the throaty whine of the snowcats being warmed up, and the high-pitched yelps of their dogs.

Taking his place in the lead snowmobile, Redmond raised his right hand overhead and commandingly shouted. "Okay, lads! The tough part's over now. We shouldn't have much further to go. So let's keep our eyes open, and stick close together. I certainly wouldn't want to lose anybody now that we've gotten this close."

As he shifted his right hand down, Cliff Ano responded by throwing back his rawhide whip and snapping it forward with a crack. Needing no more encouragement, the harnessed dogteam lunged forward, and the squadron of Canada's best was once again on the move.

Admiral of the Fleet Mikhail Kharkov couldn't believe their good fortune. Not only had they successfully escaped the Imperialist torpedo salvo, but the resulting blast had fractured the pack ice allowing the *Neva* a free ride to the surface. A look of genuine astonishment had graced their young captain's face as he'd realized the situation and quickly acted to take the best advantage of it. Then, after sharing a brief cry of relieved joy with his shipmates, Sergei Markova barked out the orders that sent the sub's radio antenna whirring up into the crisp Arctic air from its home in the enclosed sail.

The admiral had been anxiously waiting for this

moment, and was standing directly behind the seated radio operator as he activated the receiver. With the band selector already set on the high-frequency channel, the seaman fine-tuned the knob and cautiously turned up the receiver's volume gain. A throaty blast of static emanated from the elevated speakers, only to be followed by a pulsating, high-pitched staccato tone that brought a shout of sheer triumph from the white-haired veteran's lips.

"Listen, Comrades, we've done it! We've found the black box!"

The sedate radio operator efficiently confirmed this fact, and proceeded to instigate a directional fix. Only when this process was completed did a hint of excitement flavor his tone.

"Why it's incredibly close, Captain. It can't be more than a half-dozen kilometers to the southeast."

Quick to join Kharkov behind the radio console was Sergei Markova. "So we have indeed accomplished our mission, Admiral. This is truly an amazing morning. Why I thought the search for the cockpit voice recorder would take days to complete."

Already mentally planning the actual recovery, Kharkov replied. "Don't forget that the tape is not yet in our hands, Captain Markova. But I'll soon remedy that. It's important that those five volunteers join me at once in the forward torpedo room so we can suit up. I want to be standing on the ice itself in another half-hour's time."

"I still think you should reconsider going along on this excursion, Admiral. That's a full-scale blizzard going on outside this hull, and there's no telling what hazardous conditions you'll meet up with once you're out there. I'm more than capable of leading the recovery squad in your place."

"Absolutely not!" retorted the red-cheeked veteran. "Don't let this old body fool you, Captain. There's thick Siberian blood within these veins, and a little snowstorm is not about to stand in my way. A short hike is just what I need to properly stretch these cramped legs. And besides, I thought I made it perfectly clear that the *Neva*'s senior command staff must remain aboard the ship at all times. I'm not about to jeopardize this vessel by sending its officers away from their stations. They must stay here, where they belong."

"As you wish, Admiral," yielded Sergei. "I will have the senior lieutenant muster the volunteers at once."

Mikhail Kharkov felt like a young man again as he excused himself and headed for his stateroom. Once in his cabin, he quickly dressed himself for the trek. His first layer of clothing was a set of long, open-mesh underwear. Next came a flannel shirt and corduroy trousers, and a triple-knit woolen parka. After slipping on two pairs of insulated socks and a rubberized inner shoe, he proceeded to the forward torpedo room to get the rest of his gear.

The Admiral of the Fleet was glad to find the five volunteers, in various stages of dress, waiting for him there. Altogether they were a robust, muscular group of lads, who didn't mind a scrap now and then, and weren't afraid to admit it. Kharkov stood in line with them as the quartermaster handed out their outerwear—caribou-fur jumpsuits that had hoods attached to them. Sealskin boots were issued to protect their feet, while double-thick reindeer-skin gloves over which woolen mittens were worn completed their outfits.

By the time all of this clothing was put on, Mikhail had broken out in a sweat. Such a flushed state could be dangerous upon exposure to the frigid air, and he made certain that the men gathered the rest of their gear as quickly as possible. This included lightweight 5.45mm Kalaishnikov assault rifles, RGD-5 hand grenades, extra ammunition, and a portable-directional finder to precisely home in on the pulsating signal.

The recessed hatchway that was cut into the sail's base, saved them the trouble of having to climb up into the attack center and then crawl up through the conning tower itself. As this hatch was opened, a blast of bitterly cold air entered the *Neva*. A shrieking wind greeted them as one by one the volunteers ducked outside. The last one to leave was Mikhail Kharkov.

"Good luck, Admiral," offered the ship's captain, in a voice deepened by concern.

"Quit worrying so, Comrade Markova," returned the Admiral of the Fleet. "Just make certain there's plenty of hot tea and cognac to go around when we get back."

Then, with the briefest of nods, the veteran crawled out of the hatchway and joined his five colleagues on the sub's frozen deck. Even with their woolen face masks and goggles in place, the blowing ice spicules stung their cheeks and eyelids. Turning their backs to the wind, they utilized a portable hand ladder to descend down to the ice pack.

Mikhail was surprised to find that the *Neva* was already encrusted in a glistening shroud of solid ice. The lead into which they had ascended had already frozen over, and from the racket the ice ridge was making, he only hoped the pressure would remain constant until they returned. For if the ice should suddenly close in on the ship, they would be left stranded. To prepare for such a worst-case scenario, it had been established that if the *Neva* was forced

307

to descend, a supply of additional survival gear would be left topside for those on the ice. And hopefully another polynya would be encountered in the vicinity so the ship might surface and effect a proper rescue.

With compass in hand, Mikhail turned to the southeast and beckoned the others in this direction. This was all that was needed to get the squad moving. Fortunately, that put the wind at their backs, and they could concentrate solely on the rugged terrain they were crossing over.

The contorted ice ridges made their progress slow at first. It took them over an hour to travel barely a half kilometer. By this time the submarine had long since disappeared behind them, and it took a bit of imagination just to realize that they were actually walking above the waters of Lancaster Sound. Only occasional encounters with open leads pointed to this fact.

Their point man was a hearty Siberian who had been born and raised in the town of Yakutsk. A torpedoman by trade, he took to the ice like a duck to water. Trusting in his judgment explicitly, Mikhail did not balk when the point man signaled for the group to halt and gather behind an immense shelf of sloping ice. With this obstacle providing a convenient windbreak, the Siberian pointed to yet another ridge that lay immediately before them.

"That looks like the coastline," he observed firmly. "From here on in we must stick close together, and constantly be on the alert for crevasses."

"Are we still on course?" quizzed the admiral.

To answer this question, the seaman who was assigned to carry the receiver slipped off his backpack and removed the compact, battery-powered homing device. A senior radio technician aboard the

Neva, he had little trouble switching on the unit, extending its long whiplike antenna overhead, and adjusting the frequency knob to the desired channel. Only when a green light began flashing did he speak out.

"That we are, Admiral. The signal seems to be projecting from somewhere over that ridge."

Following the direction of his outstretched finger, Mikhail made a brief alignment with his compass. "We will continue on bearing one-four-zero," instructed the veteran.

As the radio technician stowed away the receiver, he momentarily began brushing away the coating of ice that had formed over his coat's length. Quick to stop him was their point man.

"Don't do that, Yuri! That ice serves as an additional insulator, and could turn out to be a real lifesaver."

Nodding that he understood, the radio man shouldered his backpack and signaled that he was ready to go. As they began to make their way toward the coastline, Mikhail found himself marveling at the professional manner in which the young sailors were behaving. Quick to help each other, they went on with their difficult mission heedless of the biting wind, the frigid temperatures, and the dangerous conditions of the ice itself. These were the kind of men that filled the veteran's heart with pride.

There were many in the Defense Department who were forever grumbling about the poor quality of troops being recruited into the Motherland's armed forces. These were the same individuals who complained that the military was not prepared to go to war because it was comprised of a vast mixture of racial and ethnic groups that could never jell as a single, unified fighting unit.

Mikhail begged to differ with such individuals. He knew it was this very racial diversity that gave the Motherland's military forces their unique edge. This morning's mission proved his point. For in his present squad were two Siberians, a Ukrainian, an Estonian, and a native Muscovite. Instead of working against each other, they each had a unique quality or talent that made the team that much stronger.

It was no different during the Great War. Faced with a continuous shortage of trained men, the military often had to make do with raw recruits who had been called to duty from the far corners of the Motherland. On many of the ships Kharkov had commanded, a good majority of his men couldn't even speak Russian. Yet regardless of this handicap, the standing orders of the day were somehow always translated, and when it came to actual hostilities, these same sailors were often the first ones to offer their lives for the sake of their country. Only in the rarest of incidents had Mikhail been forced to deal with acts of cowardice under fire or desertion. And he'd soon learned, it was just as likely for a Great Russian to abandon his post when the shells began flying as it was for a raw recruit from Azerbaijan.

The Admiral of the Fleet only wished that the bureaucrats from whose mouths these groundless complaints issued could be here now. They'd all too soon see the errors of their ways, and learn to praise the military for the difficult job it was doing, instead of constantly bellyaching. Of course in the new world order that would soon be upon them, these same spineless public officals were doomed to lose their positions of power. Most would be sent packing to the far eastern frontier, where they would be reeducated in the virtues of hard work and humility, virtues they had somehow lost sight of while serving

310

behind the insular walls of the Kremlin.

With such thoughts to keep his mind occupied, Mikhail Kharkov ignored the bitter elements. With his eyes glued to the feet of the seaman immediately ahead of him, the veteran readily matched the squad's pace. And before he knew it, they were helping each other scramble up over the raft of inverted ice that had brought them to the snow-covered plains of Baffin Island's Brodeur Peninsula.

It proved to be the mad howling of the wind outside that broke Ootah from his sound slumber. As his eyes popped open, he was immediately greeted by the bright, flashing red light of the mysterious black object Arnuk had found partially buried in the snow. The compact, rectangularly shaped box sat in the center of the domed room, exactly where he had left it earlier.

On the opposite side of the snowhouse, Akatingwah could just be seen beneath the furs on the sleeping pallet. Their son was in her arms, and for a second Ootah fought the temptation to crawl in beside them. Yet a greater duty called to him as he fondled the bone amulet that hung from his neck, and he somewhat reluctantly sat up to continue his lonely vigil before the enigmatic object that had fallen from the heavens.

With his eyes focused on the constantly blinking light, he kneeled down directly before it. In a matter of minutes, a heavy, drowsy feeling overcame him. It was all he could do to keep his eyes open as his heartbeat pounded away to the rhythm of the flashing strobe.

Though Ootah really wasn't certain if he had fallen asleep or not, his inner eye began filling with a vibrant vision. In it, Nakusiak appeared before him and beckoned his son to join him outside. Ootah did so, and found himself in a grass-filled valley. Wildflowers painted this meadow with vibrant color, while above the sun glistened in all of its summertime radiance.

As Ootah followed his father deeper into the valley, he spotted a herd of shaggy musk oxen. Instead of quickly forming a defensive circle, the massive, horned beasts continued grazing, completely ignoring the human's presence. This strange behavior bothered Ootah, who was to get an even greater shock upon viewing a pack of gray wolves peacefully interspersed amongst the musk oxen. These perpetual hunters, who were even a danger to man, merely lay basking in the warm sun, at total peace with the world around them.

Ootah was preparing to point this strange sight out to his father, when a cold wind hit him full in the back. And in the blink of an eye he was transferred to the center of a frozen lake. A circular breathing hole cut in the ice lay before him. Floating on the water's surface was a disturbingly familiar eider feather.

Though his instincts warned him to back away from the edge of this open lead, his feet were stuck to the ice below, and any escape on his part proved impossible. Forced to look down into the waters of the circular pool, he viewed a series of bubbles rise up from the depths. This disturbance increased, until a constantly blinking, intense red light could be seen glowing from the water below. This blindingly bright strobe seemed to have hypnotic powers, and began rising from the depths with a frightening swiftness. Again Ootah struggled to flee, yet he could only stand there and tremble in terror as a huge, black rectangular object broke through the ice and towered above him. Two men in fur parkas could be seen standing in a well that had been cut into this monolith's top. One of these men had snow-white hair and bright red cheeks. Above this figure, the flashing strobe incessantly blinked away from its perch on a thin black pipe that extended high into the heavens.

It was at this point that Ootah snapped awake. The pictures this trance had painted were still disturbingly real. This was especially true of the flashing strobe that continued blinking from the floor of the igloo before him. Vainly trying to make some sort of sense out of this macabre vision, the Inuit could suddenly hear his dogs barking in the distance. There was an intense urgency to these yelps, and Ootah stiffly rose to see what this commotion was all about.

He hastily pulled on his caribou-skin parka and crawled out the tunnel-like entryway. The icy wind greeted him like a slap to the face as he scanned the horizon. Though the muted dawn was just forming, he could see his dogs perched anxiously beside their tether pole. They were howling away like Tornarsuk himself was after them, and Ootah made his way through the snow to attend to them.

It was because of the whinings of his lead dog, Arnuk, that Ootah directed his gaze to the northwest. Here a line of men were visible. These figures were dressed in strange fur parkas, and had rifles slung over their shoulders. The Inuit's instincts warned of trouble, but he walked out to greet them anyway.

The strangers seemed to be of immense size. Because of the woolen masks they wore, Ootah was unable to see their faces. Yet this was soon to change when one of the figures who had been traveling at the back of the pack walked out and raised his voice in greeting.

Though this stranger's words were of a strange dialect the Inuit had never heard before, they were spoken with a forceful directness that hinted this man was the leader. Only when it was apparent that his words weren't sinking in did this figure pull back his hood and yank off his mask. Taking in this stranger's face, Ootah shuddered in horror. For staring back at him was the white-haired, red-cheeked man whom he had just encountered in his vision!

"I show a green light on laser activation, proceeding to interface with the *Defiance*'s Nav system."

Dr. Laurie Lansing's words rang out through the control room. The crew had long since adjusted to the presence of the hard-working scientist, and continued to pursue their individual duties without the least bit of distraction.

Captain Matt Colter was thankful for this fact. As he stood at the chart table watching the attractive civilian efficiently address the new surface-scanning Fathometer's keyboard, he found himself inwardly hoping that the new device would function properly. Not only for the *Defiance*'s sake, but for Lansing's as well.

"Skipper, we should be just about at those coordinates our last radio fix relayed to us."

The XO's observations caused Colter to shift his line of sight back to the chart that lay spread out before them.

"I don't think we're going to be able to get much closer to the coastline," said the captain.

"It shouldn't be more than a kilometer hike," observed Al Layman, who pointed to the north shore of the Brodeur Peninsula with the well-chewed stem of his pipe. "And if our fix is accurate, another kilometer or so inland should bring us right there."

Matt Colter intently studied the chart and thoughtfully responded. "I'm glad it's not much further than that. Our last meteorological reading showed that blizzard still blowing with a fury topside. A hike on the ice is dangerous enough, even without this storm."

"We'll manage, Skipper. Besides, at least we don't have that Russian sub to worry about anymore."

Colter looked up and directly met his XO's stare. "Can you really say that for certain, Al. I know we heard our three fish explode, but after that, all that followed was the sound of fracturing ice. We copied absolutely no evidence that indicates a successful hull penetration."

The XO shook his head. "Even if we didn't hear their hull imploding, the chances are good we did enough damage to at least knock out their propulsion system. Why I'll bet they're sitting up there dead in the water right now, trapped beneath the ice cover."

"Either that or they've scrammed their reactor on us and are playing possum," offered the captain, who turned around when a woman's voice excitedly called out behind him.

"The lasers show thin ice above us. Thin ice!"

Scrambling over to the scientist's side, Colter studied the green-tinted monitor screen. Unlike their old ice machine that printed out its information on a crude piece of graph paper, the new Fathometer provided a three-dimensional sketch of the exact conditions existing on the surface. It proved to be the alert civilian technician who explained just what he was looking at.

"The lasers indicate a polynya precisely five hundred and ninety feet long and two hundred and thirty-one feet wide. An inverted ridge extending some twenty feet deep surrounds the north face of the lead, while the southern edge is composed of relatively young ice, barely three feet deep."

"That should be more than sufficient," replied the captain. "Did the *Defiance*'s nav computer accept your interface?"

Laurie Lansing pointed to the green light located to the right side of the monitor screen's lower edge. "I show a definite lock, Captain."

"Well, from here on in I guess the rest is up to you, Doctor. You may proceed with an automated ascent. And please, don't hesitate to call out the second something doesn't look right. I'll be standing close by to go manual if needed."

"Let's hope that won't be necessary, Captain," returned the civilian. She then took a deep breath and began addressing her keyboard.

Matt Colter wasted no time informing the diving officer that the *Defiance* was now being driven by the computer. It looked strange to see the two seated helmsmen release their steering columns, and watch as the wheels began turning on their own.

As the vessel began a wide banking turn, the ballast pumps automatically activated. To a soft, muted whine the ship was lightened, and ever so gradually, they began ascending.

At a depth of one hundred and ten feet, the *Defiance* hit an unexpected pocket of colder water and began rising more quickly than anticipated. Matt Colter watched as the depth gauge lost over thirty feet in a matter of seconds. He was just about to order a manual override when Laurie Lansing intervened in his place.

"Sensors show a temperature inversion. Computer is compensating by taking on additional ballast."

Before these words were out of her mouth, the pumps once again activated, this time drawing water into the ship's tanks. The *Defiance*'s rate of ascent immediately stabilized. And a minute and a half later, the *Sturgeon* class vessel was safely floating on the surface of Lancaster Sound.

A relieved chorus of shouts and applause briefly filled the normally hushed command compartment. Speaking for the crew was its captain.

"Dr. Lansing, we'd all like to congratulate you on completing the US Navy's first automated ascent in ice conditions. If this device continues showing such excellent results, it will revolutionize Arctic operations and make our difficult profession not only a bit easier, but a lot safer as well."

Laurie Lansing blushed and humbly replied. "Thank you, Captain Colter. But your kind words are really addressed to the wrong person. This was my father's dream, and he spent almost three decades of his life making it come true. I only wish he could be here to see the results."

The civilian's response was followed by the deep voice of the quartermaster. "Captain, the radio room reports a strong, pulsating high-frequency signal coming in on bearing two-two-zero."

As he absorbed this information, Matt Colter firmly addressed his XO. "You may take the Conn, Mr. Layman. I'd better get below and throw on some long johns. I'm afraid it's going to be a little nippy where I'm off to next."

"Aye, aye, sir," snapped the XO, who facetiously added, "And don't forget to keep an eye out for polar bears, Skipper."

Colter grinned. "Thanks for the warning, Lieutenant Commander. I'll keep it in mind."

With his lips still turned in a smile, the *Defiance*'s captain smartly pivoted and disappeared through the aft hatchway, his thoughts already refocusing on the unusual job that now faced him.

Chapter Fifteen

Behind an ice-encrusted ridge, Lieutenant Jack Redmond lay on his stomach, his binoculars focused on the snow-covered plateau that stretched out before him. At his side, Sergeant-Major Cliff Ano did likewise. Both of the Arctic Rangers took in a domed snowhouse. A single, fur-clad individual with a rifle slung over his shoulder stood beside this structure's entryway.

"I don't like this situation one bit," offered the concerned Inuit. "I'm almost certain the rifle he's carrying is a Soviet-made Kalaishnikov."

Jack Redmond grunted. "You could be right, Sergeant-Major. But what in the hell is a Russian doing out here? And where did he come from?"

"It's obvious they've come for the same thing we have," returned Ano. "As to how they got here, who knows, perhaps they were dropped by parachute."

Redmond shook his head. "I doubt that, my friend. This storm has only just begun to lessen, and even now, a parachute operation would be extremely risky."

Their gazes locked on the igloo, they watched as five individuals proceeded to crawl out of the snowhouse's tunnellike entrance. Each of these figures wore a fur parka, though only four carried rifles.

"I'll bet you that unarmed one is the original occupant of the igloo," offered the Inuit. "Look, the others are pointing their weapons at him, and seem to be instructing him to harness up that dog team."

Jack Redmond watched this scene unfold and whispered forcefully. "That does it, Sergeant-Major. Something's definitely not right down there. Since our last radio fix points us directly onto this same plain, we'd better not delay any longer."

Crawling back off the ridge, Redmond began sketching out in the snow their plan of attack.

"It's obvious that we've got them outnumbered. And since they appear to be on foot, our snowmobiles will give us the element of mobility as well. We'll break out the weapons and divide the squad in half. Three of the snowcats under my command will move in and circle the igloo on its northern side, while the other three under Corporal Eviki's leadership will approach from the south. You'll move straight in on the dogsled."

"Sounds good to me, Lieutenant. But do you really think we'll need our weapons?"

There was a somberness to Redmond's tone as he answered, "If they're indeed Soviet military, we'll need them all right. So share this with the men, and make certain to remind them this isn't just another exercise."

Nodding that he understood, Cliff Ano stood and scrambled down the ridge to join the squad. Jack Redmond crawled in the opposite direction and took one last look at the assortment of armed men gathered in front of the igloo. An alien tightness gathered in the pit of his stomach, and for the first time in his twenty-year career, the commando prepared himself for real live combat.

Five minutes later, a bansheelike whine filled the air as the now-armed Rangers started up their snowcats and shot out from the shelter of the ridge where they'd been hiding. The six sleek vehicles split up as planned, with Sergeant-Major Ano following with his team of howling huskies.

The snow was deep, and as Jack Redmond drove his snowcat through a shallow ravine, he could clearly see the five armed men reacting to their surprise appearance by diving to the ground for cover. Seconds later, a variety of exploding bursts in the snow around Redmond's snowcat indicated they were being fired upon. The veteran commando was hoping the armed party would see that the odds were against them and would peacefully surrender. Yet this was not to be the case, and Redmond pulled his vehicle to a halt behind an elongated hummock of ice, all the time signaling for the two snowcats that followed him to do likewise.

"Take cover behind the ridge and return fire!" ordered Redmond.

With his own M16 in hand, he crawled up to the lip of the hummock and cautiously peeked over its ice-encrusted lip. Less than an eighth of a kilometer away lay the igloo. The armed party they were after had taken cover behind some sort of circular berm that most likely had originally been used to shelter the dogs. These same terrified huskies were harnessed to a nearby sled, and were really barking up a storm. Only a stout tether kept them from taking off on their own.

A series of sharp, explosive cracks sounded to his right, and Redmond knew his own men were responsible for this racket. His squad was primarily composed of decorated Inuit marksmen, and these men utilized their rifles efficiently, their shells probing the berm for any weaknesses. Originally trained as hunters, the Inuit depended upon their marksmanship to shoot prey such as minks and beavers right through the eye if possible, so as to not ruin the pelts. With such acquired skills, the shooting of a human being was hardly a challenge.

Before putting his own rifle into play, Redmond scanned the clearing in an effort to locate the other three snowcats. Hoping that Corporal Eviki had found a similar hummock to hide his men behind, he cringed upon spotting those snowmobiles zooming by the opposite side of the berm. They seemed to be drawing an inordinate amount of small-arms fire that was augmented by a series of deep, resonant explosions. These deafening blasts were most likely from hand grenades, and as the veil of debris thrown into the air cleared, Redmond spotted a thick column of black smoke rise up into the frigid air. His worst fears were realized as he spotted the remains of an overturned snowcat engulfed in a blazing pyre.

The soldier who had been perched beside Redmond saw this sickening sight also, and cried out in horror. "My God, Lieutenant, they got all four of them!"

Though the prudent thing for Jack Redmond to do was to wait for the enemy to run out of ammunition and then order his men to attack, this tragic loss caused something to snap deep inside the veteran. Blinded by anger and the need for instant revenge, he cried out passionately.

"Back to the snowcats, men! We're going in to

322

eliminate that bunch of scum right now!"

A unified cheer arose from his men as they scrambled back to their tracked vehicles. To the high-pitched whine of the igniting engines, Redmond addressed the occupants of the two snowcats that were parked beside him.

"We'll charge straight in at them, at full throttle. Then at the last second, you'll pull off to the right, and I'll go left. This should cause just enough of a diversion for Private Etah to lob in a grenade and take them out. Can you handle that, Private?"

The Inuit who was seated in the back of Redmond's snowcat answered without hesitating. "Just get me within range, sir. I'll take care of the rest."

"Then let's do it!" cried Redmond. "And properly revenge our brothers who just gave their lives so that Canada can remain free!"

After snapping the snowcat into gear, the enraged veteran opened up its throttle and the vehicle jumped forward into the deep snow. Only when he was certain that the other two vehicles were close behind him did he floor the accelerator and steer toward the beckoning berm.

Oblivious to the hail of gunfire that whined overhead and ricocheted off his snowcat's nose, Redmond ducked his helmeted head down beneath the windshield and continued on an unswerving course. Only when the snowcat was so close to its goal that he could actually see the muzzle flashes of the gunfire aimed their way did he briefly touch the brakes. This allowed the two pursuing snowcats to catch up with him. The Rangers in these vehicles had long ago put their weapons into play, and just when it appeared that the three vehicles were going to smack right into the wall of ice, they abruptly separated as planned.

There was the briefest of pauses as the enemy was forced to readjust their line of fire. This was all the time Private Thomas Etah needed to pull the pins out of a pair of grenades and toss them upward over the berm's bullet hole-pocked, sloped walls. A resounding explosion followed. Yet this blast all too soon faded to be replaced by only the buzzing whine of the tracked vehicles and the incessant howl of the gusting wind.

The five remaining snowcats rendezvoused beside the still-burning wreck of the vehicle that had once held their co-workers. The fire had been so intense little remained of the equipment or the four men who had manned it.

"I can't believe it!" mourned one of the soldiers, who had been driving one of the two surviving snowcats of the original trio that took this route. "Corporal Eviki was just trying to create a diversion for us to outflank them when this happened. My God, there's hardly anything left to even bury!"

This macabre remark was met by the distant barking of dogs, and Sergeant-Major Ano could be seen on his sled passing by the igloo. A look of disbelief etched the Inuit's face as he pulled the team to a halt beside them.

"What in the hell happened here?" quizzed the distraught commando.

"It was Corporal Eviki and three others," returned Redmond painfully. "I'm afraid they got a little too close and the snowcat took a direct grenade hit."

"Damn it!" cursed Cliff Ano. "They were only a bunch of kids."

"Like hell they were!" snapped Jack Redmond. "They were Arctic Rangers, and as such were well prepared to give their lives for Canada without question."

"But what in the hell did they give up their lives for?" queried Ano, whose grief was very real.

Redmond sensed his subordinate's shock and answered with a bit more compassion. "That remains to be seen, Sergeant-Major. I hope there's something left inside that berm for us to identify. We took it out with two direct grenade hits."

"Maybe he can explain what's going on here!" shouted one of the commandoes, as he pointed toward a parka-clad figure who apparently had been buried beneath the snow beside a nearby dogsled.

"I bet you that's the guy they were forcing at gunpoint to hook up that team," offered Cliff Ano.

As this dark-haired, confused-looking man stood and began brushing the snow off his clothing, yet another newcomer emerged before them. This individual was armed with a pistol, and crawled out of the igloo's entranceway, pulling two others along with him. Yet long before the Rangers could put their weapons into play, this white-haired stranger shouted out in broken English.

"I wouldn't shoot if I were you, comrades. For if you do, these two will go with me."

His hostages were a young woman and a small child. Both were Inuits. Though Redmond's patience was running low at this point, he nevertheless instructed his men to lower their rifles.

Seeing this, the stranger once more voiced himself. "Now that's more like it, comrades. But you'd make me feel so much better if you'd drop those weapons altogether."

Again Redmond conceded, and instructed the Rangers to comply with this unpopular directive.

"You are most wise, comrades. Perhaps now I could have a personal word with your leader?"

Jack Redmond stepped forward and somberly introduced himself. "I'm Lieutenant Jack Redmond of the Canadian Arctic Rangers."

"Good morning, Comrade Redmond. I am Mikhail Kharkov, commander in chief of the Red Banner Fleet. I am genuinely sorry about this intrusion on your territory. But such an act was necessary to recover valuable property belonging to the Union of Soviet Socialist Republics."

The woman the white-haired Russian held in his arms began squirming at this point, and the Russian instantly tightened his grasp. Jamming the pistol he carried up against her neck, he added.

"Easy, my little Eskimo flower. Or I'll blow your scrawny neck off!"

Though the Inuit known as Akatingwah could not understand her captor's strange tongue, his firm grip convinced her that any escape on her part would be impossible. With his hostage thusly calmed, Mikhail Kharkov continued.

"May I ask what has happened to the men who accompanied me here, Lieutenant?"

Redmond beckoned toward the still-smoking berm. "I imagine you'll find what's left of them over there."

The admiral shook his head. "Ah, I should have known. They were such headstrong lads. Yet I'll miss them all the same."

"No more than I'll miss the four brave Canadians that died by their hands," spat Redmond.

"So it seems that both sides have been bloodied," observed Mikhail Kharkov. "Though such a poor showing by my five men can't be excused. Why a

326

soldier of the Soviet Socialist Republic should at the very least be worth two second-rate Canadians."

This uncalled for remark infuriated Redmond, who took a step forward, fists ready to strike out. To halt the Rangers advance, Kharkov pushed the barrel of his pistol deeper into the Inuit's throat.

"Easy does it comrade. I was only making a little joke as you call it. Any loss of life is deeply regretted, but such things will happen when armed men confront each other."

Redmond vented his frustration verbally. "Must I remind you that you are trespassing on the sovereign property of Canada, Admiral? It looks like what we have here is a direct and willful act of war."

"I'm sorry that you see it that way, comrade. Though if you continue to behave yourself and do what I say, perhaps you'll live long enough to learn why such an incursion was necessary. Now, all I'm going to need from you is one of those tracked vehicles, and a promise to stay away from your weapons until I'm out of range."

"And if I agree to such conditions?" queried the Ranger.

"Then the Eskimo lives," retorted Kharkov.

Having witnessed enough senseless bloodshed for one day, Jack Redmond nodded. "You can have this vehicle, Admiral. But I'm warning you, your country is going to pay for this senseless slaughter."

"I imagine our United Nations ambassador is in for a busy week," reflected Kharkov, his tone suddenly firm. "Have one of your men bring this vehicle over to the side of the igloo, and instruct him to leave it running."

"How do I know you'll keep your half of the bargain and release the hostage?" questioned Redmond.

"Since the word of a Soviet officer is obviously not enough, I'll tell you what I'll do. You can have this woman and child right now, if I can take a substitute in their place."

Redmond briefly considered this offer and replied. "That can be arranged, Admiral. Will I do?"

Mikhail Kharkov slyly grinned. "I suppose you would like to go along for the ride to see what this is all about, wouldn't you, Lieutenant? But instead of wasting more of your valuable time, I'll take that one over there."

With his free hand, Kharkov pointed to the confused, parka-clad figure who had been buried beneath the dog sled. Jack Redmond needed the assistance of Cliff Ano to communicate with this Inuit, whose name was Ootah. Without a second's hesitance, Ootah agreed to the switch.

While one of the Rangers started up a snowcat and drove it over to the igloo's side, Redmond learned that the now-freed female hostage was named Akatingwah. She was Ootah's wife, and though she wasn't exactly thrilled to see her husband take her place, she conceded for her young son's sake.

With his gun now aimed at Ootah's neck, the Russian bent down and pulled yet another object from the snowhouse's entryway. This rectangularly shaped box was painted black, and had a blinking red strobe light attached to its top surface. After carefully placing this device in the snowcat's storage compartment, Mikhail Kharkov boarded the vehicle, with the Inuit directly in front of him.

"This should make for a cozy ride," said Kharkov, as he activated the throttle mechanism with his free hand. The engine whined in response, and as the veteran turned the snowcat around, he offered one last parting remark. "So sorry that I have to run like this, Lieutenant. Remember now, stay away from those guns. See you in the UN, Comrades!"

Flooring the accelerator, Kharkov was thrown backward as the snowmobile lurched forward. Yet he quickly regained control and, before turning for the northwestern horizon, whipped past the remaining vehicles and put a bullet directly into each snowcat's engine cowling.

"Damn!" cursed Jack Redmond, as he violently kicked the snow at his feet. Looking on impotently as the Russian disappeared behind a distant ridge, he angrily cried out to his men. "Will one of you stop gawking and go see if he's left us with an operational snowcat!"

As several of the men sprinted off to fulfill this request, Cliff Ano walked over to confer with Redmond.

"So it was the Russians all along," offered the Inuit. "We should have figured that they'd go and try to pull something like this off."

"But why all this useless bloodshed?" returned Redmond. "And what's so important about that damn black box anyway? I'm sure Ottawa was eventually going to give it back to the Soviets once we had a chance to check it out. Why not wait until then?"

The perplexed Inuit could only shake his head.

Then one of the men screamed out behind him. "The snowcats are finished, sir. All five of them have bullet holes right through the engine block."

This revelation was accented by the report of a distant gunshot. Each of the commandoes turned to search the northwestern horizon where the Russian admiral had last been seen fleeing with his hostage. Seeing this, Akatingwah let out a wail and began sprinting out through the snow to determine her husband's fate.

As Cliff Ano ran out to grab her, one of the Rangers called out excitedly.

"We've got more visitors, Lieutenant! This party's coming in from the northeast on foot!"

"Pick up your rifles, and form a defensive formation along that snow ridge," ordered Redmond. "If it's more Russians, this time we'll teach those Red bastards what the fear of God is all about!"

After retrieving his binoculars from the storage compartment of his disabled snowcat, Redmond took up a position on an elevated hummock and attempted to identify these new intruders.

"There's five of them altogether!" he informed his men. "But they don't seem to be carrying Kalashnikovs. Instead, they're armed with M16's!"

Cliff Ano had calmed down the distraught Inuit by this time. He left her in the care of one of his associates, and joined Redmond on the hummock.

"Lieutenant, I'd like to volunteer to follow that Russian's trail. I could use the dogsled, and find out what that shot was all about."

"Permission granted," returned Redmond. "But if you smell the least bit of trouble, get back here on the double, and we'll move in with some reinforcements. This squad's been hit hard enough as it is."

"Will do, Lieutenant," answered the Sergeant-Major, as he ran down to his sled and got the dogs moving with a snapping crack of his whip.

With Ano gone, Jack Redmond called Private Etah to his side. "Private, you've just been made a

330

corporal. I want you to pick out two of the best marksmen that we've got. Position them on this hummock. I'm going to leave you in charge while I go down to find out who these newcomers are."

"But isn't that a risky proposition, Lieutenant? Why not wait until they come to us?"

The grizzled veteran looked the young soldier directly in the eyes and retorted. "Now that you're a corporal, I'm going to share with you leadership rule number one — never question an order from a superior officer. Do you read me, soldier?"

"Yes, sir!" answered the Inuit. "Just be careful, Lieutenant."

Touched by the youngster's concern, Jack Redmond slung his rifle over his shoulder, walked down the hummock, and began to make his way over the adjoining plain. Cliff Ano's barking team could still be heard in the distance, though the sled itself had long since disappeared behind a sloping ridge.

With the two sharpshooters providing cover fire from behind, Redmond plodded through a deep snow drift, jumped over a narrow fissure, and without unstrapping his weapon, called out to the rapidly advancing party. "Hello out there!"

This remark was met by a friendly wave, and a deep voice that boomed out in perfect English. "Hello to you, whoever you are!"

Jack increased his pace at this point, and all too soon made the acquaintance of Captain Mathew Colter, commander of the US Navy nuclear attack submarine *Defiance,* and four of his shipmates. There was a look of relief on the Canadian's face as he explained both his mission and the tragedy that had just taken place on the plain behind them. Yet he was genuinely shocked to learn that the Americans had been sent here for the very same reason that the Arctic Rangers had. And for all their trouble, the Russians had beaten the lot of them!

Mikhail Kharkov felt like a child again. With an innocent joy, he steered the speedy snowmobile down a sloping grade that led directly to the frozen surface of Lancaster Sound. It had been many years since he had last traveled on such an exhilarating means of transportation. Yet as a native Siberian, he was certainly no stranger to such tracked vehicles. Why he could even remember a time when the only expedient way to travel over the snow was by horse-pulled sleighs.

His father had had a gorgeous team of black stallions, and a hand-tooled sled that he had built himself. As a youngster, it was Mikhail's duty to harness the team. And he was always available to drive if needed. Many of his fondest memories were of such sleigh rides, sitting bundled in a thick fur blanket, with the crisp Siberian wind in his face and the sound of the sled's bells twinkling to the hollow clops of the horse's gallop.

The arrival of motorized sleds doomed this innocent era. Though much more efficient, such vehicles were loud and belched noxious fumes. They also sped along so rapidly that it was often difficult to even get a glimpse of the passing countryside.

The snowmobile he currently drove was quick and easy to steer. Its speed was even further enhanced when he got rid of his additional passenger. This he'd done soon after leaving the plain where the black box had been found.

The Eskimo he had taken hostage was a cowardly,

foul-smelling brute. As they sped away from his igloo, he began trembling with fear, and Mikhail was expecting him to break out in tears at any moment.

What the veteran mariner hadn't expected was the moment the idiot tried to break out of his grasp. This abrupt move caused Mikhail to temporarily lose control of the vehicle, and it went plowing into the face of a snow drift. Mikhail had been thrown right out of his seat by the force of this collision, and as he scrambled to his feet, he spotted the eskimo desperately digging into the overturned vehicle's storage compartment. There was no doubt in Mikhail's mind that the savage was after the cockpit voice recorder, and his hand went straight to his holstered pistol. At the exact moment Mikhail raised his Kalashnikov, the Eskimo turned to face him, and the veteran shot him a single time square in the chest.

As the native went sprawling to the snow, Mikhail righted the vehicle and after a bit of effort, finally got its motor started. It had been whining away with a vengeance ever since.

With a bone-jarring jolt, the snowmobile dropped down upon the pack ice. It would be on this frozen medium that he would find his lift back home to the Motherland. While checking the dashboard-mounted compass to make certain his course was correct, Mikhail opened the throttle wide. As the vehicle zoomed over the ice, his thoughts returned to the last time he had killed a man face-to-face.

It had been during the closing days of the Great War. As the Nazis retreated to make a last stand at Berlin, both the Soviets and their western allies rushed in to fill the void. Mikhail had been sent to occupy the German port complex at Danzig. Here at the Schichau shipyards, a revolutionary new class of German submarine was being constructed. Known as Type XXI, this vessel represented a last-ditch effort by Admiral Dönitz to turn the tide of war. Able to dive deeper for a longer period of time and at a greater speed than any previous class of submarine, the Type XXI was an engineering masterpiece. Yet it went into production too late to serve the Nazi cause, and Mikhail's job was to complete the five hulls that had already been laid down in Danzig.

It was while touring the partially completed engine room of the boat known as U-3538 that he'd been attacked by a German engineer. The grease-stained Nazi was high on schnapps, and came at Mikhail with wrench in hand. Even though the German was powerfully built, Mikhail was able to take advantage of his drunken state and throw his attacker down to the deck. Without giving the German a second to catch his breath, Mikhail jumped down upon the man's heaving chest and began strangling the life out of him. With his hands tightly gripped around the Nazi's neck, Mikhail watched the German die. During the last frantic seconds, their glances directly met, and he actually saw the manner in which death took him.

That incident had taken place over four decades ago. Yet it was still so fresh in his mind that he could actually smell the scent of fear that exuded from his attacker's pores.

And now, forty-five years later, fate had once again put him in a position to directly take another's life. And once more, he felt strangely stimulated by this godlike power. This was the case even though the Eskimo was nothing but a subhuman. The savage was little more than a beast, and shooting him was like putting an injured horse out of its misery.

Back in Siberia, such natives were welcomed as an integral part of the Motherland. They were educated and taught a trade, and today their culture flourished like never before. It was on account of them that vast tracts of Siberia were able to be developed, as centers of mining, hydroelectric power, and animal husbandry.

Their Canadian cousins were in vast contrast. Exploited by their government, they were forced to live like wild beasts, dependent upon the fickle whims of mother nature and an occasional government handout. They lived in incredible squalor, as the igloo Kharkov had just visited amply showed, and drowned their sorrows in vast amounts of cheap alcohol.

Such a waste of humankind was a pity. But the Capitalists only cared about exploiting their ancestral homes for oil and minerals, leaving behind nothing but a legacy of pollution and broken dreams.

Under the new world order that would shortly come to pass, such imbalances would be corrected. The exploited masses would be freed from their chains, as brotherhood and equality became the chants of the day.

Unfortunately, there were many who had to be sacrificed along the way so that this Socialistic dream could come true. Premier Alexander Suratov had been one of these unlucky ones, as were the five brave sailors who would not be returning to the *Neva* with him, and the pathetic Eskimo as well. Each of these individuals had been called before his time, to serve as fodder for the great revolution that would soon sweep the world.

The key to this uprising's success lay locked away

inside the snowmobile's storage compartment. Here a single cassette tape would soon change mankind's very destiny. Stored in the cockpit voice recorder's interior was the certain proof that his colleagues in the Politburo had demanded in exchange for their support. And once this support was given, the reins of power would be his!

That thought thrilled the white-haired veteran, who was forced to turn his current means of transport hard to the left when a sudden lead of open water showed itself before him. His heart pounded away as the thin ice beneath him cracked in protest. Yet the great speed at which he had been traveling kept the ice from fracturing altogether, and he was spared a certain fatal dunking.

As he zoomed over an elevated ice ridge, the horizon suddenly opened up and he spotted the distinctive silhouette of an immense, low-lying, black-hulled object seemingly entombed in the distant ice. Looking like a lonely beached whale, the *Neva* beckoned like a long-lost friend, and Mikhail dared to open the throttle full.

The snowmobile lurched forward in response, and the Admiral of the Fleet knew that it wouldn't be long before he'd be returning to the Motherland in utter triumph. And one of his first treats to himself would be a visit to his cherished dacha on the shores of Lake Baikal. With the flat, frozen white landscape whipping by him in a blur, he mentally visualized yet another corner of this great planet. Here an ancient wood stood in all its inspiring glory. And unlike the desolate, ice-encrusted wilderness he currently crossed, this forest was a shrine to life itself. Surely by now the first real snows had fallen, and the pines would be matted in fluffy shrouds of white. Yet the tumbling brook would still be flowing, the diverse creatures that inhabited its banks now leaving their tracks in the powdery snow.

How he missed this peaceful, pastoral haven! It was the real source of his vision, and without it, he'd be as empty as the jagged ice fields that presently surrounded him. Thus inspired, Kharkov felt a new sense of urgency as he charted the quickest route back to the *Neva*.

understand why. . . .

Chapter Sixteen

It was noon, and the Arctic sun still lay low in the heavens, as Matt Colter returned to the *Defiance*. His weary, bone-chilled party included two new faces. One of these individuals had to be carried aboard on a makeshift stretcher, while the other stood erect on the ice-covered deck where he wished his shore-based co-workers a hearty goodbye.

"I'm leaving the squad in your capable hands, Sergeant-Major. Please try to assure the Inuit woman that her husband appears to be all right. That bone necklace he was wearing most likely saved the poor bugger's life, but it will be up to the pharmacist's mate to bring him back to consciousness.

"While I'm gone, have the men start combing that plateau for other debris. And then you've got the somber task of holding a proper burial.

"By the way, in your absence, I made Thomas Etah a corporal. I know he's young and inexperienced, but he seems to be a quick learner and the men respect him. Give him his fair share of responsibilities, and perhaps he'll grow into the job like you and I did years ago."

"Pardon my asking, Lieutenant, but I still don't

understand why you'll be sailing with the Americans. Isn't our job over at this point?"

Cliff Ano's question brought a firm response from Redmond's lips. "Most definitely not, Sergeant-Major. Captain Colter feels there's a chance he'll be able to intercept the Soviets before they get out into the open sea. Don't forget, these waters are still Canadian territory. And though both submarines are technically trespassing here, my official presence sanctions the *Defiance*'s mission while possibly allowing us to complete ours as well."

The boarding party had made their way safely below deck, when a parka-clad seaman approached Jack Redmond from behind.

"Excuse me, sir. But we'll be diving soon and the captain requests that all hands clear the deck."

After nodding that he understood, Redmond took one last look at Cliff Ano. "I've got to be going, Sergeant-Major. Give my regards to the lads, and keep those ruffians busy and out of trouble!"

The last remark was met by a crisp salute. And the last Redmond saw of his subordinate, Ano was positioned behind the runners of the dogsled, spurring the huskies onward with crackling snaps of his whip.

A narrow steel ladder led Redmond down into an alien subterranean world. He soon found himself in a fairly spacious, elongated compartment. A blast of soothing, warm air engulfed him, and as he gratefully stripped off his fur parka and mittens, he checked out his new environment. The walls were completely lined with flashing consoles and snaking steel tubing. Manning this sophisticated high-tech equipment were a number of young men dressed in matching dark blue coveralls. Each of them seemed to give him the briefest of polite stares before industriously returning to their duties.

He was surprised to find one of these sailors a woman. Also clothed in blue coveralls, she sat before a large monitor screen, busily attacking the keyboard. Her dark hair was tied in a knot, and from what he could see of her face, she looked extremely attractive.

"Ah, there you are, Lieutenant." The deep voice came from his left.

Turning his head, the commando took in the now familiar face and figure of the *Defiance*'s Captain. At this blond-haired officer's side stood a tall, thin, mustached figure, who had a scarred bit of a pipe between his lips. It was Matt Colter who initiated the introductions.

"Lieutenant Jack Redmond, I'd like you to meet Lieutenant Commander Al Layman, the ship's executive officer, or XO as we prefer to call him."

"Pleased to meet you." The XO, gave Redmond a warm, firm handshake. "From what the Skipper tells me, you had some trouble with some old adversaries of ours topside. I sincerely regret the loss of your men, and hope that we can help you even the score."

"That would be most appreciated," returned Redmond. He liked the way this officer looked him right in the eye and spoke directly.

"The bridge is secure, Captain," said a voice from behind.

"Very well," retorted the captain as he scanned the control room. "Prepare to dive."

Taking Redmond by the arm, Matt Colter guided him over to a console covered with dozens of switches and gauges. A dual line of button-sized lights dominated this console, with only the top row

340

currently lit a vibrant green. A slightly built, red-headed sailor watched them approach, and snapped into action the moment the Captain said, "Take us down, Mr. Marshall."

With fluid ease, the sailor then hit a variety of switches and buttons, and the compartment was filled with a muted, whining sound. It was Colter who explained what this racket meant.

"That noise is coming from the ship's ballast pumps. In order to dive, seawater is drawn into the specially designed tanks that line our hull. As these tanks fill, the *Defiance* loses its positive buoyancy and we begin to sink beneath the surface. Special trimming tanks are then utilized to adjust the ship's weight until it has neutral buoyancy and is balanced fore and aft."

The captain pointed toward the two sailors seated to the right of the diving console. Both these individuals wore safety harnesses and gripped airplane-like steering columns.

"Over here are our planesmen. Once we're underway at speed, they'll influence the ship's up-and-down movement by controlling the tilt of the diving planes located on our sail and at the stern."

There was a loud grinding noise as the submarine broke free from the grip of the ice and began sinking down into its intended medium.

"Take us down to three hundred feet, Mr. Marshall. All ahead one-third."

Even as the vessel's turbines engaged, there wasn't the slightest hint of forward movement. Yet Colter showed him otherwise as he pointed to the digital speed indicator mounted on the bulkhead before the planesmen.

They had attained a velocity of ten knots when

Colter once more addressed his crew. "Bring us around to course zero-four-zero. Dr. Lansing, do you see anything that might get in our way overhead?"

This time it was the seated woman who answered. "We should be fine at this depth, Captain. Though my laser scan shows an inverted ridge off our port bow, that extends some two hundred feet down into the water."

"We'll be staying well away from that monster," returned Colter, who next led his guest over to the chart table.

Here they joined the XO before a detailed bathymetric map of the Lancaster Sound. There were a confusing series of colored lines and x's on this chart, yet before asking what they all meant, Redmond softly vented his curiosity.

"You know, I never realized that the US Navy had women aboard its submarines."

"We normally don't," answered the captain. "Dr. Lansing is on temporary loan from the Naval Arctic laboratory. She's currently operating a prototype surface-scanning Fathometer that uses lasers to determine the exact state of the ice conditions topside. It was such a device that helped us surface as close to the northern edge of the Brodeur Peninsula as we did."

"We're at depth and on course, Captain," said a voice from behind.

This revelation seemed to reenergize Colter, whose face suddenly turned in a broad grin. "Now, Lieutenant Redmond, I'll show you how we're going to catch up with a group of very nasty Russians."

"All ahead, flank speed!" he ordered firmly. "And someone better call the boys in the torpedo room and the sound shack and let them know that the season for Ivan hunting has officially opened!"

In the locked confines of Viktor Belenko's cramped cabin, both of the *Neva*'s senior officers were in the midst of an intense hushed conversation.

"I tell you Sergei, as sure as the snows fall in Siberia, our esteemed admiral is holding something back on us. Why did you see his face when he got back to the ship? He looked like a little boy who had just been given the keys to the candy shop!"

Sergei Markova grunted. "I know what you mean, Viktor. That smirk was painted all over his face, and he could barely tone it down when he matter-of-factly informed us of the deaths of all five of the men sent along with him."

"He certainly was possessive about that cockpit voice recorder," observed the senior lieutenant. "From what I understand, he wouldn't even let any of the men help him with it as he whisked it off to the safe in your stateroom. It's just too bad our Zampolit chose this inopportune moment for the weekly Komsomol meeting. Instead of giving the speech he'd promised to present, the admiral could be analyzing that precious tape that he's been ranting and raving about ever since we left Murmansk. Do you really think that the Americans would have the audacity to shoot down the *Flying Kremlin,* Sergei?"

The *Neva*'s captain hesitantly answered. "I don't know what to think anymore, Comrade. Though I do know that it was a big mistake to incur the wrath of that *Sturgeon* class vessel like we did. We had no business ramming them in the first place. We should have just gone ultraquiet and let them pass on their merry way in peace. Then we could have gone on and completed our mission with Uncle Sam none the wiser."

"The old fox certainly did some job of stirring us up to a feverish pitch," Viktor commented. "With all that talk of launching torpedoes, you would have thought there was actually a war going on."

Sergei sighed. "We were lucky to get by with our lives. And for what, may I ask? A damn black box, that we could have just as easily have asked the Canadians to retrieve for us."

"I still think Kharkov's trying to pull something off on us, Sergei. At the very least, he should have postponed that damn Komsomol meeting and gotten right down to the analysis of that cockpit voice-recorder's tape like you asked him to do. Why the way he looked at you when you made this request, you would have thought you had asked him to burn his Party card!"

The captain nodded. "The way I read Kharkov, it appears he's not in a rush to analyze that tape because he already thinks he knows what's on it. And no matter what it contains, he's still going to blame the crash on the Americans."

Viktor absorbed this thought, then leaned forward and lowered his voice even further. "From what I hear, the Admiral of the Fleet and Premier Suratov were not exactly kissing cousins. Tanya has a niece who's a secretary in the Ministry of Defense, and she says it's no secret that the admiral has gone on record as opposing Alexander Suratov's peace initiatives with the West every step of the way. Why when Kharkov heard of the Premier's Arctic demilitarization proposal, he supposedly threw a nasty fit that included overturned furniture and torn-out phone wires. For an old-timer, the old fox certainly has some fire left in him."

"I'll say," said Sergei. "He's in remarkable physical shape for his age. To even think he was out there on the ice the whole day, and we almost froze our buns off just standing on the bridge to greet him."

Viktor sat back, and absentmindedly picked up his roommate's portable cassette player. While studying its compact lines, a thought suddenly came to him.

"You know, I was talking to Chief Koslov earlier, and he was telling me that he worked for Aeroflot two years before enlisting in the navy. One of his jobs was to replace the cockpit voice-recorder tapes. Did you know that the latest models are designed to fit into a machine as small as this one?"

There was a devilish look in the senior lieutenant's eyes, and Sergei responded, "If I get your drift, I gather you'd like me to open the safe and listen to the tape. Am I correct?"

Viktor smiled, and Sergei was quick to add. "Don't you think such a move on my part is a little rash, comrade? After all, the admiral will be done with his meeting eventually; we can surely wait until then."

"Come on, Sergei," urged his old friend. "You know those Komsomol meetings can last for hours on end. And besides, if this tape really is so important, I think that it's in the best interest of the Motherland to listen to it at once. As for the seriousness of such an infraction, how can you get reprimanded for breaking into your own safe? After all, you're still the captain of this ship, and nothing it contains should be held back from you."

This argument hit home, and Sergei took a deep breath and reflected. "I must admit that your proposal is most tempting, Viktor," he finally said. "But could I make sense out of the tape's contents even if I heard it?"

"There's only one way to find out," returned the grinning senior lieutenant as he handed his shipmate the portable recorder. "You have a listen, while I stand guard outside.

Driven by insatiable curiosity and a desire to express his dominion over every square centimeter of his vessel, Sergei Markova accepted his roommate's challenge.

Once a week like clockwork, the Zampolit of the *Neva* called together the ship's Party members for a meeting of the Komsomol. At this time, issues were discussed in a forumlike environment, issues that touched upon the past, present, and future direction of Soviet Communism.

When Konstantin Zinyagin had learned that they would have a distinguished guest on this patrol, he'd made certain to prepare a stimulating agenda for the Admiral of the Fleet's behalf. With over a dozen seamen packed into the enlisted men's mess hall, the Zampolit took a second to reintroduce Mikhail Kharkov, who sat in the front row of chairs. The admiral had promised to give a special presentation on the role of the Navy as an instrument of State policy, and Zinyagin opened the meeting with a brief speech of his own.

However, the Political Officer's "cursory" introduction had already turned into a forty-five minute discourse on the history of the Soviet Navy, from its inception as a limited coastal fleet to its current worldwide status. Utilizing a variety of charts that he had prepared himself, Zinyagin stood at the rostrum that had a picture of Lenin tacked to it's front. With his clipped beard, mustache, full brows, and piercing dark eyes, Zinyagin looked remarkably like the founding father of Socialism, though this was as far as the physical similarity went.

The Zampolit was in the midst of explaining the current state of the modern Soviet Navy, and his scratchy high-pitched voice whined on with a monotonous sameness. ". . . So you see, the Soviet leadership has at long last awakened to the all-important value of a powerful Fleet. Beyond its use in war, our Navy can be used to support our friends in times of crisis. The great mobility of our fleet and its flexibility in the event that limited military conflicts are indeed brewing permit it to have an influence on coastal countries, and to employ and extend a military threat to any level, beginning with a show of military strength and ending with the actual landing of forces. . . ."

As the Zampolit continued to ramble on, his white-haired guest began to fidget. Mikhail Kharkov had heard this same speech time after time, and he found himself in no mood to sit through it once again. His back and legs hurt after his long ordeal on the ice, and besides, there was still important work to be done back in his cabin.

Though the black box was securely locked away in the safe in his quarters, it still had to be opened and the switch of tapes made. Only after the original had been destroyed would he be able to relax completely. And since the Zampolit showed no signs of bringing his remarks to an end, the weary veteran had no choice but to take matters into his own hands.

It was as the Political Officer briefly halted to display a chart showing the current composition of the fleet, that Mikhail loudly cleared his throat and stood.

"Pardon me, Comrade Zampolit. But I must take this opportunity to regretfully excuse myself. Though I find your well-researched observations most astute, my physically demanding journey on the ice is finally catching up with me. This old body needs rest, and though I was looking forward to this meeting to share my own thoughts with your members, I'm going to have to take my leave early."

A look of disappointment came to the Political Officer's face as he turned from the chart and protested. "Are you certain you can't stay but a little longer, Admiral? Why I was just about to initiate my closing remarks. And all of us were so looking forward to hearing you speak. Why we might never have such an honor again."

Mikhail stretched his sore back and stifled a yawn. "No, comrade, I'm afraid this old man's had it. But I'll tell you what. Once I've had a good rest, I'd be happy to continue on with this inspiring program. Is tomorrow afternoon at this same time convenient for you?"

The Zampolit looked out to the other occupants of the room and politely nodded. "Though all of us will be sorry to see you go, we'd be honored to reinitiate this discussion in twenty-four hours. May your rest be peaceful, comrade."

As Mikhail anxiously ducked out the aft hatchway, the Political Officer wasted no time returning to an explanation of the chart he had just uncovered.

Kharkov's pace was somewhat slowed by an alien pain in his calves and knees. This was most likely an aftereffect of his hike through the deep snow drifts earlier. A couple of aspirin and a hot toddy would soon take the aches away, so he might focus on the vital task that still faced him.

As the admiral hurriedly crossed through the officer's wardroom, he was somewhat surprised to find the *Neva*'s senior lieutenant standing idly in front of the shut door of Mikhail's cabin. Viktor Belenko seemed to be an efficient officer who had been rather emotionless and tight-lipped to this point. Yet upon spotting Kharkov, his eyes opened wide and he immediately stepped forward to greet him.

"Why, Admiral, you're just the man I was thinking about. How did the Komsomol meeting go? It certainly didn't last very long."

Mikhail grunted. "Actually, I excused myself early. I'm afraid the aftereffects of my excursion on the ice have finally caught up with me."

"I thought that might be the case," offered the senior lieutenant somewhat nervously. "I can't help but admit that I was surprised when you agreed to attend the Komsomol meeting so soon after your return. How about me getting you some lunch? The cook has brewed up a pot of his specialty—Ukrainian borscht—and I'm certain you won't be disappointed. Just come and have a seat at the wardroom table, and I'll take care of all the rest."

The admiral shook his head. "You're much too kind, Senior Lieutenant. But right now fatigue has overcome my hunger. After a couple of hours' rest, I'll be happy to take you up on your offer."

"It's not healthy to go to bed on an empty stomach, Admiral. You could get ulcers that way."

Mikhail patted his stomach. "Your concerns are noted, comrade. But this old belly of mine has served me well, and a missed meal now and then hasn't seemed to have bothered it any. So if you'll excuse me, I'll be off to my bunk now."

Seemingly deaf to this request, Viktor Belenko voiced himself anew. "Before turning in, perhaps you'd like to see that stealth equipment you were asking about earlier. We're just about to activate it, and this is the perfect time to see how this amazing system operates."

A bit aggravated by the officer's persistent rambling, Mikhail's tone sharpened. "Please, Comrade Belenko! All I want to do is to get into my state-room. Is that too much to ask?"

Without waiting for a response, he pushed the senior lieutenant aside, inserted his key into the door's lock, and after quickly ducking inside, slammed the door shut behind him. He was in the process of exhaling a breath of relief, when he realized with a start that he wasn't alone. Seated at the cabin's cramped desk, a pair of lightweight headphones clamped over his ears, was Captain Sergei Markova. At his feet was the now opened cockpit voice recorder!

As his face flushed with anger, the admiral asked, "Are you finding anything interesting, Captain?"

Sergei Markova's astonishment at being discovered was tempered by the equally shocking contents of the tape he had been listening to. Taking a moment to switch off his cassette player, he peeled off the headphones and replied.

"As a matter of fact, I am, Admiral. Because as you'll soon hear for yourself, it wasn't an American F-15 that was responsible for taking down the *Flying*

Kremlin, it was a bomb!"

As a look of puzzlement etched the veteran's face, Sergei excitedly said, "Here, listen for yourself. The voices are a bit muddled, but the sequence of events is startling clear. It all seems to have started when an incendiary device ignited inside the console holding the Il-76's communications' equipment. As they lost the effective use of their radio, the fire spread, until the plane's operational systems were affected. At this point the Il-76 lost altitude and swerved off course, as the crew valiantly fought to control the choking flames. And in the process of this desperate struggle, yet another bomb was found attached to an avionic's panel. This device had yet to detonate, and appears to have been controlled by some sort of timing mechanism, for you can hear the frantic cries of the flight crew as they struggled to disarm it."

Taking a moment to control his rising emotions, Sergei somberly continued. "Soon afterward an ear-shattering explosion overrode their shouts of concern, and was followed by the sickening, wrenching sounds of the plane breaking apart and proceeding to fall from the skies.

"Yet one thing still confuses me, Admiral. Upon opening my safe, I found yet another cassette tape lying beside the sealed black box. It proved to be constructed exactly like that tape inside the cockpit voice recorder. It had the same stainless-steel casing. Yet when listening to it, I found it filled with nothing but undecipherable static."

"You had no business doing such a thing!" the enraged admiral protested. "I demand that you hand over both of these tapes at once, Captain Markova. Or the severest penalties possible will be applied to you."

"And why is that?" Sergei dared ask. "Is it because you knew what was on the original tape, and intended to switch it for the other one you brought along?"

Conscious that the intuitive young officer still had no real proof of this, the veteran mariner decided to try another tack. Instead of trying to directly confront him, he would now attempt to win him over. With a shrug of his shoulders, and the barest of forced smiles, the Admiral of the Fleet addressed Markova.

"You are most astute, Captain. And since it would be a waste of my breath to attempt to deceive you, I'll be frank. Yes, my friend, it was a series of bombs that took down the Premier's plane. And not only did I know this long before I recovered the aircraft's black box, I was responsible for having these devices placed in the Il-76 as well."

This shocking revelation caused Sergei to gasp. "But that would mean you intentionally murdered Alexander Suratov!"

The Admiral of the Fleet nodded somberly. "But before you condemn me to the firing squad, please take a moment to listen to our motives. For you see, I was not alone in this plot. Dozens of the highest-ranking members of the Defense Ministry worked at my side to see it through. And don't think that it was an easy thing to do.

"Alexander Suratov was a dedicated public servant. I knew him well, and to order his death and that of his staff and the *Flying Kremlin*'s flight crew was one of the most difficult things I have ever had to do in my five decades of service to the Motherland. But believe me, Captain, I had no other choice!"

Fighting to control his emotions, the veteran continued. "It all started when Suratov began making those unprecedented peace overtures to the West. Though we all desire to see a world free from war, our naïve Premier was trying to make it come to pass without establishing the proper groundwork. This really came to the forefront when he secretly announced his plan to demilitarize the Arctic in conjunction with the United States and Canada. As you can expect, the Imperialists jumped at this opportunity, and the Ottawa summit was hastily set up to seal the agreement in treaty form.

"As a submariner, I don't have to remind you of the utter importance of the region Suratov was about to ban all weapons of war from. Though the Motherland is the largest country on this earth, we have historically suffered from a severe lack of warm-water ports. Those we do have are so poorly placed our fleet is forced to travel through Imperialist-controlled choke points to get to the open sea.

"The only ports that are completely free from outside interference lay above the Arctic Circle. Though harsh weather and severe ice conditions make operating from them difficult, we have learned to make the most of it by building the greatest fleet of icebreakers and submarines the world has ever known.

"In the frozen expanses of the Barents, Kara, and Laptev Seas, and beneath the Arctic Ocean itself, we have positioned the ultimate revenge force. The *Typhoon* and *Delta* class submarines that patrol these waters have one purpose, to survive an Imperialist sneak attack, and to answer such a bolt-out-of-the-blue strike with one of our own.

"Dozens of attack vessels like the *Neva* here, have

been assigned the all-important task of protecting this bastion. I don't have to remind you that a ballistic missile-carrying submarine is the most survivable of all our strategic weapons, and for us to lose our only true protected bastion for such platforms would be foolishness of the worst type. Before Alexander Suratov stripped the Motherland of its most effective weapons' system with a single sweep of his pen, the difficult, painful decision was made to intervene."

Impressed by this impassioned plea, Sergei nevertheless retorted. "But why did you have to go to such an extreme as murder? And why even bother with this childish switching of tapes when you could merely have destroyed the black box before anyone was the wiser?"

Mikhail Kharkov sighed heavily before responding. "Believe me when I tell you, Captain, that we tried to talk some sense into our headstrong Premier before he even made the West the initial offer. But Suratov was completely deaf to our arguments, so we had no other course open but to eliminate him before he sold us out.

"As for the substitute tape, I can only answer you by appealing to you in strictest confidence. For what I am about to share with you will all too soon change the political balance of the world as we now know it."

As Sergei Markova nodded for the admiral to continue, the veteran took in a deep breath and did so.

"There is a civilian element within the ruling Politburo that has no understanding of strategic issues, unlike you and I, Captain Markova. These individuals would have just sat back and watched Suratov strip the Motherland of her most important bastion while the Imperialist powers gave up absolutely nothing in return. To readdress this serious imbalance, and to check the continued threat of Imperialist expansion once and for all, it was decided to create a fictitious scenario in which it would appear that an American aircraft had shot down the *Flying Kremlin*. The substitute tape you discovered would have supported this supposition by broadcasting nothing but static. For even if it had been discovered that the cockpit voice recorder had been inoperable during the flight, we had more than enough proof to sway the vacillating members of the Politburo to join us, the prize being the ultimate one—their support in authorizing an immediate nuclear strike against the Imperialist bloc nations!"

Sergei's eyes opened wide with disbelief. "Let me get this right, Admiral. You're going to launch a nuclear attack against the West for an act that they didn't even commit?"

"Pretty ironic, isn't it, Captain?" returned the beaming veteran. "At long last we can cripple the Imperialists with a surprise counterforce strike, and all for the cost of a single static-filled tape. This is an unparalleled opportunity, that will allow our great Socialist dream finally to be shared by all of mankind. And you, Sergei Markova, will be one of the founding fathers of the new world order that will follow."

"If there happens to be a world left," shot back the young captain disgustedly. "I can't believe that anyone in his right mind still thinks there can be a winner in a nuclear conflict. For our initial strike will generate a counterstrike, and the West will hit the Motherland a crippling blow with their own

355

submarine-launched ballistic missiles. And this great dream that you speak of will turn into nothing but a nuclear nightmare.

"No, Admiral, I want no part of this madness. And you can be assured that I'll do everything within my power to see that your insane, twisted machination is exposed."

Fearing just such a response, Mikhail slowly walked over to the room's single cot, reached under the pillow, and pulled out a shiny Kalashnikov pistol. With a steady hand he proceeded to aim this weapon directly at the *Neva*'s startled commanding commander.

"You leave me no other alternative, Captain Markova. Now hand over those tapes! Then perhaps I'll take compassion on you, and give you a chance to yet change your mind, before being forced to eliminate you right here and now."

"You wouldn't dare do such a thing on my ship," Sergei spat out.

Mikhail Kharkov responded by abruptly cocking the hammer of the Kalashnikov and centering his aim on Sergei's forehead. "We've already been forced to sacrifice much already, Captain. One more life is inconsequential."

Certain that the veteran meant it, Sergei decided it was time for discretion. After putting his hands up in a mock gesture of surrender, the young captain got to work to supplying Kharkov with the two tapes he had demanded.

Sergei Markova's hands were trembling as he opened his portable cassette player, and seeing this, the admiral commented, "Easy now, Captain. I will only put this Kalashnikov into use if you force me to do so. And since I've already killed one man today while on the ice, I don't find such a prospect very entertaining.

"It would be a tragic waste to have to shoot you, especially since I've taken such a sincere interest in your career throughout the years. Though I never had a son of my own, you were the type of individual I would have liked to have raised."

Surprised to hear such a thing, Sergei finished removing the cassette, and cautiously handed it to the Admiral, along with its blank twin.

"Don't look so shocked," reflected the white-haired veteran as he pocketed the tapes. "For I've been a silent admirer of yours since you first entered the A. A. Grechko Academy. Did you know that I personally saw the video tapes of each of your oral exams? Why I probably know your academic record better than you do, and it was I who was responsible for getting you that first commission you so wanted—on that attack submarine. So come to your senses, comrade, and listen to your benefactor. Even though he is currently holding a gun to your head."

Aware that compromising would put him in the best position to expose the veteran's twisted scheme, Sergei nodded. "You are right, Admiral. Perhaps I have been too hasty in my initial reaction. It's just that the prospect of nuclear war scares me so I instinctively revolt at the very idea of such a tragedy befalling mankind."

"And rightfully so," retorted Mikhail Kharkov, who realized that the tense standoff was over. As he uncocked and lowered the pistol, he added. "If I had a beautiful young wife and child waiting for me back in Murmansk, I would likely most have reacted much as you did. But if you'll just take some time to hear me out, I believe I can convince you that the

357

attack plan we've chosen to implement all but eliminates the chance of an Imperialist counterstrike. Why with our new superaccurate, MIRV'd warheads, we can take out not only their missile silos, airfields, and port facilities, but the very communications installations that are responsible for passing the word to their missile-carrying submarines to launch. And would you believe that we can thusly decapitate our enemy with a mere one-hundred warheads on our part? Why it's going to be incredibly easy, with a minimum of resulting radioactive fallout."

Though Sergei was well prepared to argue otherwise, he held his tongue and sheepishly responded. "I'd be most interested to see this attack plan, Admiral. But first I've got to get us safely back to Murmansk."

This prophetic remark was met by a firm knock on the door. As Mikhail Kharkov proceeded to hide the pistol that he had been holding under the folds of his sweater, Sergei spoke out.

"You may enter."

Quick to do so was the concerned senior lieutenant. "Please excuse me, comrades. But I just heard from Chief Magadan in sonar that we could have some company following us into Baffin Bay."

"I'll bet it's that damned *Sturgeon* again!" cursed Mikhail Kharkov.

Sergei replied while standing and shaking out his tense limbs. "Whoever it is, the best place to learn their intentions is the *Neva*'s attack center. Shall we, Comrades?"

In no mood to argue, the Admiral of the Fleet gave the young captain the briefest of supportive winks as he followed the ship's two senior officers out into the passageway.

Chapter Seventeen

There was a light spring to Petty Officer First Class Stanley Roth's step as he ambled down the passageway and entered the door marked Sound Shack. His hard-working assistant, Lester Warren was studiously hunched over a console, and Stanley gave him a punch in the upper arm to let him know that his replacement had arrived.

Seaman Warren looked up and the grin stretched across his associate's face told him the checkup had been a good one.

"So you're going to live after all," observed the Texan, as he watched Roth scoot past him to get back to work.

"It appears so," replied Stanley, who quickly seated himself and reached out for his headphones. "Pills says that the swelling has gone down substantially, and there's not even a hint of infection. He even wanted to know if I wanted him to try fitting me for a false tooth."

"I didn't think a mere pharmacist's mate was capable of doing such a thing," replied Lester seriously.

Stanley playfully punched his assistant in the other arm and responded. "No, I'm only kidding you. There'll be plenty of time to get a spare once I'm back in New London, though this time I'm picking my own dentist. Besides, right now I'm not about to bother Pills with designing a false tooth. From what I saw, he's got his hands full with his new patient."

"Do you mean the Eskimo we took aboard back on Baffin Island?" queried Lester.

Stanley nodded. "The very same, my friend. I got a peek at him laid out on his bunk, and he was still out for the count. Pills says the bruise on his chest indicates he was most likely shot. It appears he was wearing something over his chest that deflected the bullet, and that's what saved him."

"He's a lucky stiff all right," reflected Lester. "Is he going to pull through?"

Stanley could only shrug his shoulders. "Who knows? Pills sure hopes so, but he admits that he still doesn't know what's wrong with the guy. Because other than the bruise and his unconscious state, he appears to be the picture of perfect health. Though he certainly could use a bath. And here I thought you Texans got funky after missing a few showers."

"Very funny," said Lester.

"Ease up, Les. I'm only having a little fun with you. What have we got out there that's got you all hot and bothered?"

The Texan replied while turning up his volume gain a notch. "The captain's sure making things hard for us, Stan. Ever since we steamed out of Lancaster Sound, he's been pushing the *Defiance* at flank speed. With all the racket produced by our own signature, it's going to take a miracle to pick up the guys we're supposed to be chasing."

"The Skipper sure enough knows what he's doing," offered Stanley as he got back to work. "Ivan's only got a single route to get back home, and since they've got that head start on us, the *Defiance* is still playing catch-up. When the time's right, Captain Colter will slow us down, and then we can do what we do best."

"Do you think we'll trade shots with the Russian's once we tag 'em?" quizzed the anxious Texan.

Stanley turned up his own volume gain and answered. "We're certainly not going to ring Ivan up on the underwater telephone and trade sea stories with him. The way I see it, they're the ones who instigated this little misunderstanding, and the *Defiance* ain't quitting until we get a chance to return the favor."

With this said, both sonar operators focused their attentions solely on the hissing rush being conveyed into their headphones, as the *Sturgeon* class attack sub entered the northernmost extremity of Baffin Bay.

The atmosphere inside the *Neva*'s hushed attack center was tense, as the ship's senior officers came storming in to counter the threat that had just been detected in their baffles. Without bothering to confer with either his senior lieutenant or his distinguished passenger, Sergei Markova wasted no time taking the initiative.

"Comrade Michman, notify Chief Koslov that we're going to need emergency speed at once. Our course will remain on bearing three-two-zero."

Quick to question these orders was the Admiral of the Fleet. "Surely you can't be serious, Captain? This is no time for running away. We must take a stand and fight. For the *Sturgeon* class submarine is the only witness to our trespass here, and must be destroyed."

Not used to having his command doubted, Sergei angrily retorted. "As captain, I'll be making the tactical decisions aboard the *Neva,* Admiral. And I say it's just too risky to take on the Americans at this time. Not only have we spent our last decoy, but the *Sturgeon* class vessel has already shown the ability to outrun our torpedoes. So before opening ourselves up to being attacked once more, I say the wisest choice is to use our superior speed to transit the Nares Strait and then head straight back to Murmansk."

"Are you saying that the pride of the Soviet Fleet is no match for a class of vessel whose first hull was laid down over two decades ago?" the unbelieving veteran asked.

Directly meeting Kharkov's icy gaze, Sergei replied. "That's not the point, Admiral. As far as I'm concerned, our mission has been completed, and now it's up to me to get us back to port as quickly and safely as possible."

"This mission is not over until I say so, Captain!" barked Mikhail Kharkov. "You forget who you're sharing this bridge with, comrade. And since you're obviously not man enough to carry out your duty, I'll have to do it for you."

Turning his head to address the other members of the attack center's complement, Kharkov cried out. "As Admiral of the Fleet of the Soviet Union, I am replacing Sergei Markova as the commanding officer of the *Neva*. Comrade Michman, I want you to personally see to an immediate reversal of our course.

"Battle stations, torpedoes, Comrades! It's time to teach the proud Imperialists a badly needed lesson in humility."

Confused by this unprecedented change of command, the Michman hesitated in carrying out his new orders. As the puzzled warrant officer looked over to the senior lieutenant for guidance, Mikhail Kharkov stormed over to the helm.

"Are you deaf, Comrade Michman?" screamed the infuriated Admiral. "Well, since it appears that you have joined the ranks of your spineless captain, I'll just have to carry out your duties for you. Helmsman, reverse our course right now! And ready the ship to attack."

Equally confused was the junior seaman currently steering the *Neva*. This was only his third submarine patrol, and all three were with Sergei Markova as commanding officer. Since he wasn't used to taking orders from anyone but his captain, like the hesitant michman, he wouldn't budge.

Seeing this, Mikhail Kharkov went into an absolute fit, and began madly ripping at the helmsman's shoulder harness, to physically remove him from his position and personally replace him at the helm. It was at this point that the ship's senior lieutenant ran forward to intercede on the helmsman's behalf.

"Now hold on one moment, Admiral!" warned Viktor Belenko. "Let go of that harness at once, or you'll endanger all of us."

As Kharkov continued furiously yanking on the harness's jammed release mechanism, Viktor reached out and grabbed the white-haired veteran by one of his arms. An intense scuffle ensued, during which time the frenzied admiral reached into the folds of his sweater and pulled out his Kalashnikov pistol. Seconds later, the compartment filled with the reverberating explosive report of a single shot. And when the confusion cleared, Viktor Belenko could be seen lying on the deck, holding his blood-soaked shoulder and writhing in sheer agony. Standing above him, with the still-smoking pistol in hand, was the suddenly sobered Admiral of the Fleet.

"Have you gone completely insane, Comrade Kharkov?" cried Sergei Markova as he ran over to disarm the veteran.

Surprisingly enough, Kharkov surrendered his weapon quite willingly. This enabled the captain to immediately turn to his wounded subordinate. As he bent to Viktor's side, he called out firmly.

"Comrade Ustreka, you are to escort the admiral to his quarters at once. Please see to it that he remains there until I say otherwise."

This time the michman didn't hesitate, and as the muscular Kiev native walked over to carry out his orders, the Admiral of the Fleet pleaded desperately, "Please Captain, I'm truly sorry I lost control. It's just that this mission is so all-important, and I couldn't bear to see anything get in the way of its successful completion. That is why you must turn this ship around and initiate an immediate attack. Please Captain, do this, or my entire life's work will be in jeopardy!"

Barely paying these words any attention, Sergei pressed a clean handkerchief up against Viktor's wound. An alert corpsman joined him, and while the seaman began staunching the flow of blood with a proper dressing, the captain stood to complete one last necessary task. Walking straight over to the admiral, he reached into Kharkov's pocket and pulled out the two steel-cased cassettes the man had stored there. With this done, the captain silently nodded toward the michman, who proceeded to lead the now-trembling old-timer out of the attack center.

"All right, comrades, that's enough of this nonsense!" shouted Sergei. "Now let's concentrate on the real threat that lies in the seas behind us. For if the fates are still with us, perhaps we'll yet have a chance to outrun them."

The call from the *Defiance*'s sound shack reached the vessel's control-room crew over the compartment's elevated public address speakers. There could be no denying the excitement that flavored Petty Officer First Class Stanley Roth's words as he issued his latest report.

"We've tagged Ivan again, Captain! Though this time it was an explosive crack much like a gunshot that gave them away. Their bearing is three-two-zero, with a range of ten thousand yards. Shall I initiate a weapons' interface, Captain?"

"That's affirmative, Mr. Roth," shot back Matt Colter. "Lock on sonar on tubes one, two, and three."

With this said, Colter turned to address his weapons' officer. "Prepare to launch three Mk 48's, Mr. Sanger. Let me know when we have a green light on sensor interface."

There was a determined look in Matt Colter's eyes as he traded glances with his XO.

"They're ours, Al," observed the beaming captain. "There's no way in hell they'll escape us now."

"We've got a green light on weapons' release," observed Lieutenant David Sanger.

"Then let's do it, gentlemen," returned the captain. "Fire one! Fire two! Fire three!"

The whining hiss of the three approaching torpedoes registered in the *Neva*'s hydrophones moments after the weapons were released from their tubes. The shocked technician who monitored this frighteningly distinctive racket almost fell out of his chair as he twisted around to share this information.

"Torpedo salvo headed our way, Captain! I count three separate weapons coming in on bearing one-four-zero, at a range of nine thousand, five hundred meters."

This was just the news Sergei Markova had dreaded to hear, and as he pounded his clenched fist into his thigh, he snapped his men into action.

"Take us down. Crash dive at speed! Begin preprogrammed evasive maneuvers, and pray that it's not too late, comrades."

The bow of the *Neva* abruptly turned downward, and as Sergei reached out to steady himself, the *Neva*'s turbines roared alive in the background. His hands straining against the cold steel tubular railing that kept him from falling forward, the captain managed to take in the digital depth gauge mounted above the helm. With an incredible rapidity, this counter ticked off their dive's progress. Yet even then, it seemed to take a virtual eternity to break the five-hundred-meter barrier. When this finally occurred, they were plunging downwards at a speed of forty-one knots. And as man and machine were once more pushed to their limits, Sergei could only wonder if even their best would be good enough this time.

"The torpedoes continue their approach," monitored the sonar operator. "Range is down to eight thousand meters and closing."

"Where's that infernal thermocline?" queried Sergei, who listened as the hull of the *Neva* began protesting under the great pressure it was now being subjected to.

"Sir, we're approaching the seven-hundred-meter mark. Will we be pulling up here?" quizzed the anxious diving officer.

"Not yet," managed Sergei as the deck began wildly vibrating beneath them. "We're going to have to push the envelope on this one, and then some."

Again the groaning sound of the straining hull filled the attack center, and Sergei was thrown violently to the side as the deck suddenly canted hard to the right. It was the diving officer who attempted to explain what this unexpected disturbance was all about.

"We've seemed to hit some sort of current, Captain. It's a struggle just to keep the helm steady."

"Hang in there, comrade!" urged Sergei. "For this current could very well be our savior."

At a depth of eight-hundred and sixty meters, the deck abruptly stopped vibrating. It was apparent that they had broken into a different strata of water, and the captain's next command was given with great relief.

"Level off the dive, and bring us up!"

Seconds later, Sergei lurched violently backward and had to hold on for dear life, as the *Neva* reversed its course and headed out of the depths like a bullet. Again the disturbed strata was encountered. But just knowing that they were now ascending made the wildly vibrating gyrations that coursed through the ship's hull, and the mere act of standing upright a challenge, all the easier to accept.

The depth gauge registered six-hundred and ninety-one meters when the disturbance ceased. This put them back out of the thermocline, that significantly cooler portion of the sea's depths in which Sergei had hoped to lose the pursuing torpedoes.

Still forced to hold onto the overhead railing to

367

keep from falling backward, the *Neva*'s captain managed to wipe the sweat off his forehead with the upper portion of his arm. And his desperate prayers indeed seemed to have been answered, when the sonar operator's voice rang out firm and clear.

"We've lost them, Captain! The torpedoes don't seem to be on our tail anymore."

A shared chorus of relieved chatter rang out, only to be interrupted by the captain's cautionary words. "I'm afraid we're not out of the thick of this just yet, Comrades. For somewhere out there that American submarine is still lurking."

Yet before Sergei could reveal his plan to negate this threat, the sonar operator's strained voice once again took prominence.

"I'm picking up a single torpedo signature, Captain! I don't know where in the hell it came from, but it's apparently been trailing in our baffles all this time. I don't think that we're going to be able to—"

These words of warning were cut short by an ear-splitting explosion and a violent concussion that rolled the *Neva* over hard on its side, and sent those crew members not constrained by safety harnesses crashing to the deck below. Sergei Markova was one of these unfortunate individuals. Thrown hard against the flat surface of the chart table, he took a wicked blow to his back and left shoulder. As pain coursed through his body, the lights failed and the attack center was shrouded in a confusing veil of blackness.

An aftershock caused the vessel to cant violently in the opposite direction, and there was a deafening racket as loose debris and fallen crew members shifted to the other side of the ship. Somehow Sergei managed to hold onto the base of the chart table, and as the ship eventually righted itself, he cried out into the pitch dark confines of the attack center.

"Someone hit the emergency lights! And I'm going to need an immediate damage report. Helmsman, is the ship still responding?"

A frightened voice timidly answered. "We seem to be dead in the water, sir. The helm is completely unresponsive."

Silently cursing this news, the captain was in the process of attempting to pick himself up when the emergency lights suddenly blinked on. The dim red illumination was just adequate enough for him to gauge the amount of damage that surrounded him. Several crew members could be seen also rising from the debris-laden deck, while others still lay prone on the floor, unmoving. Broken glass and overturned equipment were everywhere, and Sergei could smell the sickening scent of burning electrical wiring.

As the ship's various departments slowly began reporting in, it was soon evident that the damage was widespread, though it was especially bad in the engine room, where the blast was centered. Here several crew members, including Boris Koslov the *Neva*'s chief engineer, had been instantly killed. The handful of survivors not seriously injured was currently trying to plug a leak that had developed in the seal that surrounded the propeller shaft where it penetrated the hull. The only good news was that somehow the sub's hull had remained intact. Yet with their engines and weapons' systems inoperable, the submarine could hardly be considered a man-of-war anymore.

"I'm having difficulty keeping the trim balanced, Captain," observed the diving officer. "That leak in the engine room must be getting worse, because the pumps don't seem to be able to keep up with it."

"Sir, the shock of the blast caused the electrical

circuits to overload, and we no longer have sonar capabilities," added the somber sonar operator.

Silently absorbing all this information, Sergei Markova grimly pondered the limited options he had. Lying dead in the water as they were, the only apparent way to save the *Neva* was to order the emergency ballast jettisoned. This would send them floating upward to the relative safety of the sea's surface. Yet since the ship no longer had sonar capabilities, there was no way for him to know whether the waters above were encrusted with ice. If they were, and the ascending *Neva* crashed into an impenetrable ice ridge, the resulting concussion would surely crack the hull of the already damaged vessel and send them spiraling into the black depths on a final dive into oblivion.

Things were vastly different inside the control room of the USS *Defiance*. Here a joyous, partylike atmosphere prevailed as they celebrated their successful attack with a round of spirited high-fives and a chorus of excited chatter. Taking a moment to celebrate himself, Matt Colter accepted a warm handshake from his XO.

"Congratulations, Skipper. I guess this makes you the first sub ace of the Cold War."

"That's a dubious honor I can easily live without," retorted the captain, as he took in the two figures standing next to his XO, beside the plotting table.

Both Laurie Lansing and Lieutenant Jack Redmond looked strangely out of place. Neither one of them had joined in on the festivities, and both looked like they were on their way to a funeral.

"Are we going to finish them off, Skipper?" quizzed the XO. "From what Mr. Roth says, they're just laying there dead in the water. Why don't we put Ivan out of his misery once and for all with a couple of well-aimed fish."

"I think that would be a tragic mistake," offered the close-lipped Canadian commando.

"And why do you say that, Lieutenant?" countered the XO. "The Russians are clearly the aggressors in this matter, and I can guarantee you they wouldn't hesitate to finish us off if our positions were reversed."

"That might indeed be true," continued Jack Redmond. "But you're forgetting what brought us here in the first place. And no matter how you look at it, the Soviets beat us to that cockpit voice recorder. If we proceed to sink them, the black box will be lost in the depths."

"He's got a point there, Al," reflected the captain. "Although I'm not really sure what we can do to help them out. It looks like they took our torpedo right in the stern, and if they're taking on water as it appears, it's doubtful if even a DSRV could get here in time to save them."

This time it was the civilian scientist who spoke up. "Captain Colter, is the *Defiance* rigged with an underwater telephone?"

"Of course we have one, along with every modern submarine that sails the ocean today," answered Colter. "Why do you ask?"

An inspired gleam flickered in the civilian's dark eyes as she responded. "Well, I think under the current circumstances it would be in our best interest to give that Soviet crew a call. Who knows, perhaps there's something we might be able to do to help them out."

"I say such a thing is just too risky," returned the XO. "To establish communications with them, we'd have to move to a closer range. What if Ivan's just playing possum, and takes this opportunity to launch his own torpedoes?"

With a heavy sigh, Jack Redmond replied. "I guess that's just the chance that we're going to have to take. Because if we ever hope to see that black box again, this is our last chance."

Knowing full well that the Canadian was correct, Matt Colter nodded. "Let's give a phone call a try. Yet just to be on the safe side, we'd better put some fresh fish in the tubes and be ready to use them."

The XO could only shrug his shoulders and get on with the task. Meanwhile, the captain instructed the helmsman to proceed on a cautious intercept course with the disabled Soviet vessel. This done, he beckoned his two passengers to join him by the fire-control panel, where a black plastic handset hung on the adjoining bulkhead.

"This is our underwater communications system. It operates just like a normal telephone, though its range is limited because seawater by itself makes a lousy conductor. Now, if we only had someone who could speak Russian . . . I don't believe any of the ship's crew is familiar with the language."

"I'd be happy to give it a try," offered the weathered Canadian. "My mother was originally from the Ukraine, and though I can't read or write Cyrillic, I should be able to converse enough to get by."

Matt Colter was impressed by this revelation. "I guess it was a good thing that we plucked you off the ice after all, Lieutenant. Now let's just hope this whole thing isn't a big waste of time. Or worse, a cleverly conceived ambush."

"Captain Markova, the men in the engine room

don't know how much longer they'll be able to hold out. The leak has worsened, and the water there is almost up their knees."

The chief's remarks were met by an emotional reply. "Well tell them that they're just going to have to do better, comrade. Otherwise the *Neva* is finished for sure. Perhaps I'd better get down there myself."

"But who'll man the attack center while you're gone?" It was the whining voice of the *Neva*'s Zampolit.

Sergei turned to face the sweating Political Officer, who had arrived in the control room shortly after the last damage report was received.

"I guess as senior officer, you'll be the man in charge, Comrade Zinyagin."

The captain's words brought horror to the Zampolit's already pale face. "But what do I know about running a submarine? Maybe I should go get the admiral out of confinement. In times such as these we could use his expertise."

Sergei was about to okay this request when the compartment filled with a harsh ringing buzz. The captain had to completely scan the debris-ridden room before spotting the device responsible for this racket.

"What the hell?" muttered the blond-haired officer as he thoughtfully approached the *Neva*'s underwater telephone receiver. Though he was certain this commotion was only the by-product or a short circuit of some sort, he nevertheless picked up the handset and spoke into the receiver.

"Hello."

With the Canadian's invaluable assistance, Matt

Colter soon learned the exact nature of the Russian sub's plight. Even his XO's suspicions were tempered as the captain shared with his crew a graphic description of their enemies' difficulties. It proved to be the only civilian present who offered any sort of viable game plan.

"Captain Colter, I'd like permission to activate the surface-scanning lasers."

"Permission granted," snapped the captain, who knew exactly what was on her mind.

While Laurie Lansing furiously addressed her keyboard, Matt Colter utilized the only foreign national in their immediate midsts as an intermediary.

"Lieutenant Redmond, find out if the Russian sub can manage any type of forward propulsion at all. I realize their reactor has been scrammed, but they must have some sort of backup system on board."

With a bit of difficulty, the Canadian managed to translate this query. It took two attempts to get the response clear in his mind.

"Captain Markova says their battery-powered system still appears to be on-line. Though because of the nature of the damage in the *Neva*'s engine room, they'll only be able to utilize it for a short duration."

"If God's with us, that's all they'll need," retorted Matt Colter, who added, "Tell the captain to stand by."

Colter's voice cracked with strain as he pivoted and yelled across the entire length of the control room. "Dr. Lansing, any luck as yet?"

"It doesn't look good, Captain," responded the civilian. "There's a massive inverted ridge directly above us, with heavy rafted ice to the south, east, and north. The only possibility lies to the west, approximately a mile distant. It's not open water mind you, but it looks to be smooth and of fairly recent origin. And there's more than enough room to fit the both of us."

"How thick does it appear to be?" quizzed the captain.

Laurie Lansing answered with a shake of her head. "That's the tough part, captain. From this depth and range, it looks to be about six inches thick, though I could be off by as much as three inches either way."

Matt Colter knew that six inches of ice was about the limit that their specially reinforced sail could take. Yet because of the uniqueness of their situation, he replied after the briefest of hesitations.

"Let's do it, Doc! Lock us on, and we'll lead our newfound Soviet comrades up out of these depths like a Seeing-Eye dog does its master."

Chapter Eighteen

It was a loud explosive crack that broke Ootah from his deep coma. The Inuit awoke with a start, and as his eyes adjusted to the alien brightness that surrounded him, he realized that he was in a strange place, the likes of which he'd never known existed.

Hoping that this was only some sort of horribly realistic dream, he attempted to sit up. Yet when he did so, an agonizing pain shot through his chest. Only then did his hands reach under the crisp white sheet that covered him, and he became conscious that he was stark naked and his cherished amulet was gone.

With this dispiriting realization, he scanned the room in which he found himself. No bigger than an average-sized snowhouse, it held a variety of strange equipment, and several empty cots like the one he lay on, stacked on top of each other. The only thing he could compare it to was the white-man's house he had once visited in Arctic Bay. But this place was even stranger still, for it didn't have a single window.

The air was warm and had a peculiar odor to it. Doing his best to ignore the pain that left him breathless and weak, Ootah sat up. It was then he spotted his clothing hanging on the wall on the other side of the room.

The floor beneath him seemed to be rolling back and forth like a floating floe of ice, and it took a concentrated effort on his part to cross the room without falling. Once, when the entire room rolled hard on its side, the Inuit was forced to reach out for a handhold in order to steady himself. The object that kept him from losing his balance altogether was known to the white man as a sink. Hanging above its smooth, white basin was a mirror. It only took a single glance into the shiny reflective surface for Ootah to see the fist-sized bruise that stained the central portion of his chest. And seeing it, a long string of forgotten memories rose up in his consciousness.

In the blink of an eye, he remembered the magical flashing object that had fallen from the heavens. And then there were the evil white men who had somehow made their way onto the ice to take the object from him. Other whites had appeared from the opposite direction, and a horrifying gun battle had ensued. Caught in the crossfire, Ootah could but dig into the snow beneath his sled, and wait for the whites to kill each other off. They didn't, and when the last bullet whined overhead, he arose out of the snow and saw an even more terrifying sight than the legions of gun-toting strangers that still surrounded him. For emerging from his snowhouse was the white-haired stranger who had visited him earlier in a dream. And in this mysterious elder's evil grasp was Ootah's beloved Akatingwah and their only son!

The Inuit could only silently petition the ancestors to intercede at this point, and his desperate prayers were indeed answered when the white-haired elder asked for Ootah to replace Akatingwah as hostage. With the flashing box in tow, the stranger forced Ootah to join him on a snowmobile. And off they went, on a pilgrimage that he was just starting to make some sense out of.

Could he ever forget the moment when his struggles caused the vehicle to crash into a snowdrift and overturn? And his memory would always be etched in horror when he recalled his white-haired captor raising the pistol and shooting practically point-blank at him. So no wonder this place in which he had just awoken seemed strange. This was no dream vision. Rather it was the first house of the land of the dead!

Chilled by this thought, the Inuit rushed over to dress himself. His clothing felt good on his skin. Only when he was completely decked out in parka, boots, and mittens did he dare attempt to leave the room, to continue this greatest of journeys from which no mortal was ever known to have returned.

A cramped passageway took him down a narrow corridor filled with snaking pipes that were marked in some indecipherable tongue. Wondering why his father, Nakusiak, wasn't there to greet him, Ootah caught a glimpse of a blue-suited, black man crossing the hallway in front of him. Quickly ducking down to hide himself, the Inuit breathed a sigh of relief only when this figure disappeared into yet another snaking tunnel. Cautiously peeking around the corner, he viewed some sort of ladder leading directly upward. A draft of cool fresh air drew him to its base, and as he looked up to see where it led, he spotted a familiar gray expanse of sky beckoning invitingly in the distance. He needed no more additional prompting to begin anxiously climbing.

On the exposed sail of the USS *Defiance,* its two parka-clad senior officers stood, studying the massive, black-hulled vessel that lay off their bow less han twenty yards distant. Over seventy feet longer han the *Defiance,* the *Sierra* class submarine had a tubby, elongated sail, and its retractable planes were mounted in its bow. A prominent pod sat upon the ship's tail-fin, and intelligence assumed that some sort of towed hydrophone array was stored here.

"Well, we did it, Skipper," reflected the XO. "Though for a while there, I really thought Ivan was going to play a fast one on us."

"I must admit I wasn't so sure myself." Matt Colter winked. "But Lieutenant Redmond helped sway me into giving this crazy scheme a try."

"And it's a good thing for all of us he was aboard to give us a hand," returned the XO, who pointed to the Russian boat's aft accessway as several sailors emerged. One of these figures had to be carefully lifted out of the hatch, and then helped down a portable ladder that led to the ice itself.

"That must be the *Neva*'s senior lieutenant," said the XO. "Pharmacist Mate Krommer deserves to get his medical license after this patrol's over. First extracting Roth's tooth, then treating that Eskimo, and now a real gunshot wound—Old Pills has really got his hands full on this trip."

The harsh buzzing sound of the intercom activating filled the bridge, and a familiar amplified voice soon followed. "Captain, this is Lieutenant Sanger. Captain Markova has arrived in the control room and would like permission to join you."

"Send him up. And make certain that our translator comes along also," replied Colter, who caught the gaze of his XO.

"This should be interesting," said Al Layman, as he pulled out his pipe and put its scarred bit between his lips.

While waiting for their guest to join them, Matt

379

Colter briefly scanned the horizon. The storm that had greeted them earlier had long since passed. The howling wind was noticeably absent, and in its place was a gentle, brisk zephyr that reminded him a bit of a New England winter's day.

A thick covering of grayish clouds drifted overhead, while the eastern horizon was just tinged with color as the Arctic dawn so slowly developed. With nothing but solid ice extending in all directions, it was hard to believe that they were currently floating on a frozen sea. And Mathew Colter was just about to share this observation with his XO, when their visitors arrived.

The *Defiance*'s captain was soon facing a solidly built, blond-haired officer, who appeared to be about his own age. With his blue eyes locked on Colter's gaze, this newcomer held out his hand and greeted the American in broken, Slavic-flavored English.

"Good morning. I am Captain Sergei Markova, commander of the *Neva*."

There was a genuiness to his tone, and Matt Colter sized his counterpart up as a hard-working, honest soul who had been caught by circumstances over which he'd had little control.

"Good morning to you, sir. I'm Captain Matthew Colter, commanding officer of the USS *Defiance*. Welcome aboard."

They shook hands warmly, and then the Russian proceeded to reach into his pocket and pull out a pair of steel-cased cassettes. At this point he began talking slowly in his native tongue, and Lieutenant Jack Redmond of the Canadian Arctic Rangers translated.

"On behalf of the crew of the *Neva*, Captain Markova would like you to have these tapes, sir. One of them is the original that he himself pulled out of the cockpit voice recorder. It will show that it was a eries of internal bomb blasts that brought the plane hey call the *Flying Kremlin* down. The other tape is proof of a plot by a twisted minority of his fellow countrymen. These few desired to blame this crash on he Western powers, and intended to initiate a nuclear strike in response."

Matt Colter reached out, took the tapes and was quick with his response. "I realize how important hese tapes are to you, Captain Markova. And I want o thank you for entrusting them to me like this. You can be assured they will be handled with the best of care, and eventually returned to the Soviet Union, once an impartial study of them has been completed."

As the Canadian completed his translation, the Soviet naval officer once again reverted to broken English to add. "And now I would like to take this opportunity to personally thank you for saving my ife and the lives of my crew. I will never forget your gallantry, and will be eternally grateful to you for the rest of my life. Why, you have given me a chance to see my beautiful wife and daughter once more!"

These words were delivered with such innocence that Matt Colter found his eyes filling with tears. This inspirational moment was abruptly broken by the shouts of his XO.

"Now what in the hell do you make of that, Skipper?"

Turning to see what Al Layman was referring to, Colter gazed over the bridge and watched as a single individual dressed in a heavy fur-skin parka, finished climbing out of the aft accessway. Without stopping to catch his breath, this stranger began to climb over the side of the *Defiance*. That done, he sat down and proceeded to use the rounded hull of the ship to slide down to the ice below. The moment he got to his feet, he turned to take one last look at the vessel from which he had just escaped. His glance centered on the exposed bridge. He seemed to realize at this point that he was being watched, and he meekly bowed in response before pivoting and beginning to quickly make his way over the ice pack.

The harsh buzzing sound of the intercom was followed by a breathless voice from below. "Captain, it's the Eskimo! He's not in sickbay, and Pharmacist Mate Krommer thinks that he might be loose in the ship."

Now knowing the identity of the party he had just been watching leave the *Defiance,* Matt Colter fought back laughter as he replied, "Tell the good pharmacist's mate I'm afraid he has just lost a patient. Maybe Pills' bedside manner needs improving, because our Eskimo friend just took off for home. And the way that he's hauling ass, it seems that he can't get there soon enough!"

The feel of solid ice beneath his feet was a joy to Ootah as the he scrambled up a steep hummock. Only when he reached this ridge's summit did he dare to halt his rushed journey. Then, with his pained lungs heaving for breath, he hunched down and slowly turned to take one last look at the mammoth, black-skinned monster from which he had just escaped.

From his current vantage point, he could see that there were two such beasts extending out of the frozen water. Both were sleek and evil looking, and there was no doubt in his mind that these demons were the legions of Tornarsuk himself. One of these creatures had swallowed him whole, and had been about to carry him off to the land of the dead when the ancestors had once again interceded on his behalf. And by the grace of the Great Spirit, he had been allowed to crawl out of the beast's belly to reenter the world of the living. This was a journey no mortal had ever returned from, and Ootah once more bowed in humble adoration because a great miracle had brought him back to the frozen land of the people.

With the muted Arctic dawn continuing to develop on the horizon, the Inuit gratefully turned for home. Though this portion of the pack ice wasn't familiar to him, that didn't matter. For he was a hunter, and he would find his way back to his snowhouse just as the salmon returned each spring to the same spawning grounds.

As he scrambled down the far face of the ridge, his hand went instinctively to his neck. But the bone amulet was long gone, and with it the last vestige of his father. Though he hated to lose this treasure, somehow he knew Nakusiak would understand. Just as their shared dream was an omen of things to come, the amulet had guided him back to the land of the living. And now he had only one mission—to keep his heart pure and clean, so that the fiery evil destined to fall from the heavens would be contained and yet another dawn of peace would ascend over the land of the Inuit.